Leaving L.A.

by

Kate Christie

2011

Copyright © 2011 by Kate Christie

Bella Books, Inc.
P.O. Box 10543
Tallahassee, FL 32302

All rights reserved. No part of this book may be reproduced or transmitted in any form or by any means, electronic or mechanical, including photocopying, without permission in writing from the publisher.

Printed in the United States of America on acid-free paper
First published 2011

Editor: Katherine V. Forrest
Cover Designer: Linda Callaghan

ISBN 13:978-1-59493-221-2

To Kris, Maggie and Corona—and to our much anticipated player to be named later…

Acknowledgments

Thanks to my editor, Katherine V. Forrest, for her invaluable suggestions on how to strengthen various elements of this novel and produce, I hope, a stronger, more personal story. I am grateful to have had the opportunity to work with her.

Thanks also to Myra Lavenue for her generous assistance with the love scenes in this novel. She gave abundantly of her time and ideas, from big picture concepts to individual word choice. Myra, you rock!

And, as ever, thanks to my wife Kris, who supported me throughout the writing of Leaving L.A. The fact that writers can work from anywhere includes a corollary rarely mentioned: A writer's spouse can work on her wife's manuscript from anywhere, too. My love and appreciation is immense, and not merely reserved for last-minute revisions.

About the Author

Kate Christie was born and raised in Kalamazoo, Michigan. After studying history at Smith College, she earned a Master's in Creative Writing from Western Washington University. Currently she lives near Seattle with her wife and their two dogs. Leaving L.A. is her second novel.

CHAPTER ONE

Nestled into the Santa Monica Mountains at the northern edge of L.A., the Barclay School occupied twenty-five acres of gentle hills and grassy fields just west of the 405 freeway. Most mornings, Tessa Flanagan drove her daughter Laya the eight twisty, scenic miles along Mulholland Drive from their house in Laurel Canyon to the school, where she dropped Laya at the circle drive and watched until she disappeared into the building that housed Barclay's kindergarten classrooms. A soon-to-be first grader, Laya had recently begun to spurn being escorted into the building—"I'm not a baby" had become her favorite refrain of late.

This particular morning, Tessa parked her Ford Escape Hybrid in the visitor's lot and headed for the school entrance, Laya urging her onward. Her daughter's kindergarten teacher had been put on bed rest with pregnancy complications, and Tessa was curious about the woman who had taken over the classroom for the last two months of the school year. Laya had barely spoken of anything else all week. Even her normal recess nature reports (featuring parrots, hummingbirds, raccoons and even, once, a coyote that school officials claimed was in fact a stray dog) had been lacking since Miss Chapin had entered her life.

They were nearly to the walkway when a jeans-clad man stepped out from behind a parked car. Automatically Tessa pulled her daughter behind her. Then she heard the click of the camera shutter, the brief sound all too familiar, and she loosened her grip on Laya's sleeve. Just another paparazzi cockroach who had somehow managed to find his way past security onto the grounds of her daughter's school.

"Come on, Mom," Laya said, tugging her hand again. "You have to hurry if you're going to meet Miss Chapin."

"There's plenty of time," Tessa said, ignoring the photographer documenting their progress.

The impromptu escort ended at the door. As they walked down the bright hallway, shoes squeaking on polished linoleum, Tessa wondered if the man would find any takers for his photos. It would have to be a slow celebrity news day for her and Laya to grace any of the usual rags. Since her official retirement from acting a year earlier, her paparazzi tail had steadily declined. Now whenever a man with a five o'clock shadow and ketchup stains on his shirt sprang from the proverbial bushes to catch her in an unflattering pose, she was more surprised than anything else.

Lila Van Arndt, Barclay's principal, waved at her from the front office, and Tessa waved back. She loved this school, which was as far from her own early educational experiences as any institution could get. Here the grounds included three playgrounds, two soccer/lacrosse fields, indoor and outdoor basketball and volleyball courts and a swimming pool. The classrooms were large, class sizes and student-teacher ratios small. One of the top K-6 private schools in L.A., Barclay offered its pupils access to every imaginable type of educational technology, from videoconferencing and programmable robots to labs where kids could build their own computers. Laya was still too young for the labs, but Tessa liked picturing her daughter in an environment where thriving was the main focus, not merely surviving.

She herself had bounced around a series of overcrowded, underfunded schools on Chicago's South Side. Her last stop had been a gargantuan brick high school bordered by empty lots where tall grass grew out of cracks in the pavement. The asphalt in the outdoor basketball court was so uneven that sometimes a dribbled ball would careen suddenly in an unexpected direction, while in warmer weather the worn track behind the school harbored homeless people who preferred cinder to pavement. Class sizes and student-teacher ratios were large, technological and other resources negligible. She could remember walking to school from her foster mother's apartment along broken sidewalks littered with fast-food wrappers, pop cans and broken beer bottles. She'd stared at the ground as she walked, careful not to catch the eye of passersby. Fading into the background was the safest bet, she'd learned—an approach she worked hard to perfect throughout childhood.

Since her rise to stardom in her early twenties, she'd worked to keep the details of her pre-Hollywood history hidden from the panopticon of the press. When she left Chicago for L.A. at the end of high school, she hadn't planned to become famous. She had simply been impatient to leave her old life behind. Once she reached California, she changed her name and petitioned the state of Illinois to seal her juvenile record. Later, as her acting career took off, she polished her back story—orphaned at age nine, juggled between relatives in assorted cities, home-schooled by a religious great-aunt in Brooklyn before finally escaping to L.A. Overall, the story was sketchy. This vagueness had led some members of the entertainment media to postulate divergent theories on her "lost years," but her agent and publicist, the people who stood to gain the most from her continued success, had managed to keep her childhood a closely held secret using tactics Tessa understood she was better off not knowing.

Her daughter's life, on the other hand, had taken place smack-dab in the center of the Hollywood fishbowl. Tessa didn't feel guilty for sending Laya to private school—public school wasn't an option.

Inside Laya's building, colorful children's drawings decorated the hallways while well-dressed students laughed and called out to one another. Walking through Laya's school always filled Tessa with optimism. These kids hadn't discovered the pills in their parents' medicine cabinets yet, or smoked their first joint out behind the neighbor's garage. Most were still just kids, eyes bright and full of hope. Like her own daughter.

Laya picked up the pace as they neared the classroom, pulling Tessa after her. "Miss Chapin," she called as they reached her room. "Miss Chapin, come meet my mom."

The teacher was standing beside a desk at the near end of the as-yet empty room, morning sunlight angling through the windows revealing gold highlights in her shoulder-length brown hair. Tessa squinted, trying to pick out features—freckles, creamy skin, a full mouth that needed no lipstick. This was her daughter's new teacher? With her athletic frame and girl-next-door smile, she looked as if she belonged on a beach, surfboard tucked under one arm, not in a classroom graced by orange handprints and cut-out paper flowers.

"Good morning, Laya," the woman said. Then she looked at Tessa, her smile slipping a little as their eyes met.

Belatedly, Tessa realized she was staring. "Hello," she said, stepping forward with a practiced smile, her hand extended. "I'm Tessa, Laya's mother. I've heard a lot about you."

"Eleanor Chapin," the teacher said, and squeezed her hand.

Tessa paused, looking for something to say. She hadn't expected her daughter's new teacher to be quite so attractive. Not that what Eleanor Chapin looked like mattered, of course. "I understand you haven't been at the school long?"

"No, but I've been a teacher for ten years." A bell rang in the hallway, and Laya's classmates began to pile into the room, reminding Tessa as they always did of unruly puppies. "I only moved to L.A. in January. Before that I taught at a private school in Boston."

Tessa realized that Eleanor had interpreted the question as a challenge to her teaching credentials. "I didn't mean—" she started, but was interrupted by a high-pitched scream.

"Give it back," a tiny girl with red braids was screeching at a larger blond boy, who grinned malevolently as he held a stuffed bunny over her head.

"James and Alexa," Eleanor said, her voice calm. "You have until the count of ten to get to your seats. James, bring the bunny up here please. One-two-three-four..."

Both children flew to their seats, the boy stopping only to deliver the stuffed animal as directed. "Thank you," Eleanor said. Then she turned back to Tessa. "I'm sorry, but the day seems to be starting without me. Is there anything in particular I can help you with?"

Perhaps she should have gotten an earlier start that morning, after all. "No, I just wanted to introduce myself. Thanks for your time." And she turned to go.

"Ms. Flanagan?" the teacher added.

"Tessa," she corrected, glancing back.

"You're welcome to stay and observe. I encourage parental participation."

She was tempted, but she was cutting it close for her breakfast date as it was. "I'll keep that in mind."

"Please do. It was a pleasure to meet you."

The word *pleasure* caught Tessa by surprise, and she blinked, forcing her eyes away from the triangle of skin visible at the teacher's throat. Such thoughts, and surrounded by milling children—it seemed illicit somehow. "You too." And she turned again to go.

"'Bye, Mom." Laya waved at her from a table near the door.

"'Bye, sweetie." Tessa waved back and ducked into the hallway.

At least now she knew why Laya was smitten with her teacher. Eleanor's predecessor, the very pregnant Mrs. Pierce, had been younger, shorter and prone to high-pitched laughter. This woman, with her firm handshake and self-possessed air, seemed more solid somehow. Or maybe it was just that she didn't exude the overly-plucked, fake-tanned phoniness of native and transplant Southern Californians alike.

The photographer had already beat a retreat by the time Tessa emerged into the sunny California morning—probably he'd been forcibly removed from campus by security. She made her way to her car, slid inside and sat motionless for a moment, elbows on the steering wheel. What had just happened? She closed her eyes and pictured her daughter's teacher again: that unruffled demeanor, the muscles in her forearms, the way her eyes had crinkled when she smiled. Not at all what Tessa had expected of the illustrious Miss Chapin.

In any case, she didn't have time to examine her reaction to a woman who would be in her daughter's life—and hers—for only a couple of months. She started her car and pulled out of the parking lot. Right now she had twenty minutes to get from Mulholland Drive down into Beverly Hills for a meeting with Jane and Elizabeth Byerly, elderly daughters of a long-dead L.A. business tycoon and partners in her latest venture—the formation of a charitable foundation.

A year had passed since she'd visited her last film set, and sometimes Tessa still couldn't believe how much her life had changed. For nearly fifteen years, she had moved from project to project, set to set, living away from home for months at a time. Since Laya's birth she had scaled back, but even though she worked primarily on smaller budget pictures with minimal travel demands, she was still forced to choose again and again between parenting and her career. After a decade and a half in Hollywood, she had finally grown tired of the profession that dictated what she ate and where she slept, the hotel rooms that blended one into another, her ghoulish paparazzi shadow. Tired of moving from one character to another, increasingly uncertain who she was herself behind the masks she was paid to wear. She had achieved more than she'd ever hoped to as an actor, and despite the groans the decision elicited from her agent, publicist and assorted studio executives, she was ready to be done with the business of making movies. So she'd retired from the film industry and focused on spending time with her daughter, catching up on her reading, and going wherever she wanted whenever she wanted—as much as any parent could do.

Not working while Laya was in school hadn't been all that satisfying, however, so she'd kept her antenna raised, on the lookout for what it was she should focus on next. Then, just before Christmas, she'd stumbled across a magazine article about the Gates Foundation in Seattle, one of the organizations she supported. As she read the description of the Gates' endeavors, an idea had crystallized. A vocal critic (along with much of the rest of Hollywood) of the avaricious social, economic and environmental policies of George W. Bush's recently ended (thank God) reign, perhaps she should consider putting her money where her mouth was. She could invest some of the exorbitant fees her agent had managed over the years to extract from the studios—at the end of her career, her salary quote was $10 million per picture, not including first-dollar gross or back-end revenues—and use the returns to fund charities whose causes matched her own interests.

She'd been giving away her money for years, and not just the amount her business manager recommended for tax purposes. But a foundation like the one the Gates had created was something that would continue giving unto perpetuity, provide jobs and, in theory, eventually run itself. It would also offer a chance for her to explore who she really was after all those years of playing other people, to figure out who she wanted to be. Besides, now she would have an official excuse to approach people with similar financial resources about giving to her favorite causes.

Her business manager had put her in touch with the Byerlys, who were also feeling the need to flex their wealth in a new way, and they'd officially joined forces a few weeks before. Her new career, unlike the old one, allowed her to continue to drop Laya off at school most mornings and pick her up in the afternoons. She was home for dinner more often than not, and she got to tuck her daughter into bed and read her a story (or two, or three) most nights. They finally had a normal life. Or as normal as life in Hollywood ever could be.

The notion of normalcy reminded her of Eleanor Chapin. She pictured the teacher's smile again, the pale skin at the base of her throat, the freckles that had gilded even her ears. The encounter had been brief, but in that short time Eleanor had seemed lovely and self-assured and possibly more genuine than anyone Tessa had met in entirely too long.

As she left the mountains for the flat, traffic-logged city, she watched the landscape change around her and pondered the appealing smile of a woman who undoubtedly occupied a decidedly different world from her own.

Eleanor didn't have time to think about her encounter with Tessa Flanagan until mid-morning, when the children parked themselves on the plush rug at the center of the room for a round of Silent Sustained Reading. As they read to themselves from books they'd chosen from the wooden box under the window, Eleanor sat at her desk staring out at the bright green lawn, sunlit as usual on this late March day. But it wasn't the lawn she saw. Rather her mind was full of the dark eyes and sleek hair of the famous actress who had stepped into her classroom that morning.

She'd known, of course, who Laya Flanagan's mother was. Laya was one of the reasons the school had asked her to sign a nondisclosure agreement. The Barclay School took privacy very seriously, especially when it came to the children of celebrities. Eleanor tried to recall what she knew of the retired actress—in her mid-thirties, never been married, known for her progressive politics and championing of liberal causes. And, rumor had it, possibly on the down-low. But Eleanor didn't give much credence to those rumors. Probably they arose out of wishful thinking.

Meeting Tessa Flanagan had made her month, Eleanor thought, smiling at her own shallowness. She wasn't a huge fan of L.A. Though she'd visited Southern California many times over the years, this was her first extended stay in the Golden State. Now, after three months in Hollywood, she couldn't wait to leave the hot, smoggy confines of the city. She'd moved out west for a change of pace after her mother's long, ultimately failed battle with breast cancer. Sunny California was nothing like New England, where she had lived her entire life. L.A. seemed like the perfect escape.

And it was, at first. She'd moved in with her college roommate, Sasha, an attorney who leased a comfortable apartment at the foot of the Hollywood Hills, and set to work on completing her applications to a handful of carefully selected Ph.D. programs in child psychology. But soon the constant press of people, the notorious traffic, the narcissistic culture of the city all started to grate on her. Before Sasha's cousin had hooked her up with the short-term position at the Barclay School, she'd been thinking of leaving L.A. as soon as she picked a graduate program. Assuming she got in anywhere decent.

Tessa Flanagan was the first celebrity she had met in the flesh. And what flesh. Eleanor had seen her films, of course, everything from romantic comedies to Oscar-winning dramas, but the big screen had not prepared her in the least for Tessa's real-life presence. She wasn't surprised that Tessa was stunning in person, even in jeans and almost no makeup. She just hadn't been prepared this morning to meet someone so—charismatic, that was the word. Some people just exuded sex appeal. Stood to reason that the movie star mother of one of her students would be one of the fortunate few.

Eleanor glanced out across the rug, making certain that her dozen miniature charges were all safely ensconced in literary exercise. Laya was as absorbed in her book as the rest, one hand curled under her cheek as she turned the pages of *Corduroy*. What was the deal with her father, again? Eleanor thought she remembered something about an anonymous sperm donor making headlines at the time of Tessa's pregnancy, news that had only fueled the rumors about her sexual orientation. Either way, at least Eleanor knew now where the girl got those long lashes. If memory served, Tessa was half-Irish and half-Filipino—a potent genetic combination, Eleanor thought, daydreaming about the actress's smile, the seeming warmth in her eyes.

Then she caught herself. Even if the rumors circulating through the lesbian community were true, Tessa Flanagan would hardly spare her a thought. On the contrary, Laya's mother had seemed mainly interested in her classroom experience. Tessa wasn't the only parent who had expressed concern over the sudden change in teachers. She was just the most notable one. Eleanor didn't find herself speechless very often. Tessa Flanagan, on the other hand, was probably well accustomed to the dazed reactions of the mere mortals she encountered in daily life.

Reaching for a stack of reports left behind by her predecessor,

Eleanor told herself to stop thinking about Hollywood celebrities and focus on her job, which on a typical day didn't afford her time to daydream.

"Guess who I met this morning?" she greeted Sasha that evening. Her former college roommate had returned from work just in time for a dinner of brown rice and tofu stir fry. Because Sasha wouldn't let her contribute to the rent, Eleanor insisted on buying groceries, cooking dinner and cleaning the apartment as often as she could. As a result, Sasha, who was straight, often referred to Eleanor as her wife.

"Let's see," Sasha said, kicking off her heels and coming to stand beside her at the stove, one arm around her waist. "Tessa Flanagan?"

"How did you know?"

"Easy, Elle. People dot com had pictures of her at your school this morning." She reached out and snagged a spoonful of broccoli and tofu. An entertainment lawyer, Sasha claimed that it was her professional duty to read the celebrity gossip dailies.

"How did she look?" Eleanor asked.

Sasha swallowed the bite and eyed her quizzically. "Um, gorgeous? How else would she look?"

"I don't know." She smiled a little to herself, remembering her first glimpse of the real Tessa Flanagan. *Gorgeous* didn't seem quite strong enough.

"Hold on," Sasha said. "I know that look. You want to get it on with Tessa Flanagan!"

"You'd want to get it on with her, too, if you met her."

"Probably," Sasha agreed, and headed for the hallway. "I've got to get out of this suit. I can't believe I actually wore a push-up bra to court today. Post-feminist, my ass."

Later, over wine and stir-fry, Eleanor rehashed her celebrity encounter. "I had no idea it would be so hard to act like a normal person. It's like I had no control over what I was doing or saying. I actually invited her to stay and observe class."

"Did she?"

"Of course not. I'm sure she's busy, even if she isn't acting anymore. I mean, she's Tessa Flanagan."

"To risk sounding trite, she's also just a person," Sasha said, wiping her mouth with a cloth napkin. In her work, she had told Eleanor, she'd come to realize just how fragile celebrities could be, especially the ones who believed their own press. PR was propaganda intended to keep a star in the limelight. The smart ones didn't take the business of selling themselves too seriously.

"I know that," Eleanor said. "I was actually surprised by how real she seemed. She was wearing jeans."

"Duh, Elle, everyone wears jeans, even mega-stars. Ten years in Boston did little to exorcise the Northeast Kingdom, I see."

"Last time I checked, Orange County wasn't exactly the Entertainment Capital of the World."

"Maybe not, but at least it's close."

They had met a decade and a half earlier as first-years at Smith College in Western Massachusetts, Eleanor recently liberated from a town of five thousand in the northeast corner of Vermont, Sasha from the southern edge of the Los Angeles megalopolis. For Eleanor, Northampton, a New England city of thirty thousand located in pastoral Pioneer Valley, represented a bridge to the larger world she was eager to discover. For her roommate, the ivy-bricked women's college and small East Coast city were completely foreign and frighteningly homogeneous—where *were* the other black people, she frequently lamented. Sasha was so homesick their first year that Eleanor was convinced she would transfer. But by the end of the year, Sasha claimed to have grown used to lily-white New England. She would go back to L.A. after college, she said—a vow she'd fulfilled the day after graduation.

Eleanor had visited Southern California annually ever since, and Sasha had returned to New England for regular reunions. At Eleanor's mother's funeral the previous November, Sasha had invited her to L.A. for an open-ended visit. Six weeks later, motherless, unemployed and newly single, Eleanor had grabbed the chance to spend quality time with her best friend. Not to mention get some much-needed perspective. Shortly after the holidays, she packed up her Jetta and drove west, following the southern route across the country. Her younger sister, Julia, took a break from her job as a graphic designer in Burlington to accompany her. They'd bonded along the way, but their mother's death had hung heavily between them. Eleanor had been relieved to reach L.A. and put her sister on a plane back to Boston.

These days, Sasha felt more like a sister than Julia did. In the past few months, they'd fallen back into the same easy routines from their college days. After dinner most nights they cleaned up the kitchen together and then went their separate ways, usually to pursue some form of homework. Tonight was no different—Sasha disappeared into her home office to work on a brief due the following morning, while Eleanor set up shop at the dining room table with scissors, craft foam, cardboard paper towel tubes, and other tools of the trade. She wanted to try out a crafts activity she'd discovered on a teaching blog. It was nearly the end of the year, so the kids should be able to cut and paste on their own by now. Still, she'd learned early on in her educational career that the better the planning, the more successful a lesson usually turned out to be. Especially when it came to arts and crafts.

As she drew floral designs on the craft foam, she considered the number of years she and Sasha had known each other: almost fifteen now. Roughly the same length of time Tessa Flanagan had been a Hollywood mainstay, if she remembered correctly. Her gaze strayed to the laptop perched on one side of the hardwood table, broadcasting an Indigo Girls mix on iTunes. She should keep working, she told herself even as she dropped the foam and pulled the laptop closer. In a new browser window, she typed "Tessa Flanagan" into the Google search box and hit enter. Immediately a search engine results page gave her the first ten hits out of millions of possibilities.

Scrolling down, she scanned the results, reading bits and pieces of a Wikipedia entry, an Internet Movie Database listing, multiple fan sites, and finally, a description of a People.com article with today's date. She clicked on the link, and after a moment the article opened in a new window. There on the page was a photo of Tessa and Laya walking up the brick walkway to the Barclay School. Tessa was holding Laya's hand and shielding the girl from the photographer's lens as she looked back over her shoulder. Eleanor stared at the photo, noting the narrowness of Tessa's waist, the sheen of her hair, the neat clogs that poked out beneath her jeans. A picture didn't compare, she decided, closing her eyes and remembering the feel of Tessa's palm simultaneously warm and cool against her own.

"What have we here?"

Sasha's drawl from the kitchen doorway startled her, and she quickly minimized the People.com window.

"Too late, I already saw," her once and current roommate said as she entered the kitchen, empty wineglass in hand. "It's okay, Elle. It's not like I don't know all about your libido."

This could have been a reference to any number of incidents. In college first semester, when Eleanor was discovering that it wasn't the fact she'd known the boys in her hometown since nursery school that made them seem unattractive, Sasha had walked in on her making out with another girl in their dorm room. To her credit, Sasha hadn't asked for a new roommate on the spot, as some other Smith first-years might have done. She was fine with the gay thing, she said, as long as Eleanor didn't try anything with her. It took Eleanor months to forgive her for this crass remark, and nearly a year passed before Sasha officially took it back.

Or it might have been a reference to an episode a month earlier when Eleanor, believing Sasha to be pulling an all-nighter at the office, had invited a woman she'd met at a West Hollywood club back to the apartment. On that occasion, Eleanor had actually been relieved at Sasha's unexpected arrival because as the three vodka tonics she'd imbibed at the club started to wear off, she found herself remembering why it was she tended to stick to serial monogamy. As the key turned in the lock, she implied that the new arrival was her jealous girlfriend, and the stranger (Jen? Jamie? she couldn't remember now) had hightailed it out of the apartment.

Then again, it wasn't as if Sasha didn't have her own closeted skeletons. "Right," Eleanor said.

Her roommate wiggled her carefully shaped eyebrows. "What does the Internet have to say about your girlfriend? Plenty, I bet."

"Shut it."

"Suit yourself." Sasha refilled her wine glass and sauntered back to her office.

As she cut out foam flowers and attached them to the cardboard tubes that would serve as stems, Eleanor wondered if she should worry. Sasha had taken to polishing off a bottle of wine most nights while she worked in her home office. She also hadn't gone out on a date since Ben, her ex, had dumped her for an older woman (a phrase you didn't often hear in L.A.—or anyplace else, really—Sasha liked to point out), and she was working more hours than ever at a job she claimed to despise. Sasha, her best friend in the world, wasn't happy. Then again, Eleanor thought, was she?

Since graduating from Smith a decade before, neither of them had achieved the goals they'd set for themselves as dewy-eyed undergrads. Eleanor still hadn't started graduate school, and Sasha was unmarried, childless and stuck as a mid-level associate at a firm practicing the kind of corporate law she'd always claimed to detest. But law school loans forced many a would-be altruist to sell out. Sasha claimed she hadn't yet decided if she was fully committed to being just another law school cliché.

At least Eleanor got to work with kids. She'd wanted to be a child psychologist since her first psych class sophomore year of college. Midway through the semester, the professor had assigned them homework that involved a visit to a residential mental health center. They could choose from the local VA, a nearby substance abuse recovery facility or a children's hospital in Worcester, an hour east on the Massachusetts Turnpike. Eleanor and one of her classmates had decided to road trip to Worcester, a twist of fate she'd always considered providential. Not many of her friends had as clear an idea of what they were supposed to do with their lives. She was lucky in that regard, she knew.

Not so lucky in other ways. The summer after her junior year, when she might have been pursuing an internship at a children's clinic, she spent driving her mother to cancer treatments in Burlington two hours from where they lived in Newport, Vermont, just south of the Canadian border. She almost didn't go back to Smith her senior year, but her mother was adamant. Her illness should not, could not, negatively impact the family.

As if that were even possible. But Eleanor hadn't wanted to upset her mother, not when she needed every ounce of energy to fight the murderous cells lurking in her bloodstream. Dutifully she returned to school and came home two weekends a month, while her father took time off from his architectural firm to care for his wife. Julia, Eleanor's younger sister, had just started her freshman year at the University of Vermont. Their parents took out a second mortgage on their 1920s bungalow in Newport, only a block from Lake Mempremagog, to help pay for their daughters' schooling, and life went on as usual. Except, of course, that it didn't.

Eleanor got up from the table and went to pour herself a glass of wine. It was a Thursday night, and back in college she and Sasha might have spent the evening hanging out in a dorm room with friends from Sri Lanka and South Carolina, drinking cheap beer or sharing a joint and debating the existence of God or democracy or some other American institution they'd implicitly believed in before beginning their intellectual journey toward adulthood in bucolic Western Massachusetts. She missed those days, missed the easy camaraderie of a women's college where girls becoming women could be themselves without worrying about what other people—their families, former acquaintances, men—thought. She missed the simpler, pre-cancer years when her future had seemed wide open, the path she would follow simultaneously exciting and predictable. Smith had spoiled her for four years by providing a secure environment in which to explore what she wanted from her life, not to mention who she might like to share it with. Sometimes she thought she was still trying to get over the rude awakening of leaving Smith and Northampton after graduation. No place since had ever felt quite right.

Turning back to the dining room table, she took a sip of wine and picked up her scissors. Though she didn't look at the People.com article again that night, she somehow still felt Tessa Flanagan's presence as she set about creating a colorful spring garden for her class.

CHAPTER TWO

Over the next few weeks, Laya continued to prattle on about the favorite new adult in her life. Tessa tried not to conjure an image of the kindergarten teacher every time Laya mentioned something new and miraculous Eleanor Chapin had said or done, but it was difficult to tune out only part of what her daughter said. She didn't want to join the ranks of the parents who replied "Uh-huh" and "Wow" without actually listening to anything their child said. She knew too many of those, both in her old life and here in L.A.

Amalia, Laya's nanny, had noticed the girl's fixation on the evidently faultless Miss Chapin, too. "This is like celebrity worship, no?" she said to Tessa one morning after breakfast had consisted of a detailed analysis of the teacher's affinity for trail running, apparently mentioned during story time the day before. "Only without the celebrity."

"Miss Chapin has her own miniature stalker," Tessa agreed.

"Do you think she knows?"

"How could she not?"

For once, Tessa had a free morning—the Byerly sisters were taking a long weekend to visit the King Tut exhibit up in San Francisco, and Tessa didn't have anywhere to be until an afternoon meeting with the consultant they'd recently hired. Perhaps, she thought as she drove Laya the short distance to school, she should stay and watch the object of her daughter's affection in action. After all, Eleanor Chapin had invited her to observe anytime. Who knew when she'd get another chance?

The April day was sunny and crisp, heat yet to descend as she guided the Escape around the curves of Mulholland Drive, Laya singing to herself in the backseat. The mountains blocked their view of the city to the south and the ocean to the west, while stucco walls and landscaped terraces camouflaged multi-million-dollar homes near the school. Tessa found herself wondering where Eleanor Chapin lived, what her commute was like. Maybe she would ask her over lunch in the school cafeteria.

Then she caught herself. It had been years since she'd attempted to befriend someone outside the film industry, for good reason. What made her think Eleanor Chapin would be interested in getting to know the real her anyway? In her experience, women (and men) were more intrigued by the plastic Hollywood version they were sure they already knew. This whole idea was preposterous. She should just drop Laya off and return home to get some work done around the house.

But she parked in the visitor's lot and joined a handful of other parents escorting their elementary-aged students into the school, ignoring the customary double takes cast her way.

"Are you coming in to see Miss Chapin again?" Laya asked as they walked, beaming up at her.

"I thought I'd stay and watch your class this morning," Tessa said, "if that's okay with you."

"Duh, Mom," Laya said, and danced across the sidewalk. "Come on!"

Inside, as they strolled down the hall hand in hand, Tessa chatted absently with her daughter—no, they weren't having pizza for dinner tonight, and yes, they could watch a movie over the weekend—and counted the doorways to the kindergarten classroom. One down, three to go. Now two, one... She took a breath and turned into the room with a smile intended to simulate the appearance of calm.

Eleanor Chapin was standing at the front of the classroom again, talking this time to a young woman Tessa guessed was her aide. As Tessa paused in the doorway, the teacher looked up and saw her. Blast it, she thought as their eyes met. Eleanor was just as attractive as she'd remembered.

The teacher stopped mid-sentence, handed a stack of construction paper to the aide and moved toward the door, her smile welcoming. The young woman had followed her gaze and was now staring wide-eyed at Tessa.

"Miss Chapin," Laya said, nearly bouncing in place. "My mom wants to watch you this morning."

It took supreme will for Tessa not to flush in embarrassment. She followed up her daughter's unfortunate choice of words with a composed, "I had a free morning and was hoping the offer to observe a class still stood."

Eleanor was already nodding. "Of course," she said, and waved the stunned aide forward. "We're happy to have you. This is Megan. Megan, this is Ms. Flanagan, Laya's mother. Why don't you help her get settled while I start the morning routine."

As the bell rang and the rest of the children filed in, chattering monkey-like amongst themselves, Tessa hid her disappointment at being handed over to the starstruck aide. She hoped the girl would recover use of her voice soon. Surely she couldn't be the only celebrity parent who had ever dropped in to observe a class?

The morning routine consisted of a variety of activities that made time pass quickly. By the time the children had recited the Pledge of Allegiance (they still did that?), discussed the weather report, dictated the morning message for Eleanor to inscribe on the blackboard and read the sentence back as a class, Megan had rallied and was directing Tessa through what appeared to be a fixed level of involvement. Parents volunteered most frequently in this and the pre-school class, she told Tessa, but the ones who hadn't passed a background check were only allowed minimal contact with children other than their own. This struck Tessa as ironic—she was the one who usually ordered background checks on the people in her employment. Or one of her lawyers did, anyway.

For most of the morning, she sat at the edge of the classroom watching Eleanor and Megan guide their students through a series of workstations that focused on literacy, the natural world, social studies and health. As she watched the children nearest her tackle a vocabulary-building computer game, she was impressed. She'd had no idea how much her daughter learned on a daily basis. Laya's dinner reports tended to focus on nature-oriented lessons or on recess, her self-proclaimed favorite part of the school day. Perhaps the ungodly amount the Barclay School charged was worth it, after all.

Despite the sustained level of commotion, Eleanor didn't ignore Tessa's presence. She smiled each time she drifted near, asked her to help with various tasks, answered her questions about particular activities. Laya, meanwhile, kept grinning and waving at her. She waved back, amazed as ever that this lovely, articulate child was hers. Not that she was biased.

Mid-morning, Eleanor announced that it was time for individual reading. After the children had each picked a book from the communal storybook box and were ensconced on the brightly colored rug in the center of the room, the teacher left Megan in charge and ambled over to where Tessa occupied one of the two adult-sized chairs in the classroom.

As Eleanor approached, Tessa wished she had something to occupy her hands. As it was, she could only pretend to be more interested in the artwork set out to dry on a nearby table than in Eleanor's lithe frame revealed in close-fitting khaki capris and a pale blue T-shirt with the image of a sun splashed across the chest. She looked like a runner, Tessa thought, suddenly more aware of her own contrasting curves.

"So what do you think?" Eleanor asked, leaning against the whiteboard at the back of the room.

"I'm impressed," Tessa said, watching her daughter and the other students mouth the words to their selections. "You certainly pack a lot in."

"Children this age, as you've probably noticed, are not great at focusing for extended periods of time. That's why kindergarten is an ADHD's dream."

Tessa laughed. "In that case, I know some directors who might benefit from your instruction." She glanced over at Eleanor, her smile fading as she noticed the color of the teacher's eyes. Green-blue, like the ocean off Kauai. Uncanny.

"Eleanor," Megan called from the front desk, where a small boy was holding his stomach.

Eleanor murmured something and hurried away. Tessa looked out a nearby window and wiped her palms against her jeans. What was she doing? She knew better than to flirt with an ordinary person. There was a reason Hollywood stars dated each other. The last thing she wanted was to set the paparazzi on the scent of an innocent bystander. Or, for that matter, to reveal too much to a woman who, despite the ridiculously complete background checks the Barclay School required for all employees, was still a stranger.

They didn't speak again until the lunch bell had rung and Megan had led the children out into the hallway, Laya waving again before disappearing from sight. Tessa approached the front of the room where Eleanor stood staring down at her desk. She didn't move, but Tessa knew that Eleanor was aware of her. She was accustomed to people losing their ability to speak in her presence. Most of the actors she knew had the same experience—utter silence or the opposite, verbal diarrhea. But Eleanor seemed to be responding in a slightly different way. Was it possible she was gay? Tessa checked her left hand—no ring. Not that that meant much anymore. Even the word "partner" had been appropriated by straight people.

"So," she said, her voice light, "how's the food around here?"

Eleanor looked up. "You're staying for lunch?"

"I have a little time before I have to get back to the city. Do you mind if I join you? I was hoping to talk to you about Laya."

Which was entirely untrue but gave her an excuse to prolong her time at the school.

"Of course," Eleanor said. "We can eat in the teacher's cafeteria. Unless you'd prefer someplace more private?" As Tessa's head tilted, she added, "To talk about Laya."

"No, the cafeteria is fine."

As they walked down the hall together, Tessa commented, "You said before that you worked in Boston until last year. Is that where you're from?"

"Close. I grew up in Vermont. But I went to school in Massachusetts and stayed there after college."

"Which school?"

"Smith. It's a women's college in Western Mass."

"Northampton," Tessa said. "I've actually spent some time there." So Eleanor had gone to Smith. If the rumors Tessa had heard about the liberal college were true, then her daughter's teacher was at least familiar with the notion of Sapphic love, if not the practice.

"Really," Eleanor said. "When were you in Northampton?"

"I worked on a film in New York a few years ago, and one of my co-stars had gone to Hampshire College. We spent a weekend in the Valley eating at wonderful restaurants and walking through the autumn leaves next to the pond at Smith—what was it called?"

"Paradise Pond."

"That's right." As Tessa followed Eleanor out into a sunlit courtyard, she pulled a pair of sunglasses from her bag and slipped them on, oversized lenses camouflaging as much of her face as possible. Here such precautions weren't necessary, though. Security was tight. While photographers might be able to sneak onto the front lawn, they could never make it into the interior of campus. Or so Miss Van Arndt had assured her on her first visit to the school three years earlier.

"I can't believe you know Smith," Eleanor said. "So few people I've met out here do. Usually I get comments like, 'Isn't that a girls' school?' Or, 'Is that like Jones University?' I'm still not sure why that one's supposed to be funny."

Tessa nodded. "Californians tend to be a little insular.

It's like they don't understand why anyone would want to live someplace else."

"You're not from here, are you?"

"No, I'm not."

They had entered a different building where students occupied one half of a large open seating area divvied up by a sliding partition, teachers and staff the other. Tessa felt a variety of eyes lingering on their entrance and automatically schooled her features into a neutral expression as she stowed her sunglasses back in her Jimmy Choo bag. She had been watched for so much of her adult life, she should have been used to it. But the weight of a crowd's appraisal still sometimes unnerved her.

"Where did you grow up?" Eleanor asked, leading her to the lunch line.

She almost said Chicago. It almost slipped out as she stood in line beside her daughter's teacher, caught by eyes that didn't have a thing to hide. "All over," she said instead, and pointed at the food spread out beneath a plastic buffet shield. "What do you recommend?"

As Eleanor advised her on the Barclay School menu—cheeseburgers and fries, mixed green salad, grilled chicken breast, pizza, homemade soups and sandwiches—Tessa reminded herself to be careful. Just because the nearness of a woman she'd only just met evoked a sense of security that had been missing from her own childhood, it didn't mean she should let her guard down. The best way to stay the self she'd become was to remain a mystery to others. And that included Eleanor Chapin.

Laya's mother, Eleanor noted as she and Tessa stood in the lunch line, was a hard nut to crack. She didn't seem to mind asking questions, but as soon as the spotlight shifted to her, she noticeably withdrew. This was not at all what Eleanor had expected. She'd assumed someone like Tessa Flanagan would be a narcissist only too eager to blather on about her life and career. Instead, Eleanor had the sense of being gently redirected anytime she came too close. But too close to what?

As they selected their meals and paid the cashier, Eleanor kept telling herself that this was really happening. Tessa Flanagan had actually appeared in her classroom that morning and invited her to lunch. Of course, she was only there to talk about her daughter, Eleanor reminded herself, trying to rein in her absurd excitement at seeing the famous actress again.

"About Laya," she said once they were seated on the teacher's side of the cafeteria. "Your daughter is one of my brighter students. She's curious, quick to learn and a fan of anything related to the natural world. She doesn't mind getting dirty, and she's often the first to volunteer when I need a helper."

"That's because she adores you. I don't know if you've noticed?" Tessa made it a question.

"Well, sure," Eleanor said, tearing apart a crescent roll and dunking it in her cup of soup. She had long since accepted the pull she had for dogs and children as a welcome gift. The fact that she could connect on a basic level with kids only reinforced her career choice. But a sudden thought occurred to her. "Is that what you're concerned about? Are you worried that Laya is becoming inappropriately attached?" Perhaps Tessa Flanagan had learned from the Barclay School administration that she was a lesbian, and wasn't comfortable having her daughter in Eleanor's class.

"God, no," Tessa said. "It's perfectly normal for Laya to be so attached to her teacher. In fact, I feel lucky that she has you to come to every day. I mean, someone who can make learning enjoyable. I don't have any concerns on that front."

Eleanor felt a tad silly for suspecting Laya's notoriously liberal mother of homophobia. Like her former school in Boston, Barclay was a fount of progressive ideas, socially, philosophically, pedagogically. But as an out lesbian teacher, she often worried about parental response. "What did you want to talk about, then?"

Tessa took a bite of her salad and chewed slowly and methodically. After she swallowed, she sipped from her bottle of water. At last she said, "I only wanted to make sure that Laya wasn't acting out in the classroom. She was quite attached to Mrs. Pierce too, and I've read that children in single-parent homes sometimes react more to disruptions in their routine."

"I haven't noticed anything." Single parent—that meant that Tessa was un-partnered, despite the linking of her name with assorted male Hollywood luminaries. (Eleanor had discovered a previously unknown interest in celebrity gossip magazines the past couple of weeks.) Who, then, was the other woman that Laya often mentioned? "Can I ask you a question?"

"Certainly," Tessa said, but her smile didn't reach her eyes.

"Does a woman named Ama live with you?"

"Yes, she's Laya's nanny, and has been with us since Laya was born. Her name is actually Amalia, but Laya couldn't pronounce it. Kind of funny—Ama means father in Tagalog. Amalia says since Laya doesn't have a father, she might as well take the name."

"And Dani?"

"He's Amalia's husband. He's in charge of the garden and does most of the cooking."

"Ah," Eleanor said. Tessa lived with a married couple, not another woman. Or man, for that matter. "The thing is, developmental problems usually occur at a higher rate in kids who experience multiple changes in circumstance. It sounds to me like Laya has a stable home life."

"I'd like to think so. Now, can I ask *you* a question?"

"Of course."

"Do you have any children?" Tessa was watching her now with a slight smile, dark eyes seeming almost to see through her.

"Nope. No kids yet."

"Too bad. You're good with them. I bet you would make a great mom."

Tessa Flanagan thought she would be a great mom? Eleanor filed the compliment away to recount to Sasha later, simultaneously cursing the Northern European heritage that made her skin tone an easy-to-read emotional barometer. "Kindergartners are easy," she said, trying to ignore the blush she could feel creeping up her neck. "They're my favorite age—developing language, learning to identify and quantify, and they're so excited about everything. It's hard to be cynical around them. Kind of redeems my faith in the world." She realized she'd waxed sentimental and stopped to take a bite of roll. Sentimentality was typically not well-received in L.A., in her limited experience. Or, for that matter, in New England.

"You, cynical? That's hard to imagine," Tessa said. An insistent beep issued from her leather bag, and she pulled out a BlackBerry. "I hate to say it but I have to get back to the city. Work beckons."

Eleanor couldn't imagine what sort of work might beckon a fabulously wealthy, retired-by-choice actress. As they carried their trays to the counter, she said, "I thought you retired from acting."

"I did." Tessa dumped the remains of her salad in the compost bin as a bell rang. "I'm in the process of starting up a charitable foundation with some other people. It's not public knowledge yet. Actually, I'd appreciate it if you wouldn't mention it to anyone," she added, frowning a little.

"I promise I won't leak the story to my numerous contacts in the press," Eleanor said.

She was rewarded with what appeared to be a genuine smile. "Thanks."

They walked back to the classroom together, and Tessa stopped in to say goodbye to Laya, who gave her a hug and a kiss before scampering off. Eleanor accompanied her out to the hallway, trying to think of something to say. Talking to Tessa had been easy over lunch, but now that it was time to say goodbye, her tongue-tied state had returned.

"Thanks for lunch," Tessa said. Her gaze dropped, and Eleanor wondered if Tessa Flanagan could actually be staring at her mouth in a distinctly non-parent-teacher way.

"My pleasure," she said, feeling her pulse spike. If Tessa had been the friend of a friend, or someone she'd met at a bar or on one of the trails around the city, she would have known what to say. But she only watched as Tessa gave her one last unreadable look, and then the movie star was turning away, walking down the hallway and out of her life while Eleanor remained where she was, wishing that Laya's mother was anyone else.

CHAPTER THREE

"You know, the whole lunch excuse sounds flimsy to me," Sasha announced as they sat on bar stools at their favorite sushi joint that night munching edamame, spicy rolls and nigiri. Luis, a fellow associate from her firm, sat with them, checking out restaurant visitors in the mirror above the bar.

"I'm with you, sistah," he said, and held up his hand to Sasha for a high five. They were always doing that—something from work, they said. Apparently most of the attorneys at Martin, Felpausch and Stein were former college athletes. Luis said he thought the partners in the firm had a rule against hiring non-athletes. Fortunately that rule didn't extend to people of color or flaming homosexuals, both groups that he was happy to represent.

"Don't sistah me," Sasha said, ignoring his raised hand.

Luis and Eleanor exchanged a look. "Not yet," she said, and he nodded.

"What's not yet?" Sasha asked.

"Nothing," Eleanor said quickly. "Back to me and my celebrity crush. What reason would Tessa Flanagan have for inventing an excuse to have lunch with me?"

"Obviously she wants to sleep with you," her roommate said, checking herself out in the mirror. The week before she'd had her extensions removed, and now her short hair stood up from her head in a baby 'fro.

Eleanor snorted. "Tessa Flanagan does not want to sleep with me, as much as I might wish she did."

"Please," Sasha said. "You know you look good. This is your longest dry spell since high school, isn't it?"

Frowning, Eleanor counted the months since she and Laurie, her girlfriend of three years, had called it quits. They'd broken up right after Eleanor's mother's funeral. She'd thought it strange that they'd made it through the stress of the final year of her mom's life and only then split up. Strange until she ran into her newly ex-girlfriend at Dyke Night wrapped around Justyn, her "best friend from work," only a week after Laurie moved out of their Davis Square apartment.

"Yeah," she admitted, "it is."

"How long has it been?" Luis asked.

"Five months." The unconsummated tryst with the girl from the club (Jess? Jasmine?) two months earlier didn't count.

"Dios mio," he said, and crossed himself.

"You're not Catholic," Eleanor said.

"Maybe not, but I am a drama queen." He looked hopefully at Sasha, who smiled and held her hand up. As he slapped it, he nodded at Eleanor. "Bingo."

Whenever she drank vodka, Sasha started slinging around the high fives willy-nilly, as if she were channeling an alternate reality version of herself. Tonight's tipping point appeared to be one and a half vodka tonics consumed in just under a half hour.

"You guys don't seriously think I have a chance with her, do you?" Eleanor asked.

Sasha shrugged. "Not if you don't grow some *cojones* and make your feelings known, *chica.*" Another high five.

The conversation moved on to the prevalence of Spanish words in Mexican-phobic Southern California and the tendency of any dominant culture to misappropriate parts of the subculture it longs to destroy.

"Wait," Sasha said, "you're saying that in this case I represent the dominant culture because I called Elle *chica*?"

Luis nodded as he caught the eye of an attractive twenty-something with shapely biceps and a six-pack evident beneath his shimmery shirt. "Precisely."

"I don't think so. Black women get paid the least and have the most violence committed against us," Sasha argued. "Not to mention we're viewed by men primarily as sexual objects. We're at the lowest end of the totem pole in this country."

"There you go again, misappropriating," Eleanor said. When Sasha stared at her, she added, "Um, totem pole? If any group of people occupies the lowest end of the totem pole, it has to be Native Americans."

Luis smirked, and reluctantly, Sasha smiled. "All right, the Indians win. You know why black people are so happy in Southern California?" The other two shook their heads. "'Cause there ain't no big trees. My people don't go camping for that very reason. You've seen the movies. Always some redneck hiding behind a tree with a shotgun."

"True dat," Eleanor said, and ducked as they chucked empty edamame shells at her.

Later, after Luis had left with the boy in the shimmery shirt and Eleanor and Sasha had gone back to their apartment to watch *Ghost Whisperer* on DVR (a guilty pleasure that could never be revealed in front of their other Smith alum friends, they agreed), Eleanor sat on the couch next to her roommate, wondering what Tessa Flanagan was doing. What was her life like? A house in the Hills, a live-in couple to watch her daughter and cook their meals and, presumably, clean up after them. Then what? What did Tessa Flanagan do after her daughter was in bed on a Friday night?

At that moment, Tessa was fielding a phone call from her agent. "I told you, Michael, no. Retired means retired."

"Come on, sweets," he said, his silky voice cajoling. "You know these offers are going to dry up if you keep toeing that party line."

"Fine with me," she said, scrolling through the onscreen guide on the television in her bedroom. Tonight was one of Ama and Dani's regular nights off, so she and Laya had made veggie lasagna for dinner and cleaned up the kitchen before bed. Fridays were her favorite night of the week, a chance to spend some quality time with her daughter and decompress from a busy week. Which was what she'd been doing before Michael had made a pest of himself, calling her cell phone and land line repeatedly until she finally picked up.

"Are you sure?" he asked. "We're talking six figures for a one-time guest appearance. You like everyone involved in this show. Good politics."

She wavered for a moment. The exposure might be good for the foundation. Then again, there would be plenty of time later to make appearances that would be more meaningful than a guest spot on a sitcom. "I'm sure," she said. "But tell them I'm flattered they thought of me."

"Will do," Michael said, and sighed audibly. Actors weren't the only ones fluent in melodrama.

After they hung up, Tessa set the TV to a classical music station and reached for the stack of books on her bedside table. She was a glutton when it came to reading fiction, from cheap paperbacks to new hardcovers, always switching between three or four at a time. She preferred to read paperbacks in bed—hard-backed books got so heavy. But right now she was working on the new Sarah Waters novel, only available in hardcover.

Like Waters' last novel, this one was a departure from her early works, well known and much loved lesbian romps through Victorian England. As she read the first chapter, Tessa found herself longing for the sexiness of *Tipping the Velvet*, or the mystery of *Fingersmith*. Ironic, she thought, that she was loathe to allow the British writer to reinvent her writing when change was what she craved herself.

Tessa had never planned on an acting career, or even dreamed of one. When she turned eighteen in the middle of her senior year of high school, she'd graduated early, packed her belongings in a single bag, and left the latest in a long line of foster families. She'd been saving her babysitting money secretly for years, waiting to leave Chicago, a city that had left her with few genuine connections. The only adult who had seemed to take an interest in her was a math teacher at the high school she'd attended sophomore year. Looking back, Tessa was pretty sure that Leticia Williams was a lesbian, and had always wondered if the young teacher had recognized the inner queer in her. But one person in eight years of foster families and new schools was not enough to tie her to Chicago.

The potential destinations on her escape list demonstrated little creativity: New York or Los Angeles, both cities where she could lose herself in the masses. Since her birthday was in January, one of the darkest, coldest months in the aptly named Windy City, the choice was easy. In L.A., no one would ever have to know what she came from. No more pity or poorly disguised trepidation in the eyes of the adults who had read her case file, no more taunting from her foster siblings. She couldn't wait to build a life where no one knew who she was. Ironic, she thought again—for despite the fact that she was decidedly recognizable the world over, no one actually knew her, except perhaps her daughter.

A few intrepid members of the press, sensing in her back story a snow job, had tried to track down names and addresses of the relatives she'd invented. But without her real name, they didn't have much to go on. And Flanagans, it seemed, proliferated throughout the Northeast United States. Her birth certificate was a closely guarded secret, and Tessa publicly claimed to share her Irish father's last name, while the relatives she had (allegedly) lived with belonged to her mother's side. She'd looked different in high school, too—she'd worn her hair in a tight braid, and unfashionable glasses and a tendency to eat when she was upset had made her the proverbial ugly duckling. Not until she reached L.A. and cut her hair, slimmed down and bought contact lenses did she begin to blossom into her pre-star self.

Only her agent, publicist and business manager knew the truth about her past—except that wasn't entirely true. Tessa was aware of at least two cases where someone who claimed to have information had approached her management team, but nothing had come of either situation. So far, at least, it appeared she'd managed to create a new life that couldn't be traced back to the old one.

That was partly why she'd had Laya. Selfish and potentially wrongheaded, maybe, but she'd longed for one person in the world connected to her by blood and genetics, a child in whom she could see herself. Once she'd held her daughter, though, as soon as she'd cradled the tiny, defenseless creature in her arms, it didn't matter anymore why she had decided to have a child, only that she was a mother. Not that the press saw it that way. During her pregnancy, the paparazzi had made such a concerted effort to uncover the father's identity that Melody had finally issued a release stating outright that Tessa had used an anonymous donor.

This was, in fact, the truth. She had purchased sperm through a high-end clinic in Switzerland that specialized in working with couples and individuals for whom privacy was a major factor in family planning while money wasn't. She'd pored over the clinic's catalog, finally deciding on a donor with a similar genetic makeup so that her baby would look like her, not a stranger they would likely never meet. Then she'd called Michael and Melody and told them she needed a good fertility doctor, one who was both accustomed to celebrity clients and willing to make house calls.

Since she was youngish and healthy, the fertility doctor Melody put Tessa in touch with suggested they try basic artificial insemination a few times, just to see what happened, before resorting to more extreme hormone manipulation. During a break between film projects, Tessa had the sperm shipped to the doctor's clinic. The next time she ovulated, he drove to her house, canister stored in a portable cooler, and, with a nurse's assistance, inseminated her right there in her own bedroom. Apparently women in her family were fertile—she'd gotten knocked up on the second try. She hadn't felt any different at first, so when she missed her period two weeks after the second insemination attempt, she was sure it had to be a mistake. But no. The half dozen home pregnancy tests she took indicated what a blood test confirmed—she was going to have a baby. What had been theory was suddenly on the verge of becoming reality.

Her pregnancy had been without complication of any kind, which was a good thing—she'd had to work through week number thirty-three on a movie that had been planned for over a year and a half. The film's producer wasn't thrilled about her inflated abdomen that had to be camouflaged in shot after shot, and Tessa didn't blame him. But she'd genuinely believed getting pregnant would take longer than a mere six weeks. As soon as news got out, her normal paparazzi shadow turned into a dedicated following. Melody's press release, viewed by some as just another celebrity subterfuge, had helped tame some of the craziness. But even so, prognostications of all types continued about Tessa's decision to have a baby out of wedlock.

She didn't particularly care what anyone else thought about her having a child on her own, though. For the first time in her adult life, she felt as if she'd made something good happen. Unlike her acting career, which had happened to her, she'd chosen to be a mother. Laya had been wanted, and Tessa planned to spend the rest of her life demonstrating that fact.

Stretched out on her king-sized bed with one of their cats curled against her, Tessa tried to focus on the words on the page before her. But she couldn't quite envision the straight characters Waters had chosen to give voice to this time around. Or maybe it was just that she was tired of straight people, sick of hetero culture imposing itself everywhere she turned—on billboards, in magazines, even in stories about her, for God's sake. Her sexuality was an open secret among the Hollywood elite, but the movie-making machinery operated on the assumption that if middle America, its main consumers, found out that its favorite action hero liked handsome boys, or that the queen of romantic comedy preferred women, those actors' market shares would plummet.

Tessa wanted to believe that this was an outdated notion, that average Americans wouldn't care if their big screen heroes and heroines were homos. But she knew that homophobia was still legal in most states, gay civil rights were routinely voted down by a majority of citizens (California's Proposition 8 was only one example among many), and gay-bashing was still regarded as boys just being boys in plenty of towns and cities across the country. So she'd let Michael and Melody talk her into staying in the closet, and she hadn't denied the fabricated gossip that linked her with various male celebrities, some of whom had closets of their own to camouflage.

Only sometimes, like today when she looked into Eleanor Chapin's eyes and read the attraction there, when she felt that tingle that comes when you're close to someone whose body chemistry matches your own, on days like today she wanted to bust out of her closet and tell the straight world where it could go. Tell her viewing public that they didn't own her. But instead of holding an impromptu press conference, she holed up at home, turned on the incredibly complex alarm system Michael had had installed (how did heat detectors know the difference between animals and humans, anyway?), and, after Laya was safely tucked into bed, escaped into lesbian land via film or fiction.

Tonight, though, Sarah Waters wasn't cooperating. The need to escape hetero land unassuaged, Tessa set the novel aside. She stepped into slippers and padded along the wood floor out into the hallway, past Laya's door—she poked her head in to make sure her daughter was asleep in her treehouse bunk bed—and down the hall to the library. When she was growing up, she'd never had any books of her own, and had had to content herself with worn paperbacks and cracked hardcovers from the public library. Now that she had more money than any one person had a right to, she bought books whenever she liked, so many that she'd had one of the bedrooms in the house converted to a library complete with floor-to-ceiling bookshelves and a ladder on wheels that swiveled around the high-ceilinged room.

She turned on the light and enjoyed the frisson of pleasure she always experienced at the sight of so many books. One of her studio-sponsored assistants had offered to alphabetize the collection, and Tessa had accepted gratefully. Now she trailed her fingers across the book spines closest to the door. Authors with M names. She moved left, checking spines as she went until at last she came to W. Finding the book she wanted, she turned out the light and returned to her bedroom, stopping once again to look in on her sleeping daughter. She loved Laya with a depth that sometimes surprised her still. Since she'd become a mother, she finally understood what the phrase "unconditional love" truly meant. And understood that it wasn't something she'd had much of in her own life.

Back in bed, she snuggled under the covers and opened her trade paperback copy of *Tipping the Velvet*. She leafed through the pages, pausing to read a snippet here, a phrase there. When she came across the scene where the main character, Nan, spent her first night with the alluring Lady Lethaby, she closed her eyes. It had been way too long since another woman had touched her. Who would have thought a kindergarten teacher could arouse such heat?

But she had, and now the question was what Tessa should do about it.

CHAPTER FOUR

On Sunday morning, Eleanor rose early, hauled Sasha's mountain bike out of the basement of the apartment building and, cycled the short distance to Runyon Canyon Park, just beyond the Hollywood Bowl. There she locked up the bike and began to jog up the trail, full CamelBak hydration pack strapped to her back.

Her first run in L.A. a decade earlier, when she'd visited Sasha the Thanksgiving after they graduated, had ended badly—as in vomiting and dehydration. Sasha had tried to warn her ahead of time that the heat was only a symptom of the real danger: aridity. Despite the palm trees and the distant sea you could visit if you were willing to brave freeway traffic or surface streets, L.A. was a desert. And people died in the desert all the time.

"Remember, you're from Vermont," Sasha had cautioned. "Your pores won't know what hit them."

Eleanor now knew to take more water than seemed necessary, to drink copious amounts as she ran, and to jog more slowly than she truly liked. In this way, she could enjoy her workout without experiencing the ill effects of dehydration, which, as a pale-skinned northern Vermonter, she seemed particularly prone to. Another reason she would be glad to leave Southern California for grad school.

So far she'd received two acceptances and four rejections. The schools that wanted her were Cornell and Stanford—on clear opposite sides of the country as well as in exceedingly different climactic and cultural environments. The one thing the two universities had in common was that both were only offering her partial funding. She knew why, but the slight still stung. Because she'd finished undergrad so long ago, technically she would be a "returning student"—one who was stepping away from an existing career to consider a new one, rather than a newbie with little life experience. Jack Mills, her Smith mentor, had explained that most programs accepted older applicants with mixed feelings. On the one hand, students like Eleanor had valuable experience to contribute to their studies. On the other, returning students could be especially stubborn and intractable. The older they were, the less likely they were to kowtow to their professors' opinions, and the hierarchy of graduate school depended on at least a modicum of blind obedience.

Assuming the last program rejected her (it probably would—Wisconsin-Madison had one of the top programs in the country; out of an average of 250 applicants, they accepted exactly six new students each year), Eleanor was going to have to decide between being broke in the Bay Area or impoverished in Upstate New York. She was leaning toward Stanford, and not just because its program more closely matched what she wanted to do, with a focus on developmental and pre-adolescent psych. The Bay Area was West Coast progressive, close to L.A. and Sasha (her roommate had vowed to never again reside outside of Southern California), and offered a vibrant lesbian community where several friends from college currently resided.

Still, Palo Alto was considerably farther away from her sister and father than she wanted to be, not to mention a thousand times more expensive than Ithaca. If she had to borrow so much money that her future career plans would be hostage to her student loans, the pedagogical difference between the two programs would be neutralized. She had just finished paying off her undergraduate loans a year earlier—her indentured servitude, as she had referred to the three hundred dollar payment automatically deducted from her bank account each month. Once, and once only, she had done the math: three hundred dollar a month for one hundred and eighteen months (she'd paid the balance off two months early) came to $35,400. A down payment on the house she didn't own, or, at least, a really nice car. She'd been so elated to finally pay off the last few hundred dollars that she was now loathe to voluntarily return to a similar state of vassalage.

As she ran up the wide, dusty trail at the edge of Runyon Canyon, early morning sun strong on her shoulders, she debated her options. Was there some way she could make a bunch of cash in a short time? There was always stripping, a field surprisingly dominated by lesbians. She was fit, but her breasts were small. Running kept her lean, a trait typically not prized in the exotic dancing field. Besides, she possessed the usual feminist aversion to participating in an industry based on the objectification of the feminine form, not to mention a commercial enterprise that encouraged violence against women. If she resorted to stripping, she would always feel like a cautionary real-life CSI story waiting to happen—*a smart girl who needed money for school, found strangled to death behind the downtown L.A. club where she pole-danced four nights a week.* She grimaced at the thought and took a generous gulp of water. The Northeast Kingdomite in her didn't like seedy urban places. She preferred evergreen forests, ancient rock walls, clear freshwater lakes, black bears who mauled your trash if you didn't keep animal-proof containers.

Nearly to the top of the mile-long climb up the rim of the canyon, she dodged a pair of panting yellow labs (Runyon was off-leash paradise) and slowed slightly. All of this thinking was causing her to run faster than was likely good for her in the heat. As she followed the trail east, she gazed over the city spread out below. The neat grid-like streets of Hollywood gradually gave way to the high-rises of downtown L.A, surprisingly unhazy on this spring morning. From this vantage point, the city looked clean, bright, futuristic. She knew better. Perhaps it was just the Vermonter in her, but certain gritty parts of L.A. felt as if they might break into violence at any provocation. Another factor of the heat, Sasha claimed, combined with Eleanor's subconsciously racist imagination. Which was probably true. Sasha was the first black person she'd known intimately. Vermont hardly went out of its way to make people of color feel comfortable, Sasha noted whenever she visited Eleanor at home in Newport, where residents sometimes did double-takes before looking away guiltily.

As Eleanor ran along the canyon edge, she passed a lone scraggly California tree with a bench placed strategically beneath it. She closed her eyes, but that didn't stop the memories from forming against her eyelids. Running with your eyes closed near a two-hundred-foot drop was not advisable, so she opened her eyes and let the images come. Fighting them didn't help, she'd learned by now.

One March several years earlier, her mother had traveled west with her to visit Sasha over spring break. Sarah Chapin had never been to Southern California, and it was something she had always wanted to do. *Before she died* was the phrase that, at the time, had recently begun to hang over them all. She'd successfully fought the first round of breast cancer, which had found its way into her lymph nodes before they caught it. For four years she was cancer-free. But then, before the all-important five-year anniversary, the cancer came back. The second time, she'd opted to have a double mastectomy and breast reconstruction surgery.

To celebrate the supposedly successful completion of the second round of treatment, Eleanor had (with her dad's help) surprised her mom with a one-week vacation to L.A. They'd stayed in Sasha's guest room, where Eleanor had awakened more than once in the night to find her mother weeping beside her in the queen bed.

But by day, Sarah Chapin rallied. The trio walked the bustling streets near Sasha's apartment each morning, visited museums and art galleries in the afternoons, even drove the four-and-a-half hours to Vegas and back for an overnight gambling adventure. Their last day in L.A., Sasha and Eleanor brought her mother to Runyon Canyon. She wanted to make it up on her own power, but by the time they neared the top, Sarah was fading fast. She sat down on the bench beneath the lone shade tree at the edge of the trail and didn't move. After twenty minutes, Sasha pulled Eleanor aside and offered to call for paramedics. They could come in the back way from Mulholland Drive, where there was an entrance to the rim of the canyon.

But Eleanor didn't want to embarrass her mother, so instead, Sasha jogged down to the parking lot and drove up Mulholland to meet them. Eleanor helped her mother to the car, feeling the fragility of her bones, the dryness of her skin. Her treatment had concluded six months earlier, but she was still so weak. That was when Eleanor began to believe her mother wouldn't make it. The cancer was waging too fierce a battle. Sarah Chapin was losing her ability to fight back.

After the Runyon Incident, as Eleanor thought of it, she and her mom stayed an extra two days "to regroup," and it turned out that the trip extension allowed them to check out a new planetarium show at the Griffith Park Observatory, one that explored the history of the universe and humanity's place in it. The show was the highlight of the trip, her mom told her on the plane home. As director of the local public library, Sarah had spearheaded a long-term capital campaign to add a planetarium to the Newport Public Library. A couple of months before she died, ground was broken on the start of the new Sarah Chapin Observatory just outside town on a hillside overlooking South Bay. Eleanor, her parents, and her sister were all there on a warm September afternoon to bear witness.

When she reached the canyon rim, Eleanor paused at a viewpoint, gazing out over the sunny, shiny city. She missed her mom so much, but she missed the younger, pre-cancer Sarah most. The disease that had killed her whittled her away slowly but steadily over its intermittent twelve-year assault, until Eleanor and her sister no longer recognized the same woman who had taught them to read before they started school, taken them hiking along the Appalachian Trail, laughed more than she cried. Losing her mother wasn't like something out of an after-school special. The illness didn't magically bring them closer or give them a common foe to fight. Eleanor, her sister and her dad were powerless to stop the spread of the disease that left her mother a trembling victim who, by the end, had seemed relieved to die.

Eleanor stared westward to the Santa Monica Mountains that edged West Hollywood. She didn't want to think about her mother. That wasn't why she'd come to Runyon. She wanted to think about something happier. Someone—but she knew who. Tessa Flanagan's house wasn't far from Runyon Canyon. Eleanor knew this because she'd copied down Laya's home address before leaving work on Friday and typed it into Google Maps the night before after a lame tween movie premiere that Sasha had dragged her to. Only in L.A. did lawyerly work functions involve spotlights and the red carpet. Eleanor had found herself checking out the crowd throughout the evening, just in case.

"Your girlfriend isn't here," Sasha had said when she caught her scoping the crowd. "This isn't her scene. Now, a black-tie dinner to raise money for AIDS treatment in Africa..."

"I can't hear you," Eleanor had maturely responded, humming to drown out the sound of her roommate's teasing.

According to Google Maps, Tessa's house was somewhere *there*, Eleanor thought now, gazing out at the hills rolling away to the west. Not that she'd ever find it from here, not even with binoculars. Too many hills in the way, and besides, the street view had only revealed a tall white stucco wall topped by an iron gate with security cameras posted at regular intervals. The Flanagans certainly took their security seriously. Not that she could blame them—Tessa no doubt had her share of scary stalkers.

Of which Eleanor was determined not to become another. She began to run down the western trail, taking the stairs built into the sand beneath the viewpoint as slowly as she could manage. One thing about being in your thirties, she'd noticed, it hurt more to fall. And the pain lasted longer. Another reason not to take up pole dancing—she wasn't a highly coordinated athlete, though she could play softball with the best of them. Pole dancing was probably something better left to professionals.

The slot machines in Vegas, on the other hand, she thought, remembering her mother's laughter as they'd walked the Strip at night, could be a boon to amateurs and professionals alike. Maybe a quick trip to Sin City would be the answer to her grad school financing woes, since she hadn't been graced with her sister's athletic endowments.

Julia had attended UVM on a partial soccer scholarship. Daddy's girl from the beginning, Julia grew up playing club soccer ten months a year and traveling to tournaments throughout Vermont and New England. Their father had been a faithful fan at all of her games, driving her to matches through rain and snow, over hill and dale. Eleanor was proud of her little sister, and had cheered her on every chance she got. But sometimes she'd wondered why the family always divided into "Eleanor & Mom" and "Julia & Dad."

Before she came out her sophomore year at Smith, Eleanor had been much closer to her mother. When she decided to be honest with her parents about who she was, though, her mother withdrew. Someone outside the family might not have noticed, but Eleanor did. Her mom no longer looked her directly in the eye, no longer asked about her life. Eleanor had believed that time would help Sarah Chapin become more accepting. She'd hoped right up until the final hours of her mother's life that she would take it all back and look at her with the same love and acceptance that had once graced their relationship. Now she never could.

That was the worst part—that her mother's story, their family's story, was over. It couldn't change, couldn't evolve over time. There was a finite beginning, middle and end. And the end had been hard. So much agony in such a small body. Her mother had finally simply faded away, color leaching out of her eyes, her skin, even her lips at the end, until she no longer resembled the woman Eleanor had loved and admired. Her mother's story was set immutably in the text inscribed on the headstone in St. Mary's Cemetery: *Sarah Westfall Chapin—Beloved Mother, Daughter, Sister, Wife. We will miss you always.* Simple but true. They would always miss her.

Although some more than others, perhaps. Six weeks after

the funeral, Eleanor and her sister had been crossing Arkansas at dusk, the day's light only a fading reminder at the horizon, when Julia informed her that their father had a girlfriend.

Eleanor's gaze had jerked away from the road. "What? What are you talking about?"

"Dad is seeing someone. It's pretty serious."

"But it's only been—I don't understand. Who is she?"

"Emma Barnes. Her husband was killed in a plane crash a while ago. Dad remodeled her house a few years back. She's great. You'd like her, Elle."

"How do you know all of this?"

"Dad told me. I met Emma at Christmas."

"Why didn't you tell me then? Why didn't Dad?"

"He thought you might need time to get used to the idea. You live so far away, and you don't come home that often. He thought you might not understand the way things were with him and Mom at the end."

"Boston is not that far away. And anyway, I took the year off from teaching so I could be home for Mom, so we could all be together."

"Yeah, well, she didn't just start dying in September."

Eleanor's gaze skittered back to Julia again, but her sister's head was turned away. She was tempted to let the matter drop, to turn up the radio and let the impersonal noise drown out the personal pain flitting about the car, but the therapist she'd been working with had helped her break away from the family mythology (a regional hazard) that talking about bad things only made them worse. She forced herself to ask the question whose answer she was pretty sure she didn't want to know. "You said he worked on her house a few years ago. How long have they been...?"

"I'm not sure," Julia said, staring ahead at the darkening road before them. "A while, though, I think. They're past the honeymoon stage—but maybe widows and widowers don't get another honeymoon."

Was this why their father had listed "Wife" last on the headstone? Because Sarah Chapin had been more beloved by the other people in her life? And had his wife known about his diverted affections?

Now as she neared the bottom of Runyon Canyon, Eleanor slowed to a walk and gulped more water. Sweat soaked every inch of her skin. Even her ponytail was wet. Back at the trailhead, she stretched out and tried to drip-dry a bit before climbing on Sasha's bike and heading back to the apartment. Maybe she'd call Julia when she got home. They hadn't spoken in a couple of weeks. Her baby sister would blow a gasket when she heard about her date with Tessa Flanagan, as Eleanor was now unofficially deeming their lunch together in the Barclay School cafeteria. It was only a small distortion, really, and anyway, what Tessa didn't know wouldn't hurt her.

On Sunday mornings, Tessa, Dani and Laya made a big breakfast in the carriage house where Dani and Ama lived. A devoted Catholic, Ama went to early mass on Sundays and usually came home just in time for the four of them to eat at the breakfast bar in the kitchen.

At first, this Sunday seemed no different from a hundred others. Tessa helped Laya cut her blueberry pancakes into manageable bites and poured orange juice into a tall plastic cup. Then she dug into her own pancakes, which were scrumptious as ever. Dani had embraced her suggestion after Laya was born that they eat as much organic, low-fat, gluten-free foods as possible. Her naturopath had recommended a vegan diet, but Tessa liked cheese and eggs too much to give up dairy. As a compromise, they ate fish and poultry but steered clear of mammals. Dani and Ama, who had grown up on a small island in the Philippines and come to the U.S. as adults, told her they'd eaten this way most of their lives.

"Until we moved to L.A.," Ama would say. "Then we started to buy Spam and Frosted Flakes. 'No pancit,' our children would cry. 'No Filipino food! Hamburgers and french fries, please!'"

"I like pancit," Laya always said. "I like french fries too. But I don't like hamburgers. I wouldn't want to eat Moo."

Moo, a big soft black and white dairy cow with expressive brown eyes, was one of her favorite stuffed animals.

This morning Laya was describing the craft project they'd worked on at school the previous week. "Miss Chapin brought in these flower stems made out of cardboard and this soft stuff, I forget what it's called—wait. Feld?" She looked at Tessa for confirmation.

"Could it be felt?"

"Doh!" Laya slapped her forehead like Bart Simpson's father, and Tessa wondered where she'd learned the move, since they didn't watch *The Simpsons* at home. "That's what I meant. Anyway, so Miss Chapin brought in the felt and we cut it up and made flowers and then she hung them up in the hall. Mine was super-duper pretty, Miss Chapin said so."

Had Laya's teacher used the word "super-duper," or was it merely a product of Laya's imperfect retelling? Tessa could picture Eleanor Chapin kneeling beside her students, helping them with the craft activity. Could see her smile, her freckles, her graceful hands. That generous mouth…

But Laya was asking her something, and she returned from her fantasies guiltily. "Sorry, honey, what?"

"I said, when are you coming back to school with me? Miss Chapin told me to tell you to come anytime."

"She did, did she?" Tessa felt herself flush, and avoided Ama's curious look. "I don't know, Laya. I'm pretty busy with the foundation."

"To help kids who aren't as lucky as me," Laya said, sighing. "I know. I just like it when you go with me. Miss Chapin likes it too."

Now Ama was staring at her, eyebrows nearly level with her hairline, eyes twinkling. "Does she?" the tiny Filipina asked, balancing on her stool.

Busted, Tessa thought.

Dani looked from his wife to Tessa and back again. Then he put his fork down and went over to the stove to start cleaning up the breakfast mess, humming to himself. Tessa gave Ama a silencing look and said, "Come back, Dani. You know cleaning up is Laya's and my job."

"You keep eating," he said. "You and that child both need fattening up."

Laya giggled. "Miss Chapin says it's not nice to call people fat."

"In this case, it's a compliment," Tessa told her daughter.

After breakfast, she managed to avoid being alone with Ama for a little while. But eventually Dani drifted outside to work in the garden and Laya went down for her afternoon nap. Tessa was reclining among the pillows in the window seat downstairs, the Sarah Waters novel open on her lap, when the pint-sized inquisitioner finally cornered her.

"What's this about Laya's teacher?" Ama asked, settling onto the love seat with the blanket she was knitting for her youngest daughter's new baby.

"I don't know what you mean," Tessa said, and stared down at the book she was determined to finish. Disliking a work of fiction simply because it was about straight people struck her as narrow-minded, a quality she would like to believe she didn't possess. Anyway, plenty of straight people enjoyed Waters' lesbian books, didn't they? At least, straight people in England.

"That's a load of hooey," Ama said, repeating a Midwestern phrase Tessa had made the mistake of teaching her. "You like her, don't you?"

Nancy, Ama's eldest, had come out as a lesbian while at Stanford twenty years earlier. It had taken Ama some time, she'd told Tessa, but eventually she'd learned to embrace her daughter's "lifestyle." By the time she came to work for Tessa, she was fine with both the idea and practice of homosexuality. Dani wasn't quite as far along as his wife, but Tessa only knew this because Ama had told her. Outwardly, he seemed unaffected by any mention of same-sex love.

One thing Ama didn't like, though, was single motherhood. She was always after Tessa to find a nice girl and settle down. She and Dani wouldn't be around forever to help out with Laya, and then what would happen? She'd once offered to set Tessa up with one of her daughter's friends, at which point Tessa had had to remind her that unlike Nancy, she needed to stay closeted for professional reasons.

Another thing Ama didn't approve of: "Too many people have worked too hard for you to hide," she often said. "Like that Harvey Milk."

Now Tessa frowned at her across the coffee table. "I do not like Miss Chapin. I mean, I like her, but I don't *like* her."

Ama laughed and muttered something in Tagalog.

Tessa's mother and her Filipina friends in Chicago had spoken Tagalog, and she'd been able to understand it as a child. But now she only remembered a few phrases, among them *magandang umaga* (good morning), *salamat* (thank you), and *malaya* (free). This last word was Laya's full name, of which Ama thoroughly approved.

"She's Laya's teacher," Tessa pointed out. "It would be inappropriate."

"Not for much longer," Ama said.

Barclay followed the college calendar rather than that of the local public schools. In a matter of weeks, Laya would be on summer break.

"That reminds me," Tessa said, changing the subject. "I was thinking of taking Laya to Kauai in June for a vacation. We could use some time away from the city. Would you and Dani like to come with us?"

Like many Filipinos, Ama and Dani both had family in Hawaii. They usually came along to the big house, as they jokingly called it, for a paid vacation in return for helping to look after Laya. Tessa had a home office at her vacation house, and while she tried to leave work behind for the few weeks they were in Hawaii, sometimes she needed to lock herself in for an afternoon.

"Not this time," Ama said.

Tessa started. She'd thought asking was just a formality. "Really? Why not?"

"Dani wants to go back to the Philippines."

"Oh. That'll be nice." Ama and Dani had visited family in the Philippines twice since coming to work for her. Each time they'd gone for three weeks, their suitcases overflowing with American T-shirts, shoes and candy bars to distribute among their relatives. Someday, Tessa wanted to go with them. She still had family there. She just didn't know where. Or, precisely, whom. "How long will you be staying this time?"

Ama set her knitting needles aside. "I've been wanting to

speak with you about this. Dani and I have been talking, and we agree. When we go to the Philippines this summer, we won't be coming back right away."

Tessa sat up, book forgotten. "But your children are here. And your grandchildren."

"They are, but you know that our parents are still in the Philippines, and they're very old, Tess. Dani's father has some heart problems lately. He needs us. Later, we can come back here. But we are tired of L.A. It's too expensive, and we would like to live near the sea again without having to listen to the smog reports."

"Of course. That makes sense," Tessa said, trying to wrap her mind around what Ama was telling her. "When were you thinking of going?"

"When you leave for Hawaii, we'll go, too."

Tessa felt her throat closing up. She looked down at her hands. They were going? And so soon? "Does this mean we won't see you again?"

"Sweet girl," Ama said, and came to sit beside her on the window seat. She took Tessa's hand and held it between both of her own. "We will always see you again. You are our daughter now, and Laya is our granddaughter. You and she do not have family, so we adopt you. We choose you."

Tessa had thought she'd worked through her abandonment issues (years of therapy before Laya's birth with an eminently discreet psychologist who catered to Hollywood stars), but Ama's words broke something inside her. Soon she was crying silently, her head on Ama's shoulder as whispered Tagalog rose into the space above them. She was going to miss them so much, this funny little couple who had shared their home for Laya's entire life. Despite what Ama said, once they left the country, would she and Laya ever see them again? She'd always thought of Ama and Dani as older because they had a daughter her age. But they came from an island where the average life expectancy exceeded ninety, they had told her proudly more than once. You just had to steer clear of the guerrilla fighters in the hills.

Eventually Ama kissed her forehead and returned to her knitting, and Tessa went back to her book, though she had a hard time concentrating on the words staining the pages, and not because the characters were straight. Now her mind churned from one worry to another—how would Laya take the loss of her adopted grandparents? Who would take over the thousand practical details Ama and Dani oversaw? And what would Tessa do with Laya when they got back from Hawaii? The foundation planning was ramping up, which meant she would need someone to watch Laya most days until school started again in the fall.

Ama had apparently been thinking on this matter too. When they heard Laya stirring in her upstairs bedroom a little later, she paused her knitting needles again and said, "You know, Mahal, I can think of a substitute kindergarten teacher who may be interested in employment."

Tessa shook her head. "Stop matchmaking, Tita."

"But I'm so good at it! My sister in Encinitas would not be happily married to this day if not for my assistance."

And she was off and running on a story Tessa had heard many times before, always a little different, but always with the all-important ingredients of doughnuts, mini-golf and true love.

CHAPTER FIVE

Eleanor was about to turn off the light in her classroom when her cell phone rang. She set her teaching bag on the nearest miniature chair, cursing as she realized her phone wasn't in its outside pocket. Where the hell was it? She searched through the bag, pushing aside a notebook and a pair of children's scissors. This was why she always tried to put everything back in its rightful place.

Just as she found the truant cell phone wedged into a set of laminated flash cards, it beeped—gone to voice mail. She flipped it open and checked the screen, but the incoming number was unlisted. Probably another wrong number from Massachusetts. She'd gotten so many that she now knew the former owner of her cell number was a guy named Nathan who had friends with uber-WASPy names like Addison West and Maxwell Alexander. Probably an Exeter grad. Likely a Harvard alum.

That was another thing she didn't miss about Boston—the hordes of lemming-like prep schoolers, recognizable by their Kennedy-esque good looks and the well-fed rosiness of their white cheeks. She knew the type only too well after teaching at private schools her entire adult life. Had it really been ten years? She'd never intended to be a teacher. Her current career was only supposed to be temporary, a pause between undergrad and graduate school. That was why she'd never taken the time to become certified—why spend the time and money on public school certification when she would soon be headed down a different career path?

Five years, she'd promised herself: Once her mother hit the magical five-year cancer-free milestone, after which she would have the same odds of developing the disease that anyone else had, then Eleanor would go back to school. But that didn't happen, and Eleanor kept on teaching private school in Boston, only a few hours from home. Over the years, she had attempted to instill in her Choate- or Concord-bound students a mistrust of privilege and a generosity of spirit that would follow them to the hallowed halls of their future academic settings. No way of knowing what kind of impact, if any, she'd had.

The phone beeped again as she slid into the front seat of her Jetta. The mystery caller had left a message. She turned on her Bluetooth headset and dialed voice mail as she left the Barclay School parking lot, waving at the uniformed attendant at the front gate. The hulking guard, a former Marine officer according to the head of school, nodded coolly back at her. As she turned onto Mulholland Drive, she was thinking about what she wanted for dinner, if the letter from Wisconsin-Madison would be there when she got home, whether or not it was too hot out for a quick run. But all of these thoughts vanished as Tessa Flanagan's voice sounded in her headset.

"Hi, Miss Chapin, this is Tessa, Laya's mother. Could you call me? I have an idea I was hoping to discuss with you. My cell phone number is 323-770-1478. Thanks. Take care."

Eleanor pressed replay and listened again to the luscious

Tessa Flanagan speaking into her voice mail. Thank the gods she had misplaced her phone. Otherwise she might actually have answered and proceeded to behave like Sydney Ellen Wade in *The American President* (one of her favorite movies) in the scene where President Shepherd calls Sydney to ask her out and she hangs up on him. Twice. Eleanor could just see herself saying, "Right, Sasha. Very funny."

Except that Tessa's voice was unmistakable, even filtered through multiple satellite relays, and there was no chance the world-famous actress was calling to ask her out.

She hit Sasha's work number on speed dial. "I need advice," she said when her roommate picked up, and quickly described the contents of the voice mail message.

"Call her back, you idiot," Sasha responded. "It's probably something related to school. Maybe she wants to hold an end-of-the-year party for her daughter's class. Stars like to do that kind of thing."

"Of course. You're right. It's probably nothing."

"That, or she's always wanted to sleep with a Vermonter."

Eleanor ended the call, cutting off Sasha's laughter. She was almost down the hill to Franklin. Should she call Tessa back right away? Didn't want to seem too eager. Right—as if playing hard to get was the reason she might delay the call instead of abject fear. She was beginning to wish she'd never submitted her application to the Barclay School.

Back at Sasha's, she found parking on a narrow side street off Beechwood and entered the building from the back. She checked the mailbox first thing—no letter from Madison yet, damn them—and made her way upstairs. The apartment was at the quiet(ish) rear of the building, top floor, with a view of the Hollywood sign from the living room window and balcony. The rent was outrageous, but for a comparable monthly mortgage payment, Sasha would have had to move to Van Nuys. She didn't want to cross over to the dark side, she said. Meaning the Valley.

By the time Eleanor had dropped her bag by the dining room table and changed out of her teaching clothes, her nervousness had abated. Mostly. She picked up her cell phone, dialed voice mail and wrote down the Flanagans' number. She could do this. Tessa was a student's mother. So what if she also happened to be a Hollywood goddess about whom Eleanor had recently taken to fantasizing?

Tessa picked up on the third ring. "Hi, Eleanor. Thanks for calling back."

"No problem. Is everything okay with Laya? I noticed she was sneezing this morning."

"Just allergies. Sometimes she sneaks one of our cats into her room at night. Sweet, but the dander doesn't always agree with her."

"Gotcha." Eleanor hesitated. "So, what can I do for you?"

"I was hoping to talk to you in person about a possible job opportunity. Do you have any free time this weekend?"

"I do." Should she put it out there that she wasn't really on the job market?

"Would you be interested in having lunch with Laya and me at our house on Saturday?"

Then again, it couldn't hurt to hear what Tessa had to say. "Saturday would be great."

"Good. I'll send a car for you at noon. You live off Beechwood, don't you?"

Was it creepy that Tessa knew where she lived, or just insanely flattering? "Yes, but I can drive myself."

"I'm sure you can." Tessa's voice sounded as if she were smiling. "The car will be there at noon. Laya and I will both be looking forward to seeing you."

"Um, yeah. Me too."

The line clicked, and Eleanor sat staring at the phone, a little stunned. Then she hit save and entered Tessa's name in her cell phone directory. A month ago, before she got the job at Barclay, if someone had told her that she would be going to lunch at the Flanagans' house in the Hollywood Hills, she would have laughed herself silly. But here she was, already wondering what she possibly had to wear to such an occasion. She dialed Sasha's office number. Good thing her best friend was straight and a native Southern Californian. For once, those qualities would come in handy.

Tessa stood inside her walk-in closet, lights turned high. This was just another professional lunch, she told herself. Only instead of a discussion of up-front quotes and gross points or, more recently, nonprofit funding strategies, the conversation today would revolve around summer vacation and nanny duties. She could have called a service, but her daughter would be losing her second mother and only father figure when Ama and Dani left for the Philippines next month. If Eleanor Chapin, who Laya already adored, agreed to take the position, Ama had argued convincingly, surely it would be better for all involved. The fact that Tessa found her daughter's teacher attractive was beside the point. Hiring Eleanor hadn't even been her idea.

She paced the closet. One side of the walk-in housed her work attire—business clothes, designer evening wear and assorted accessories, most from top tier designers who sent her clothing at no charge in exchange for a free PR boost. A couple of times a year, she donated her freebies to silent auctions and other charity fundraisers. She used to complain to Michael that he was forcing her to wear drag whenever she dressed up in Hollywood glam. Over the years, though, she'd come to enjoy the sleek lines of a Vera Wang dress and even, on occasion, the look of her legs in Christian Dior stilettos. Did that make her a lousy lesbian? Probably. Then again, she wasn't exactly winning any HRC awards with her closeted status.

The other side of the walk-in held real-life clothes—jeans, capris, shorts, sweats, tank tops, collared shirts and sweaters. She settled on a dark red V-neck wraparound shirt that showed a modest amount of cleavage, paired with blue jeans and her favorite around-town clogs. Maybe a little dressed up for lunch at home, but it was, after all, a job interview. She'd asked Eleanor to come to the house not only so that the teacher could get a feel for what the position would entail but also so that Ama and Dani could meet her. It was just possible that her own judgment might be somewhat clouded when it came to her daughter's teacher.

Downstairs, she checked with Dani to see how lunch preparations were coming—fresh-squeezed juice, green salad and a variety of sandwiches on spelt bread—then went outside to the patio. The heat had descended early, and Laya was splashing around the shallow end of the pool, yellow inflatable arm bands keeping her afloat under Ama's watchful eye. Almost from birth, Laya had demonstrated an impressive ability to amuse herself. She seemed happiest immersed in her own make-believe world, talking to animals and inventing stories about her immediate environment. Briefly, as she watched Laya leap off the edge of the pool into the water, Tessa wondered if self-reliance was a learned trait or if, instead, it might be something she had passed down to her daughter along with almond-colored eyes and delicate ears.

One thing was certain—Laya had inherited her love of nature from her grandmother. As a girl growing up on a tiny island in the Philippines, Tessa knew, Benita Reyes had spent most of her time outdoors, riding water buffaloes and climbing trees. She couldn't wait to explore the wide world she imagined was waiting on the other side of the ocean, which was why she'd moved to the U.S. on her own with minimal family support. But when she reached Chicago, her adventurous spirit couldn't help her find employment. A college-educated teacher back in the Philippines, she finally ended up taking a job in a textile factory in Chicago, where she met Tessa's father, another immigrant living far from home.

Each summer, Benita had tended a small garden on the porch at the back of their building, growing vegetables and herbs in pots alongside sampaguita, a species of jasmine native to her homeland. Tessa shared her mother's love of the tropical plant, whose sweet-smelling blooms opened at night and closed in the morning, the opposite of most traditional sun-worshipping flowers. At her vacation house in Hawaii, she'd had sampaguita planted throughout the grounds, and loved to sit out on the deck there at night knowing the flowers were silently opening in the darkness around her. Her mother would have loved the Kauai house.

The sound of a car door slamming came from the driveway, and Tessa took a deep breath. From her lounge chair near the pool, Ama smiled and offered a thumbs-up, a gesture her daughters had taught her.

Dani leaned out the door that opened onto the patio. "She's here."

Laya started to climb out of the pool, but Ama stopped her. "You wait here with me, my little clownfish."

"We'll be right out," Tessa assured her daughter.

Smoothing her palms against the soft denim of her jeans, she returned to the house, pausing inside the patio doors. Eleanor was just entering the kitchen, looking around with interest as Dani hovered at her elbow. Tessa tried to see it through her eyes. The light, open kitchen with its butcher block island and limestone flooring merged directly into the dining area and family room where a fireplace, window seat and exposed beams framed a comfortable living space. This was her favorite part of the house, and she, Ama, Dani and Laya spent most of their waking time here. Or outside—French doors led from the family room to the patio, where a wisteria-draped trellis kept the midday sun at bay. She, Ama and Laya often gathered there at day's end to watch the sun set over the distant ocean while Dani puttered about the kitchen or garden. He was not a fan of staying still, not when there was "always so much to do," Ama would mimic him, smiling indulgently.

When Eleanor's gaze stopped on her, Tessa smiled. "Hi. Did you meet Dani?"

"I did," Eleanor said, turning a friendly look on the older man.

"Good." She paused. "Would you like something to drink? There's fresh-squeezed pineapple-orange juice, if you'd like. Or we have milk or sparkling water." Tessa stopped. No need to run through the entire contents of their refrigerator.

"Juice would be great."

As Dani poured, Tessa added, "I thought we might talk on the patio over lunch."

"Sounds good." Eleanor glanced around again.

She seemed nervous too. She was dressed in dark brown capris and a collared shirt open at the neck. Her freckles stood out against the white of her shirt, and Tessa wondered if she had them all over. She was staring again, she realized, and averted her gaze. What was wrong with her? Maybe this wasn't such a good idea after all.

They had barely stepped outside when Laya ran up to greet her teacher, bouncing from one foot to the other, her bathing suit and dark hair plastered to her skin.

"Miss Chapin! Want to see me do a cannonball?"

"Of course," Eleanor said, grinning.

And just like that, the ice was unceremoniously broken. Tessa introduced Eleanor to Ama, who shook her hand enthusiastically and cast Tessa a sideways glance of evident approval. Then the older woman returned to her lounge chair by the pool, leaving the two women to chat over sandwiches and Dani's fresh-squeezed juice.

"Your home is beautiful," Eleanor said, her gesture encompassing the house, the patio, the canyon view.

"Thank you." The sunlight that filtered through the wisteria revealed the highlights in Eleanor's hair, Tessa noticed, just like the first morning they'd met. Real, or bottled?

"How long have you lived here?"

"I moved in when I was pregnant with Laya. I wanted a house that felt more like a home. Before that I lived on the beach in Malibu in one of those glass-walled houses with way too much space."

"Do you miss the beach?"

"Not really. Photographers used to anchor their boats offshore and take shots through the windows. Here there are only a few ways in that don't involve climbing a sheer canyon wall." Talking about security concerns, it occurred to Tessa, might not be the best way to convince her guest to take a job looking after Laya. "Anyway, I know you went to Smith, you're from Vermont and you used to teach in Boston. What brought you out to California?"

"My college roommate is from here and I needed a break from New England." She hesitated. "I guess it was just time for a change."

"Do you think you'll stay in the area?"

"No. Actually, I'm starting grad school in the fall."

Definitely not part of the plan, Tessa thought, and took a sip of juice. "I see. What will you be studying? And where?"

"Developmental psych, but I'm not sure where yet," Eleanor admitted. "I just heard from the last school yesterday, and I got into three."

"That's great, isn't it?" Tessa's admiration for her daughter's teacher clicked up a notch. It had taken her nearly a decade to finish her own B.A. from UCLA.

"It would be great if any of them had offered me full funding. Unfortunately, they didn't."

Which meant she needed money for school. Ah-ha—an angle. "Maybe I can help," Tessa said, reworking her intended spiel on the fly.

Eleanor tilted her head. "What do you mean?"

"I invited you to lunch because Ama and Dani are moving back to the Philippines next month," she said, lowering her voice so that Laya wouldn't hear. She wanted to finalize the replacement nanny plan before she shared the news with her daughter. "That means I need to hire someone for the summer to look after Laya while I'm at work. Ama and I thought you might be a good option."

Eleanor had just popped a cucumber sandwich into her mouth. She seemed to swallow it nearly whole before choking out, "Me?"

Tessa nodded. "You're already part of Laya's life, and I need someone I can trust. You're great with her, and you're clearly overly qualified for the position. It's only for a few months." As Eleanor looked out at the pool where Laya was floating happily, eyes closed and face raised to the sun, Tessa added, "The position pays twenty-five hundred a week." A generous salary, perhaps, but it would go toward a good cause—the education of a future child psychologist.

Eleanor stared at her. "Are you serious? That's way too much."

"Now I know you're not from around here," Tessa said, smiling. "Anyway, you don't know what I'd ask of you. You'd have to spend a lot of time here at the house, and sometimes I keep odd hours. Early on, in fact, I would ask you to come to Hawaii with Laya and me."

She watched Eleanor frown and toy with a loose thread on her shirt sleeve. Tessa was used to poker-faced industry executives who considered it unprofessional to reveal any sign of emotion. Eleanor appeared to have no such compunction.

"Will you at least think about it?" Tessa asked.

"Of course. It's a very generous offer, and Laya is a great kid."

Whew. "Good. If you wouldn't mind letting me know soon, I'd appreciate it. I'll need to make other arrangements if you're not available."

Eleanor glanced out at the pool again. "Would tomorrow be soon enough?"

"It would," she said. "I do hope you'll take the job. I think it could be a great summer for everyone involved." Her eyes dropped to Eleanor's lips, and then she averted her gaze again as she saw the blush tingeing Eleanor's throat. Great, now she was officially sexually harassing her daughter's teacher.

If Eleanor took the job, Tessa thought, reaching for her juice glass, she would have to figure out a way to douse the flare of attraction between them. It wasn't like anything could really happen, not when Eleanor was headed to graduate school in the fall. But just then, with the sun's rays deflected by the winding boughs of wisteria and the sounds of Laya's poolside delight plainly audible, September seemed impossibly remote.

CHAPTER SIX

That night, Eleanor went out for Thai food in West Hollywood with Luis and Sasha. As she rode in the passenger seat of her roommate's father's hand-me-down BMW, she watched the lights pass beyond the window and wondered how she'd gotten here.

She knew *how*, of course. The cross-country drive a few months before had been memorable, and not just for the scenery—eight southern states she'd never before laid eyes on, not to mention a two hundred foot tall cross just off the freeway in Texas to put the Bible in Bible Belt. She and Julia hadn't spent so much time together since before Eleanor left for college. Her little sister had grown up, as evidenced by nightly phone calls to James, her boyfriend of four years who, she'd confessed one night in a darkened Motel 6 room that smelled of carpet deodorizer, had begun to drop hints about marriage and kids.

Julia had a job she liked and someone she loved waiting for her back in Burlington, a whole life already in progress not far from where they'd grown up, while Eleanor was temporarily employed and currently un-partnered, crashing at her college roommate's apartment three thousand miles from home.

Lunch with Tessa and Laya had reminded her of what she had lost—her mother—and what she had yet to find—a family of her own. After the job talk, they had strolled through the gardens above the canyon with Laya holding their hands and swinging fearlessly between them, her laughter rising above the koi ponds and into the fruit trees that lined the stone pathway. Eleanor had caught herself thinking that the summer could be just like this—the three of them together among the flowers and shade trees at the edge of the canyon. And just for a moment, she'd felt more at peace than she could remember since her mother's death, the loneliness she'd carried around these last months temporarily forgotten.

Just before Laya's nap, Tessa had walked her out to the driveway. As the limo driver held the back door open, the actress touched her arm and said, "I'll look forward to hearing from you."

Eleanor had glanced sideways at her, aware of Tessa's hand lingering against her skin. "I thought that was my line."

"Not in this case. The job's yours if you want it."

"Right." She hesitated. "I'll call you tomorrow."

"Okay." Then Tessa did something that made Eleanor doubt even more the sagacity of accepting the offer: She leaned in and kissed the air near Eleanor's right cheek. "Thanks for coming to lunch."

Eleanor swallowed hard. "Thanks for inviting me."

Then the driver was opening the back door of the limo, and Eleanor was giving a half-wave as she slipped into the car. She was tempted to glance back through the tinted window to see if Tessa still stood on the drive, but she stared straight ahead. She thought she was picking up on certain signals from the star, but what if Tessa just enjoyed being worshipped? What if she was another insecure beautiful woman who needed everyone to love her? For a woman like that, no amount of attention would ever be enough.

At the same time, how could she turn down the job when it offered her a respite from another round of indentured financial servitude? Probably she should just pick a school, move there as soon as Barclay's term ended, and get a summer job to help defray tuition costs. But no job in the world would pay what Tessa was offering. The Madison program, her top choice, was the cheapest one on the list and, like the others, had offered her partial funding. If she agreed to be Laya's nanny for the summer, she wouldn't have to worry about taking out loans for at least the first two years of the five-year program. Could she pass that up?

She'd argued with herself all the way home, then mentally debated the issue some more while she waited for Sasha to return from playing tennis at her club. If she took the job, she'd be getting paid exorbitant sums to hang out with a kid she already liked. Laya was still testing boundaries and learning when to push, when not to. But she was a secure and confident and kind-hearted kid. She was loving and, obviously, well-loved. Eleanor hadn't expected such balance from someone like Tessa. Before they'd met, she'd pictured the stereotypical career actress more interested in herself and the Hollywood scene than in her offspring. But Tessa was engaged, an active parent, seemingly unplugged from the film industry by choice. And she wanted Eleanor to join their family for the summer.

Over appetizers, Sasha filled Luis in on Eleanor's continuing celebrity adventures as they munched vegetarian spring rolls and coconut prawns.

"I can't believe Tessa Flanagan invited you into her inner lair," Luis said. "Bitch—I don't know if I should be jealous or kiss up."

"Kiss up, my friend," Sasha said. "Tessa asked our little Elle here to be her daughter's nanny for the summer. If Elle plays her cards right, she'll be in the inner lair almost daily."

"No she didn't," Luis squealed, reminding Eleanor of the sounds her students made at recess. He cleared his throat and lowered his voice. "I mean, that's fantastic. You are going to say yes, aren't you?"

Eleanor sipped her pomegranite margarita. "I don't know yet."

He stared at her, apparently stunned speechless.

"I know, right?" Sasha said. "I've been trying to get to the bottom of this bizarre response. When the Tessa Flanagans of the world invite you into their private circle, even if it's only as a paid employee, the answer is always yes. Particularly when they offer to pay you two-K plus a week."

Luis whistled. "Damn, girl. Are you sure it's babysitting she wants you for? She didn't mention booty calls by any chance, did she?"

Eleanor glared at him. "Of course she didn't. She was completely professional." No need to mention the seemingly more-than-friendly looks Tessa had occasionally leveled at her, or the air-kiss when they parted. Probably Tessa hadn't meant anything by that, either.

"Sorry, *chica*," Luis said placatingly. "No need to get your panties all in a bunch."

She could feel Sasha's eyes on her and took a deep breath, releasing the sudden anger Luis's flippant remark had ignited.

"A bit sensitive, aren't we?" Sasha commented. "Wait—that's why you're thinking of running off to Wisconsin, isn't it? You're afraid something might happen with her."

"Don't be ridiculous," Eleanor said. "The only reason she even offered me the job is that Laya has a major case of hero worship going. That, and Barclay has done all of the heavy lifting—you know, background checks, fingerprints, the promise of my firstborn child."

"Please. As if you'll ever have a child," Sasha said. Then she looked down at the table and sighed audibly. Her biological clock had recently shifted into high gear. Everywhere she went, she told Eleanor, she saw babies or pregnant women. The night they'd broken up over dinner at Spago's, she'd been sure Ben was finally going to ask her to marry him. Instead he'd told her he was leaving her for a recently divorced co-worker at his PR firm, a woman with whom, incidentally, he'd worked closely for longer than the five years he and Sasha had been together.

Eleanor couldn't decide if she should smack Sasha up side the head or squeeze her hand in sympathy. She exchanged a look with Luis, who shrugged helplessly.

"I can see you both, you know," Sasha said, and took a sip of her Thai coffee spiked with Jack. "Now, tell us what the house looks like, Elle, and don't leave anything out."

Dutifully she launched into a description of Tessa's house, a vintage English country estate in the Hollywood Hills with a Tudor façade, ivy-covered walls, and orange and lemon trees in the garden overlooking the canyon. They'd spent more time outside than in, so she was better able to describe the elegantly curved swimming pool, matching hot tub, wisteria-shaded patio, and distant ocean views than the interior of Tessa's beautifully appointed home.

"She lived on the beach before, didn't she?" Sasha asked. Their entrees had arrived by now, and she scooped brown rice onto her plate before covering it with chicken cashew stir-fry.

"In Malibu," Eleanor said. "Apparently the paparazzi used to anchor boats offshore and stalk her from afar." No wonder Tessa had moved into the more easily defensible foothills—like the royals of old who built their castles on promontories and dug moats all around. Just like that.

"Those guys are snakes," Luis said. "It may be legal to harass people the way they do, but it's definitely not ethical, if you ask me."

"You sound almost as idealistic as this one here," Eleanor said, nodding at her roommate. "Maybe you guys should break off and form your own firm that does good deeds. You know, start the next Legal Aide."

"We would be so much more effective than they are," Sasha said. "The talent they hire is abysmal. Half the time they don't even know how to file a brief."

As the conversation moved on to lawyerly topics, as it almost always did, Eleanor tuned out. She pictured a gang of photographers storming Tessa's beach house, a cross between *Saving Private Ryan* and *Gia*. Good thing Tessa had retired. Not that retiring meant she was immune to scrutiny. But even Eleanor, who lived on the other side of the country and was more attuned to advances in literacy pedagogy than the state of the film industry, knew that the public spotlight had shifted from Tessa Flanagan in recent years to younger, hotter actresses. She would always be Hollywood royalty. She was just no longer one of its undisputed queens.

Eleanor dug into her basil fried rice and tried to put thoughts of Tessa Flanagan out of her mind. Easier said, of course, than done.

Tessa wasn't used to waiting. Actually, that wasn't true. Being an actor was a lot like being a soldier, according to the research she'd done for a role in a movie about Desert Storm—the motto "Hurry up and wait" fit both occupations equally well. On a movie set, each scene required the completion of a thousand or more tasks: sets had to be built, camera tracks laid, hair and makeup perfected, new tracks laid when the director of photography decided to change the shot, and so on. After a dozen years in the movie-making business, Tessa was accomplished at waiting.

What she wasn't used to was having her personal life depend on someone else's decision. For the past ten years or more, other people had sought her approval, her agreement, her acceptance. Now that she was the one waiting for another person's verdict, she wasn't sure she liked the feeling much—a sign the experience was probably good for her. A voice came out of the past, her father's laughing baritone with an echo of County Derry: "It'll put hair on your chest, love." And her own laughter, just like Laya's now—high-pitched, carefree. Hard to remember she'd ever felt that free.

On Sunday morning, after a semi-sleepless night, Tessa had already been reading for an hour when she heard Laya pad down the hall and pause outside her half-open door. "Come in, munchkin," she called, and her daughter stumbled sleepily around the edge of the door.

Laya was dressed in her favorite PJs, a plaid cotton top and mismatched light blue pants with pink bunnies on them. Tucked under one arm was one of her stuffed animals, a giraffe named Gerri who came up to her belly button. "Hi, Mom," she said, throwing Gerri up onto the king-sized bed and climbing up after him.

"How did you sleep, my sweet?" Tessa asked, planting a noisy kiss on her cheek.

Giggling, Laya swiped at her cheek and threw herself across the pillows. "I dreamed Miss Chapin lived with us. Do you think she could come back again sometime?"

"I hope so," Tessa said, rubbing at a smear of what was probably peanut butter stuck to Gerri's right ear. "Was it a good dream? Did you like having Miss Chapin around?"

"Of course," Laya said, looking at her as if she were crazy for even asking. "You like it too, don't you?"

"Sure." She closed the Sarah Waters novel—almost done, finally—and grabbed her daughter, tickling her belly. "I think it's time for pancakes!"

Laya squirmed and shouted, "Pancakes! Let's find Lolo!"

As they dressed in matching bathrobes and tramped downstairs, Tessa was relieved once again that her child could so easily be distracted with promises of food. Like mother like daughter. One of the first things she'd done after landing her first paying gig—five thousand dollars for two lines in a James Cameron film had seemed like a fortune to her then—had been to go to the grocery store and stock up on all of her favorite foods. As a foster child and then a struggling college student, she'd survived for longer than she cared to remember on canned goods and day-old bakery products. As a working actor, she could finally afford the good stuff. She'd never looked back and never planned to. That was why she had hired the Midas of financial advisors, Howard Duffy, business planner to the stars.

Over the years, Howard had carefully hoarded her money and helped her spend only the interest on her principal investments. At his urging, she owned a restaurant in La Jolla, real estate in Hawaii and Mexico, and an investment portfolio focused on long-term growth, while at her insistence Howard gave away a good chunk of the profits from her investments to a list of her favorite liberal causes. When she'd decided to look into starting a charitable foundation, she'd called Howard first, and he'd pointed her toward the Byerlys, her co-conspirators in trying to fill the hole Princess Diana's death had left in the celebrity-giving scene. Their words, not hers, but an ambition she didn't mind sharing.

Ama was still at mass and the pancakes still in liquid form when Tessa's BlackBerry rang, Eleanor Chapin's name flashing on the caller ID. Tessa left Dani and Laya in the carriage house discussing where eggs came from and took her cell phone outside. On the one hand, she was glad she wouldn't have to wait all day for Eleanor's decision. But what if the answer was no?

She flipped her phone open. "Good morning."

"Good morning," Eleanor said, her voice cool.

Shit, Tessa thought, and paced toward the shallow end of the pool. She hadn't let herself dwell on what it would feel like if Eleanor turned her down. The sinking sensation in her stomach was nearly unfamiliar: disappointment. She'd insulated her life so carefully these last years, she'd almost forgotten what it felt like.

She forced her voice to sound upbeat. "So have you thought about my offer?"

"I have," Eleanor said gravely. "It's a very generous offer, as I said yesterday. Too generous, in fact. I'd like to accept, but I'm not sure it's a fair wage."

Wait, she was taking the job? Tessa couldn't stop the grin that split her face. "Obviously no one ever taught you how to negotiate. You're supposed to ask for more, not less."

"Private schools don't have unions," Eleanor said, and Tessa thought she detected a matching smile in her voice. "I'm not going to talk you down, am I?"

"Nope. So you're saying yes? You're going to spend the summer with us?"

"I am," Eleanor said. "If you still want me to."

"Of course I want you," Tessa said, then instantly regretted her word choice. Nothing like a Freudian slip to out your less-than-honorable intentions. Not that she *intended* anything dishonorable toward her daughter's future nanny. "Anyway," she added quickly, "I'm delighted to hear the news and I'm sure Laya will be too. Ama and I will tell her today and I'll get in touch with my lawyer this week. There'll be some paperwork for you to fill out at his office, the usual W-2 and more NDAs. Is it okay if I have his assistant call you to set up an appointment?"

Eleanor said it was, and then asked, "When would you like me to start?"

They decided on the first of June to give Eleanor a couple of weeks with Ama and Dani still around. Then in mid-June, Tessa, Eleanor and Laya would fly to Kauai. By the time they returned to California, Ama and Dani would be settling back into life in the Philippines.

Plans complete, another silence set in. Tessa wondered if Eleanor was at the Beechwood apartment she shared with her college roommate or if she was somewhere else in L.A., strolling a boardwalk or a city street. Tessa could hear traffic in the background, but her own L.A. apartments pre-fame had been noisy, community affairs. She didn't miss the sound of buses or feuding frat boys.

"I'll be in touch, then," she said finally. She didn't want to hang up yet. She remembered how Eleanor had sat cross-legged on the wicker couch on the patio, smiling affectionately at Laya, watching Tessa bemusedly. She longed to invite her over again. They could swim, or walk in the garden or read quietly in the sun. But she couldn't ask that, not of someone who would be on her payroll in a matter of weeks. Anyway, soon enough she would see Eleanor nearly every day.

"Thanks, Tessa," Eleanor said, using her name for the first time. "I look forward to working with you." Despite the formal words, her voice was light. "Tell Laya hi for me, and I'll see her tomorrow."

"I will," Tessa said. "See you soon."

"Yes," Eleanor said. "Soon."

They hung up, and Tessa held the cell phone to the front of the ancient Sea World T-shirt she'd slept in, smiling out at the view from her patio. Eleanor would be with them for the next three months. "Eleanor," she murmured. She liked the sound of the old-fashioned name. No one in Hollywood picked names like that anymore, not for themselves or for their children.

"What did I miss?" Ama asked, bustling across the patio, her purse and an umbrella slung over one arm.

"She said yes," Tessa announced, turning to smile at the older woman.

"That's wonderful!" She slipped her arm through Tessa's and tugged her toward the carriage house, umbrella bumping against her side. "We'll have pancakes and orange juice to celebrate."

"You know, Tita, it isn't raining," Tessa said as they walked.

"I thought it might earlier, but it was just that pollution," Ama said, and shook her head, grumbling under her breath.

Tessa squeezed the older woman to her side. She was going to miss her so much. Maybe Eleanor's presence would help ease some of the loss. Maybe Eleanor would fill the space—before she left, too, Tessa reminded herself. Everyone left. It was inevitable. Even Laya would someday depart to lead her own separate life. Fortunately, not for a while, she thought as they opened the door to the carriage house to find Laya and Dani busy stacking pancakes on yellow Fiestaware plates.

"Hi Mom! Hi Lola!" Laya said, gazing on them happily. "Time for pancakes!"

And they were mighty tasty too.

CHAPTER SEVEN

Eleanor had never flown on a private jet before. She could get used to this sort of air travel, she decided as she stretched out in a comfortable recliner, feet extended. Tessa sat on another recliner nearby reading the Sunday edition of the *New York Times* while Laya slept, head on her mother's lap. As Eleanor watched, Tessa glanced up and smiled at her over the top of the newspaper. She smiled back until she felt warmth rising in her cheeks, then looked away, focusing on the book in her hands. When would she stop blushing like a starstruck schoolgirl? She had practically lived with the Flanagans for the past two weeks, spending most days looking after Laya while Tessa worked and Ama and Dani packed up the carriage house.

To keep Laya out of everyone's hair, Eleanor had taken her on day trips to a variety of local sights, from the aquarium and the children's museum to Disneyland and Sea World. The days had been fun, for the most part. From teaching, Eleanor knew the art of distraction and blood sugar management. If Laya got cranky, either food or a nap was usually in order. If neither of those worked, a favorite book or a dip in the pool usually turned the girl's mood. Eleanor still couldn't quite believe she was getting paid a small fortune to entertain a child. New England, with its Puritan notions of frugality and hard work, seemed a world away.

Currently her charge was snuggling with her mother. This flight was the most time Eleanor had spent with Tessa since starting the job, a change that would supposedly stick now that Tessa was officially on vacation. Eleanor wondered what the word "vacation" meant to her, since her version of "retirement" had no apparent bearing on reality. Most mornings back in L.A., Tessa had left for the city shortly after Eleanor arrived, and stayed away all day. The actress-turned-humanitarian usually reappeared in plenty of time to join them for dinner, but then it was bedtime for Laya. While Tessa read her daughter a bedtime story, Eleanor would drive downhill to Sasha's apartment to fall nearly directly into bed herself. She'd thought teaching a dozen kindergartners was exhausting, but full-time "parenting" allowed few breaks, she was learning.

She glanced surreptitiously at her employer again. Tessa seemed tired, the skin under her eyes bruised, her mouth taut. Ama and Dani had seen them off at the airport in Burbank. Laya had sobbed, and Tessa and Ama had wiped their eyes continuously as they hugged and kissed goodbye on the tarmac outside the private terminal. Even Dani had seemed bright-eyed and forlorn, waving disconsolately as Eleanor and the Flanagans climbed the steps to the small, sleek jet that would take them to Kauai. Tessa and her daughter had both watched out the window as the plane took off, Laya waving furiously long after Ama and Dani had shrunken to mere dots on the gray tarmac. Eleanor had buried her nose in a book and left them to their shared grief.

Now, almost as if she sensed Eleanor's scrutiny, Tessa looked up. "How are you doing?" she asked, raising her voice slightly to be heard over the jet's engines.

"Fine. How about you?"

"Fine. Good."

They'd been on the plane for over an hour already. The flight from Burbank to the Princeville Airport on Kauai's northern coast would take five hours. And then they would have two entire weeks to spend on the Hawaiian island nicknamed the "Garden Isle" for its lush greenery and sparkling beaches (according to Eleanor's guidebook). She had never been to Hawaii before. This summer, she had a feeling, was bound to supply a variety of firsts.

"What are you reading?" Tessa asked.

"*Persuasion*, by Jane Austen."

"That was her last novel, wasn't it?"

Eleanor tried to hide her surprise. Despite the books proliferating throughout Tessa's house, this was the first time she'd seen the actress sit still long enough to read. "It was. Her family published it after she died, along with *Northanger Abbey*, her first novel. I reread all of Austen's books every few years, usually in the order she wrote them. This summer I thought I'd read them in reverse."

"Once you start graduate school, you probably won't have time to read for fun, will you?"

"Probably not." She paused. "How's the news?"

Tessa dropped the newspaper to the carpeted floor. "The usual—war, famine, pestilence."

"Is that why you decided to start a foundation? To take on those things? Or was it..." Eleanor trailed off. She was fairly certain it would be rude to ask one of the richest women in America if she was trying to give money away to assuage her guilt at being a have in a world of have-nots.

"An ego thing?" Tessa supplied. "I know it probably looks like a ploy for attention, but really it isn't. I just never planned to make this much money. I'm not sure anyone does."

"I don't know about that," Eleanor said, picturing some of her Smith classmates. Old money legacy and new money first generation Smithies, all with one thing in common—the expectation of greater wealth than their parents.

"I should have said that no one I knew growing up planned to make so much money," Tessa amended.

"That's probably why you don't mind giving it away."

She shrugged. "I don't have a problem with higher tax rates for the wealthy, either. What I do have a problem with is helping bankroll a war I don't believe in, not to mention an administration so deceitful and manipulative that I still sometimes find myself wondering if 9/11 might not have been some sort of conspiracy."

Eleanor's eyebrows rose. "Not a Dubya fan, I take it?" She already knew the answer, but couldn't resist commenting. Usually Tessa seemed so carefully reserved, so deliberate about what she said and did.

"Hardly. You?"

"Not exactly." Eleanor had attended protest rallies up and down the eastern seaboard during the too-long years of the Bush administration. "What's your personal favorite? Cause, I mean."

"Kids," Tessa said. "Children should be able to be children, and yet so many of them are in situations where they're physically and emotionally abused. I wish I could change that." Her eyes seemed to come unfocused for a moment. Then she turned a practiced smile on Eleanor. "Apparently we have that in common. Developmental psychology is a fancy way of saying you want to help kids, right?"

Eleanor nodded. "It is." As the plane sped westward, she found herself telling Tessa about her first trip to the juvenile mental health care facility in Worcester a million years before, back when Bill Clinton was president and anything seemed possible.

"If you knew you wanted to be a child psychologist back then," Tessa said, absently toying with her daughter's curls as she slept, "why are you only now going back to school?"

She wasn't sure why she hadn't told Tessa about her mother yet, except that since she'd been in L.A., her circle of contacts had split into two distinct groups: people who had known her before her mother's death and people who hadn't. From now on, for those in the latter category—like Tessa—she would always and forever be motherless.

"Well," she said, and was about to admit to the family crisis that had derailed her professional plans, when the flight attendant drifted into their section of the cabin. Laya woke up with a hankering for french fries, and Eleanor was saved from having to delve into her family's drama.

Which was good, she told herself, watching Tessa patiently try to redirect Laya's post-nap crankiness into a more agreeable form of communication. She wiggled her toes in her Teva sandals and thought back over their conversation as she waited for her own veggie burger and fries. Tessa was intelligent and thoughtful, self-effacing and ironic, all traits Eleanor appreciated. Was this what life would be like now that Ama and Dani were gone and Tessa was officially on vacation? Hours spent talking politics and books and personal histories while they soaked in the Hawaiian sunshine?

In midair, with the Pacific stretching from horizon to horizon, Eleanor shivered in anticipation. Capitalism was a pestilence that, in tandem with industrialization, had caused the decimation of the natural world, it was true. But she wasn't going to let that stop her from enjoying her Kauai vacation with the Flanagans. For once, she was going to guiltlessly revel in someone else's luxury. After all, it was temporary.

As the plane banked low over the ocean and turned to line up with the narrow landing strip at Princeville, Tessa watched the familiar landscape take shape below. There were the manicured grounds of the Princeville resorts with their golf courses and oceanview condominiums. There was Hanalei Bay, a perfect half-moon indentation in the coastline bordered by her favorite Kauai small town. Inland, to the south, lay the green mountains and thick foliage of a dozen protected forest reserves. After the desert of L.A., the lush greenery of the island was always a welcome change. She loved Kauai, and she loved the property she owned on the island more than anyplace else in the world. Which was saying something, considering the variety of locales she'd inhabited during her career.

On the other side of the cabin, Eleanor had her face pressed to the window. Laya was buckled in next to her now, and was leaning across her former teacher to point out landmarks she claimed to recognize from their regular pilgrimages to the island. Tessa listened to her daughter incorrectly identify the nearest bay and shook her head. Geography was not Laya's strong point. Blindly insisting she knew something she didn't, though, was. Tessa noticed that Laya's hand rested on Eleanor's wrist, and for a moment she envied her daughter the ease with which she demonstrated her affection. Laya had a big heart. Almost too big sometimes. Saying goodbye to Ama and Dani that morning had left her empty and exhausted. She'd perked up a little after lunch, but Tessa suspected her grief would return. At least Eleanor was here. Her steady, warm presence might help coax Laya out of her funk.

The Princeville Airport consisted of a single runway that paralleled State Highway 56 at the north end of the island. Once they were on the ground, Tessa thanked the flight crew and led Laya and Eleanor toward one of the two small hangars.

"Now we get to ride on the helicopter!" Laya announced, literally jumping up and down as they walked.

Eleanor grinned at Tessa. "Sounds like we've got a future pilot on our hands."

Tessa liked the sound of the word *we* coming from Eleanor's luscious-as-ever mouth. It was different somehow from Ama's *we*, different from any other incarnation of the possessive pronoun. She looked away from Eleanor's friendly smile, telling herself to stop ogling her employee. She'd managed to avoid any additional sexual harassment episodes in the two weeks Eleanor had been in her employ. Of course, she'd accomplished this feat mainly by staying away from the house when she knew her daughter's nanny would be there. As a bonus, she'd managed to avoid having to watch Ama and Dani preparing to leave L.A.

"First helicopter ride?" she asked Eleanor as one crew member secured their luggage while another helped them inside and handed out headsets.

"Yes," Eleanor confirmed, buckling her seat belt and looking around with apparent interest.

The helicopter was small and new, and would whisk them the short distance to the estate at Kahili Bay in a matter of minutes. The estate was only a quarter of an hour from the airport by car, but Laya had fallen in love with helicopters the previous year and Tessa had thought that a ride in a "twirly-bird," as her daughter sometimes called them, might cheer her up. Both of them, actually. She knew she was trying to buy her daughter's happiness, a tactic she would like to believe she didn't often stoop to. But this would be their first trip to Hawaii without Ama and Dani, not to mention half of the extended Mercado clan.

Christmas last year had included Ama and Dani's four grown daughters, their significant others, and their children. Laya had been in heaven running around with Ama and Dani's grandkids. Tessa had even caught herself thinking that it might be time to give Laya a sibling. While she was pregnant, she'd purchased extra vials of sperm from the original donor, enough for a dozen additional tries. The vials were in storage at the clinic in Switzerland, available any time she wanted them. But being a single parent to one child could be difficult enough at times, even with her resources. She wasn't sure if she was up to lone-parenting two.

As they flew to Kahili Bay, Tessa watched Eleanor. Though she had seemed nervous at takeoff, her face relaxed and her eyes began to glow as the helicopter followed (at Tessa's request) the coastline east from Princeville out toward the Kilauea Point National Wildlife Refuge, with its diverse seabird population and postcard-perfect lighthouse. There was nothing quite like a helicopter ride to provide an aerial introduction to a place. A trip on an airplane offered few opportunities to pause—if a plane's speed decreased, it lost altitude. But in a helicopter you could take your time, drift closer to an object of interest, hover, as their pilot was doing now just offshore from the Refuge, far enough away to protect the flora and fauna but close enough to clearly observe the lighthouse and the bird-covered cliffs.

Laya was busy listing the species she knew—wedge-tailed shearwaters, Laysan albatrosses (which sounded like her name, she pointed out) and red-footed boobies (which made her snicker)—when the pilot turned the chopper and pointed at a dark shape in the water just off the coast.

"What is it?" Eleanor asked.

"A humpback whale," Tessa said.

"They're in danger," Laya confided.

"Endangered," Tessa corrected. "We're lucky to be seeing them."

They watched the whales surfacing, distinctive humps visible in the midday sun above the blue-green water, until one of the whales dove deep and displayed its tail fluke. At that, the pilot turned the helicopter toward Kahili Bay.

"It's a good sign to see his tail, isn't it, Mom," Laya said, settling her hand in Tessa's.

"Yes, it is." She squeezed her daughter's fingers. Until today, she'd only seen humpbacks in the winter, and even then they were rare.

The pilot landed his machine on a flat section of road just outside the entrance to the estate, where Robert, a gray-haired native Hawaiian who served as the year-round caretaker, met them. He and Eleanor carried the bags to the golf cart, and then the helicopter lifted off again, Laya waving at the pilot from her seat in the back of the cart as they drove through the security gate. As soon as they were inside, Robert hit a remote mounted on the dash, and the tall, iron-pronged gate slid closed behind them.

Tessa slouched in the front seat and looked out over the colorful flowering bushes and low fruit trees that crowded the long drive. Robert allowed the jungle to grow thick and tangled here at the edges of the estate to provide a natural protective barrier. Almost home, she thought, rubbing her sore neck. She was exhausted. The night before she'd barely slept as she, Nancy and Evangeline, another of Ama and Dani's daughters, had helped the older couple finish packing. Ama had insisted on cleaning the carriage house from top to bottom despite Tessa's protests, and around three in the morning, Evangeline had produced a fat joint that Tessa and Nancy had been only too happy to share with her out on the patio, away from Dani's disapproving gaze.

Staring up at a few stars barely visible through the light and air pollution, Tessa had only taken a couple of hits. That's all it took to relax her these days. She'd gone through a near wake-and-bake phase when she was younger—at first, a hit of pot was the only thing that kept her calm enough to run her lines in front of the dozens of people on a typical film set (gaffers, grips, camera operators, director, director of photography, first assistant director, studio rep—the list seemed endless at times) without breaking out in hives. Early on in her acting career, she was convinced everyone would see her for the fraud she was. But as the years passed and no one outed her, sexually or otherwise, she grew more secure. Until a woman she'd decided to trust proved that she'd been right to worry all those years. She shut her eyes briefly against the memory. She must be tired. Normally she didn't have any trouble not thinking about Nadine.

As they rounded a curve and the house came into sight, a well-ordered oasis in the middle of the jungle, Tessa put thoughts of the past out of her mind. She and Laya were on vacation in a beautiful place where no one and nothing could hurt them.

"Welcome to Mele Honu'ala," she said, turning to Eleanor.

Well, almost no one.

CHAPTER EIGHT

Eleanor hung her beach towel on a hook near the slate-tiled hot tub and slipped into the water. The sun had set a little while earlier, and the sky to the east above the sliver of lagoon visible from the hillside still bore traces of pink against the dark gray clouds that hung low over the island. Sighing, she sat down on the smooth stone ledge that lined the tub's interior and leaned her head against a conveniently placed pillow. In the dying light, she could just make out the pale strip of sand at the bottom of the hill seeming to undulate as the ocean rose and fell with a rhythmic pounding she could hear from where she sat immersed in the gently humming hot tub, steam rising about her.

This was her third night on Kauai, and already she'd fallen in love with Mele Honu'ala, Tessa's island getaway. The name meant "Song of the Sea Turtle," according to her host, and though Eleanor had yet to encounter a sea turtle, which like the humpbacks were "in danger" in Laya's terminology, she could easily imagine the giant gentle creatures skimming through the clear waters off the coast. The Flanagans' slice of Kauai was jasmine-scented heaven. She wasn't sure why anyone would ever want to leave.

Tessa's estate consisted of four buildings—a cottage with attached garage near the gate where Robert lived, a studio off the garden, the main house and a yurt. Except for Robert's cottage, the buildings occupied the hillside above a private, crescent-shaped lagoon. The studio, which Tessa used as an office, was the first building off the driveway, and resembled a Japanese single-story pagoda with exposed wooden beams and a tiled roof.

The two-story main house also had Asian accents. With only three rooms downstairs (kitchen, dining room and living room) and three bedrooms upstairs, it boasted just half the square footage of Tessa's Hollywood home. A local artist had finished the exterior with tasteful ceramic tiles of native plants interspersed with tan, dark gray and maroon slate stonework, while the wood-frame living room walls had been built on sliders and could be rolled away so that the house opened to the hillside and a view of the lagoon on one side, the back garden with terraced rock walls and colorful native plants on the other. Years before, the previous owner had rented out the house as a wedding site. Sometimes, Tessa said, wedding planners still called to see if she might be interested in renting the space out. She wasn't. She prized her privacy too much to open her house to the public.

The hot tub where Eleanor was currently relaxing was accessible from the yurt's deck. It wasn't your average yurt, of course, but rather a deluxe brown and green canvas structure with separate partitions inside for changing rooms that flanked a living space, and a wide platform deck outside. Tessa kept all of her beach and other outdoor gear here, even though the actual beach was a hike down the long hillside. The previous day, Eleanor and Laya had spent the afternoon on the private beach, building castles and animals in the sand and dozing in the sun, while Tessa "took care of a few things" from her studio office. Despite the 45 SPF sunscreen Eleanor applied liberally all over her body, she still returned to the house more freckled than she wanted. Meanwhile Laya, who was half-Filipino (Tessa had mentioned that she'd selected a sperm donor who, like her, was both Filipino and Irish), toasted a light brown beneath her sunscreen.

Today had been more active with a visit to the Kilauea Point National Wildlife Refuge they'd seen from the helicopter along with a tour of the nearby Na Aina Kai Botanical Gardens. Again Tessa had spent the afternoon in her studio office, leaving Eleanor to explore the local sights with Laya. After admiring the picturesque white lighthouse and the cliffs at Kilauea Point, they drove the short distance to the botanical gardens, where Judy, a friendly middle-aged woman, led them on a prearranged private tour of the grounds. The tour started in the gardens and included a stop at a waterfall-fed lagoon where Eleanor and Laya fed by hand the iridescent Koi fish who lived there, followed by an hour of play in the Under the Rainbow Children's Garden.

After a box lunch and some cooling-off time in the wading pool, Judy led them away from the gardens toward the rocky Kaluakai Beach. As they crossed the Makai Meadow on the way down to the beach, Judy pointed out several Laysan albatross chicks, identifiable by their darker feathers. In the next month, she told them, the chicks would finish fledging and join their parents at sea, where they would remain for three to five years until they were ready to take a mate. Laysan albatrosses mated for life, and returned to land from November to July each year to hatch and fledge their young. The rest of the time they were at sea.

Eleanor was still pondering the notion of seabirds who mated for life when Judy clapped her hands and pointed to the path behind them—not twenty feet away, a wild boar was crossing from one set of trees to another, followed closely by several of her young. At Laya's urging, Eleanor snapped a few quick shots with Tessa's digital camera.

Later, at dinner, Laya had used the digital pictures to frame her narrative as she told Tessa about their day. Eleanor found herself once again admiring the girl's intelligence. Not many six-year-olds would think to tell a story in chronological order, let alone devise a system of keeping the narrative on track. Or mostly on track.

"I'm sorry I missed it," Tessa had said when Laya finished relating the events of the day.

Eleanor heard the genuine regret in her voice. "Did you get your work done?" she asked.

"I think so." Tessa glanced at her daughter obediently finishing the milk in her plastic cup. "But even if I didn't, it can wait. We're on vacation, right, Mahal?"

"Right, Mom."

"From now on, no more work," Tessa declared.

"Really?" Laya's eyes were wide. "You promise?"

"Yes," her mother said. "I promise."

Now, as Eleanor luxuriated in the hot water that eased the aches from her joints (the bed in the guest bedroom was a bit firmer than she was used to), she hoped Tessa would keep her word. For Laya's sake.

"Mind if I join you?"

She started at the now-familiar voice. Tessa was walking along the lamp-lit stone pathway that led from the main house, her hair pulled back in a ponytail, a short robe tied loosely at her waist. Eleanor gulped. "Of course not," she said, and started to rise. "I can give you some privacy, if you'd like."

"Don't go," Tessa said as she pulled a baby monitor (tuned, no doubt, to Laya's room) from her robe and set it on a nearby patio table. "Unless you'd rather go inside."

"No, I just thought you might want some time to yourself."

"I've had plenty of that lately," Tessa said, pausing to hang up her towel and shed her robe. "Anyway, what's the point of paradise if you don't have anyone to share it with?" She turned, smiling down at Eleanor from the deck.

Afterward, Eleanor hoped her sudden intake of breath hadn't been audible. Over the past couple of weeks, she'd become accustomed to Tessa in tailored business suits, casual outfits, even in pajamas on a few occasions. But unclothed, her lovely breasts only just restrained by a skimpy black bikini top, a tiny triangle of cloth clinging to the apex of her thighs, Tessa was stunning. Her light brown skin was supple and smooth, her body curvy in all the right places. Eleanor's girlfriends had been attractive, certainly, but none of them could compare to the woman descending into the hot tub before her. And then Tessa was dropping down next to her on the stone seat, closing her eyes as the water rose to her chest. The sigh she gave was definitely audible.

Eleanor forced her gaze away and looked out over the lagoon. In the ten minutes since she'd arrived, the sky had darkened even more so that now she could pick out a few stars that had begun to appear overhead, including the easily recognizable Big Dipper. Maybe if she concentrated on constellations, she would stop drooling over the gorgeous woman whose silken thigh, she was pretty sure, had just brushed against hers. Then again, even the sight of the Milky Way stretching away above her into the depths of space couldn't have taken away from the fact that she was sitting in a hot tub on a bluff overlooking the Pacific Ocean with a woman she hadn't been able to get out of her mind since the moment Tessa had walked into her classroom.

She swallowed hard again. "Is she asleep?" When she left the house, Tessa had been upstairs reading Laya her bedtime story.

"Sound asleep. Just to warn you, I turned the alarm on before I came out."

Sometimes Tessa seemed overly obsessed with security, but Eleanor didn't doubt she had her reasons. "What story did she ask for tonight?"

"She wanted me to make one up."

"Let me guess—something with a talking animal?" Laya, Eleanor had learned in the past month, highly prized homespun stories that featured anthropomorphized protagonists. Usually mammals.

Tessa inclined her head. "In honor of your wildlife experiences today, a wild boar."

"I'm guessing you didn't mention their omnivorous diet. Probably wouldn't want to paint a picture of Mama Boar chomping on a baby rabbit right before bedtime, would you?"

Tessa laughed, her eyes dark, the light from the yurt a halo behind her head. "You didn't tell your students the truth about polar bears in the global warming unit, did you?"

"What, that they eat penguins and baby seals? No, that didn't come up." She shifted on the stone bench, stretching her legs out in front of her. "Ideology targeting the kindergarten set tends to be uniformly nonviolent. Not to mention, vegetarian-positive."

"I know. Have you ever noticed that films for kids are usually pro-environment and anti-business?" Tessa asked.

"Anti-hunting, too. I have a theory that children's movies are actually liberal propaganda. Like environmentalists realized, hey, if we get the next generation when they're young and vulnerable, then there won't be as much of a battle later about saving wetlands or protecting owls. Or, say, abolishing the meat industry."

Tessa was staring at her, and Eleanor wondered if she'd crossed some invisible Hollywood insider-outsider boundary. Did she not get to say critical things about movies? This idea didn't thrill her. On the other hand, Tessa was currently within arm's reach nearly naked, and ideals were such a small thing to sacrifice.

"I didn't mean that in a negative way," she added. "I'm all for instilling an environmental ethic in the next generation."

"That's not it." Tessa paused. "It's just, I said almost the exact same thing in an interview with *Entertainment* magazine a few years ago. Pixar and DreamWorks were so pissed that Michael, my agent, convinced me I had to work on their next project as a show of good faith."

"Really? Maybe I should start reading *Entertainment*. You know, for the articles."

"Ha, ha." Tessa shook her head, but she was smiling at Eleanor through the steam rising between them.

Eleanor sat back in the tub, telling herself it was just the hot water making her feel flushed. Right. She looked away from Tessa's eyes, out at the black sky now playing host to several dozen stars. Maybe they would see the Milky Way tonight, after all.

"Nice, isn't it?" Tessa asked.

"I can't imagine living in L.A. knowing this is here waiting for you."

"Whenever I'm here I wonder how I'll ever be able to leave. But this is where we come for a vacation. It isn't real life."

"I guess not."

Eleanor glanced at Tessa. Was this real? The actress was watching her through half-lidded eyes with a look that Eleanor felt resonate in her own body. Then Tessa turned her head away. Eleanor blinked. She must have imagined the look. There was no way that Tessa Flanagan could be attracted to her, a skinny, freckly nobody from Vermont who had been mistaken for a teenage boy more than once during her radical days at Smith when she buzzed her hair and tromped around in men's boots. Tessa Flanagan dated fellow celebrities. Male celebrities.

Too bad—all Eleanor wanted to do right now was slide between Tessa's parted legs, push her back against the side of the tub, and meld their lips in a long kiss. What would their bodies feel like pressed together in the warm water, separated only by a few strips of thin material? She imagined running her hand along the string bikini bottom, cupping Tessa's hip and the curve of her ass, releasing her breasts from the swimsuit top. Her breath quickened, and she felt heat rising in her chest. Not to mention certain other places.

Wow, she thought. Maybe now would be a good time to get out of the hot tub.

Shivering slightly, she rose and made her way across the hot tub, conscious of her body exposed in the lamplight as she climbed the steps to the deck. Her new swimsuit was a two-piece but covered her body almost as thoroughly as her favorite racing suit. Sasha had insisted she replace her old one-piece. She'd also insisted that Eleanor splurge some of her newfound cash on a professional bikini wax before the trip. As she reached for her towel, she was glad she'd listened to her roommate.

"Where are you going?" Tessa asked.

"It was getting a little hot in there."

"Ah." Tessa lifted an eyebrow, a gesture Eleanor had watched her make on the big screen more than once, usually in a romantic comedy when Tessa's character was trying to appear wry and vulnerable at the same time.

For a moment, she tried to figure out what her own role

was as she wrapped the beach towel around her waist. Then she remembered that this wasn't a movie, and Tessa was a real person, just like her. Well, maybe not just like her.

"I think I'll head in," she said, staring down at the deck.

There was a moment of silence. Then Tessa said, "Okay. Goodnight, Eleanor."

"Goodnight."

Back in her room a little while later, she lay in bed in the dark remembering the sound of her name on Tessa's lips, the fleeting touch of Tessa's thigh against her own. What had she gotten herself into? And how exactly was she going to make it through two more weeks in Hawaii, let alone two more months in L.A., without giving herself away?

Whenever they came to Kauai, Tessa slept with the curtains open in her bedroom so that the light of the rising sun would wake her. From her king-sized bed in summertime, she could look out through the sliding glass doors at the sun emerging from the ocean at the start of its trek across the sky. Then she would slip from bed and do a little yoga until Laya heard her moving and came running in to tackle her.

This trip was different, though. Normally she slept soundly on the island, lulled by the scent of sampaguita and plumeria and the nearby sound of the ocean. But this time her sleep was fitful, interrupted often by the sound of nocturnal animals or the house shifting on its foundation. Four days in, and she had yet to sleep a full night through.

The previous evening she'd followed Eleanor out into the hot tub. For a few minutes, Tessa had enjoyed her proximity, knowing that her bare skin was tantalizingly close. But Eleanor had fled after only a short time. As she'd drifted past on her way out of the tub, Tessa had nearly given in to the urge to pull her close. Would Eleanor have struggled, or acquiesced readily? She'd imagined peeling Eleanor's swimsuit down over her narrow hips, across her long thighs, over her lean calves. But instead she'd watched Eleanor slip out of the hot tub, dark hair falling over one side of her face, the other side in shadow. Hidden in plain sight, impossible to read.

All night Tessa had started awake every few hours from dreams that were detailed, lucid. Not to mention, lurid. After one dream too many, she lay awake waiting for first light. In her dreams, Eleanor had been simultaneously firm and yielding, hot and cool, wet and—well, wet. As Tessa was now, imagining her legs entwined with Eleanor's in the hot water beneath the starlit sky.

Lusting after the hired help was a Hollywood cliché. But it wasn't as if she were some middle-aged star acting out his midlife crisis, and Eleanor was no nubile teen looking to explore daddy issues. Who would it hurt if their relationship turned personal? Laya, she thought immediately, picturing the worshipful gaze her daughter regularly leveled at Eleanor. But no matter what, Eleanor was Wisconsin-bound come fall. Either way, Laya would lose her newfound hero.

Wisconsin bordered Chicago's northern suburbs, but Tessa wasn't sure she'd ever ventured that far north. In her old life, she'd been more of a South Side girl. On the rare occasions she willingly channeled thoughts of Chicago, she saw the same fleeting images over and over again—the brick row house near the El that shook each time a train went by; a group of Filipino women in the oval living room with its shag carpet and plaid wool couch, laughing loudly over a game of Mah Jong; her mother tending the potted herbs and flowers on their back porch in the summer, teaching her the plant names in English first, Tagalog second; her mother shrieking at her father, whose temper always ratcheted up quickly to match his wife's, Tessa creeping away unnoticed to hide in the front closet in among the shoes that smelled comfortingly of leather; warm, sunny afternoons spent in a park near their house, the scent of cut grass and spring flowers in the air, her father pushing her on a swing, urging her to jump at the top of the arc, catching her in his strong arms as she fell toward earth; her mother tucking her into bed at night with noisy kisses and laughter; and on the last good day, the police officer at the door of her fourth-grade classroom, waiting for her.

After that her memories revolved around an endless succession of schools and foster homes, some memorable for the "siblings" she had to fight off, some for the "fathers" whose eyes and hands lingered too long on her leg, belly, breast. Until finally the bus to L.A., where her Filipina features and high school Spanish landed her a job waiting tables at a Mexican restaurant. She hadn't wanted to be an actor then, not yet. That first year of freedom, she'd luxuriated in the tiny studio apartment she rented in the shadow of the 101. Noisy, but no worse than some of the apartments she'd been forced to inhabit in Chicago. And all hers.

Sometimes now she thought she actually missed the Midwest. Missed seasons, and practical, no-nonsense people who withstood winter temperatures tens of degrees below zero with a philosophical shrug of the shoulders and the sincere assertion that no matter how bad things got, they could always be worse. California in general and L.A. in particular were full of whiners, weather wusses who complained when the temperature edged below sixty, who wore wetsuits to swim in ocean waters that Chicagoans would have considered balmy. Sometimes she hated the idea of raising Laya without snow in a desert city where the passing of seasons was barely noticeable. Of allowing her daughter to grow up in a city whose residents cared more about mani-pedis and plastic surgery than the environment.

In a way, she envied Eleanor. At the end of the summer, she would pack up her car and head to the center of the country—the flyover states, as Californians and New Yorkers referred to the Midwest. What would Madison be like? Other than butt-ass cold in the winter, of course. Tessa had Google Earthed it, wandering the small city's neighborhoods and landmarks via satellite. Madison had a reputation as a liberal college town, a mecca for Midwestern gays and lesbians. Was that why Eleanor had picked it? Was she a lesbian?

Tessa closed her eyes against the light flooding her room and pictured Eleanor as she must look right that second, sleeping down the hall in the bedroom that overlooked the garden. She imagined herself pushing open the guest room door and stealing quietly across the room, pulling back the covers and slipping into bed beside her daughter's nanny... So this was what it felt like to want to stalk someone. The temptation to let herself into Eleanor's room—she was so close, after all—was nearly irresistible.

Fortunately, the Hawaiian sun had its usual effect on her daughter. Even though it was barely six, Laya soon bounded through the door, Moo in tow, and launched herself onto the bed, effectively squashing any and all stalkerish urges.

"What's on tap today?" Eleanor asked at breakfast a little while later, munching a bowl of cereal across the kitchen table.

"No work allowed," Laya declared, staring hard at Tessa.

"I wouldn't dream of it," she said, even though there was a conference call that Jane Byerly had asked her to sit in on. But while there would always be a conference call or an important meeting, Laya wouldn't be six for long. And Eleanor—well, their time together had a definite expiration date. For now, they were on vacation. High time she acted like it.

"How about a hike on the Na Pali Coast?" she suggested.

Laya dropped her toast and clapped her hands. "Really? Can we go to Hanalei too?"

"You betcha," Tessa said. "What about you, Eleanor? Do you like to hike?"

"I'm from Vermont," she said, as if this answered the question.

Tessa's gaydar pinged. As she watched Eleanor add cream to a giant mug of coffee, she added up the clues—Smith alum, unmarried, no reference to a boyfriend, hot in an androgynous, natural beauty way. And, now, a fan of hiking, that all-American West (and apparently East) Coast lesbian pastime.

Remembering her own decidedly Sapphic dreams, Tessa drained her orange juice. Perhaps her subconscious was trying to tell her something. Namely, that she hadn't had sex in way too long. Damn Ama for convincing her to invite this intriguing woman into their lives. Or should she thank her? Tessa had yet to decide.

CHAPTER NINE

Eleanor watched Tessa over the top of her wineglass. They'd put Laya to bed a few minutes earlier—she had requested that they tandem-read one of her favorite stories, *Rikki Tikki Tavi*, that evening, in honor of the large snake they'd glimpsed on the Na Pali Coast trail—and returned to the living room to finish the bottle of wine from dinner. Eleanor was currently stationed on the couch, while Tessa had selected an armchair a short distance away.

All day Eleanor had thought she'd caught Tessa watching her, though the actress had been quick to look away or hide her eyes behind dark glasses. Now, with half a bottle of wine warming her belly, Eleanor worked up the courage to inquire, "Is there something you want to ask me?"

Tessa's eyebrows rose. "Are you psychic too, in addition to your goat-like powers?"

Laya and her mother had nicknamed Eleanor "Billy" on the trail that morning as she sped up the narrow path ahead of them, kicking up red dust with her trail shoes. She kept having to force herself to slow down to match the pace of the easily distracted little girl, who wanted to use her magnifying glass, sketch a plant in her outdoor journal, or check her compass every dozen or so feet. She was a National Park Services Certified Junior Ranger, she'd announced in the car on the way to the trail, a designation that apparently carried with it certain responsibilities and obligations.

Now Eleanor tucked her stocking feet under her and smiled. "Not a good psychic or I would already know what was on your mind."

"Valid point." Tessa drained the rest of her wine and set the empty glass on the coffee table between them. "I guess I was thinking about a conversation we had on the flight out here. You never got a chance to tell me why you waited so long to go back to school."

While Eleanor didn't believe in psychic abilities (at least, not in the way the average resident of California probably did), she could read people, and she knew that this wasn't the question on Tessa's mind. Still, it was out there now, and she could either answer truthfully or invent some safe, alternate reality. After all, Tessa was her boss, not her friend. And yet there was something genuine about the actress, something beyond her outer beauty, distracting as it could be, drawing Eleanor in. Again, if Laya's mother had been anyone else, Eleanor would have sworn there was an entirely mutual attraction smoldering between them. But she wasn't anyone else.

"Well," she said, running her finger over the rim of her glass as the quiet sounds of a Sarah McLachlan album floated down from hidden speakers, "my mom was diagnosed with cancer my junior year of college, so everything sort of got put on hold." She remembered the phone call she'd fielded one February night in her dorm room, the double off-campus ring that usually signaled a treat but this time heralded the battle to come. For months after that call, she flinched every time she heard an off-campus ring.

"I'm sorry to hear that," Tessa said, her voice serious. "Is she okay now?"

"Not exactly." She took a breath, bracing herself for the matter-of-fact recitation of her mother's passing. She had arranged her life the last few months so that she hadn't had to say the words out loud very often. "My mom died in November. That's why I didn't teach the whole year. I took time off to be with my family in Vermont."

"Oh, Eleanor. I'm so sorry." Tessa leaned forward, the usually smooth skin between her perfectly shaped eyebrows drawn into a V.

Eleanor was almost certain the empathy she read in Tessa's gaze was real. Then again, hard to be sure with an Oscar-winning actress. "It's also why I needed a break from Boston. That, and my ex shacked up with another woman right after the funeral."

"You're kidding."

"Unfortunately not." So far they had both avoided identifying pronouns, but now Eleanor could read the question clearly in Tessa's eyes. Was this what she wanted to know? After fourteen years of living out and proud, coming out was not a new process for Eleanor. Normally she announced who she was right off the bat to anyone who would be in her life for any significant period of time. "It seems so long ago," she added, "I don't actually remember what I saw in her."

The room was quiet, the only sounds the faint hum of the dishwasher running in the kitchen, the distant thrum of the ocean crashing against the beach, the melodic croon of Sarah McLachlan's voice. Eleanor bit her lip. Why wasn't Tessa saying anything?

Then she nodded. "I knew my gaydar couldn't be that off."

Gaydar? Did that mean…? Eleanor felt an absurd hope welling up and tried to quell it. Even if Tessa were as queer as, say, Ellen and Portia, it didn't mean she would magically return Eleanor's crush.

"Besides," Tessa said, "Ama had you pegged from the start. And that little woman is rarely wrong when it comes to Sapphic sisters."

With difficulty, Eleanor schooled her features. It was one thing for Tessa to be lesbian-friendly, but for Ama to be fluent in queer culture? Still, the smile on Tessa's face was overly smug for Eleanor's liking. She may have only been a kindergarten teacher, but she was also from New England, a land where sarcastic understatement and gruff rebuffs were the norm.

Emboldened by the wine, she asked, "Are you familiar with the term gaydar because the rumors about you on After Ellen dot com are true, then?"

Tessa blinked several times before arranging her face in a casual smile that Eleanor had learned was one of her stock expressions. "Don't believe everything you read on the Internet," she said, and stood abruptly. "I think I'll head up now. Sleep well." And without waiting for a reply, she slipped from the room and made her way upstairs.

Eleanor sat where she was on the couch, suddenly alone. Overhead, she heard Tessa traverse the hallway, footsteps muffled on the thick runner, and then the door to one of the bedrooms creaked audibly. Eleanor gripped her wineglass, looking around the empty living room. What had just happened? One moment they'd been sharing deep, dark secrets, and the next Tessa was running off without warning. Or at least, Eleanor had shared secrets. Apparently she had crossed a line with her last comment, but it was a line that existed only in Tessa's head. She was the one who had started this conversation, after all, the one who had been watching Eleanor all day as if she wanted to get inside her head and sift through what she found. Jesus. The woman was infuriating.

And also, seemingly, gay-friendly if not an actual friend of Dorothy herself. The fact that Tessa had suspected she was a lesbian when she hired her, when she invited her to Kauai with them, when she came out to the hot tub the night before, had to mean something. But why did it feel as if every time they started to get close, Tessa withdrew? Probably because that was exactly what kept happening.

Eleanor leaned her head against the back of the wicker couch. What did she know about Tessa, really? She knew that she was a devoted parent and a hard worker, had a B.A. in English with a concentration in Asian American lit, drank decaf coffee because the "hard" stuff made her jittery, was kind to nearly everyone they encountered, worried about Laya, loved to read and that Nutter Butters were her secret guilty pleasure. But these were mostly observations Eleanor had made over the past few weeks since joining the household staff. In that time, Tessa had shared little information about herself that didn't directly impact their current plans or activities.

Meanwhile, since they'd met, Eleanor had found herself describing her childhood in Vermont, her educational experiences at Smith, her time teaching private school in Boston. The questioning had been subtle, and Eleanor had been flattered that Tessa was interested. So flattered she hadn't really noticed when the actress dodged her own questions with vague answers or a change of subject. But she was noticing now. The only personal information she knew about Tessa was what she'd read online. And yet she suspected she knew a side of the actress that few others did.

When she'd mentioned her mother's death, she was sure she'd glimpsed genuine emotion in Tessa's eyes. For a moment she had even thought Tessa might come to her on the couch, take her in her arms, comfort her. But it was just a fantasy, albeit a compelling one. She wanted Tessa to hold her the way Laurie hadn't after the funeral, wished Tessa would tell her that everything would be all right even though she knew it wouldn't, imagined the actress kissing her eyes, her hair, her lips…

As the fantasy inevitably took on adult themes (she couldn't seem to keep her thoughts of her employer G-rated), Eleanor shook her head. Despite the tantalizing glimpses Tessa had revealed, Eleanor was still alone in the living room of the actress's vacation house, the sound of the ocean muted in the distance.

Upstairs, Tessa sat in a mission-style rocker in a corner of Laya's darkened room, gazing out through the wide windows at the moonlit sea rising and falling seemingly just out of reach. Laya was asleep, the sound of her breathing audible in the otherwise quiet room. Her allergies had been acting up since they'd arrived on the island, which meant that her snoring was worse, too. It used to amuse Tessa that Laya snored. Made her wonder if this was a trait her daughter shared with the unknown, unknowable father Tessa had selected from a sperm bank catalog.

How many times had she sat in this very room watching Laya sleep, the ocean shimmering jewel-like in the background? Sometimes in L.A., she dreamed of this room, this house, this corner of the island where time seemed to both slow and quicken at the same time. In her dreams, she often found herself in the ocean swimming toward shore, where she could see the house lit up as if for a movie premiere. But no matter how hard she pulled against the saltwater waves, the current took her farther and farther out to sea, away from her daughter.

She had that sense of inevitable distance now, a result of her conversation with Eleanor, no doubt. While she'd suspected Eleanor's sexuality might fall in the "other" category, she'd had no idea she'd lost her mother less than a year before. Wasn't that the sort of thing the Barclay School's background check should have included? Perhaps a death in the family was considered a private matter, not applicable for the purposes of the report. But to Tessa it seemed incredibly applicable. Like her, Eleanor was motherless in the world, only newly so.

Instead of going to Eleanor as she'd longed to, instead of offering her a shoulder or, at the least, a consoling touch, she'd run off as soon as the spotlight had shifted her way. She couldn't help it. The wine had lowered her defenses, as had the company, and she hadn't been able to pretend that the idea of Eleanor reading celebrity gossip sites to glean information about her wasn't somehow unsettling. Tessa, who had won two Best Actress Golden Globes in addition to the coveted Oscar, had been unable to hide her discomfort at the notion that Eleanor might know things she'd rather not be known.

Which was ridiculous. The material on the Web was public property, and wasn't even accurate in most cases. She'd never dated Tom Cruise (as if) or Jude Law (though they had gone for drinks a few times), and she certainly hadn't spent her teen years in Brooklyn with her father's nonexistent great-aunt. Anyway, so what if Eleanor had read up on her? Hadn't she thoroughly researched the Byerly sisters before partnering with them? It was the same idea. And yet, somehow, it wasn't.

But that wasn't the real reason she'd turned tail and run. Sometimes she had a hard time letting people in. Women in particular, as her longtime friend Will liked to either gently point out or harass her about, depending on his mood. Since Laya's birth, he claimed, she'd used her daughter as an excuse to keep any romantic encounters casual, brief. Perhaps, but as a single mother, she'd reminded him more than once, she had to look out for her child. She couldn't very well parade people in and out of Laya's life willy-nilly. Even she knew this was a joke. Other than the occasional hook-up, she hadn't gotten involved with another woman in years, not since Nadine.

Looking back, she still couldn't believe she'd opened her life to a woman who, it turned out, had been willing to sell the intimate details of their relationship to the highest bidder. At least she'd escaped the affair without permanent damage—Nadine had skeletons of her own, ones that would land her in jail on a probation violation should they be revealed, and that threat had been enough to ensure her silence. That plus the buy-off Michael, her agent, had tried to talk Tessa out of offering. But she'd known that more than anything, Nadine craved attention, which was why she'd been such an easy mark. Money could buy all the attention anyone needed, for a while anyway.

She still felt an odd sense of dislocation when she thought about Nadine, who, though not an actor, had managed to create a persona Tessa hadn't thought to question. She'd known nothing about the younger woman's drunk driving or rehab history until Michael brought it to her attention. Part of it was that Nadine had been clean for more than a year when they met at a release party, and managed to remain so through nearly the entirety of their relationship. Nadine's father, Bradley Simmons, was a powerful producer known for taking big risks that nearly always paid off. Tessa had worked with him before, and initially refused Nadine's advances because of who her father was. But Nadine was charming and persistent, and enough of a Hollywood insider that Tessa thought she was safe.

Until she came home early one day to find Nadine hooking up a camera in the bedroom of the Malibu beach house. A hidden camera. Nadine had sobbed dramatically, begging forgiveness, but for Tessa it had been simple. She'd kicked Nadine out, changed the locks, and never spoken to her again. Michael dangled the open threat of probation violation and slipped her an envelope of cash, and that was that.

Tessa knew that Eleanor was nothing like Nadine. A teacher committed to helping kids reach their potential, she hadn't grown up a stereotypical poor little rich girl in a city known for glitz and glamour, she hadn't partied her way through her twenties and landed in rehab, and best of all, she didn't know a thing about the business of making movies. Was that why Tessa was attracted to her? Maybe a little. But she was more interested in who Eleanor was than who she wasn't. By now, Tessa had watched her closely enough to know that she was generous and open, smart and funny, lovely despite some occasionally klutzy tendencies. And, maybe, a little bit lost since her mother's death. Tessa knew what that felt like.

She rocked the chair slowly as a cloud passed before the moon, momentarily casting a shadow over the island. She liked Eleanor, enjoyed her dry sense of humor, loved the fact that she reread the work of Jane Austen, arguably one of England's earliest feminists, every few years. Admired her cool confidence, her dedication to helping kids, the obvious intelligence in her eyes. Found her incredibly sexy too, but it was more than just physical attraction drawing her to her daughter's nanny. Ultimately, that sense of something more was what had sent her skittering upstairs to Laya's room. Because if she and Eleanor were to give in to the heat between them, what would happen at the end of the summer?

As the cloud passed from in front of the moon, Laya rolled over and sighed, clutching Gerri the giraffe closer. Safe in her rocking chair in the corner of the dark room, Tessa clamped down on temptation and listened to her daughter breathe as moonlight spilled across the island and reflected off the sleeping ocean.

CHAPTER TEN

Over the next few days, Eleanor became convinced that Tessa was avoiding her—as much as anyone could avoid someone sleeping in the next room. The actress didn't work much when Laya was awake, but as soon as her daughter trudged upstairs for her afternoon nap (usually grumbling that she wasn't a baby and didn't need to take naps anymore, a yawn nearly always punctuating this grouchy avowal), Tessa would vanish. Sometimes she went to "check e-mail" in the studio. On other occasions, Eleanor would glimpse her strolling alone down the hill toward the lagoon, chin lowered, shoulders hunched against the temperate trade winds. And she would wonder—what sort of quandary would someone like Tessa Flanagan have to weigh her down?

At night, once Laya was in bed, Tessa would set the alarm, say goodnight in a neutral tone and retreat to her bedroom, leaving her door slightly ajar in case Laya needed her. Eleanor would creep quietly past, fighting the urge to look through the gap to where her employer probably lay in bed in her plaid pajama pants and a beat-up UCLA T-shirt. She wasn't sure if the cold shoulder meant Tessa was upset with her or merely had other things on her mind. The mystery kept her up at night, literally, as she tried to keep her mind on Jane Austen and found it instead wandering to the woman sleeping down the hall. A couple of times she rose and paced the length of her room, but she never ventured into the hallway. The realization that Tessa might be genuinely uninterested in her kept her from opening the door.

The rest of their first vacation week passed uneventfully and somewhat lonely, with Eleanor spending the bulk of her time with Laya or by herself. Sometimes Tessa took her daughter for walks or drives or down to the beach without Eleanor, and she was left on her own trying to figure out if she'd imagined Tessa's initial friendly overtures. What about the encounter in the hot tub? Had the attraction been one-sided? Not that that should surprise her. Tessa could have any of a horde of willing men or women. A kindergarten teacher from Vermont could hardly expect to compete with the likes of Jude Law. Or even Lindsay Lohan.

As the first week on the island drew to a close, Eleanor finally called Sasha for help puzzling out her employer's mysterious behavior. Her former roommate suggested the actress might suffer from PMS. Or perhaps she was off her meds.

"Do you think she's on something?" Eleanor asked, keeping her voice low as she lay on the cover of her bed, afternoon sunlight and sea air pouring in the open window. Tessa and Laya were off on another of their strolls, leaving Eleanor to kick around by herself. Again.

"Everyone in L.A. is on something," Sasha said. A male voice sounded in the background, low and fluid. "I have to go. Some of us actually have to work to earn our exorbitant salaries." And the line clicked.

Eleanor shut her eyes and dropped her cell on the bed. This vacation wasn't turning out the way she had anticipated. Not even close. Could Sasha be right about Tessa's state of mind? She didn't remember seeing Tessa take anything other than her daily multivitamin. But then again, who was to say that the pill she popped at breakfast was, in fact, a vitamin?

And then, just as suddenly as Tessa's boycott of Eleanor's company had begun, the unofficial blockade ended. At breakfast the morning after Eleanor's emergency phone call to Sasha, Tessa asked Laya if she'd like to go to Waimea Canyon.

"Yeah huh!" the girl replied, smiling widely around a half-chewed bite of toast. "Elle, do you want to go?"

"Of course." The previous afternoon, she'd been studying Hawaii's Grand Canyon, as the park was known, on the map she'd ordered from Amazon. Had Tessa noticed? But as Tessa cast her yet another unreadable look before turning an indulgent smile on her daughter, who was "thrilled" by the idea of returning to one of her (many) "favorite places" on the island, Eleanor wasn't sure Tessa had meant to include her in the invitation.

Whatever, she groused inwardly as she went upstairs to pack a bag. It wasn't as if she required Tessa to be anything other than professional. After all, she'd lived quite happily—or at least, not terribly *un*happily—for thirty-plus years without the Flanagans. So what if she had once told Laurie, her ex, that Tessa topped her *Friends*-inspired list of celebrity freebies? No one actually believed they'd ever meet anyone on their list.

By now Laurie had probably heard through the grapevine that she was working for Tessa. Eleanor had e-mailed a few friends back in Boston to gloat, but the NDAs she'd signed kept her from answering in any detail her friends' numerous queries, the most common of which involved the actress's rumored lesbianism. She tried to picture Laurie's face at the moment she learned that Eleanor was working for her number one celebrity freebie as an "educational consultant." (Tessa had jokingly coined this title, but Eleanor found herself using it at times—as a Smithie, it was difficult for her to admit publicly that she was working as a nanny, however temporary and lucrative the position might be.) As she attempted to summon an image of her ex-girlfriend, she realized suddenly that she couldn't remember exactly what Laurie looked like. She could call up individual features—oval face, hazel eyes, ready smile, straight brown hair that moved like water in certain lighting—but not the overall package.

What about her mother? Had she lost her too? Fortunately, her mother's face came back to her easily, in full detail. She relaxed, relieved—until she realized that the image she was remembering was in fact her favorite photo of her mom, taken at the crest of Monadnock Mountain during the first remission when they still thought everything might be all right.

It had begun. She was losing even her memories of her mother now.

The half-open door snapped back on its hinges as Laya entered the room. "Come on, Eleanor! Quit dillydallying!"

"I do not dillydally," Eleanor said in a dignified tone. Then she grabbed Laya and planted a noisy zorbert on her forearm, smiling as the girl's peals of laughter rang out. Thank God for little kids, she thought for easily the thousandth time in her adult life.

A little while later, Eleanor embarked on her second-ever helicopter ride. This trip was considerably longer than the first and took them over and around the mountains and valleys that adorned Kauai's interior. The center of the island was surprisingly untamed, all trees and rivers and jungle with no sign of human habitation for miles at a time. Eventually the ocean appeared in the distance again, and then they were setting down at a makeshift landing pad at the parking lot of what turned out to be a coffee plantation on the outskirts of the southwestern town of Waimea. A gray-haired ex-hippie who both Tessa and Laya already seemed to know greeted them and waved the small party toward a mud-splattered Jeep Wrangler parked outside the plantation gift shop.

As they approached the vehicle, Tessa insisted Eleanor take the front seat. "You get motion sick in the back, don't you?" the actress said, seemingly genuinely concerned.

Eleanor nodded grudgingly, refusing to be touched that Tessa remembered this fact, and slid into the front seat next to Pete, a retired geology professor who, it turned out, knew everything there was to know about Waimea Canyon. As they drove up the windy state highway that led into the canyon's interior, the drops at the edge of the road increasingly impressive, Pete explained the plate tectonic history of the Hawaiian archipelago and the geology of Kauai, a former volcano and the oldest of the Hawaiian islands. When the paved road ended, Pete parked the Jeep and took them hiking on trails that lined the rim before dipping down into the red-brown canyon, where he related colorful Hawaiian myths as they walked up and down through cloud forests.

A couple of hours in, they stopped for lunch at the edge of a thousand-foot drop. As she munched the PBJ sandwich Tessa had fixed her that morning, Eleanor was enchanted. She'd visited the real Grand Canyon once with Sasha on a road trip a few years back and could see why this canyon had earned its nickname. The reddish earth fell away in dramatic fashion here too, lava flows leaving etched basalt ridges further scored by rainfall from the island's central peak, Mount Waialeale, one of the wettest places on earth according to Professor Pete. The green of Kauai's pervasive vegetation, another result of all that rainfall, gave the canyon a friendlier cast than the Arizona desert, though, while overhead, cumulus clouds sped past on omnipresent trade winds, casting shadows over the canyon walls.

The day passed quickly, Tessa and Laya recording their adventures on the family digital camera, Eleanor asking the professor question after question. Much too soon they were making their way back to the coffee plantation where they found the helicopter pilot waiting for them in the parking lot near the gift shop. But as Pete drove off, waving in the rearview mirror, Tessa didn't immediately head for the waiting chopper. Instead she turned to Eleanor.

"Interested in a tour of the plantation?"

"Not really." Eleanor associated the word "plantation" with America's history of slavery. "But I'd love a look at the gift shop. I thought I might send some coffee to my dad."

"Is he as big a dark roast addict as you?" Tessa asked, smiling a little.

"Where do you think I learned to be such a coffee snob?" Eleanor felt her pulse speed up and cursed her seditious body. True, this was the most attention Tessa had given her in days, but that didn't mean she had to react like a dog starved for its master's notice.

"Ah—so you admit that Northeasterners are snobs."

"I didn't say that." As Tessa lifted an eyebrow, she added, "Okay, maybe the Northeast has that reputation for a reason. But New England and the Northeast aren't the same thing, you know."

At that moment, Laya, grouchy after a busy day without a nap, suffered an official meltdown, which prevented Tessa from pressing her further on the pretentiousness of the opposite coast.

They lured the whining girl into the "boring" gift shop with the promise of ice cream, and soon Laya was chomping on a sugar cone while Eleanor browsed the aisles, seeking out souvenirs to send to her family and friends. She'd rarely gone on vacation as an adult, except to visit Sasha or other college friends in various parts of the country. For Christmas one year when she was in high school, her family had visited London, where her mother still had relatives. And in their first year together, Laurie had surprised her with a week in France during summer break. Then, with a less than impressive bank account, she had sent only the occasional postcard home. But now her checking account was fairly brimming, and she hadn't spent a cent so far during their sojourn on the island. Why not splurge a little?

"Geez," Tessa said a half hour later as they made their way out to the parking lot. "I had no idea you were such a serious shopper."

Eleanor had paid the gift shop to ship packages of coffee and other goodies to her father, sister and Sasha, spending a couple hundred dollars in the process. "I'm not usually, but I didn't have to pay for a plane ticket," she pointed out. "And besides, they're all worth it."

"I'm sure they are," Tessa said.

Eleanor glanced at her, but the actress was already slipping her sunglasses on and smiling down at her daughter, who skipped along between them riding the crest of her sugar high. With their matching dark green fishing hats (Laya had picked them out before the trip because she said they looked like real ranger hats), they were adequately camouflaged. Only a handful of tourists in the shop had pointed and whispered, seemingly uncertain of the veracity of their celebrity sighting.

"Ama and Dani will like their T-shirts too, won't they?" Tessa said to Laya.

"Uh-huh. And Uncle Will. I miss him. When do we get to see him again?"

"When we get back to California," Tessa promised. "I'm sure he misses you too."

Will Knight, Eleanor knew, was Tessa's personal trainer. Were they more than friends? He hadn't been around much before the trip, but that didn't mean anything. Laya seemed on awfully familiar terms for him to be just a trainer.

The helicopter ride interceded to distract her from this unpleasant line of thought, and she enjoyed the seemingly slow-motion transit of the island's interior. Besides, what Tessa did or didn't do with Will Knight was none of her business. Likely, it would stay that way.

That night, Laya nearly fell asleep at the dinner table. Afterward, while Eleanor read her a good-night story, Tessa retired to her own bedroom and locked herself in for the night. She was tired from the day's adventures too, so after reading a few pages of the most recent book by Arundhati Roy, another of her favorite writers, she fell asleep quickly. But she awoke in the middle of the night and lay in bed, moonlight streaming in her window as she strained to detect any sound from Eleanor's room. So close. So tempting. And ultimately such a bad idea.

So far so good. She'd managed to keep Eleanor at a distance, which, though not entirely satisfying, at least allowed her to feel in control of the situation. Since the night she'd learned about Eleanor's mother, she had avoided being alone with her daughter's nanny for long periods of time. Another week and they would be back in L.A., and then she could return to the old schedule—leaving for work shortly after Eleanor arrived in the morning and coming home in time for dinner, after which Eleanor would return back down the hill to Sasha's apartment. On the weekends, Tessa would practice being a single mom, something she was going to have to get used to come fall. She'd decided not to hire another nanny after Eleanor left at the end of August. Her job was in L.A. now, and she wanted to see if she could handle parenting on her own. She'd already hired a landscaping company recommended by her friend Margot Trivers, film producer and mother to Laya's best friend and Barclay classmate, Rayann. Lawn work aside, she planned to assume the role of a normal mother once Eleanor left for Wisconsin.

Sometimes Tessa daydreamed about leaving L.A. herself, especially when they were on vacation in Hawaii. Perhaps it was genetic memory—her parents had each come from tiny, verdant island nations—but she felt comfortable on Kauai, her world bounded by sand and jungle, the ocean never far off. Not just tenants of her garden, sampaguita flowers grew wild across the island. The locals called the plant "pikake" and made leis from its fragrant petals. Each time she noticed the scent, Tessa thought of her mother. Had she survived, Benita Reyes would have celebrated her sixtieth birthday this November, lines etched about her eyes like Ama, her body thicker around the middle. Would her legs still be strong and shapely or would her muscles have slackened with age? It was hard for Tessa to imagine her as anything other than the young, laughing woman she remembered, as the few photos she kept hidden away in her bedroom dresser showed her to be. In a year, Tessa would be the same age her mother was when she died. Was she already that old herself? Could she really be on the cusp of surpassing her mother's lifetime?

She thought of Eleanor's mother too, so recently lost. Eleanor seemed fine most of the time, stoic in the face of grief. But Tessa understood now the question she sensed in Eleanor: What was she supposed to do now? She recognized the urge Eleanor had succumbed to—the impulse to leave, to go as far away as she could from the place she had always lived and, perhaps, the person she had always been. Tessa had read once that when you lost a loved one, you were supposed to stay put and let yourself grieve. And maybe there was something to that. But, like Eleanor, she had longed to leave the before part of her life behind. And, mostly, she'd succeeded.

Just as she'd succeeded in keeping Eleanor at a distance. At least, in daylight. At night, her imagination refused to toe the boundary she'd set. In the dark quiet of her room, she still dreamed about the long-limbed, freckle-faced woman in the next room—X-rated, entirely unprofessional dreams.

Perhaps avoiding Eleanor really wasn't necessary, Tessa had found herself thinking the last day or two. After all, they were adults. They'd managed to keep their clothes on so far. Besides, it wasn't often that she met someone who shared her values, political beliefs, interests. She wanted to know more about Eleanor—her favorite writers other than Austen, what kind of music she liked, and, of course, what types of movies she was into. In the Flanagan household, movies were a necessity of life.

The morning after their tour of Waimea Canyon, rare clouds drifted in to obscure the island. By lunchtime, rain was falling in tropical torrents, flooding the hillside below the house.

"It's raining, it's pouring," Laya sang, munching potato chips as water gushed from the gutters outside.

"Whatever will we find to do?" Tessa asked, wiggling her eyebrows meaningfully at her daughter.

The girl clapped her hands. "Can we watch *Finding Nemo*?"

"I'm up for it," Tessa said. "What about you?"

Eleanor looked up from her tuna sandwich. "Me?"

"Yes, you," Tessa said.

"Yes, you," Laya echoed.

"Okay," Eleanor said, her smile tentative.

No more distance, Tessa decided as they cleaned up the lunch mess. There was no reason they couldn't be friends. Not like she had all that many.

To prepare for the afternoon's film screening, they popped a bowl of microwave popcorn and sprinkled it liberally with salt. Then they dashed through the rain to the studio where, at the touch of a button, shutters dropped into place over the windows and a movie screen descended from the ceiling.

Finding Nemo was Laya's favorite movie, and she knew the dialogue practically by heart. She sat on the couch between them, her feet pressed against Tessa and her head against Eleanor's shoulder. Tessa glanced at Eleanor occasionally. She looked happy, and even seemed to like the movie. She'd seen it twice before, she told Laya when the girl asked. This, in Laya's opinion, was nowhere near enough times.

Even Nemo couldn't compete with naptime, however. Halfway through the film, Laya's snores began to rise above the voices of the animated characters. Tessa turned down the volume and glanced over at Eleanor, whose face was lit by the play of light and color across the screen.

"She's really out," Eleanor said.

As if in agreement, Laya let out a particularly guttural snort, and Tessa had to bite her lip to keep from laughing.

"Such a lady," she said.

"Like mother like daughter."

"Tell me about it. I used to complain that my agent was forcing me to wear drag whenever he convinced me to squeeze myself into a dress and heels for the red carpet. It's a miracle I never fell flat on my face on camera."

Eleanor glanced back at the screen as a flock of animated seagulls chased Dory and Marlin while calling out in creepy monotones, "Mine? Mine?" Tessa imagined the wheels spinning in Eleanor's mind at the reference to drag, and decided it might be time to take pity on her.

"You know," she said, "you were right. Some of those rumors online are true."

Brow knit slightly, Eleanor looked at her again. "I'm sorry if what I said the other night upset you. It wasn't my intent."

"You don't have to apologize." Tessa forced herself to return Eleanor's open, forthright gaze. "I might have overreacted a little. It's just difficult knowing that complete strangers can find out such random information about you. Not that you're a stranger. But for a while, I couldn't blow my nose without wondering if someone would snap a shot and sell it to the dailies."

"I can't even imagine," Eleanor said. "Technology probably just made everything worse. Along comes the Internet and camera phones, and suddenly everyone's a reporter."

Tessa hadn't expected someone outside of the business to have such insight. "That's exactly how it is. Anyone you meet could be secretly filming you in order to score a payday from some celebrity stalker site." She stared down at her bare feet, clad in simple Armani flip-flops. She needed a pedicure. She hadn't had time before the trip.

"I can't imagine what it's been like," Eleanor repeated, voice as gentle as the hand that reached across Laya to settle on Tessa's. "And I am sorry. I didn't mean to touch a nerve."

"It's okay. I know I can trust you." She paused. "Besides, you've signed away any future royalties should you decide to write a tell-all memoir about your summer with us."

Eleanor drew her hand back. "Lucky for you I'm not a very prolific writer. I'm definitely not looking forward to having to write papers again. Yuck."

"Really? I loved writing essays. One night my freshman year I just kept writing, and I didn't even realize what time it was until my upstairs neighbor, who bartended until two every night, came home and started pounding around his apartment." She shook her head, remembering what it had felt like to forget time and place. She hadn't had that luxury for a while now.

"Me, not so much. I used to get Sasha to help me with my papers, and even then I'd barely eke out a B. That's why I stuck with the social sciences. Not as much emphasis on topic sentences and paragraph transitions."

Tessa watched the animated characters dance across the screen. "Sounds like you and Sasha have been friends for a long time."

"The powers that be matched us as roommates our first year of college."

"Have you and she ever, you know…?"

"Sasha?" Eleanor laughed. "Definitely not. She's straight. Well, except for the requisite collegiate lesbian experience, which wasn't with me." She raised a hand to her mouth suddenly and gazed at Tessa through wide eyes. "Don't tell her I told you that. She would kill me."

"Don't worry. Mum's the word." Knowing that Eleanor

wasn't living with an ex-girlfriend cheered her, for reasons she didn't think she would examine too closely.

A moment later, Laya snorted herself awake. As Tessa and Eleanor exchanged an amused look over her head, she rubbed her eyes. "What? What did I miss?"

"Nothing, Mahal," Tessa said, and rubbed her daughter's feet, dirty from going barefoot on the estate.

As they settled back in to watch the rest of the movie, Laya snuggling sleepily between them, the rain tapered off beyond the darkened windows of the studio. Probably there would be a rainbow later. Maybe they could take a drive after the movie for a little rainbow-hunting. And then they would have dinner together, just the three of them.

Somehow, Tessa couldn't remember a Hawaiian vacation ever feeling quite like this.

CHAPTER ELEVEN

The following morning, Eleanor slept late. By the time she came downstairs, lured by the rich scent of coffee, the sun was well above the horizon. The house was quiet, and it took her a moment to remember that this was the day Tessa had planned to take Laya on a day of mother-daughter bonding on the southern side of the island. A note on the kitchen counter in Tessa's nearly horizontal script wished her a great day by herself and promised that the Flanagan women would be home in time for dinner, with pizza in hand.

Eleanor stood at the counter, her fingers tracing the curve of Tessa's writing. She should have been excited—she hadn't had a day off in weeks. But spending time with Tessa and Laya hardly felt like work. Anyway, what was it Tessa had said the night in the hot tub? Wasn't much fun visiting paradise if you didn't have someone to share it with. This seemed especially true now that Tessa's withdrawal seemed to have ended. Eleanor still didn't know what had been behind her employer's moodiness. Maybe Sasha was right and Tessa had wicked PMS. Wouldn't be the first woman Eleanor had lived with who displayed temporary hormonal insanity. Laurie had suffered from endometriosis, a condition that caused debilitating cramps and borderline personality disorder two or three days each month.

Not that she was living with Tessa. This time next week she would be back in L.A. spending her nights at Sasha's apartment and her days with Laya while Tessa went off to work in the city each day. This was a somehow depressing thought, and she turned to the coffeemaker, green light glowing on its base. Tessa must have ground the beans and measured the water before she and Laya left. Eleanor poured a cup and added cream and sugar, then tasted it carefully. Not bad. Apparently Tessa knew how to make coffee, even if she didn't drink it herself. Definitely a good quality in a woman. Or a good quality in an employer, anyway.

By the time she'd finished her cup of coffee, she'd decided that a day on her own, with hour after hour pursuing whatever activity she chose instead of entertaining a mercurial six-year-old, was a gift. The garage near the gate, she knew, held certain treasures, including an expensive racing bike that Tessa had confessed she rarely used but that Robert kept tuned and ready. Since joining Tessa's employ, Eleanor had managed to find time to run but hadn't been on a bike much. What better way to see the island and get in a low-impact workout at the same time?

Within a half-hour she had scoped out a route on her map, filled a small backpack with sunscreen, snacks, water and her current Austen fare—*Emma*, her favorite of the six novels—and was wheeling Tessa's beautiful road bike from the garage. With a wave at Robert, who had solicitously asked after her itinerary, Eleanor tightened the helmet strap and swung her leg over the seat. Her pioneering bike trip in Hawaii. Nice.

The first couple of miles, she rode past open fields and sprawling villas set back off the road, security gates and encircling walls matching those of Mele Honu'ala. As she rode through humid island air, inhaling the pungent scent of vegetation with each breath, Eleanor wondered who owned these mansions and how much time they spent on the island. L.A. and Hawaii were both studies in contrasts, with the wealthiest Americans living and working side by side with the poorest. But she couldn't help admiring the view of the ocean in the distance, the well-tended homes as she approached the village of Kilauea, the beautiful stone church just before the junction with the state highway.

Too soon she was turning onto Highway 56, the only route between Tessa's house and Hanalei, her intended destination. She picked up the pace as she rode along the wide shoulder, careful to stay as far from the car lane as possible. Road riding wasn't her favorite type of cycling. In Boston, she'd regularly rode out the Charles River bike path, a car-free eighteen-mile loop between downtown and Watertown. The trail, along with the variety of landscapes and people-watching it afforded, was one of the few things she missed about Boston. This fact surprised her. She'd thought she was happy in the largest city in New England, or as happy as someone with a desperately ill family member could be. But since leaving the city, she'd found she didn't particularly miss the grouchy New Englanders and entitled college students who crowded Boston's streets in warm weather, cold winter winds that sliced through even the warmest coat, tourists who crowded the Commons and Faneuil Hall every fall on their way to tour the autumn leaves beyond the city's confines.

She missed her family, of course, but she hadn't felt like she really belonged with them for a while. Her mother's emotional distance and her father's obvious preference for her sister's company, not to mention Julia's happily hetero mate, had gradually combined over the years to create in Eleanor a definite sense of otherness whenever she was around her nuclear family. Now, with her mother gone, her father ensconced in a new relationship, and Julia engaged in a life Eleanor could picture all too well but couldn't imagine ever wanting herself, there seemed nothing left to anchor her to New England. No reason to spend every other weekend driving the familiar stretch of I-93 between Boston and Newport, listening to books on tape as she drove the three and a half hours each way.

After more than a decade of arranging her time according

to her mother's chemo or radiation treatments, participation in a new trial, or visits to specialists across the eastern seaboard, she had come unmoored. That part of her life was over, and with it, so were her twenties. Now she would have to find something else to do. Fortunately, she had a built-in plan. While L.A.'s heat, sprawl and laidback culture were a needed change from her old life, the green mountains and pristine beaches of Kauai gorgeous, she was just marking time until grad school. Then her real life would restart and she would put down roots in Madison, a college town known for its residents' collective irreverence.

Only one problem: Eleanor wasn't entirely certain she wanted to be a child psychologist anymore. She wasn't the same person who had visited the clinic off the Mass Pike in the mid-'90s. She hadn't been that person for a while, and yet she had held on to the notion that someday, somehow, she would achieve her "life's dream." Lately she'd been thinking about having a child of her own, someone in whose smile her mother might live on, someone she could take care of and nurture the way her parents had done for her and Julia. She and her sister had been luckier than most, despite losing their mother early. Maybe her life's work should include taking care of her own children, not just those of other people. Not that the two were mutually exclusive. Look at Tessa—she'd continued to act after Laya was born, and was now pursuing an entirely different career path.

In any case, Eleanor thought as she rolled along toward the little town of Hanalei, she supposed it was no use worrying now. Soon enough she'd be in Madison, starting the five-year program she'd committed to. Being back in school would help her decide if a Ph.D. was really what she wanted. Nothing like homework and deadlines and stress to help you see what was important in life. Then again, her mother's illness had already done that, to some degree. And after watching her mother suffer, she wasn't sure she wanted to spend five years kissing faculty ass as a lowly grad student. After all, no one could be sure how long they had. What if she spent the next half decade worrying about supplemental reading and department politics only to be diagnosed at the end of it with breast cancer herself? Her mother had only been forty-two at the first diagnosis. No way for Eleanor to know if diseased cells were even now wending their way through her bloodstream.

When she reached Hanalei, she guided Tessa's bike down a side street to the local beach, where Tessa had taken her and Laya for a stroll to the end of the pier the day they hiked the Na Pali Coast. Her legs were tired, and she was happy to lock the bike to a rack and find a space on the beach to spread out her towel. She was also glad to be there alone. Even disguised in a floppy hat and wide sunglasses, Tessa had been recognized by locals and tourists alike while they wandered Hanalei and the beach park. Most people had refrained from approaching, but the stares and whispers and pointed fingers had been enough to make Eleanor long for the peace of anonymity. Which today, on her own, she could enjoy.

Stretching out on the towel, she closed her eyes and tried not to imagine what Tessa and Laya might be doing on the other side of the island.

While she was glad to have an entire day with Laya, Tessa missed Eleanor's company. A few days before, when she'd still been on her short-lived avoid-Eleanor kick, she'd called John Alvarez, an outfitter she knew on the southern end of the island, and arranged for a guided half-day kayak and tubing tour of the Hule'ia River. As they navigated the tranquil river, John, owner of Kipu Falls Ranch, provided Tessa and Laya with a running commentary on the flora and fauna of the National Wildlife Refuge they were traversing. When Laya commented on adding the Hawaiian stilt they caught a glimpse of to her "life list" of birds, Tessa wished she could share the moment with Eleanor, who she was certain would have understood her simultaneous pride in Laya's intellectual ability and uneasiness regarding her social skills.

Laya was "totally bummed" at not having her nanny along too, a comment that led to Tessa initiating a conversation about Eleanor's future plans as they floated along the gentle river, paddling around submerged trees and watching the shores for wildlife.

"I know she's not staying forever," Laya said, pushing back her fishing hat. "But it's only June. We still get to have her for a while."

Tessa couldn't argue with that.

After a half day of kayaking, tubing and swimming beneath picturesque waterfalls, they made their way back to civilization and stopped for lunch at a little shop in Poipu, a resort community at the southeastern end of the island. Unfortunately, the teenage girl behind the counter recognized Tessa and proceeded to text everyone she knew within a fifty-mile radius. By the time their order was ready, the sidewalk outside the shop was jammed with tourists and locals craning for a look. The owner, thankfully, sneaked them out through a back door, and Tessa drove to the nearby Sheraton, where they took their picnic to the hotel beach and borrowed a pair of guest-only chaise lounges.

Laya wanted to go swimming again, this time in the ocean. They spread out their towels on the beach and waited for their food to digest so that they wouldn't "get cramped." As her daughter dug holes and built sand sculptures with her bare hands, Tessa kept her hat low and read a newspaper someone had left on one of the lounge chairs. The beach wasn't crowded and no one seemed to recognize them this time, not even when she joined Laya in the water for a round of body-surfing. Laya was slippery as an eel in the shallow water, and just as comfortable. Was a love of saltwater programmed into her DNA too?

Later, on the way home, they stopped to pick up a pizza and do some shopping at Hilo Hattie's in Lihue. They picked up a gift basket and more "Wish You Were Here" postcards for Ama and Dani (Laya had phoned the couple half a dozen times already since their tearful parting at the Burbank airport) and matching Hawaiian shirts for themselves. Laya insisted they get a third shirt for Eleanor so that she would know she was part of the family. Tessa found herself imagining what it would be like if their family really did include Eleanor, then banished the thought. Eleanor was a paid employee, nothing more, nothing less.

When they reached the house, Robert met them at the gate and told them that Eleanor had taken off that morning on a bike ride to Hanalei. Tessa placed the pizza in the oven to stay warm and sent Laya, whose eyes had kept drifting shut on the drive home, to her room for a nap. Soon enough, Eleanor would return to compare days over dinner. Laya would be excited to tell her nanny all about their adventures. Would Eleanor be as eager to share details herself? Maybe she'd been relieved to have an entire day on her own. Maybe she was tired of spending all her time with just the two of them.

To distract herself, Tessa picked up a book, *The Complete Guide to Getting Funded*, and turned to where she'd left off. Since she was a newbie to the grant-making business, she thought she might as well learn what she should be doing from as many angles as possible before the foundation announced that it was ready to begin receiving applications from worthy causes. That day was still a ways off. They had yet to define their specific areas of interest—needy children was apparently much too broad, according to the consultant they were working with—let alone hire an executive director. So far Tessa hadn't liked either of the men the Byerly sisters had vetted and sent her way.

Jane had accused her of being sexist, and though Tessa hadn't bothered to explain that while a woman could certainly be prejudiced toward a man, no member of an oppressed minority possessed the power to systematically subjugate a member of the majority, she also didn't deny that she would prefer a woman director. After her years in Hollywood, where female directors and executive producers were still rare and the old boys network alive and thriving, she was tired of dealing with powerful men. It was her foundation. She would hire who she wanted.

The sun had begun its downward trek by the time Laya came stumbling down the stairs rubbing her eyes.

"Where's Elle?" she asked, looking around the room as if her former teacher might be hiding behind a potted plant.

Good question. Tessa closed her book. "Tell you what. You go wash your hands and put on a sweatshirt and I'll try her cell. She probably just lost track of time."

Grumbling that she wasn't cold, Laya nevertheless did as she was told. When Tessa pressed the send button on her cell, a phone started up in the kitchen. She followed the sound of "Life in the Fast Lane," the ringtone Eleanor had assigned to her as a joke (or so she claimed), and discovered the cell on the counter still hooked to its charger. Now what?

Before her concern could overly foment, she buzzed Robert on the intercom.

He picked up immediately. "Yes, ma'am?"

"Has Miss Chapin returned yet?"

"No, ma'am, I haven't seen her. Should I take the truck out for a look?"

"That's okay," Tessa said. Then she paused. "Actually, on second thought, why don't you, if you don't mind. And could you take your cell? That way I can let you know if she turns up." Or vice versa. But she didn't want to think about that possibility.

"Yes, ma'am," he said and signed off. She'd told him he didn't have to call her ma'am, but Robert was a retired police officer from Maui and had never seemed able to overcome the habit.

When Laya came back downstairs, she was frowning. "Mom, is Eleanor all right? You don't think she's hurt, do you? Remember the time I fell off my bike?"

Did she. A few months earlier, her daredevil daughter had crashed her training wheels-bedecked kiddy bicycle into the stone wall at the bottom of the drive and come up dripping blood. A quick trip to the celebrity wing of Cedars-Sinai had revealed that nothing was broken, thanks to the elasticity of children's limbs. Still, Tessa didn't think she'd ever forget the way her heart had initially stopped at the sight of the red stains on Laya's T-shirt.

"I'm sure she's fine," she told Laya. "Robert's out looking for her. Why don't we set the table? By the time we finish, they'll probably be back."

But they weren't. Tessa put the pizza on the kitchen island and she and Laya dug in half-heartedly. They were nearly done with their first pieces when the door to the garden finally opened and Robert led a scraped and bloodied Eleanor into the kitchen.

"Elle," Laya exclaimed, and jumped down from her stool.

"Careful, honey," Tessa said, sliding from her own stool as Laya stopped uncertainly before Eleanor, whose bike shorts were torn and stained, her left elbow sticking out at an odd angle. "Jesus, what happened to you?"

“I had a little accident,” Eleanor said, looking sheepish.

“Are you okay? Do you need to go to the hospital?” Tessa hovered nearby, wanting to go to her but staying back. A cut above Eleanor’s right eye had leaked blood down the side of her face, along her neck and beneath her sky blue tech shirt.

“No, I’m fine. Just banged up.” She reached out with her good arm and mussed Laya’s hair. “Hey, champ. How was your day?”

“Awesome! We kayaked on this river near this wildlife refuge—”

“Laya,” Tessa interrupted, her eyes on the gash on Eleanor’s forehead. “You can tell Elle about our day later. Right now she needs to get cleaned up.”

“Your mom’s right,” Eleanor said. She glanced up at Tessa. “By the way, I’m really sorry. Your bike is, well…” She trailed off, looking to Robert for help.

He still hulked in the kitchen doorway, broad chest barely covered by his customary tank top. “It needs some work,” he said neutrally. “I found her walking back along the main road. I was going to call,” he added, “but the miss here didn’t want you to worry.”

“Thanks, Robert.” Tessa nodded at him. “Can I ask another favor? Would you mind staying with Laya for a little while? I think Miss Chapin might require some assistance.”

“I’m fine,” Eleanor protested.

“I don’t need a babysitter,” Laya said, rolling her eyes.

Tessa ignored Eleanor and directed her comments to her daughter instead. “I thought you could keep each other company. Besides, Robert might like some pizza.”

“Sure thing, ma’am,” he said, and smiled down at Laya. “I meant to tell you about some turtle sightings from the other day, anyway.”

The girl’s eyes widened, and she apparently forgot to be annoyed as Robert settled his heft on an empty stool and reached for a piece of pizza.

“It’s okay,” Eleanor insisted as Tessa ushered her out of the kitchen and up the stairs. “I can take care of it.”

"Somehow I doubt you're coordinated enough to pick gravel out of your own elbow."

Eleanor smiled ruefully. "Coordinated is probably not what I'd call myself right now."

"Are you sure you don't want to go to the hospital? I could call a helicopter and we could be in Lihue in no time."

"No, really. My pride is hurt worse than my body."

Tessa doubted that but kept quiet as she led Eleanor through her bedroom into the master bath that sat between her room and Laya's.

Eleanor gazed at the slate-tiled floor, twin sinks, walk-in steam shower and stand-alone whirlpool tub. "This room always makes me think maybe capitalism isn't *completely* evil."

"I know. A small family could live in here." Usually she didn't feel guilty about the way she lived, chalking it up to luck of the draw, but Eleanor somehow managed to remind her what was real and what wasn't. "Have a seat," she said, pointing at the toilet.

As she crossed the bathroom, Eleanor caught sight of herself in the mirror. "Wow," she said, fingering the cut on her brow. "That's going to leave a scar."

Tessa rummaged in a cupboard below the sink, coming up with hydrogen peroxide, Neosporin, Q-tips, tweezers and a small plastic tub. She stacked them on the counter. "This probably isn't going to feel very good."

"That's okay," Eleanor said, perching on the toilet lid. "It's what I get for being stupid."

Tessa ran a clean washcloth under warm water and eyed Eleanor as the small tub filled. "You, stupid? Doubtful."

"You won't say that when you hear how I crashed your bike."

Leaning against the sink, Tessa turned off the water and arched one eyebrow in the gesture that had made her famous. "Try me."

Eleanor's expression was half-smile, half-grimace. "Well, you know how there are all these chickens around?"

"Uh-huh." Kauai was famous for its renegade wild chicken population. Nonnative to the island, the birds had been brought by early settlers. In 1992, Hurricane Iniki was thought to have blown apart many of the chicken coops on Kauai, according to one theory, thereby freeing the birds and causing a surge in the number of wild chickens roaming the island.

"There was this rooster on the side of the road, and, um, apparently I got a little too close to one of his lady friends," Eleanor explained. "He attacked, and I crashed."

Biting back a smile at the ridiculous image, Tessa said, "The important thing is that you're okay."

"If it was you who had provoked the mighty rooster, I'd be laughing my butt off."

"Maybe, maybe not." She set the tub of water on the counter near Eleanor and held out the damp washcloth. "Ready?"

"Not really." But she took the warm cloth from Tessa's outstretched hand and began to slowly clean away the dust and blood.

Tessa stayed where she was and tried not to stare too obviously. What was wrong with her? To distract herself from the slide of the cloth over Eleanor's flesh, she said, "Which Austen book are you on?"

"*Emma*," Eleanor said, wincing as the cotton threads brushed over the exposed skin on her hip, where her bike shorts had been shredded in the fall. "It's my favorite. What about you? Are you an Austen fan?"

"I am. I'm half-Irish, you know, so I'm genetically predisposed not to like English writers. But she's so good."

Wringing dirt and gravel from the washcloth, Eleanor glanced up at her. "What about Sarah Waters?"

"Love her, too."

"I know. Who knew Victorian England could be so delightful? I mean, sexy. Sorry—whenever I read Jane Austen I find myself saying things like, 'Upon my word' and 'What a welcome sensation.'"

"The English, always so understated and controlled. I think that's why I find them a bit dull, to be honest."

"You probably wouldn't like New Englanders much, then."

"I don't know. If you're representative of the lot, I haven't found much not to like so far." As Eleanor looked down, a blush coloring her neck beneath the bloodstains, Tessa added, "Anyway, perhaps unsurprisingly, my favorite British author is a multiracial woman. Have you read *Wide Sargasso Sea* by Jean Rhys?"

"Sophomore year for a Women's Lit class. I don't remember the multiracial part, though." She squeezed her eyes shut as she rubbed her swollen elbow.

"Born in the Dominican, but to a Welsh father and Creole mother." The first time she'd read Rhys's best-known novel, told from the perspective of a character based on Rochester's insane wife in Brontë's *Jane Eyre*, Tessa had recognized in the short work the story of her own family torn apart by secrets, jealousy, rage. "Rhys once said she felt that Charlotte Brontë had something against the West Indies and it made her angry. That's why she wrote the novel."

"You're a serious reader, aren't you?"

"Surprised?"

"Maybe a little," Eleanor admitted.

"Like I said, you can't believe everything you read online."

"Apparently not."

When the scrapes had been washed, Tessa offered to check for foreign objects. Eleanor seemed to hesitate a moment before nodding. Tessa knelt on a thick rug beside her and carefully picked tiny shards of gravel from her torn skin, cleaning the abrasions with hydrogen peroxide as she worked. She had to grasp various body parts to accomplish her task: calf, thigh, hip, elbow. Resolutely she kept her eyes lowered, wondering if she imagined the tautness in Eleanor's body matching her own growing tension. This was the first time they'd touched so intimately, and she had to force herself to focus on Eleanor's injuries to prevent her mind (and, more importantly, hands) from wandering over the tantalizing expanse of freckled skin before her. But the temptation was delicious, if tormenting—a sensation to which she was becoming accustomed the more time she spent around Eleanor.

"You're very fit," she said at one point.

"Thanks," Eleanor said, her voice a little husky. From pain, or something else? "You're not so bad yourself."

"I work out. But I eat more junk food than you do, so it's a requirement."

"I know, I'm a little obsessed. My sister's the same way. We both run and buy organic vegetables and try to eat all the foods on the anti-cancer list."

Tessa frowned. That particular concern had never occurred to her. "Do you worry about getting sick?"

"Sure. Women whose mothers have breast cancer have twice the risk of developing it. Plus I've got other risk factors—my mom was diagnosed the first time before she turned fifty, I like wine and I haven't had a baby yet."

Yet? Did that mean she wanted to have a baby? Tessa pictured Eleanor pregnant, her belly swollen, eyes and cheeks glowing. She would be even lovelier than she was already.

"I thought red wine was supposed to be good for you," she said.

"It is, for heart disease. Not so much for breast cancer."

"Have you noticed no one agrees on what can kill you anymore? I saw Ellen DeGeneres do a routine once where she made fun of fear-mongering on local news programs—'Tonight at 11, how the food you're eating for dinner may be killing you. And now, back to *Wheel of Fortune*.'"

Eleanor smiled. "I saw her do the same show in Boston. I love her."

Tessa looked away from Eleanor's smile and back at the scrape on her knee. Focus, she told herself. This wasn't supposed to be fun.

When she finished a few minutes later, she reluctantly stood and stretched her legs. No doubt about it, she was getting old. It no longer felt good to kneel on the floor for a quarter of an hour. Not that such a position had ever felt good, exactly. A flash of Nadine, this time on her knees at the edge of Tessa's bed in Malibu, popped into her head, and she blinked it away. What was up with the parade of memories lately?

"Thank you," Eleanor said, and stood up. "You're right, I never would have been able to reach my elbow." Without warning, she reached out and pulled Tessa into a hug.

Conscious of the softness of Eleanor's breasts pressed against her own, Tessa stood unmoving in the circle of her arms. Of course she would give excellent hugs, and of course it would feel amazing to be held by her. Better than amazing. Tessa's desire, which she'd thought she had managed to tamp down, flared up again, and she worked to modulate her voice as she pulled away. "You're welcome. As Laya's mother, I've had to hone my nursing skills over the years."

"I'll bet," Eleanor said, her eyes fixed on Tessa's. Then she stepped back. "I guess I should let you get back to dinner."

"You're coming down, aren't you? You should put some ice on that elbow and take some ibuprofen." Doing her own stunt work had led to more than a working knowledge of swelling reduction tactics.

"I'll be there in a bit. I just need to change into something more presentable," she said, waving at her mangled shorts and blood-stained shirt.

"Of course." Tessa moved toward the hallway, aware of Eleanor behind her. "I'm glad you're okay. I—well, Laya was worried about you."

Eleanor grinned and turned toward her bedroom. "Takes more than a chicken to keep a Vermonter down."

As she headed downstairs, Tessa pictured a furious rooster throwing himself through the air at Eleanor as she guided the bike over the Kauai roadway. The image was laughable, but at that moment, she didn't feel much like laughing.

CHAPTER TWELVE

The next morning, Eleanor lay in bed taking stock of body parts that hadn't fared well in the bike crash. The pain oozing along with pus from her many scrapes had kept her from deep sleep throughout the night. Which was actually fine—she'd taken advantage of her recurring wakefulness to revisit the scene from the bathroom, where Tessa had knelt before her and, with probing, gentle hands, tended to her injuries.

From her elevated position, Eleanor had noticed the sheen of Tessa's hair, the muscles in her upper arms, the tiny freckles dotting her nose. She'd never noticed the freckles in any of Tessa's many films or photos. Did she cover them up with make-up? Focusing on minute details had helped distract her from the feel of Tessa's hands on her body. All in all, Eleanor thought, she had managed fairly well at pretending to be unaffected. At least, until The Hug.

Closing her eyes, she remembered the way she'd pulled Tessa against her. Tessa couldn't have missed the intimacy of the gesture, the crossing of the employee-employer boundary. Then again, she was lucky she hadn't gotten kissed. Eleanor hadn't been that close to another woman in months. Not to mention she'd already wanted to throw herself at Tessa (preferably naked) before the extended feeling-up episode in the bathroom. Too late to take back the embrace now. Better just to pretend it had never happened. Judging from Tessa's behavior at dinner the night before, that was the tack she was taking.

Eventually Eleanor heaved herself out of bed, showered briefly, wincing as she soaped the areas affected by road rash, and pulled on long khaki shorts and a long-sleeved T-shirt. She would have to be especially careful of sun exposure in the coming days—a sunburn on top of road burn was not a sensation she was eager to experience.

Downstairs, mother and daughter were seated quietly at the dining room table, Laya hard at work coloring a picture, Tessa reading the *New York Times* (delivered every day here and in L.A.). They glanced up in unison when Eleanor appeared, matching smiles on their faces, and she almost missed the single step down into the kitchen. The Flanagans were a beautiful lot.

"Hi, Elle," Laya said. "Bawk, bawk, bawk," she added, giggling almost too hard to eke out her poultry imitation. The joke apparently hadn't gotten old yet—Laya had clucked and flapped around the house for much of the previous evening once she heard the reason for Eleanor's bike accident.

Tessa cast her an apologetic look. "How did you sleep?" she asked.

"A little rough," Eleanor admitted, and looked away from the appealing sight of Tessa in her pajamas, hair mussed from sleep.

Like the house in L.A., the kitchen here opened onto the dining room, which meant she could see Tessa and Laya as she made a quick breakfast of cereal and toast. Tessa had phoned in a massive food order their first night on the island. A uniformed boy from the nearest gourmet grocery store had carried in a half dozen laden bags, sneaking glances around the villa as if trying to memorize details. Eleanor had been playing a game of Uno with Laya at the dining room table and, sensing the boy's eyes on her, had wondered idly if straight people knew of the rumors about Tessa's flexible sexuality. Somehow it always seemed as if queer people knew who was and who wasn't in Hollywood, while straight people had little clue. Perhaps this was a symptom of heterosexism: don't ask on the part of the straight folks, don't tell on the part of the gays.

Now she carried her breakfast to the table and took a seat next to Laya, who smiled distractedly at her and returned to her work of art—a drawing of a dark-haired woman on a bike, an impressive red rooster in midair beside her, legs and wings extended.

Tessa lowered her newspaper and they exchanged a knowing look—ah, the beauty of being six and having a one-track mind. And yet the picture was sweet too, because the fact that Eleanor was the subject of today's art piece showed how important she was to Laya. They managed to communicate all of this without saying a word, and then, with an almost shy smile, Tessa went back to her paper.

Eleanor started in on her cereal. Leaving L.A., she was starting to think, was going to suck.

They took it easy the next few days, lounging around the grounds pursuing assorted pleasurable pursuits while Eleanor's wounds healed: soccer in the driveway until the ball disappeared into a tangle of jungle vine; badminton on the garden lawn; junior rangering on every corner of the estate; reading and more movie-viewing in the studio. Tessa ignored the work demanding her attention and relaxed fully, enjoying the time they had together on the island, just the three of them.

But the week steadily dwindled until soon there were only two days left of their vacation. That morning, the sun had barely crossed the horizon when Laya shot into Tessa's room. "Get up get up get up!" she crowed, pouncing on her mother's inert form.

Blearily, Tessa sat up, holding her squirming daughter away with one arm. "Where's the fire?" she asked, and yawned.

"Duh, Mom, there isn't really a fire or you would smell smoke. Now come on. It's time to get up!"

Laya wouldn't tell her what the rush was, just ushered her out of bed and downstairs for breakfast. Eleanor was already there, prying her eyes open with the help of her usual dose of caffeine. She seemed to favor flavored creamer, and Tessa wondered absently if Eleanor's lips would taste like vanilla or hazelnut this morning.

As Eleanor and Laya exchanged a significant look, Tessa glanced from one to the other. "What are you two up to?"

"Well," Laya said, one hand on her hip, "it wasn't fair that I got to have Eleanor-only and Mom-only days, but you didn't. So today I'm going to Camp Hyatt and you're having a Mom-Eleanor day." She stopped and smiled up at Tessa. "Cool, huh?"

Tessa put on what she hoped looked like a genuine smile of pleasure. "Very cool," she said. "You're awfully sweet to think of such a thing." She kissed the top of her daughter's head and glanced up to find Eleanor watching her.

Laya prattled on through breakfast about Camp Hyatt and the plan she had concocted—with Eleanor's help, of course. Apparently they had booked a full adults-only safari with the outfitter: hiking, ziplining, kayaking, swimming and canoeing. A pair of guides would accompany them every step of the way.

"It's the same people we went kayaking with," Laya said. "It was Eleanor's idea to go there."

Tessa glanced at Eleanor across the table. "Thanks for that." She already had an NDA on file with Kipu Falls Outfitters that stipulated they couldn't take any photos or other media recordings without her consent.

"No problem," Eleanor said. "I know how difficult it is to find people you trust."

Their eyes held, and Tessa felt her pulse speed up at the look in Eleanor's eyes. She glanced away quickly, reaching for Laya's crumb-filled plate. As she carried it to the sink, she said lightly, "We'd better get going. Don't want to be late for Camp Hyatt, do we?"

"No way," Laya said, and sprinted upstairs to change.

As Tessa rinsed her daughter's plate and stowed it in the dishwasher, Eleanor approached, breakfast dishes in hand.

"You okay with all of this? I probably should have checked with you, but Laya really wanted to surprise you."

She should have checked. "It's fine."

"You don't mean that," Eleanor said. "I'm really sorry. I asked Robert and he said Laya spends a couple of days at the Hyatt every summer. I thought it would be okay."

Tessa was being a control freak and she knew it. Sometimes, though, it was hard to let go, especially when you never knew what—or who—might be lurking nearby. "It is okay," she said. "One of the things I like about Kauai is how safe it is here. And anyway, the Hyatt is used to celebrity kids."

"That's what the woman on the phone said, but I'm glad you think so too. I know Laya is everything to you."

They were standing close together at the sink, watching each other in the early morning sun beaming through the picture windows and across the dining room. Was Laya everything to her? Of course. But might there not be room for something else? For someone else?

Eleanor looked away first, the tips of her ears red. Tessa saw the color and hid a smile. Would she always have such an effect on Eleanor? Then, with a pang, she remembered that "always" in this case had a time limit.

"Anyway," she said, "we should get ready."

"Don't forget your suit," Eleanor said, rinsing out her cereal bowl.

"Don't you forget sunscreen."

"Yes, ma'am."

Upstairs, Tessa moved about her room, distractedly packing a bag for Kipu Falls Ranch. The day together, just her and Eleanor (and a pair of guides), stretched ahead wide open, and she had to admit she was glad for her daughter's scheming. Did Laya sense something between them? Were soon-to-be first graders capable of such discernment? And what would she think if something did happen between her mother and her nanny?

That bridge, Tessa reminded herself, should never be crossed.

But she was starting to think that crossing the Eleanor-Tessa bridge might be inevitable.

As they drove toward the southern side of the island in Tessa's Volvo Cross Country wagon, Laya singing a made-up song to herself in the backseat, Eleanor tried to figure out what the actress was thinking. Eyes hidden behind her usual oversized sunglasses, lips pursed, brow slightly furrowed, Tessa might be considering firing her for helping Laya with her little plan, or she might be pondering who to hire to oversee her foundation. That was the problem with Tessa—she was impossible to read, and she looked out on everyone and everything with such wary eyes. What was she hiding? It could have been anything or nothing at all.

Eleanor glanced into the back of the car where Laya was buckled into the center seat, short legs dangling into space. She was dressed in board shorts and a matching Lycra surf tee, and with her brown skin and dark eyes, looked for all the world as if she belonged here on this tropical island. At least she hadn't inherited her mother's need for secrecy. Or maybe it just hadn't had a chance to develop yet.

"You ready to have some fun?" Eleanor asked, flashing on Sasha and Luis as she held up her hand for a high five.

"Heck yeah," Laya said, slapping her palm as she uttered one of the many adult-isms that Eleanor knew simultaneously amused and dismayed Tessa. Out of the corner of her eye, she saw Tessa flinch a little.

"What's your favorite thing to do at the Hyatt?"

"Last year we got to talk to this parrot and he could talk back and I got to hold him on my arm and I asked Mom if we could get one but she said no. Did you know parrots don't really talk? They whistle the words."

"I didn't know that." Laya's ability to retain information about any and all animal species continued to amaze her. She wondered if the girl would maintain her creature interests throughout childhood or succumb to peer pressure and abandon her somewhat nerdy naturalist tendencies, then realized she would probably never know. Once the summer ended, she would only learn how Laya fared from the occasional celebrity news item.

"What else did you do last year?" she asked.

Unsurprisingly, Laya had numerous Camp Hyatt stories in her arsenal—hula and archery lessons, lei making and other crafts activities, not to mention the ever popular waterslide at the pool. She kept up a steady chatter until they reached Poipu.

Eleanor waited in the parking lot while Tessa met with the Camp Hyatt director and got Laya settled. Then Tessa returned, slid behind the wheel again and guided the Volvo away from the hotel. Eleanor sat silently in the passenger seat, noticing how much quieter the car's interior seemed without Laya's energy to fill it. As they headed back toward the main road, Tessa turned the stereo on. An old Indigo Girls CD started playing, one Eleanor had listened to compulsively her freshman year of college.

"Is this okay?" Tessa asked, eyes on the road.

"Fine," Eleanor said, singing along softly as Amy and Emily described looking back on their lives every five years or so and having a good laugh.

Whenever she heard this song, one of her favorites, she tried to look back on her own recent past with humor. Right now, though, all she could think of was realizing that her mother would die and then waiting for it to happen, neither of which was remotely amusing. During the most recent half decade, she used to catch herself laughing or enjoying a particular moment and feel indescribably guilty. Hard enough for a native New Englander to let herself enjoy life, but for one whose mother was terminally ill, taking pleasure was unacceptable.

This, she knew, must have made her not-so-great as a girlfriend. Poor Laurie—which seemed strange as Laurie had left her for another woman only a week after her mother's funeral. But looking back now, Eleanor could see she hadn't given her ex much choice.

The November night she ran into Laurie with her new girlfriend, Eleanor had left the club and made her way alone into the blustery Boston night. Laurie caught up with her at a nearby T station, touching her arm hesitantly as Eleanor stood waiting for the train to take her back to their half-empty apartment, the rent for which she couldn't afford on her own. At Laurie's touch, she'd turned to face the woman she'd spent the last three years with, and tried to figure out how she should react. But she didn't feel anything. Her mother hadn't been gone long and she was still numb. Or maybe she'd been numb for a while.

"I'm so sorry, Elle. I didn't mean for this to happen," Laurie said as they stood together on the platform. "But you haven't really seen me in months. Each night I would wait for you to look at me, really look at me, and you know, you almost never did. Justyn sees me. She wants to see me."

"Good," Eleanor replied, aiming to wound, "because I don't care if I ever see you again."

This wasn't exactly true, but the knowledge that Laurie would go home that night with Justyn and sleep in a strange bed in an unfamiliar apartment while Eleanor went back to the home they'd built together, the home that Laurie had recently dismantled, was enough to induce her to break one of the cardinal rules of dating women: staying friends after a break-up.

Laurie's eyes filled with tears and Eleanor turned away, looking down the tracks for the next train. She didn't see Laurie walk away. The air just felt different, emptier. When she glanced over her shoulder, Laurie was gone. They hadn't spoken since.

In the past few months, Eleanor's numbness had thawed, and now when she remembered the tears in Laurie's eyes it actually hurt. Laurie was right. She'd been nearly consumed by her mother's cancer, a collateral victim of the voracious cells. Laurie had been right to leave her, just as Eleanor had been right to leave her old life. The six months she'd spent away from the East Coast had been good for her. By immersing herself in an entirely new environment, surrounding herself with different people and plants and trees, changing her diet and the way she exercised and now, briefly, the continent she resided on, Eleanor had found the change she'd craved. She wasn't numb anymore, not by a long shot.

She smiled as Tessa turned the car onto a road marked by a subtle sign, "Kipu Falls Ranch," and navigated down the unpaved driveway.

"What?" Tessa asked, glancing over at her.

"Nothing. I'm just happy to be here."

Tessa didn't say anything for a long moment. Then she nodded. "Me too. You and Laya did good."

Eleanor looked out the window and watched the tropical jungle drift past as they wound along the road. It was good to be alive, she decided, gazing up at the patch of sky visible through the thick vegetation. *Hope you're with us today, Mom*, she thought. Back in Boston, she would have been terrified to even think about trying something like ziplining, where you could most certainly die if something went wrong. But right now she wasn't in the mood to give in to "what-if" fears. And anyway, she didn't feel like she was going to die anytime soon. At least, she hoped not.

At the end of the long drive, a rustic building with a covered veranda and a much larger sign came into view. Tessa parked the Volvo in the crowded parking lot—looked like Kipu Falls Ranch was popular. Two guides were waiting for them on the veranda, both men. The older one, John, greeted Tessa familiarly and shook hands with Eleanor. He was polite and jovial, his skin dark from the summer sun, a canvas fisherman's hat protecting his balding head from the UV rays. The younger man, Christian, looked like he had stepped out of a surfer movie complete with a blond ponytail and an open shirt that revealed a six-pack Eleanor would have killed for. Somewhat predictably, he eagerly shook both their hands but his gaze kept returning to Tessa. When he called her "Miss Flanagan," Eleanor expected Tessa to tell him to call her by her first name. But she only nodded coolly and turned back to John.

"I understand my daughter wanted me to experience the full safari adventure she isn't old enough yet to try herself."

John laughed. "She's a spitfire, that little girl. Wanted to make sure you got the whole kit and caboodle today—kayaking, ATVing, ziplining, hiking, canoeing. She especially wanted to know if there would be a rope swing over a swimming hole. I told her there would be two."

"Guess I can't disappoint her, can I."

"Wouldn't if I were you," he said. "You know, in another couple of years she'll be old enough to try the safari herself."

"Look out then," Eleanor said. She could already see Laya flinging herself through the air on a zipline, hooting and hollering high above the treetops.

"Your daughter sounds like a handful," Christian put in.

Tessa eyed him. "She's got a mind of her own."

Like mother like daughter, Eleanor thought, relieved that Tessa didn't appear overly impressed by the young guide's muscle-bound body. Despite the *Finding Nemo* incident, she still didn't know for sure which way Tessa swung the bat. For all she knew, the actress might be a switch-hitter.

Inside the main building, they dodged other tour participants, Tessa's floppy hat and sunglasses guarding her identity while they picked out gear and signed waivers. After a brief safety and instruction course in the clearing behind the "kayak shack," they were ready to put their two-person crafts in the water and head downriver. John suggested they each ride with a guide, but Tessa said she'd rather share a boat with Eleanor.

"Since I just kayaked this stretch of river a few days ago," she added, "I'll take the back. That way, Eleanor, you can see what's coming."

"Sounds good to me. Does this mean I get to sit back while you do all the work?" she asked teasingly.

"Hardly," Tessa said. "I expect my partners to work just as hard as I do."

Eleanor held her breath as Tessa brushed past her, wondering if she'd imagined the flirty tone. Christian moved into her line of vision, weighed down with paddles and PIDs. He met her gaze and smiled innocently, white teeth blinding in the sun. She didn't trust men who bleached their teeth. At least, not straight men.

They pushed away from shore and floated down the peaceful Hule'ia River, sun shimmering on the surface, calls of birds and insects on the air. It took some practice, but after snorting with laughter as they turned their kayak in a full circle, she and Tessa got the hang of paddling together and soon were gliding smoothly with the current. John described the area's ecology as he and Christian drifted along beside them. Eleanor remembered Laya's enthusiastic description of the Hawaiian stilt they'd seen in a pool on this same river. For a moment, she missed Laya's ebullient presence. She glanced over her shoulder to catch Tessa watching her, feeling her chest tighten as Tessa smiled at her, a slow, lazy smile that hinted at something more to come. Then again, it was nice to have an adults-only day every once in a while too.

Sunshine warmed her skin as she listened to John wax eloquent about the jungle-lined river that stretched out before them, the endangered birds who made the wildlife refuge their home, the dark green mountain towering in the distance, and for a moment, she could almost convince herself that this vacation from reality wouldn't ever have to end.

CHAPTER THIRTEEN

Tessa clung to a handrail at the edge of a wooden platform forty feet above the ground. A harness connected her to the zipline, and John was telling her that all she had to do was step forward off the edge. Easier said than done.

This particular section of zipline extended two hundred and fifty feet downhill over the top of a waterfall. John had buckled her and Eleanor into their harnesses, while Christian waited far below to help them dismount at the end of the ride. They'd had to ascend an extensive network of platforms and bridges, including an eighty-foot long suspension bridge, to reach this platform on an enormous tree house built around a giant banyan tree. The structure looked like something out of *Swiss Family Robinson*, Eleanor had commented as they scaled the walkway to the platform, echoing Tessa's thoughts. The novel was one of her childhood favorites, read at a time when being shipwrecked on a tropical island with her parents and a bunch of brothers and sisters had seemed appealing.

All she had to do was step forward, Tessa told herself now. But somehow she was finding it hard to take that first step off the wooden platform into open space. Her fear surprised her. A decade before, she'd worked on the first of a trilogy of action movies inspired by a comic book about a female version of Indiana Jones. Will had trained her for months ahead of time, and she'd done most of her own stunts, including a base jump off a skyscraper in Dubai. But she'd been in her mid-twenties then and had believed she might well live forever, or at least for quite a bit longer. Now she was older and, more importantly, she had Laya. The idea of leaving her daughter alone in the world the way she had been left terrified her.

"It's okay," Eleanor said, standing a few feet away attached to a line that ran parallel to Tessa's. They were supposed to zipline at the same time, tandem style. "We're pretty well tied in. It's perfectly safe."

Easy for her to say. She didn't have a child who would keep her spirit earthbound were she to die in, say, a ziplining-gone-wrong accident. "Things do sometimes go wrong, you know."

"Maybe, but not today. Watch—I'll go first." And she smiled at Tessa, moved forward, and took off into midair.

All at once, Tessa didn't want her to get away. Without letting herself think about what she was doing, she stepped forward off the wooden platform. After the first sickening drop, the line tautened and away she flew. Eleanor was just ahead, spinning around and laughing, and Tessa heard a shout of excitement that she belatedly realized was her own. The waterfall and a wide swimming hole approached and receded below, glowing in the midday sunshine, while the river and mountains formed a serene backdrop to their flight. This was freaking awesome, even better than helicopters. Why hadn't she tried it before? Up here above the earth, she wasn't Tessa Flanagan, Actor, anymore. She was just herself, flying freely, seemingly weightless. The only other person who could see her was Eleanor.

They ziplined half a dozen courses that day, including

another tandem line that stretched a whopping twelve hundred feet across a forested hillside. Each time they took flight, Tessa forgot everything but the sensation of being alone with Eleanor speeding through the air side by side above the earth, laughing and calling out to one another, the forest a one-dimensional, seemingly smooth canopy beneath them.

In between zipline courses, they picnicked on the shore of the river, swam beneath waterfalls, and dove from rocky cliffs into crystalline pools. Eleanor photographed her flying on a rope swing out into the middle of a pond and letting go to execute what John called a perfect "rip"—a clean landing, as opposed to a "wash" (a not-so-clean splash) or the dreaded belly flop. Eleanor performed rip after rip herself, and except for the younger guide's occasionally over-attentive presence, Tessa thought the day was going beautifully. She'd been working too hard lately, worrying about Laya and Ama and Dani and the foundation. Her daughter, brilliant creature that she was, had recognized that she needed a break.

God, she was lucky, Tessa thought as she watched Eleanor swim across a blue-green pool toward her. She would have to remember to thank Laya later.

Eleanor paused before her, treading water. Ten feet away a cascading waterfall cast spray into the air, where sunshine caught in rainbow droplets.

"What do you think?" Eleanor asked, shaking wet hair out of her eyes.

"I think it's lovely," Tessa said, moving closer until only a few inches separated them. "I think you're lovely." Eleanor gazed back at her, eyes glowing. Impulsively Tessa leaned forward and planted a quick kiss on her cheek. "Race you. Last one to shore has to make dinner!"

Tessa took off, arms moving clean and sure through the warm water. She'd arrived in L.A. unable to do more than doggie paddle. As soon as she could afford to, she took adult swimming lessons at the YMCA in Van Nuys, where she was joined by half a dozen immigrants of varying nationalities. As a newly minted Californian, it had seemed important that she know how to swim.

As she pulled herself out of the pool and reached for a Kipu Falls Ranch beach towel, Tessa saw Christian turn away. Then Eleanor climbed onto the shore beside her, a fair goddess with an impish grin on her luscious mouth, and Tessa remembered that she had kissed her before racing away.

"How about stir-fry?" Eleanor asked as she toweled herself dry.

Tessa removed her gaze from the hint of cleavage revealed by Eleanor's two-piece suit. "What?"

Eleanor smiled some more, and Tessa knew she'd been busted. "Dinner tonight," she clarified. "I was thinking stir-fry."

"Sounds perfect," Tessa said, smiling back at her. *And later, after dinner,* she thought... Well, time enough when they were alone to find out what the look in Eleanor's eyes meant. Maybe girls' day out would last beyond sunset. Just then, she couldn't remember why it shouldn't.

Surprisingly, Eleanor thought, Laya stayed awake on the ride home, listening to their stories and examining the digitized evidence of her mother leaping from the rope swing earlier that afternoon. She even tried to keep up her end of the conversation over the rice and tamari tofu stir-fry Eleanor whipped up back at the house, regaling them with occasionally disjointed tales of her adventures at Camp Hyatt. But toward the end of dinner, she lost the battle and put her head down on the table, too tired to remain upright any longer.

"You can take her up if you want," Eleanor said. "I can clean up."

Tessa shook her head. "You cooked, which means I'm on clean-up duty. Do you mind munchkin duty?"

Eyes still closed, Laya giggled.

"Not at all," Eleanor said, thinking that it was, in fact, her job. But she didn't want to remind Tessa that she was The Nanny, not when they both seemed to be pretending that the contract she'd signed at the lawyer's office back in L.A. didn't exist. Tonight it felt like they were more than employer-employee, chopping vegetables together, chatting about their day over dinner, helping Laya when she struggled to pronounce a particular word.

The sensation only intensified as she carried Laya upstairs. The girl's arms were around her neck, and she smelled like tamari and peanut butter and sea salt. Eleanor felt her heart expanding, her love for the girl surrounding them both in a cozy cocoon.

In her room, Eleanor helped Laya change into pajamas and crawl beneath cool sheets. Then she brought her a glass of water from the bathroom and sat down on the bed beside her. "All set, kiddo?"

"Uh-huh. I'm glad you're here, Elle," Laya said sleepily.

"Me too, Mahal." The Filipino term of endearment, which she'd heard Ama and Tessa both use, slipped out, and she remembered Luis and Sasha discussing the tendency of the dominant culture to misappropriate the language of the oppressed minority. In this case, she represented the dominant culture, even though Tessa had more money than many third-world nations, according to *O* magazine.

Laya picked up Eleanor's hand, turned it over, and placed her much smaller palm against it. "Mommy needed a friend. She was lonely. I mean, I've got Luke and Rayann," she said, naming two of her regular playdate pals back in L.A., both of whose parents were film bigwigs of some sort, "but she didn't have anyone. That's why I wanted her to meet you."

Eleanor blinked, trying to decide which line of questioning to pursue. It probably didn't mean anything that Tessa had failed to introduce Laya to any of the men she'd been linked to in the press. Or, apparently, to any women, for that matter. "What do you mean, you wanted her to meet me?"

"She came to school with me that one time because I asked her to. I knew she would love you as much as I do and now she does." Laya yawned, squeaking like a puppy one of Eleanor's students back in Boston had brought to school for show-and-tell.

Eleanor smoothed the girl's hair back from her face. "I love you too, Laya."

"Ditto, pal," she said, a reply that Eleanor knew drove her mother crazy. Then she rubbed her eyes with her fists. "Do you mind if we don't read a story tonight? I'm 'zausted."

"I don't mind. Sleep well, sweetie. See you in the morning."

"Not if I see you first," Laya mumbled, eyes already closed as she recited the line Ama had taught her years before.

Eleanor brushed her lips against the girl's forehead and left the room, closing the door quietly behind her. So Tessa hadn't come to school that first time to scrutinize her teaching skills, as Eleanor had believed, but rather at Laya's behest. Why, then, had she come back?

Downstairs, the feeling of familiarity continued as she and Tessa stood together at the kitchen sink finishing up the dishes. They talked about Laya as they worked, Tessa sharing stories of past trips to Kauai and the scrapes she'd managed to get herself into with the assistance willing participation of the other kids from Camp Hyatt sometimes, Ama and Dani's grandchildren at others.

"Speaking of scrapes," Tessa added as they carried their wineglasses out onto the patio where a wicker love seat faced the ocean, "yours didn't seem to bother you today."

Her road rash had scabbed over rapidly, so much so that Eleanor had almost forgotten about the accident. "No, I'm fine," she said, sitting down on one side of the love seat and gazing up at the sky. Tinged pink by sunset, it stretched toward the distant point where ocean and sky melded into a single line.

"I'm glad you're okay," Tessa said. "You had me worried."

"Did I?" She glanced over and felt her breath catch at Tessa's beauty—those dark eyes and long lashes, her mane of curls and full lips. Eleanor had thought that with time she might become accustomed to the way Tessa looked, but whenever she focused on her, she still felt the same jolt, the same sense of incredulity that this stunning woman was with her. Not that they were really *with* each other, she reminded herself, glancing back out at the ocean.

After a moment, Tessa took a swallow of wine, set her glass on an end table and said, her tone light, "So I have a question for you."

Relieved by the mood change, Eleanor said, "Shoot."

"What does your middle initial stand for? I saw you write it on the waiver this morning."

She took a quick gulp of her own wine, thinking fast. She couldn't really tell her, could she? "Right. Well, I'm gonna have to plead the fifth on that one."

"Come on. You know I could find out if I wanted to."

That was undoubtedly true. Gazing out across the idyllic scenery, Eleanor thought that nothing seemed real here. Or was it the opposite, that everything seemed more real here?

"All right," she said, "but don't laugh. Promise?"

"No."

She was going to laugh. This was why Eleanor didn't tell people. "It's Rigby."

"As in...?"

"Yes, as in the Beatles song. Apparently it was my parents' favorite song of all time. Personally, I think they were high when they picked my name. Vermont in the '70s—you do the math."

Tessa was laughing openly now. "Go Mr. and Mrs. Chapin. But isn't that song about a woman who never got married? Do you think that's why you're gay?"

"Shut it," Eleanor said, elbowing her.

Unexpectedly, Tessa caught her arm and tugged her closer. What was she doing? Only Eleanor knew—it was what she'd wanted to do herself but couldn't quite work up the nerve. Tessa took the wineglass from her and set it on the end table. Then, her eyes on Eleanor's mouth, she murmured, "If you don't want me to kiss you, you might want to say so now."

Finally, Eleanor thought, and closed her eyes as she leaned in. Then they were kissing, lips pressing together tentatively at first, and then more insistently as the heat rose quickly between them. Tessa tasted of lip balm and red wine, the scent of roses mixed with an earthier fragrance wafting from her skin. For a moment, Eleanor couldn't breathe without filling her lungs with air that passed from Tessa's lips to hers, couldn't focus on anything except the feel of Tessa's mouth burning against hers. Then—she was making out with Tessa Flanagan, she thought incongruously. And just like that, the realization of who she was kissing kicked her out of the moment.

As if sensing the change, Tessa pulled back. "Are you okay?"

“I don’t know.” Eleanor shook her head and stood up, trying to put some distance between them. The breeze off the hillside felt cooler suddenly, and she wrapped her arms around her body.

After a moment, Tessa came to stand beside her, carefully separate. “I’m sorry,” she said. “I thought you wanted to.”

“I did,” Eleanor said. “I’m just not sure…”

“It’s okay,” Tessa said, her voice cool. “I shouldn’t have… Let’s just pretend it never happened, okay?” And she turned away, heading inside.

Eleanor stayed where she was, watching Tessa through the picture window as she strode across the living room and vanished up the stairs. Why had she stopped? Was she crazy? Tessa Flanagan wanted her and Eleanor wanted her right back. But for her, it was more than simple desire. She already cared way too much about both Flanagans at this point to protect herself if sex was all Tessa wanted. Right now, she couldn’t begin to guess what Tessa wanted from her other than sex. Which would be amazing, she thought, her pulse speeding up again, thighs tingling as she thought about the touch of Tessa’s lips on hers. If a simple kiss could get her this hot, what would the feel of Tessa’s naked body against hers do?

If she had any sense, she would run upstairs this instant and throw herself at Tessa. But what if Tessa turned her away? Maybe it had been a temporary, one-time-only offer born of the exhilaration of ziplining, the romance of Kauai.

“Damn it,” Eleanor muttered, hunching her shoulders. Now what? She couldn’t go upstairs yet. She sat back down on the love seat and picked up her wineglass. No need to let the alcohol go to waste. Like everything else she owned, Tessa’s wine selection consisted only of the finest labels.

One of these things is not like the other, Eleanor thought, lifting the glass to her lips.

CHAPTER FOURTEEN

An insistent beep from the bathroom woke Tessa. The sun was up and she could hear voices downstairs. Laya and Eleanor.

Eleanor. Tessa pulled the covers up and buried her head under a pillow. The reason she hadn't slept well came rushing back to her, and she groaned a little, feeling like Meg Ryan in *When Harry Met Sally* as she tried on the sound for size. Felt good. Her BlackBerry, charging in the bathroom, repeated its adamant alert, and she groaned again. Maybe Eleanor had left her a message saying she quit, or that she was pressing charges for sexual harassment. Tessa had nearly gotten up a hundred times during the night to go to her, but each time the urge struck, she reminded herself that Eleanor was the one who had pulled away.

Flopping onto her back, Tessa pulled the pillow over her

head again, blotting out the sunlight streaming in the window. Why did it always have to be sunny? She was sick of unrelenting sunshine that seemed to demand unceasing positivity. When she was a kid, she'd enjoyed the luxury of moping on days when the clouds, indistinguishable from one another, formed a solid wall of gray that somehow matched the lump in her chest that had materialized the day the woman police officer came to tell her about her parents.

For some reason, whenever something upset her she ended up going back to the day when everything changed. That last morning, she had awakened to a world where she was safe and both of her parents were alive and loved her. But by the end of the day, she was sleeping in a bed among strangers in a women's shelter, waiting for Child Protective Services to find her someplace to live. Both sets of grandparents lived overseas, and Tessa had never met or even spoken to either. None of her mother's friends stepped forward to claim her. Maybe they were afraid of interacting with the authorities. Most of the men and women her parents knew were immigrants too, at least some among them probably in the U.S. illegally. Not one of them had come forward to offer her sanctuary.

Enough, Tessa told herself, casting the pillow to the floor. Enough drama. Time to get up and see who had called this early on a vacation morning.

As soon as she unlocked the BlackBerry screen, a cold feeling wormed its way into her belly. Five voice mails and three text messages. That could not be good. For some reason, she thought of Eleanor. Had something…? The ghost of Nadine flickered into her mind, but she shook her head. Eleanor was nothing like Nadine.

The first text message was from Michael and said only, "Call me—red flag day." Their code for major scandal. The second text was from Melody, her publicist, and echoed the need to talk ASAP. Christ, Tessa thought, running a hand over her sleep-tangled hair. She had to get to her computer and check the news. Had someone found out about her past? And if so, how?

Skipping the rest of the messages (none were from Eleanor), Tessa pulled on sweats and a clean tank top and jogged downstairs barefoot. Eleanor was in the kitchen at the stove, while Laya perched on a stool at the island. When she saw Tessa, she jumped down and launched herself through the air. "Mom!"

Tessa caught her and swallowed back her impatience with difficulty. It wasn't Laya's fault that a crisis had arisen in the night. "Hi, baby. How are you?"

"Awesome. Eleanor made pancakes."

"I see that," Tessa said. She waited a moment, then steeled herself. "Good morning, Eleanor."

"Morning. You might want to check the laptop," Eleanor said without taking her attention from a pair of flapjacks heating in a skillet.

Tessa reached past Laya and opened Eleanor's laptop where it sat on the kitchen island. Slowly the screen returned from sleep mode, and Tessa stared in mingled horror and fascination at the browser window open to People.com and a large color image of her and Eleanor in a tranquil pool, a gorgeous waterfall behind them, looking for all the world as if they were about to kiss. Beneath the image ran the headline, "Who Is She?" The intimate expression in both of their eyes, fixed indelibly in digital pixels, mesmerized her more than the headline. The look made the image almost more damning than if they had been caught in an actual kiss.

She closed the laptop, but not before Laya had seen the photo.

"You look so happy!" she said. She was used to seeing Tessa's and her own picture online and in print, and seemed to accept as a given that Eleanor should appear there as well.

"We do, don't we, sweets." And all at once, it didn't seem to matter why Eleanor had backed off the night before. Tessa clearly wasn't alone in her feelings. Film didn't lie. Well, actually, it often did. Just not this time. "Are you done with breakfast, baby?" she asked. "Elle and I need to talk." Out of the corner of her eye, she saw Eleanor shoot a quick look in her direction, the first since she'd entered the kitchen.

"I'm done," Laya said, frowning now. "Did I do something bad?"

Tessa knelt down so that their faces were level. "No, we just need to have a private, grown-up conversation. Could you go play in your room for a few minutes? I'd appreciate it."

"Sure thing, chief," her daughter said solemnly, then turned and ran for the stairs.

Straightening again, Tessa leaned against the kitchen island, arms folded across her chest. For her, appearing on a Web site to millions of viewers was nothing new, but for Eleanor it probably felt as if she'd awakened this morning to an alternate reality. Tessa wanted to go to her, wanted nothing more than to slip her arms around her and tell her everything would be okay, but the night before still hung between them.

"So?" she said, and waited as Eleanor turned off the burner and set the last of the pancakes on an already overflowing plate.

"So." Eleanor turned at last to face her, eyes seeming to focus somewhere just beyond her left ear.

"We should talk this out, don't you think?" she prompted. "After all, we are lesbians," she added, trying to lighten the mood.

Eleanor frowned. "Are you? A lesbian, I mean?"

"Well, yeah. I thought you knew that."

"You were a little vague the other day."

"Oh. Well, yes I am," Tessa joked, quoting Melissa Etheridge. As Eleanor stared levelly at her, she ducked her head. "I know, it's not funny. I'm sorry. For everything, actually."

Eleanor squinted at her. "You're not angry with me?"

"Why would I be angry with you?" John Alvarez at Kipu Falls Ranch, on the other hand, had some explaining to do. Or, more likely, his hired hand Christian.

"You should read the article. Sasha called me this morning to find out why I'd been holding out on her. Apparently their source is quoted as saying that we were talking openly about being a couple. Seems there's a video too."

There was always a video. Tessa tried to seriously consider what it meant that the press was covering their supposed love affair. But all she felt was relief—she wouldn't have to hide this part of her life anymore. There was still her past to worry about, but this was one secret she would be more than happy to relinquish.

"Honestly," she said, "it's fine. I'm out of acting, and even if I wasn't, I'm tired of hiding who I am. I haven't been in a serious relationship in years because every time I came close, the person either didn't want to deal with my closet or turned out to be someone I couldn't trust." *Person* slipped out—she meant *woman*, but the habit of hiding her sexuality was deeply ingrained. Not anymore, she thought as a new sense of freedom overtook her. Holy shit. She'd been outed.

"I thought you would hate me," Eleanor said. "Especially after last night."

"Hate you? What kind of crack are you smoking?" She wanted to say more, but her BlackBerry beeped. Michael. Not to mention Melody, Will and Margot. "Look, I have to make some calls, and then I think we need to pack up and head home. My house is the only place equipped to repel the paparazzi invasion this photo has probably already launched."

"Of course, whatever you think."

"Good," Tessa said. "Okay." She hesitated. She wanted to ask Eleanor what the look on her face in the photo meant, wanted to find out why she'd pulled away the night before. But talking would have to wait until they were safely ensconced behind the gates of her house in L.A. Bloody press, she thought for easily the thousandth time in her adult life. And yet, thanks to the AP, her closet door was now wide open. Maybe there was a reason this was all happening now.

Eleanor reached out and touched her shoulder. "Everything will be all right," she said, the warmth of her hand seeping through Tessa's tank top.

Tessa couldn't remember the last time someone had tried to reassure her. She nodded. "I know."

Twelve hours later, Eleanor stood alone in the dimly lit family room in Tessa's Hollywood home, staring unseeingly at the wall of books on either side of the glowing gas fireplace. That morning she'd awakened before dawn in the guest room at Mele Honu'ala, and now as the last bit of daylight leaked from the sky, she was back in L.A. She didn't think she would ever get used to the displacement of air travel.

That morning, while Tessa made travel arrangements and discussed strategy with her agent and publicist, Eleanor had entertained Laya and cleaned the house, even though Tessa had insisted the cleaning crew would take care of it. Picking up kept her occupied, and anyway, Eleanor's only experience with a house cleaner had come during her mother's bouts with chemo when Sarah was too rundown to keep the house as pristine as her lowered immune system required. Chapins didn't pay strangers to pick up after them.

By early afternoon, their bags had been packed and the jet ready to take them back to the mainland. On the way back to L.A., Eleanor had stayed on her side of the cabin and pretended to sleep. In reality, every time she looked at Tessa, the memory of their make-out session came rushing back. Had it really happened? And had their picture really made *People*? A ranting message from Sasha on her voice mail that morning had informed her of their unwitting public display of affection. Ironically, she'd turned her phone on in order to call Sasha and rehash the previous evening's incident.

The photo itself was fairly innocent, she'd told Sasha when she saw it. And the video didn't show anything at all. She could almost hear her friend's eyes rolling over the telephone line.

"It's not *what* you're doing, Elle," she'd said with exaggerated patience. "It's how you're *looking* at each other, as if you're in the climactic scene of a romantic comedy. Or tragedy, maybe."

"Thanks for the optimism."

"Just calling it like I see it." Sasha paused. "Although in this case, I suppose I might be a little jealous."

Given that a large percentage of straight women confessed to fantasizing about Tessa, Eleanor wasn't surprised by this admission. Like many Smithies, especially those who had close lesbian friends, Sasha had spent a semester toward the end of college kissing girls. Or, rather, kissing one classmate specifically—Paige Thomas, now a successful journalist working for the *Washington Post*. Although technically a "hasbian," her roommate still occasionally admitted a latent attraction to women.

Before they hung up, Sasha had told her that Tessa would probably want to return to L.A. immediately. Forewarned, she hadn't been surprised when Tessa said they had to go, though the warmth in her eyes this morning had taken Eleanor aback, as had the apology. She'd thought that Tessa would almost certainly distance herself again, given what had happened the night before combined with her public outing. But she hadn't. At least, not yet. Eleanor supposed there was still time. They'd just gotten back from the Burbank airport, and Tessa had asked her to wait while she put Laya to bed so that they could discuss strategies for handling "the situation."

Eleanor still couldn't believe that she was the subject of tabloid speculation. Turning from the bookshelves, she opened her cell phone and scrolled through the as-yet unanswered text and voice mail messages stored there. Quite a few of her friends and family had taken note of the image blasted worldwide by the AP. Had Laurie? Not that she cared. Really. In the morning, she promised herself, she'd make some calls. After all, no matter what was or wasn't happening between her and Tessa, her current life was temporary. These experiences were on loan only.

That was one of the reasons she'd been reluctant to leave Kauai. There, on vacation, she could pretend that this was how life would always be, just her and Tessa and Laya finding ways to pass their days together: bird-watching at the wildlife refuge, reading in the sun beside the lagoon, building sand castles and playing Frisbee on the beach. She'd felt so at peace there (if you didn't count the previous night's incident), but she doubted the feeling would carry over to L.A. Especially not given their current situation.

"I thought we were beyond all this," Tessa said from behind her. "I retired so we could have a shot at a normal life. So that Laya wouldn't have to grow up like this."

Eleanor closed her phone. Tessa was still in the jeans and tank top she'd worn on the plane, her hair pulled back in a loose French braid. Her face was drawn, dark smudges visible beneath her eyes. Eleanor felt a pang of guilt. She'd thought Christian, the guide, might be trouble. She should have kept a closer eye on him.

"I'm sorry," she offered as Tessa moved toward her.

"It's not your fault." She stopped a few feet away. "The thing is, I'm not sure you going back to Sasha's tonight is such a good idea. I think you should probably just stay here."

Eleanor's pulse sped up at the insidious image that popped into her head: the two of them entwined in bed, naked. "Really?"

"Yeah. I mean, the gate is being watched. If you try to leave, someone will follow you back to Sasha's and then she'll be involved too. It might be easier if you stay in the carriage house until all of this subsides."

The carriage house, where Ama and Dani had lived. Her pulse slowed to normal. "Of course. Whatever you think."

"Shouldn't take too long," Tessa added, her tone distinctly cynical. "Hollywood scandals have a half-life of about a week. Odds are someone else will steal the headlines sooner rather than later. We'll still have to be careful after that, but the initial blood-in-the-water frenzy should pass pretty quickly."

"Right," Eleanor said.

"Okay, then." Tessa hesitated. "I am sorry, Elle. This is going to get a lot nastier before it gets better. Right now they don't know who you are, but it's just a matter of time before someone figures it out. And then... Have you seen the movie *Notting Hill*?"

Eleanor smiled crookedly. "I'm Hugh Grant, aren't I?"

"I can honestly say I'm thankful you're not. But this is much bigger than that movie made it seem. Once the press figures out who you are, you're going to be the subject of a massive amount of scrutiny, as will your family, friends, former colleagues, supposed buddies from high school whose names you don't even remember. By the time this blows over, you just might hate me."

Eleanor stared at her. "That won't ever happen."

"I hope not." Tessa turned away. "Anyway, the carriage house should be all set. Ama left clean sheets on the bed. Let me just get you the key."

Eleanor watched her rummage through a kitchen drawer. All day Tessa had seemed smaller, vulnerable somehow, unlike her normal competent, confident self. Was it the paparazzi assault, or could it have something to do with the night before? *People* at least seemed to think Tessa was harboring romantic feelings toward her.

"Here it is." Tessa came back into the family room and held out a sand dollar key ring.

Eleanor reached out to take it, but instead her hand closed around Tessa's. "Hey."

Tessa watched her, eyes luminous in the light from the gas fire. "What?"

If she wasn't Tessa Flanagan, Eleanor thought, what would she do? This—she tugged Tessa toward her. "I won't ever hate you," she said again, holding her close.

After a moment, Tessa's arms slid around her waist. She was only a few inches shorter, but the difference meant her head fit perfectly under Eleanor's chin. Eleanor felt Tessa's shoulders sag, the breath leave her body in a long sigh, and they stood in the quiet room together, the only movement the gas flame flickering behind the glass fireplace screen.

Tessa leaned against Eleanor, too exhausted to think. All day she'd been on the go, from the moment her BlackBerry had awakened her with its insistent beckons until a few minutes before, when she'd tucked Laya into bed and kissed her goodnight. She'd come downstairs intending to explain to Eleanor how these sorts of situations worked, to let her know that Melody would try to nip this whole thing in the bud before her reputation got too trashed. Instead, she found herself finagling a way to keep Eleanor close.

True, having her stay in the carriage house was probably the best way to minimize her exposure to the uglier side of life with an A-lister. But that wasn't why Tessa had suggested it. In actuality, she wasn't ready to say goodbye. Once Eleanor stepped foot outside the gate, it would be nearly impossible to get her back in. At least, not until some other joker grabbed headlines and the whole crazy episode passed.

Tessa hid her face against Eleanor's neck and closed her

eyes. She still didn't know why Eleanor had pulled away the night before, but at this point, she would take what she could get. Being held felt too good.

But Eleanor was pulling away again, and Tessa opened her eyes. What…? Then Eleanor's lips met hers and they were kissing, and Tessa was twining her arms around Eleanor's neck and pulling her closer. As their tongues met, Tessa forgot to be tired. She had wanted this for so long. Needed it, even.

When a sound from the patio caught her attention, it was Tessa's turn to break away mid-kiss. "Did you hear that?" she asked, staring through the picture windows out onto the floodlit patio and pool area. The alarm was set. In theory, they would know if someone made it onto the grounds.

"I think it was just the wind," Eleanor said, her voice unsteady.

Tessa turned back to her, closing her fist over the carriage house key. "Are you sure you're okay with this?"

In answer, Eleanor led her to the love seat and kissed her again. They stayed like that for what might have been hours but was probably only a matter of minutes, side by side on the love seat exploring each other's lips and skin, shirts and bras cast aside so that they could lie breast to breast. When they finally came up for air, Tessa rested her head on Eleanor's shoulder and whispered, "I don't want you to go."

"I don't want to go," she murmured back.

"Then stay."

"Are you sure?"

"I'm sure."

It was that easy. They shrugged back into their shirts, pocketed their bras and headed upstairs together, Tessa leading the way. She could feel Eleanor close behind her, and she could also feel her heart beating nearly double-time. It couldn't be nerves, could it? She'd been with her fair share of women since she'd figured out her first year in L.A. why her crushes always seemed to be on women. But it had been a while since she'd been with someone she knew as well as she now knew Eleanor. Usually she relied on brief hook-ups with near strangers for a release of pent-up tension, like the woman she'd slept with at her ex-girlfriend's wedding in New York the previous fall.

Soon they were passing Laya's partially closed bedroom door and padding quietly down the carpeted hallway to the master suite with its bedroom, sitting room and palatial bathroom. Tessa had never allowed anyone back here—at least, no one she was romantically interested in. Ama had been in her bedroom, of course, as had a few personal assistants, housekeepers and other assorted professionals. But in the way that counted most, Eleanor would be the first.

As she closed the bedroom door behind them, Tessa felt nervousness sparking through her body again. This was it, she thought, switching on a bedside lamp. Now everything would be different. She flicked off the overhead light and turned to face Eleanor.

Eyes on hers, Eleanor moved closer. "If you don't want me to kiss you, now would be a good time to say so," she said, and leaned forward to touch her lips to Tessa's.

Shivering slightly, Tessa opened her mouth to Eleanor's, feeling the heat rise again between them as their tongues met and the kiss deepened. Eleanor's fingers slid to the back of her neck, and Tessa ran her hands along Eleanor's waist, tracing the increasingly familiar curve of her body. Then she arched her back, pressing herself fully against Eleanor and hearing her sharp intake of breath. This was really happening. This was actually going to happen. She couldn't help the smile that creased her lips.

Eleanor leaned away from her. "What?"

"Nothing. I'm just glad you stayed," she said.

"I'm glad you wanted me to stay."

For a while, she was conscious of everything—the beauty of Eleanor's body in the lamplight as they undressed; the contrast between their skin colors, one cream, the other closer to caramel; the lushness of her own curves compared to Eleanor's leaner, more angular lines. But then she lost the ability to think, overwhelmed by the sensation of Eleanor on top of her, breast to breast, hip to hip, pressing her into the mattress; Eleanor's hands and lips moving over her body, gentle now, then insistent, demanding a response she would have been unable to prevent even if she'd wanted to.

She was so wet, and Eleanor's mouth was unrelenting at her

breasts while her hand traced sensual circles across her stomach, moving lower and lower until she was exploring Tessa's slick folds lightly, almost teasingly. Tessa closed her eyes, fists clenched at the sinuous pressure that approached but never seemed to reach the spot that craved it most. Then Eleanor moved back up her body to kiss her again. When Tessa's lips parted, Eleanor's tongue stroked into her mouth at the same moment her fingers entered her, pressing deep inside. Tessa gasped, her hips lifting as Eleanor's thumb massaged her swollen clit rhythmically, fingers rubbing skillfully against the sensitive nub within.

Tessa moaned softly, her own hands sliding downward to squeeze Eleanor's taut nipples. But Eleanor had other ideas. Shifting to one side, she paused her ministrations to grasp both of Tessa's hands and pin them to the pillow above her head. Then she lowered her mouth to Tessa's, tongue slipping inside as her free hand dipped lower again. Tessa writhed against the sheets, even more turned on by the inability to move. Eleanor angled her fingers further into Tessa, thumb rubbing steadily, fingers flexing, until all Tessa knew was the tension building inside her, centered on Eleanor's hand. She couldn't think, couldn't move, could only let herself be carried along until the pressure reached a sudden crescendo. Her hips bucked convulsively, and she squeezed Eleanor's fingers tightly between her thighs.

Eyes shut, she gasped against Eleanor's lips. "Don't stop."

"I won't," Eleanor murmured. "I've got you." And she kept up the tempo, fingers sliding in and out, thumb circling her engorged flesh until the last tremor subsided.

Eventually the waves receded, and Tessa's awareness gradually returned. Eleanor had released her hands and was lying beside her now as she gently stroked her, one leg over both of Tessa's. They traded easy kisses, pausing to smile at each other in the low light as their heartbeats slowed. Tessa stretched, feeling a glow spreading through her limbs.

She shifted onto her side so that their heads were cradled by the same pillow. "Thank you," she said quietly.

"My pleasure." Eleanor ran a finger over Tessa's lips. "God, you're beautiful."

Tessa had heard this particular compliment many times in

her life, but coming from Eleanor, it felt somehow new. Tessa leaned in to kiss her, and Eleanor inhaled quickly, her hips arching against Tessa. Smoothly Tessa rolled on top of her, pushing her down into the eggshell mattress. She couldn't wait to make Eleanor feel as good as she did. Better, even, if that was possible. But there was no rush. For once, she could take as much time as she wanted.

Slowly she traced a line of kisses down Eleanor's neck to her breastbone, then dipped down to flick her tongue around the edge of a pink nipple. Their colors were so different, as was almost everything else about them. Tessa was generally hairless, while Eleanor appeared to be covered in a pale, nearly invisible peach fuzz. Her breasts were high, areolas light pink and small, while Tessa had retained the full figure wrought by motherhood, her nipples dark and wide. She brought her breasts against Eleanor's, slowly rubbing their nipples together. Eleanor stared up at her, eyes darkening. Tessa felt new desire stirring as she lowered her mouth to Eleanor's, their tongues weaving together. She'd never wanted anyone quite this much, had she?

Legs entwined with Eleanor's, Tessa rubbed herself against her, slowly at first, then faster as Eleanor's hips rose to meet her. They moved in unison, faster and faster, breathing ragged as their rhythm caught and held. Reaching between Eleanor's legs, Tessa slid her fingers through her hot wetness, entering her in one swift move. Eleanor gasped, and Tessa kissed her hard, tongue probing her mouth as they strained together. Eleanor was close, she could tell.

All at once, Tessa stopped, and Eleanor whimpered slightly as she shifted away. She didn't want her to come too soon. She had been dreaming about this ever since the night in the hot tub.

"It's okay," she murmured, and placed a gentle kiss on Eleanor's lips.

Taking her time, she left a trail of hot kisses across Eleanor's breasts, down over her narrow ribcage, dipping her tongue into her navel and sucking lightly on her angular hip bones. Eleanor moved restlessly beneath her, groaning quietly, and Tessa smiled, enjoying the effect she was having. Then she slipped between Eleanor's legs and pressed her thighs apart.

This was one of her favorite places to be—between another woman's legs, a willing instrument of someone else's pleasure. She used her hands to spread Eleanor wide, inhaling the mild, musky scent rising from her neatly trimmed bush. Dipping her head, she took her first taste, tongue delicately exploring the exposed ridges and folds. Above her, she heard Eleanor moan, and the sound reignited her own desire. She ran her tongue across Eleanor's center, reaching her swollen clit and sucking it into her mouth greedily. At the same time, she slipped her fingers inside Eleanor, seeking and quickly finding the receptive spot within.

It didn't take long. She was already so close, and soon Tessa felt Eleanor's muscles contracting around her, heard the muffled cry as Eleanor came, hips rising up from the mattress. Tessa was close too. Her mouth still on Eleanor, Tessa drove her own pelvis into the bed, rubbing urgently. After a moment her body tensed, and she hid her face against Eleanor's damp thigh as waves of release broke over her again.

"Jesus," Eleanor murmured eventually, her voice gravelly.

"No kidding." Tessa crawled up the bed and collapsed, head on Eleanor's shoulder, arm across her belly. The perspiration that had pooled at the small of her back was rapidly cooling now that they were still. She shivered, only partially from cold.

Eleanor tugged the sheets and comforter up over them and rubbed her back. "Better?"

"Mm," Tessa said, and closed her eyes. She couldn't remember the last time she'd felt this relaxed.

In the past when she'd gone to bed with someone new, she'd often been too aware of her own celebrity status to let go completely, certain the other person was making love to Tessa Flanagan, Star. But with Eleanor, she hadn't felt like that at all. Eleanor knew her as a serious reader and an attentive mom, a woman who enjoyed ziplining and longed to make a difference in the world. Eleanor knew her, and that was what had allowed Tessa to let go and give herself over to the feel of another woman's body, lips, fingers bringing her so far inside herself she forgot, for once, to worry.

"That was incredible." Eleanor kissed Tessa's forehead

and brushed her hair back from her face. "Can I tell you something?"

Tessa opened her eyes. "Um, okay."

"I'm really glad you're a lesbian."

She smiled. "Ditto, pal."

As they lay together under the covers, silence blanketing the house, Tessa could feel sleep tugging at her.

"Do you want me to go to the carriage house?" Eleanor asked.

"No," she said without stopping to consider, and then realized it was true—for the first time in years, she wanted to fall asleep next to someone she'd made love with.

"Are you sure?"

"I'm sure. Unless—do you want to go?"

"No."

"Then stay." She tightened her grip on Eleanor. She should probably let her go. After all, Laya usually found her way into her room first thing in the morning. But she couldn't bear to watch Eleanor leave, not tonight. She was tired of being alone, and the old reasons—her closet, her career—no longer held.

"I'll set my alarm," Eleanor said, fiddling with her watch.

When she'd finished, Tessa clapped twice and the bedside lamp shut off.

In the dark, Eleanor laughed. "You do not have The Clapper in your bedroom."

"What can I say? I'm lazy," she mumbled.

"Are not," Eleanor said, but her voice sounded sleepy, too.

Tessa moved closer to her, sighing as Eleanor's warmth seeped into her. "Goodnight, Elle."

"Goodnight, Tess."

Lovely was the last word she thought before succumbing to the pull of sleep.

CHAPTER FIFTEEN

When Eleanor's alarm went off, she automatically felt for her watch, eyes still closed. Then she noticed the warm body pressed against her side. Her eyes shot open. She was in an unfamiliar room, high-ceilinged and decorated in dark red and tan accents. Beside her lay sleeping the woman whose body she had ravished the night before and who, in turn, had ravished her. The night before had been better than anything Eleanor could have (and had) imagined. Their bodies fit together perfectly, and Tessa seemed to know just where and how to touch her. This didn't surprise Eleanor especially, given Tessa's intuitive powers in their non-horizontal interactions.

She shifted onto one side and stared at Tessa's face in profile, memorizing the features that she already knew well—shapely eyebrows (not plucked to death like some women in Hollywood), full lips, faint smile lines at the corners of her eyes and mouth relaxed now in sleep. Tessa didn't believe in Botox or collagen injections, she'd said publicly often enough. Jokingly, she'd told Eleanor that was why she'd had to retire from acting. Who wanted to pay to see a non-surgically-altered thirty-four-year-old woman's body when they could drool over the next up-and-coming teenage starlet's perky breasts and firm ass? Personally, Eleanor thought, lifting the covers slightly to continue her observation of Tessa's body unobstructed, she would take a mature woman over a nubile youth any day. Particularly this mature woman. Her breath quickened as she traced Tessa's curves—her luscious breasts, shapely hips, the narrow triangle of dark hair between her thighs. Eleanor remembered the sound of Tessa's sharp gasps the night before, the softness of her breasts as she'd lain on top of Eleanor, the feeling of being inside her. Maybe there was time yet before Laya...

Tessa stirred, and Eleanor dropped the covers quickly. No need to scare her off first thing—Tessa was jumpy enough as it was, what with the caravan of photographers who had staked out the gate the night before shortly after they'd driven in. Most of the paparazzi had believed they were still on Kauai. With the element of surprise, they'd managed to get home without encountering much in the way of stalkers. Frankly, Eleanor had been a little disappointed. Here they were hopping flights and riding in limos with tinted windows, and the red-carpet entourage she'd expected to encounter at the gate to Tessa's driveway had been late.

"Good morning," she murmured now, watching Tessa closely as she opened her eyes and blinked at Eleanor a few times. Any sign of regret?

Tessa's lips curved upward in a smile that warmed her eyes. "Good morning," she said, and stretched her arms above her head, yawning. A squeak escaped her, reminding Eleanor of the time Laya had yawned like a puppy.

"That is so cute," she couldn't help saying.

"You're so cute." In one fluid move, Tessa rolled over on top of her. "How are you?"

"Good. Except I'm kind of being crushed at the moment."

Eleanor could feel her arousal kick up another notch at the feel of Tessa's silky nakedness.

"Didn't seem to bother you last night." Tessa lowered her head to kiss her.

Eleanor squirmed away. "Wait, I have morning breath!"

"Now the Puritan comes out. Isn't it a little late for that?"

"Actually, it's a little early. Not until I brush my teeth, okay?"

Grumbling, Tessa rolled off her and slipped out of bed. "Whatever," she said and strolled toward the bathroom, seemingly unselfconscious.

Then again, Eleanor thought, enjoying the view, why wouldn't she be?

More than anything, Eleanor wanted to brush her teeth and tackle Tessa back into bed, but Laya could appear at any moment. Sighing, she reached for her discarded clothing strewn across the foot of the bed. Tessa Flanagan's bed, she thought, testing herself. But the name no longer held the same power it once had. She knew Tessa well enough now to understand that the public image was just that—a mirage projected to keep American movie-goers happy. Last night, Eleanor had made love with the woman she'd gotten close to these last few weeks, not the icon her fans adored.

In the bathroom, the toilet flushed and the sink ran. Then the door opened and Tessa came out, a lightweight robe tied loosely around her waist.

"What are you doing?" Tessa asked.

"Getting dressed so your kid doesn't find me in your bed." Eleanor pulled her jeans on commando-style, the previous day's underwear tucked into a back pocket.

"Ooh, no panties." Tessa came over and wrapped her arms around Eleanor, pinning her arms to her sides.

"No fair," Eleanor protested, inhaling the minty scent of toothpaste.

"It's okay. I brushed for both of us." And she leaned in and kissed her slowly, softly, lingeringly. "See you downstairs?"

"You know it," Eleanor said, glancing down the robe's partially open front. Damn, she had nice breasts.

Tessa pushed her away. "Later." She smiled, lifting one eyebrow suggestively.

"Later," Eleanor repeated, and ducked out of the bedroom. She practically skipped down the hallway, amazed at the level of conversation she'd managed to maintain despite the early hour (ten to six) and her lack of coffee. Apparently sleeping with Tessa agreed with her. She felt better rested than any night in recent memory.

In fact, this was the first morning in a long time that she hadn't remembered her mother's death immediately upon awakening. Her steps slowed as she moved down the staircase. Was that a sign she was moving on with her life, or should she feel guilty that she'd forgotten about her mom? The New Englander in her mandated guilt, while the twenty-first century psychology student-to-be viewed her delayed memory as an indicator of improved mental function. Probably, the psych student was right.

She paused in the front entry to retrieve her suitcase and carry-on, both forgotten overnight, before continuing through the kitchen to the family room. Her luggage held the clothes she would need if she were to camp out in the carriage house for the next week, along with the all-important toothbrush. If last night's events became a habit, she might have to keep a second toothbrush in Tessa's bathroom... She clamped down quickly on the thought and headed toward the patio doors. No need to be a typical lesbian and start fantasizing about their future nuptials. She was still leaving in a couple of months, and besides, Tessa's life was already full. Just because they'd acted on their apparently mutual attraction didn't mean they were going to have a genuine relationship.

Her hand was on the doorknob when she heard footsteps on the stairs and Tessa's voice calling, "Wait, Elle!"

But it was too late. She'd already broken the seal on the French doors. She jerked her hand away as an ear-splitting siren started up, accompanied by a rhythmic clanging and a voice that intoned, "Intruder, intruder," like something out of *Lost in Space*. Christ, what a noise! Dropping her bags, she covered her ears and turned to see Tessa hurrying to a console on the wall near the refrigerator. She typed in a code and the horrible sounds ceased immediately.

"I'm so sorry," Eleanor said, still frozen in place near the patio doors. "I totally forgot."

"No, I should have reminded you."

Just then, Laya's voice carried down the stairwell. "Mom," she wailed.

The phone decided to add to the chaos, and Tessa shook her head at Eleanor, laughing helplessly. "Can you get Laya? I have to talk to the alarm company or they'll send out a team."

"Sure," Eleanor said, checking to make sure her underwear was secure in her back pocket. "Sorry," she mouthed as she brushed past Tessa, who nodded distractedly, already on the phone repeating the safe word to the alarm company: *Luzon*, the main island of the Philippines.

Eleanor sprinted up the stairs to find Laya standing in her pajamas at the top, eyes wide. She was holding her arm at a funny angle, and as Eleanor knelt before her, the girl pointed at three jagged scratches just inside her elbow.

"Hey, sweetie," Eleanor said, taking the proffered arm. "What happened?"

"Totoy got scared," she said, sniffling a little. Her eyes were wet, and she rubbed her nose. "He doesn't like the alarm."

"I'll bet. Neither do I," she confessed.

"It's so loud, it hurts my ears."

"I know, I'm sorry. It's my fault. I forgot about the alarm."

Laya accepted this with a stoic nod. "It's okay, Elle. Everyone makes mistakes. Why are you wearing the same shirt as yesterday?"

"Am I?" Eleanor looked down, pretending to be surprised at her shirt selection. "Oh. Well, I, um, left my suitcase here by accident last night."

"Can we have pancakes for breakfast again?"

"Sure. If we have milk and eggs. Otherwise it might have to wait until we order some groceries."

"Ama always made sure we had milk when we got home," Laya said, her voice small. She sighed and rubbed the scratches on her arm. "Oh, well."

This morning was turning into a monster guilt fest. Not really what she'd anticipated when she first awoke this morning, comfy and warm in Tessa's bed.

"Come on, kiddo," she said. "Let's wash your arm and put some ointment on those scratches, okay? Then your mom and I will worry about groceries."

"Okay," Laya said, and allowed herself to be led back down the hall to her room.

As she washed her hands and tended to her charge's wounds, Eleanor remembered the evening not too long ago when Tessa had helped her with her own scrapes and bruises from the encounter with the rooster. Less than a week had passed, but her bike wreck felt like it had happened an entire lifetime ago. In a good way, she told herself. Definitely in a good way. An image of Tessa leaning over her the night before, naked, flashed into her mind, and she blinked it away.

"Thanks, Elle," Laya said when the cat scratches had been treated. She reached out and wrapped her arms around Eleanor's neck. "I love you."

"Ditto, pal," Eleanor said. Then she heard a sound behind her and turned to see Tessa standing in the doorway.

Laya released her and launched herself at her mother. "Totoy scratched me but Eleanor fixed it, see?" she said, holding up her arm for Tessa's inspection.

"I do see," Tessa said. She looked at Eleanor for a moment, eyes serious, before turning away. "Anyway," she added, "now that we're all awake, what do you say we get some breakfast in that belly?" And she tickled her daughter until she squirmed away and ran screeching down the hallway.

Eleanor put away the medical supplies, wondering what had happened to chase away the open, happy Tessa from earlier that morning. It couldn't have been the fact that she'd set off the alarm, could it? Someday, Eleanor thought as she closed the medicine cabinet, she hoped to be able to break through the walls Tessa seemed able to raise at will between herself and the rest of the world.

Tessa sat alone at the kitchen island after breakfast, finishing her herbal tea. The morning so far had been a jumble of contrasting experiences. She'd awakened to find Eleanor watching her, and unlike with previous liaisons, she'd found herself smiling at the sight of the person she'd made love to the night before still lying beside her. Eleanor's morning-breath shyness was sweet too, though something that would have to be overcome—assuming, of course, they intended to repeat the previous night's activities. For her part, she hoped they would. Even now, her body felt languorous, replete. She was, simply, happy.

The incident with the alarm had jolted her from her state of near bliss, though, and then Laya's cat scratches had led to Tessa overhearing her daughter telling Eleanor she loved her and Eleanor returning the sentiment. Tessa had stood in the doorway remembering suddenly that this moment, the way the three of them were right now together, couldn't last. No matter who loved whom.

Still, a little of the feeling of harmony she'd awakened with had returned as Eleanor showed them how to make oatmeal in the microwave using a canister of Quaker Oats she'd found in one of the cupboards, insisting that it would be even better than the pancakes Laya had requested. She'd added generous servings of maple syrup and raisins to each dish, and even Tessa had had to admit that the end result was surprisingly good. Eleanor had beamed at her, and it was all Tessa could do not to reach across the corner of the kitchen island and kiss her. She was just too cute.

After breakfast, Eleanor had taken her suitcase over to the carriage house to get settled in, Laya going with her "to help." Now Tessa sipped her tea, wishing she could go back to bed. The paparazzi assault had just begun and already she was exhausted. Unfortunately, she knew she had to take advantage of the temporarily quiet house to make phone calls even though it was only half past seven. Resigned, she reheated her cooling tea and made her way to her home office.

Her agent and publicist were first on the list of must-calls. During a hastily arranged conference call, Tessa informed them of the mystery woman's role in her household, bracing herself for the response she knew would follow. Sure enough, Michael and Melody were of the same opinion: Tessa would have to go on someone's daytime talk show as soon as possible and deny that anything had happened with her daughter's nanny, who was just a good friend she'd gotten to know when Eleanor worked at the Barclay School. Then she should "let it slip" that she was seeing someone of the male persuasion. Melody offered to make a few phone calls to see who they could get at short notice to stand in as her beard. She actually used the term beard.

Tessa let the two of them duke it out for a while. When they finally paused for breath, she intervened. "I think I'd rather go with a no comment. You know, complete radio silence."

"Tess, that's like admitting it's true," Melody said.

"You saw the photo, didn't you? It wasn't fake. No Photoshop or anything."

"That's not the point," Michael said.

"Isn't it? I'm out of the business, guys. I know everyone is convinced I'll be back next year looking for a good project, and who knows, maybe I will. But for now, I'm out, pun fully intended. I'm done with movies and I'm done hiding who I am. I've done it for way too long."

They were both quiet. At last Melody said, "She sounds like she means it, Michael."

"God bless her," he said, though Tessa was pretty sure he would have liked to use another phrase. "All right, Tess. No beard. But the media is going to have a field day. You sure that's the way you want to go?"

"I'm sure," she said, remembering how it had felt to wake up in the middle of the night to find Eleanor curled around her from behind. Safe and warm, cared for even. If she were to deny the relationship publicly and claim that she was seeing a man, she had a feeling she wouldn't get a chance to experience that feeling again—at least, not with Eleanor. Besides, Laya was getting older, and Tessa had to think about the message she was sending her daughter by staying in the closet. She had taught

Laya to respect adult relationships of all kinds, whether they were between people of different races or the same gender. If she hid who she was much longer, she would be modeling hypocrisy for her daughter. Sooner or later Laya would recognize this.

After the conference call, she dialed up Ama and Dani. Ama had sent her an e-mail early that morning that said only, "You go, girl!" so she knew the news had reached the Philippines. Somehow she doubted the rest of the heavily Catholic country, which had adopted her as its shining example of emigrant success, would be quite as happy about her love life.

L.A. was fifteen hours behind the Philippines, which meant it was nighttime there, so Tessa only talked to Ama for a few minutes. The older woman was thrilled about the apparent match and reminded Tessa that it had been all her idea. She also wanted details, but Tessa only allowed that she and Eleanor had grown close during their time on Kauai. Laya wasn't to know about it yet. She didn't want her daughter getting her hopes up unnecessarily.

"What about your hopes?" Ama asked in her customary bluntly insightful way.

"I don't know," Tessa admitted. "We'll see."

Will, her longest friend in Hollywood, was next. He picked up his cell on the tenth ring just as she was mentally rehearsing a message.

"Well, if it isn't the next Ellen," he said, sounding slightly out of breath, wind rattling his phone.

"You know I would never want my own talk show," she responded, smiling at the sound of his voice. "Where are you?"

"Running on the track at my club." His voice got farther away for a moment. "That's it, Tom, don't slack off just because I'm not leading you out."

"Tom? I thought you said you wouldn't work with him again."

"I thought you said you were straight."

"Not to you I didn't."

"Let me be the first to congratulate you on detonating your closet door, sweets."

"Ooh, sorry, Ama already beat you to that one."

"Damn that wily little woman. I have to run, but let's make a date for lunch soon. I want details."

"How about a date for a workout instead? I don't think I'll be leaving Laurel Canyon anytime soon."

"Got it. Call Becky and she'll set something up."

"Will do. Give Tom my best."

He snorted. "I think he'll want to be staying as far away from you as possible right about now. You know, in case busted closets are somehow catching."

"Right," she said, rolling her eyes as they hung up. Hypocrisy and panic were alive and well in the fertile breeding grounds of Hollywood.

The last call on her list had to wait until Laya's afternoon nap. Once Laya was down for the count, Tessa tore herself away from an enticing Eleanor, who was sunning herself by the pool in very little clothing, and locked herself in the office to make the dreaded call to the Byerly sisters. Both in their seventies, she wasn't sure what her business partners would have to say about the headlines she was currently garnering. Particularly when she told them that the supposition about her sexuality was true.

As she frequently did, though, she discovered she'd worried unnecessarily. The Byerlys were glad to hear from her after the way she'd been so out of touch these last weeks, they told her over speaker phone. They talked for a few minutes about what the press blockade of her driveway meant in terms of the foundation and agreed on a plan for her to work remotely until the ruckus died down. And that was it.

"How did it go?" Eleanor asked, closing her book of crossword puzzles as Tessa crossed the pool deck and dropped onto the chaise lounge next to her.

"The Byerlys say they don't care if I'm gay," she told Eleanor, who was looking noticeably fit in her two-piece swimsuit. "They do, however, care that I'm not available to interview executive director candidates. They're right, you know. I should be working."

"And I thought Protestants had a corner on the workaholic market," Eleanor commented.

"Please. I'm first-generation, not to mention Asian. You think you have pressure."

She was joking, but Eleanor tilted her head and appeared to consider her words seriously. "Not really anymore. Not since my mom got sick. It's funny. I used to be so driven when I was younger. I had this image of who I was going to be and what I was going to accomplish, and then she got sick and all of that just didn't seem to matter anymore. You know?"

"Kind of." Tessa hesitated. "I was only a little older than Laya when I lost my parents, so it was different for me. But I do remember that the day I found out they were gone, my life became separated into these very distinct before and after parts."

"What was the after part like?"

She didn't want to lie to Eleanor. "Lonely," she said. "Before L.A., I felt invisible, like no one really cared whether I lived or not."

Eleanor reached across the space between their lounge chairs and took her hand. "Now thousands of people adore you, and the paparazzi is camped out in your driveway. Kind of the opposite extreme."

Tessa squeezed her hand, remembering for a moment just what those fingers were capable of. "Those people, my 'fans,' they don't really adore me. They don't even know me."

"I do," Eleanor said. "And I care whether you live or not."

Tessa glanced at her, wishing she could see Eleanor's eyes behind her sunglasses. She was so sweet, so normal. What would she think if she knew the truth about Tessa's parents? Would she feel differently about her and Laya?

"What are we doing about dinner?" Eleanor asked, her thumb tracing circles against Tessa's palm.

She suppressed a shiver, thinking again of Eleanor's hands on her. Inside her. "You have a one-track mind."

"Just trying to keep up my strength."

Eyes closed against the sun, Tessa could feel desire coiling inside her at Eleanor's touch. All at once she couldn't wait for nightfall, when she and Eleanor could wend their way upstairs again and have their way with each other. As she pictured their naked limbs entwining beneath her sheets, she smiled slowly. She was starting to think she just might enjoy this paparazzi-enforced house arrest, after all.

CHAPTER SIXTEEN

Despite the early morning fiasco with the alarm system, Eleanor's pre-coffee giddiness lasted throughout the day. Her friends and family, meanwhile, were in shock. Not that she blamed them. They'd thought it out of character for her to pick up without warning and head out to California in the first place, let alone take a job working for Tessa Flanagan. Now the press claimed she was having an affair with the world-famous actress? Admittedly, it was a bit much to fathom, particularly given her former seemingly virtuous kindergarten teacher existence.

Midway through that first morning, she'd sent Laya back to the main house and set about returning the calls and e-mails the Kipu Falls photo had elicited. First there was her father, who had phoned "to make sure you're okay." Though they'd been nothing but welcoming to the girlfriends she'd brought home, he and her mother had never been comfortable discussing her love life. She could only imagine his displeasure now. Then again, he was the one who'd had a girlfriend while his wife was dying. Eleanor wasn't sure he had the moral high ground here.

"I'm fine, Dad," she said when she reached him at his office in downtown Newport, only a few blocks from the house she'd grown up in. "The photo wasn't what it looks like. We were just swimming. You know how the press is—always making something out of nothing."

"I thought that must be the case," her father said. "You're not the type to get caught up in all of that Hollywood nonsense. You have too good of a head on your shoulders to get involved with someone like Tessa Flanagan."

Eleanor was sitting on a stool at the kitchen counter in the carriage house, which was larger and better furnished than any of her prior residences. "Actually, Tessa is fairly intelligent herself," she said, trying not to bristle at her father's words. "She's got enough books to make a pack-ox sweat." Ama had described Tessa's library in these terms once, and the phrase had stuck in Eleanor's head.

"Oh," her father said. "I didn't mean to imply that she wasn't intelligent. I'm sure she'd have to be to accomplish what she has. I just meant that the movie business has a reputation for sleaziness, and you are as far from sleazy as they come. If I can objectively say that about my own daughter."

Through the window, Eleanor could see Tessa and Laya taking up residence on the patio with books and an Uno deck. She rubbed her forehead, glancing away from the tranquil scene. Her father couldn't help that he'd been born in Vermont and had only ever moved a single state away to attend Dartmouth back when it was still an all-male bastion.

"Anyway, Dad," she said, "I'll let you get back to work. I have a few more calls to make this morning."

"I imagine you do," he said. "Thanks for checking in, honey. Take care."

"You, too." She was actually relieved to hang up, she realized. She didn't seem to know how to talk to him anymore.

Had he changed, or had she? They still hadn't talked about his relationship with Emma Barnes yet, though Julia had told him she knew. Was he waiting for her to bring it up? If so, he'd be waiting a long time.

She looked out at the patio again. It was another beautiful day, still cool this early. But it was always cooler up here in the hills, with plentiful trees and a steady breeze to keep the hot air from settling the way it did down in the city. Not such a bad place to be marooned temporarily. Not such bad company, either, she thought, eyeing Tessa in her skimpy bikini. Not that Laya wasn't a joy to be with, but Eleanor couldn't wait to be alone with her mother again.

The other calls had gone more smoothly. Sasha had said, "Told you so," and "Invite me to dinner when this breaks." Eleanor had a hunch that Sasha and Tessa would like each other. She hoped so, anyway—Sasha was notoriously stingy with praise for Eleanor's girlfriends. Not that anyone was anyone's girlfriend, she'd reminded herself, and dialed the next number. To her sister and a handful of friends back east, she'd hedged that she wasn't sure where she and Tessa were headed. She'd also sworn the people closest to her to secrecy, and warned that they might be contacted by reporters once the press figured out who she was.

This was accomplished by the end of that first day. Somebody somewhere let it be known that the woman in the photo was Laya's nanny, Eleanor Chapin, a thirty-three year old school teacher from Boston. Within hours, her senior picture from Smith had made its way into the news cycle, accompanied by an article about her college years. One of her exes (though which one was unclear) had apparently come forward and claimed that Eleanor's name had been linked romantically with more than her fair share of fellow students. In other words, the article all but stated, Eleanor was a lesbian slut who had somehow managed to worm her way into the Flanagan household and seduce her wealthy employer.

"You don't believe that, do you?" Eleanor asked Tessa worriedly that night. They were reclining in Tessa's bed on top of the covers, Eleanor's laptop propped up on a cushion between them. The browser window was tuned to People.com, where the story of their alleged affair was being updated every few hours.

"Of course not," Tessa said, rubbing the back of Eleanor's neck. Her voice was soft, her fingers gentle. "I asked you to come work for me, remember? If anyone's to blame, it's Ama and her compulsive matchmaking."

Eleanor closed the laptop and set it aside. "No wonder you stayed in the closet. I know you said the press would be bad, but it's really, really awful. I'm so sorry."

"Please," Tessa said dismissively. "I've had much worse said about me. It's you I'm worried about." She hesitated. "You know, we could make it go away pretty easily."

"What do you mean?" Eleanor rested her chin on her upraised knee.

"Well, I could deny that anything is going on between us. You know, pretend I'm dating someone else. As in, a man. Michael and Melody tried to convince me to let them round up a beard. There are always actors willing to lend their name to the closet cause. No publicity is bad publicity, and all that."

It hadn't occurred to Eleanor that Tessa's publicist and agent would try to convince her to shore up her closet walls, but of course they would. "What did you say?"

"I told them I don't want to hide who I am anymore." She shrugged and picked at a seam on the comforter cover. "But at the same time, this whole thing isn't exactly fair to you. You've done nothing wrong and the press is already painting you as some kind of sexual predator. Me staying silent is like throwing blood in the water, and it's only going to get worse. I would understand if you wanted it to stop."

Silence, to Eleanor, seemed like the opposite of coming out. But not to the press, and that was apparently what mattered. She reached out and covered Tessa's hand. "I don't need it to stop. I've been out since I was eighteen, and remember, I'm a Vermonter. I can take it if you can."

"Oh yeah?" Tessa smiled a little, turning her hand over to stroke Eleanor's suggestively. "I think I can take it."

The sultry tone struck an answering chord in Eleanor, and she caught Tessa's wrist, tugging her closer. "What else can you take?" she asked. Maybe the press was right. Something about Tessa did seem to bring out the seductress in her.

Tessa pulled her wrist free and eased on top of Eleanor. "I'll just have to show you," she murmured, and leaned forward to nibble one of Eleanor's earlobes.

Eleanor closed her eyes and gave herself over to the desire that shot through her at Tessa's slightest touch. Who really cared about the press anyway? Just then, made-up stories of her past and present seemed too far away to matter.

Over the next few days, though, as the media continued to work itself into a frenzy over the first-ever outing of an A-list movie star and the stories began to pile up, Eleanor wondered if she should reconsider her initial disregard for the power of the printed word. Once the lesbian seducer angle had appeared, suddenly there were quotes from co-workers Eleanor had never met recounting stories of her near-legendary promiscuity and suggesting that perhaps she should never have been allowed near children.

This last insinuation hurt the most, probably because it touched a nerve every gay teacher she'd ever met possessed—the *If you're a sexual deviant, you must be a child molester* nerve. The problem with that, of course, was the assumption that homosexuality was a form of sexual deviance, that consenting sex between adults could somehow be compared to pedophilia. She wasn't sure who had started the horrible urban legend that a majority of pedophiles were gay (the Catholic Church? Right wing fundies?), but she did know that studies revealed conclusively that most pedophiles were in fact straight married men with wives and children of their own. Unfortunately, the media and the general public both seemed willfully ignorant of this fact.

Even more frustrating, Eleanor was powerless to respond to her detractors in the press. All she could do was write scathing letters to the editor in her head about journalistic responsibility and professional ethics. Not at all satisfying, really, and as the articles mounted up, she could feel her sense of humor threatening to go MIA. Perhaps permanently.

On day three of the siege, as she and Tessa had begun to refer to it, she brought her laptop out onto the patio after breakfast. While Laya colored and Tessa read (she was rereading *Emma* now too), Eleanor spent an hour skimming the latest lies and bemoaning the new unflattering photos the press had managed to unearth overnight. When she released a particularly disgusted sigh at the sight of her junior high school self in overalls, pigtails and braces (where had they gotten *that*?), Tessa lowered her book.

"You have to stop doing this to yourself, Elle."

"I'm not doing it. They are!" she said, scowling at the computer screen.

"Do you want some advice from someone who's been there?"

Reluctantly Eleanor looked up at her. "What?"

"Sometimes the best way to handle this situation is to institute a media ban. Just ignore it. They're going to say whatever they want and there's nothing you can do about it—except choose not to listen."

Eleanor wasn't sure she could stick to such a plan, or even that she wanted to. The photos and articles were like a car wreck she couldn't help staring at as she passed. "What does a 'media ban' entail, exactly?"

Until the entertainment press tide shifted, Tessa told her, she should read only books and non-current magazines and watch only DVDs and the occasional pre-screened episode of Ellen, Jon Stewart or Stephen Colbert, their mutually favorite television shows. Other than that, she could check her e-mail but not any online news sites.

Eleanor pursed her lips. Maybe being out of the loop would be better than finding out just how low *ET* or *Star* could sink. Tessa had been a Hollywood star for a long time. Surely she knew what she was talking about.

She closed her computer. "Okay, I'll try it. On one condition."

"What's that?"

"You monitor the news and let me know if there's anything I absolutely have to know about—you know, like peace in the Middle East or a cure for cancer."

"Deal," Tessa said, and held out her hand.

Eleanor shook it, holding on to her fingers longer than was necessary. They shared an intimate smile over Laya's head, and Eleanor felt her mouth go dry at the look in Tessa's eyes. So far, she had yet to sleep in the carriage house, a trend she was more than happy to continue.

With the media prohibition in place, their days took on a comfortable routine. Each morning they rose and made breakfast and checked to see if the piranhas were still circling the estate. They always were, so the next step was to set a plan for another day at home. She and Tessa actively worked to tire Laya out so that she wouldn't be bored being stuck at home, with the added bonus that their evenings could be about them. Unfortunately, swimming and playing soccer and riding bikes in the driveway tired them out too, so they ended up falling asleep after making love and dragging themselves out of bed early each morning to keep Laya in the dark about their relationship. Or, at least, Eleanor dragged herself out of bed and out of the house. She didn't forget the alarm again.

In the middle of the day, when Laya took her naps, or sometimes when she was paddling happily around the shallow end of the pool or otherwise entertaining herself, Eleanor and Tessa talked. Conversation flowed easily, and they rarely broached the same topic twice. It was as if the finite amount of time they had to spend together meant that they had to learn everything they could about each other while they had the chance.

"Can I ask you something?" Eleanor said one day as they strolled through the garden, Laya running ahead to climb her favorite eucalyptus tree.

"Sure."

She checked to make sure Laya was out of earshot. She was. "Were any of the stories about your supposed relationships true?"

"No," Tessa said, "unless you're talking about Nadine Simmons."

Eleanor sat down on a bench near the koi pond, one eye on Laya hanging from a tree branch a little ways away. "Never heard of her."

"Her father is Bradley Simmons, the producer."

"Him I've heard of. So you and she were together?"

"For a little while, right before I had Laya."

"What does that mean if you were in the closet? What kinds of things could you do? Other than the obvious," she added, frowning as Tessa lifted an eyebrow suggestively.

"We double-dated sometimes with Will and whatever guy he happened to be dating. And sometimes we went to parties for closeted Hollywood people, thrown by other closeted Hollywood people. Those were fun. Everyone signed NDAs, but there was still this sense of danger, even if it was basically a mirage."

"Wait, like in the *L Word*?" Eleanor asked. "Like when Tasha and Alice went to that party at the producer's house and Alice took the picture of the NBA point guard on her phone?"

"Right. Only in reality, that never would have happened. The parties I went to all had a security checkpoint. You had to leave your electronics at home or check them at the door."

"You're kidding," Eleanor said. "That is so crazy."

"L.A. is its own worst nightmare," Tessa said, then winced suddenly.

Eleanor followed her gaze to see Laya hanging upside down from the branch by her knees. "Careful," she heard Tessa murmur under her breath, but she stayed where she was, letting her daughter explore her limits. Eleanor admired her restraint. Not all parents were able to rein themselves in. Would she be able to do so herself if she were to have a baby? She pictured an infant with her eyes and Tessa's hair, then blinked the image away. Not even biologically possible, just to begin with.

"Did you ever date any other actresses?" she asked, returning to the subject of Tessa's romantic history.

"Occasionally, but probably not anyone you would know," Tessa said, much too vaguely for Eleanor's taste. "By the way, most women in Hollywood prefer the term *actor*. You know, levels the playing field. As if that's how the movie business works." She shook her head. "The sad thing is, the casting couch stereotype is still alive and kicking. Or blowing, as the case may be."

Eleanor recoiled slightly, her Puritan New England upbringing raising its ugly head.

"Sorry," Tessa said. "I didn't mean to be so crude."

"That's okay, I didn't mean to be such a prude."

"I would hardly call you a prude," Tessa said, her voice low and sexy.

Eleanor felt her face grow warm. Naturally, Laya picked that moment to run over, an orange in hand. "Look what I picked," she said, and wormed her way between them on the bench. "Mom, can you peel it for me?"

"Sure," Tessa said, still smiling slyly at Eleanor.

Tessa was enjoying this, Eleanor thought, and tilted her head against the back of the bench, squinting at the sunlight cutting through the trees. Then again, so was she. This was paradise, despite the very public assassination of her character currently taking place in the world beyond the walls encircling the estate. Soon enough the press would lose interest, Tessa kept assuring her, and they could go back to normal life. The thing was, Eleanor wasn't sure what normal life looked like anymore. Would she have to go back to Sasha's when the paparazzi decamped from Tessa's driveway?

She closed her eyes and listened to Laya and Tessa chatting beside her. She was in trouble, exceedingly pleasurable trouble that had little to do with the lies being spread about her in the real world.

Whenever the press decided to invade her personal life, Tessa usually felt trapped, immobilized by the reach of camera lenses and bloggers' posts. But this particular scandal afforded her the opportunity to extend her vacation with Eleanor and Laya. Not that they told Laya the real reason they were holed up at home. Laya seemed so happy to have them to herself that the fuzzy reason they offered her for the photographers' encampment—that someone had told a lie about Tessa and Eleanor and the photographers were there trying to find out if it was true—seemed to suffice.

Tessa had rarely had a chance to spend this much quality time with her daughter, not since the first year of Laya's life. As a new mother, she'd been enamored with every move her baby made, lulled by the rhythm of new life when all she had to think about was food and sleep and poop and food and more sleep. This time, though, instead of hanging out with her newborn child, Tessa was being given the opportunity to get to know Eleanor better.

One afternoon while Laya took her daily nap, the two women lay together on the couch in the family room. Tessa was remembering the previous night's activities. Eleanor certainly knew what she was doing when it came to a woman's body. But then she'd apparently had plenty of experience, judging from some of the stories she'd related.

"You came out at Smith, didn't you?" Tessa asked, tracing the map of freckles along Eleanor's forearm. Her skin was so soft.

"Yeah—first semester freshman year."

"And at a women's college. That must have been fun."

"It was," Eleanor admitted, smiling nostalgically. "First semester, I started to wonder about my real reasons for picking Smith when this senior field hockey player caught my eye. She was a total BDOC—Big Dyke on Campus—who lived in the house next door."

"House?" Tessa repeated, resting her cheek against Eleanor's shoulder.

"That's what they call dorms at Smith. Anyway, so Becca, this field hockey player, notices me mooning over her at a house party the second week of school and invites me upstairs to her single for a backrub."

"Smooth."

"That's what I thought. She put Enya on the stereo and started rubbing my back. But then she stops and says it would be better if I took my shirt off."

Tessa snickered. "And you fell for that?"

"Honestly, I didn't know what she had in mind until she asked if she could kiss me. I was like, 'Um, okay.' And then I was in heaven for the next two weeks, until she ditched me for a soccer player."

"Poor girl," Tessa said, nibbling her ear and trying to dispel the image of Eleanor being seduced by a faceless field hockey player with muscular thighs and a plaid kilt.

"Sucked at the time," Eleanor said, slipping her hand around to stroke the edge of Tessa's breast. "But it was pretty typical for Smith."

"What do you mean?" Tessa moved Eleanor's hand to a less provocative spot. Laya had been asleep for a while already, and all they needed was for her to sneak up on them and ask what they were doing.

"Everyone knew Smith's reputation," Eleanor explained, "which meant that everything you did was seen through this lens of sexuality. Not that I minded. But there was just so much gossip, especially about anyone who was openly gay."

Sounded like Hollywood. Tessa hesitated, then plowed ahead with the question that had been on her mind all week. "Have you dated a lot?"

Eleanor cast her a sideways glance. "Depends on what you mean by *a lot*."

"Well, how many women have you been with?"

"I don't know. I haven't kept track."

Either she wasn't being honest or she had been with too many women to count. Tessa found the latter option much more worrisome. "What are we talking—twenty, fifty, a hundred?"

"God, no!" Eleanor exclaimed. "I told you, the press was making that stuff up. I've probably only slept with like fifteen women, total."

"Fifteen?" Tessa repeated. Eleanor's libidinous adventures made her own handful of affairs seem tame.

"Your name has been linked with quite a few fellow celebrities, I'd like to point out."

"The difference is that I wasn't having sex with any of them, idiot."

"Oh. Well, enough about me," Eleanor said quickly. "What about you? When did you realize you liked girls?"

"Here in L.A.," Tessa said, willingly changing the subject. She wasn't sure she wanted to hear more about Eleanor's dating past. Ever. "My first year out here, I was waiting tables and taking a couple of classes at UCLA. Over the summer I met this woman, Tory, a sophomore theater major from Seattle. She's the one who convinced me to take my first acting class."

"So acting wasn't your idea?"

"Never even occurred to me. But when I took that class with Tory, I realized that acting was like being invisible, only the opposite somehow."

Eleanor stroked her hair. "And this appealed to you?"

"I seemed to be good at it." She shrugged. "It's easy to like something you're good at."

"How did you get your first big role?"

"This girl at UCLA convinced her cousin who was an agent to come to one of our school productions." She paused, remembering the night the agent, a junior associate in Michael's firm, had approached her backstage. Remembered, too, the incredulity in Tory's eyes followed quickly by crushing disappointment. Acting had been her dream, not Tessa's. "Tory couldn't handle that I was the one getting offered the break. She left for New York after college to try to work on Broadway."

"Wait—are you talking about Victoria Bradshaw?"

Tessa nodded. "We're still friends. I was at her wedding last fall."

"Wow, Victoria Bradshaw and you. If I weren't a little jealous, I would totally think that was hot." She shook her head. "Anyway, it sounds like if you weren't gay, you never would have started acting."

"I hadn't thought of it quite like that."

"That's what I'm here for. Well, not only that." She pulled Tessa on top of her. "What was your first time with a woman like?"

Tessa placed her hands against the couch on either side of Eleanor's head. She could already feel her pulse rising, the flow of blood increasing to certain sensitive body parts. "Well," she said softly, pressing her hips into Eleanor's, "she came back to my apartment with me after class one night and we drank a bottle of wine. And then she kissed me."

"Like this?" Eleanor asked, tugging Tessa down and covering her mouth with her own.

They kissed slowly and lingeringly, the taste and feel of

Eleanor's mouth familiar to Tessa after nearly a week of nights spent together. Yet each kiss still felt different from the last. What didn't change was the electric effect Eleanor had on her. Tessa felt her body curving willingly against Eleanor's, yielding to her.

"Then what?" Eleanor whispered against her mouth.

Tessa tried to catch her breath. "Then she lifted my shirt over my head..."

"Like this?" Eleanor tugged at the hem of her tank top.

But as the thin material slid upward, Tessa pictured Laya's face. "We can't," she said, holding her shirt in place. "Laya—"

"—is asleep, and if she gets up, we'll hear it on the monitor," Eleanor said, reaching for the zipper on Tessa's capris.

With supreme effort, she pulled herself out of Eleanor's arms and stood up, running a hand across her hair. "I told you, I don't want to risk her finding out like that."

Eleanor sat up, rubbing her eyes. "No, you're right. I'm sorry. I just get next to you and... Well, you know."

"I do." Tessa dropped down beside her on the couch again, careful not to sit too close. "Tell you what. Tonight we'll send Laya to bed early and I'll make it up to you. Sound good?"

"Better than good. In the meantime, I think I'd better cool off." She pecked her on the cheek chastely and retreated.

As Eleanor disappeared through the patio doors, Tessa remained where she was on the couch, staring into space. Eleanor had led such a different life. Close-knit family, elite Eastern college, a plethora of girlfriends and a ten-year teaching career. What would she think if she knew what kind of background Tessa came from?

I can't tell her, she thought. There was too much at stake. But keeping her past a secret was starting to feel like a burden she might not want to carry much longer.

Outside she heard a splash. Rising, she walked out onto the patio and watched as Eleanor cut a clean swath through the pool, arms and legs churning steadily.

CHAPTER SEVENTEEN

The paparazzi seemed especially determined this time, Tessa couldn't help but notice. It had been a week already, and still they prowled the gates looking for a way onto the estate. As if that would happen. She was tempted to have Melody set up a tell-all interview with *People*, complete with photos of her and Eleanor with their arms around each other, just to piss off the slimy bastards camped out on her driveway. But she was pretty sure Melody would have refused.

The more malicious news stories had bothered Eleanor, Tessa knew. She remembered in the early days of her own career, back before she'd had Melody and Michael watching out for her, how devastated she'd been when she read a fabricated article that claimed she had to be homeschooled because she'd been unable to keep up with her public school peers in Brooklyn. The source of this report was an anonymous school official who probably didn't even exist, not that she could convince anyone else of that fact.

Overall, though, Eleanor was handling the storm better than Tessa would have expected. No one had ever mentioned Eleanor's name in print before, let alone put her photo in a national publication. This was her fifteen minutes of fame and despite some of the low blows, she seemed to be taking it in stride, even, on occasion, intrigued by the attention. Perhaps if Tessa had had Eleanor's background or had come to fame later in life, she wouldn't have been so vulnerable to the capricious nature of the entertainment press—lauding her one moment for her talent and progressive politics, knocking her down the next as a closet case unable to accept herself for who she really was. According to the current mood of the media, it had taken her daughter's nanny to get Tessa to overcome her seething self-hatred and internalized homophobia.

"It's such bullshit," she told Will when he stopped by for a training session a little over a week into the siege. They were stretching out in the gym that occupied one-half of her garage, a two-story structure that housed her cars and a game room in addition to the four hundred square foot workout facility. Sometimes she felt as if she had spent half her life in this room. Her body had been her job for so long that over the years, exercising and eating right had become well-ingrained habits. At this point, she was addicted to the endorphins Will was an expert at inducing.

"What's bullshit?" Will asked as he leaned against her shoulders from behind, stretching her lower back.

"The trash they're writing about me. I'm starting to think I should go on national TV and tell the truth about Hollywood."

"You mean name names?"

"Not that. More like I've been happily queer my entire adult life and the studio heads were the ones who were less than happy about it." Tessa leaned forward, feeling her hip flexors tighten. They'd been seeing more action recently than usual.

"Don't you think Americans already know that some of their action stars and romantic leads are homos, but they just prefer to pretend otherwise?"

"I don't have any idea what Americans may or may not know. At this point, I've been away from real life for so long I don't even know what goes on out there."

"You're probably better off that way," he said. "After all, fifty percent of 'real Americans' voted for Dubya."

"Not so fast, Fox News. Fifty percent of *presidential election voters* voted for Dubya. Allegedly. Although there was no paper trail in several states, so even those numbers might have been made up."

"Whatever." He grinned at her. "Come on, I have a new circuit I want you to try. Time to mess with your muscle memory."

Will was Tessa's best friend in Hollywood. They'd met when she was nineteen, new to the movie business and still in the process of losing her final ten pounds of "baby fat," as he'd kindly referred to it. He was young then too, a newly minted personal trainer just starting out at one of Hollywood's trendy clubs. Now he ran his own celebrity training business and gym, and Tessa was lucky to see him twice a month when they were both in town.

As she ran through the circuit he'd set up, Will filled her in on various celebrity reactions to her being outed. Some people were happy for her, but the predominant reaction seemed to be coming from the duck and cover quarter, stars who immediately wanted nothing to do with her in case proximity caused the press to look more closely at their personal lives.

"Oh, darn," Tessa panted, throwing a medicine ball back at Will and dropping into push-up formation. "I'm so hurt."

"Straighten your back," he said. "Now hold it… No cheating."

"I'm not, bitch," she said, and jumped to her feet in time to catch the medicine ball and fire it back at him before resuming the push-up position.

"You're looking very flexible," Will said a little while later. "Is it the nanny keeping you fit?"

"Don't you wish you knew," Tessa said, glad her face was already flushed from exertion. Was blushing some sort of contagious condition? She and Will had always talked about their sex lives—at least, back in the day before he got married and she had Laya and they both retired from the scene. For a time, the press had been convinced that Will was the father of her child, a fact that still amused his partner, Scott, a special education teacher from Pasadena.

"Wait, are you blushing?" Will asked. "Must be serious. She's not your typical slutty starlet, is she?"

"No," Tessa said as she performed lunges in a line across the room, a ten-pound dumbbell in each hand, "she's not. And it isn't serious. It can't be. She's leaving L.A. at the end of the summer."

He whistled, lunging next to her in a parallel line. "Bummer. So why don't you do something about it?"

"Like what?"

"Like asking her to stay? In case you haven't noticed, you're a fairly good catch."

"I can't," she said, frowning. "It's complicated."

"The good ones always are," Will said. "Straighten your shoulders, girl. No cheating."

"I don't cheat, unlike some people. How's that open marriage thing going?"

"It's mostly open in theory. Neither of us has been attracted to anyone else for a while."

"My God, is the famous Will Knight settling down? Or are you just getting old?"

"If I'm old, you are too," he said, reaching the far wall before she did. "Just for that, I'm going to make you wall-sit for an extra minute."

"Aw, man," she said dutifully, knowing he liked to hear his clients complain.

Later, as they pedaled a pair of stationary bikes to cool down, she asked, "How about we both ended up with teachers?"

"Something sexy about do-gooders, I guess."

"Must be." She hesitated. "Does Scott ever ask about your clients? You know, like gossip?"

Will glanced at her. "You know nothing you tell me goes beyond this room, Tess."

"I didn't mean that. I just think it's odd—Eleanor never asks me for dirt on anyone. She knows I know Tom and Kate and

Will and Jada, and everyone else I've worked with over the years, but she doesn't ask me what anyone is like. Doesn't that seem strange?"

Will laughed. "Not at all," he said. "She must have figured out the big secret—stars are just richer, prettier people who aren't necessarily any more interesting than the rest of us."

"Thanks a lot," she said, and threw a hand towel at his shaved head. "Jackass."

"You know you love me. Hey, when the blockade is over, let's have dinner. Scott and I would love to meet this woman."

"Definitely," Tessa said, even as she wondered if they'd have the chance.

That night, after Laya had gone to sleep, Tessa and Eleanor took strawberries and chocolate with them to bed and gorged themselves as they debated politics in their lifetime—the shallowness of the Reagan years when Baby Boomers discovered their capacity for greed; Bush senior's short-lived reign and the first Gulf war; Clinton's decade, a balm to the previous one; and, of course, the recent setback to democracy in America that was George W's legacy.

Tessa told Eleanor that she'd met Obama once at a fundraising dinner. She, like the rest of Hollywood, had been happy to support the young, dynamic politician, though in truth she'd voted for Hillary Clinton in the California primary. Now she wished more than ever Hillary were president. Obama was doing an okay job, considering the state of the nation he'd inherited from his predecessor. Tessa just didn't think he was living up to some of the promises he'd made, particularly to queer Americans.

"I agree," Eleanor said, sucking on a strawberry until its juice leaked from the corner of her mouth. "He's completely behind the curve when it comes to gay and lesbian issues. But other than that, he ran as a centrist Democrat so I'm not sure why people are surprised he's leading as a centrist Democrat. What's he like in person? Is he really as dorky as he seems?"

"He is. But he's married to this awesome woman, so you know there must be something more there." She paused. "You know, that's the first time you've asked me about anyone famous. Why don't you ever ask about other celebrities?"

Eleanor shrugged, staring at her with those clear, green-blue eyes. "Obama's the president, so of course I want to know about him. But you're the only celebrity I care about."

She meant it, Tessa could tell. Leaning forward, she licked the strawberry juice from Eleanor's mouth. "Good."

The media siege unofficially ended two days later when a young up-and-coming actor overdosed on prescription drugs. In the space of an afternoon, all attention immediately shifted to the tragedy of his untimely death, and Tessa and Eleanor's romantic involvement was relegated to pop culture's back burner. Still simmering, according to Tessa, just no longer boiling over. Eleanor was relieved to see an end to the tales that had been spun about her (depending on who you asked, she was both predator and victim) but also disappointed, as she'd known she would be, that their extendo-vacation was finally, unavoidably over.

That night after dinner, Eleanor took Laya upstairs for her bedtime story. When Laya begged for a second story, Eleanor quickly acquiesced. She even read a third book without being asked. By the time she finished, Laya's snores were echoing through the tree house bunk bed, amplified by the hollow faux trunks on either end. Eleanor tucked the blanket around her, placed the books back on the large shelf under the window and got her a glass of water. Then she stood in the doorway watching Laya sleep.

Tessa found her there a few minutes later. "Everything okay?" she asked, peering over Eleanor's shoulder into the room lit by a nightlight painted to look like a tropical frog.

"Fine," Eleanor said, not meeting her eyes.

"Come downstairs, then," Tessa said, twining her fingers through Eleanor's. "I made us a sundae, and it's melting."

Eleanor held tightly to Tessa's hand and followed her downstairs, trying to ignore the words that kept looping through her head: *Now what?*

The ice cream sundae was delicious, and they took turns kissing chocolate sauce from each other's mouths. Eleanor was beginning to think that maybe things could just stay the way they were when Tessa leaned away from the kitchen island and eyed her.

"You're not going to mention it, are you?"

"What?" Eleanor stalled.

"You know—the fact that you're finally free to leave."

"Oh, that. I was going to bring it up. I assume you need to get back to work?"

"I have a meeting in the city tomorrow morning." Tessa licked a dollop of hot fudge from her spoon. "So what's the deal, Elle—do you want to start going back to Sasha's again at night?"

Tessa was in acting mode, her eyes blank and unreadable, her smile of a distinctly professional variety. Eleanor looked down at the ice cream dish. "I can do that. I'll just call her tomorrow and let her know."

Silence hung over the room.

"I'm not saying I want that," Tessa clarified after a moment, "not unless you do, in which case I completely understand."

Always in the past Eleanor had scoffed at friends who moved in together at the start of a relationship, but this situation was different. They weren't really living together. Anyway, it wouldn't be forever. Couldn't be. "I kind of like things the way they are. What about you?"

"I like having you here," Tessa said. "But I don't want you to do anything you don't want to do. Technically, I'm still your boss."

Smiling a little, Eleanor leaned forward and kissed the corner of her mouth. "You go ahead and keep telling yourself that."

Tessa rolled her eyes, looking for a moment just like her daughter. "You know what I mean."

"Don't worry. If I don't want to do something, you'll know."

"Really? Just a second ago you were all set to go back to Sasha's. I thought you said Vermonters were tough."

"We are. If you need someone to climb a mountain or make maple syrup, I'm your girl. But emotional risk-taking? Not so much."

"Good to know," Tessa said, and dug her spoon into the sundae.

Normal life, which Eleanor hadn't been able to imagine while they were in siege mode, commenced the following morning when Tessa headed into the city after breakfast, leaving Eleanor to entertain Laya. The first thing they did was drive to Malibu for a long overdue playdate with Rayann, the six-year-old daughter of the woman who had produced the comic book trilogy that launched Tessa's action film career. While Tessa and Rayann's mother, Margot Trivers, were often too busy to interact themselves, their daughters usually got together once a week when both families were in town. Today Eleanor watched the two girls while Rayann's nanny Olivia "ran some errands." After a round of badminton, a game of indoor bowling, grilled cheese sandwiches for lunch, and an extended afternoon dollhouse session, Olivia returned and Eleanor drove Laya home, reaching the house just before Tessa arrived with plenty of time to hang out and make dinner before Laya's bedtime.

The next morning they got up and did it all over again, minus the trip to Rayann's house. Soon the days settled into a predictable routine. Eleanor rose each morning and breakfasted with the Flanagans and kissed Tessa goodbye (when Laya wasn't looking) and planned a day that involved entertainment and education in equal measure for Laya, who had officially assumed the role of her favorite kid ever. Their post-siege summertime adventures included day trips to the San Diego Wild Animal Park (twice); Disneyland (only once—honestly, Laya was more interested in non-human-made attractions, she confided to Eleanor); Santa Barbara's Zoological Gardens and Andree Clark Bird Refuge; and assorted other nearby natural landmarks and wild places they researched together online.

At night, after Laya went to bed, often so did Eleanor and Tessa. Occasionally they lay in bed just talking—about the foundation, about Laya, about their lives before they met. Other nights, they stripped down quickly, barely waiting to shed their clothes. As they moved together in the dark, skin sliding against skin, lips and hands caressing every curve and indentation,

Eleanor still couldn't quite believe her luck. Tessa became more and more beautiful to her as the weeks passed, not less. Each night when Tessa's car sounded in the driveway, Eleanor's heartbeat speeded up a little and she waited for the moment when Tessa would enter the house, a matching smile on her face and in her eyes. Eleanor knew the honeymoon period was working its mushy magic on them, but sometimes she suspected the reason they slept each night wrapped around each other might be the threat of separation shadowing them. The end of the summer loomed in the background of every interaction, the elephant in the room that neither of them seemed to want to bring up.

One Monday shortly after the Fourth of July, Laya had another playdate at Rayann's house. This time, Eleanor dropped Laya off at the Trivers' residence and poked around Rodeo Drive by herself, wondering if anyone would recognize her. No one seemed to, probably because in her ponytail, capris and cropped tee she looked nothing like she had in the photos the press had gotten their hands on. Her twenty-something buzz cut, flannel shirts, and the popular baggy jeans of East Coast dykedom were a far cry from her current bland private school teacher ensemble.

A little before noon, she left Beverly Hills and headed up the 101 to Universal City, where Sasha was waiting for her outside the shiny silver and glass building that housed Martin, Felpausch, and Stein.

"How's Martin Fel?" Eleanor asked as Sasha slipped into the front seat of Tessa's Hybrid Escape.

"Same old same old." Sasha gave her a quick hug and pulled her seatbelt on. "Rolling in environmentally friendly style, I see."

"I had to drop Laya off in Malibu and this gets better mileage than my car."

"Right," Sasha said, managing to imbue the single word with an impressive amount of sarcasm.

"You're just jealous. Where to for lunch?"

They settled on Indian food and Sasha guided her to a restaurant in nearby Studio City. They picked a quiet table in the back well away from the sunlight streaming in the front windows, ordered a feast of their favorite foods to share, and set about getting caught up. They'd e-mailed and talked on the phone the last few weeks, but that didn't really count, they agreed.

"What's it like being involved with Tessa Flanagan?" Sasha asked.

"Incredible," Eleanor said, tearing apart a piece of steaming naan. "She's so different from what I expected. She's a really good person, you know? She gives away obscene amounts of money every year, and not just for the tax benefits. In fact, she's working on creating this charitable foundation so that she can give away obscene amounts of other people's money, too."

"She is? I'd heard rumors she was working on something, but nothing substantial."

"Please don't mention it to anyone yet," Eleanor said, pretty sure she'd just broken the terms of the NDA she'd signed. "You have no idea how paranoid she is about her privacy. I can't say I entirely understand it, but then I haven't been living under a microscope my entire adult life."

"Just the last few weeks," Sasha said. "But don't worry. My lips are sealed. I would hate to get you in trouble with your girlfriend."

"She's not my girlfriend," Eleanor said.

"No? Then what is she?"

"We haven't really talked about it. Anyway, how's work going? Any exciting cases you're not allowed to talk about?"

"As it happens, I am working on a case that involves a certain high-profile television journalist." And she was off and running on ambiguous professional gossip.

Their entrees arrived, and they chatted about legal issues while they ate, cataloging the GLBT and other civil rights measures on the local and national fronts. Sasha was a firm supporter of GLBT rights, but she still bristled at times when Eleanor compared the battle for gay and lesbian rights to the black civil rights movement. Recently, though, she'd been willing to acknowledge that there were, in fact, more than a few similarities between the two.

"How's Wisconsin for queer folks?" she asked at one point, dipping a chunk of naan into her chicken biryani.

"It's the Midwest, so not great. There's a constitutional

amendment as well as a law on the books against gay marriage."

"Sounds like overkill."

"Some of us don't like to use the words 'kill' and 'homo' together," Eleanor said in her cheerful teacher's voice.

"My bad. What's the deal with grad school, anyway? You've barely mentioned it. Do you have a place to live yet?"

"No. I need to get out to Madison to look for an apartment, but to be honest, I haven't been thinking that much about it. Can I tell you something?"

"Of course," Sasha said. "You know anything you tell me stays between us. Probably. Most likely."

"I'm serious."

"Gotcha. Serious it is," she said, frowning in mock concentration.

"It's just that, well, I've been having second thoughts about going back to school."

"I don't blame you. It's a massive amount of work. But what brought this on? Miss Flanagan and her cushy lifestyle, by any chance?"

Eleanor shook her head, toying with her fork. "I know that's what it looks like, but I think it's more about my mom. I'm just not sure the old life plan fits anymore. Does that make sense?"

"Of course it does. People change, Elle. You decided you wanted to be a psychologist when you were nineteen. I remember—I was there. But I've also seen what it's been like for you since then. No one would blame you if you didn't want to spend the rest of your life taking care of other people."

"It's not that. I like taking care of people. But my sister said something when we were driving out here that made me realize maybe I had spent all of this energy on other families and not enough on my own."

Sasha frowned again, this time for real. "Don't let Julia revise history. Your parents are the ones who pushed you away after you came out. You were there for them as much they would let you be. I know it and you know it. Or at least, you should."

Eleanor felt her throat tighten as they sat at their corner table, flanked by murals of elephants and pre-colonial India. "Thanks, Sash."

Her friend reached across the table and squeezed her hand. "You don't have to thank me. I'm more your sister than that little soccer-playing kiss-ass, anyway."

"I know." She turned her palm up to Sasha's. "Look out—someone might see you holding hands with me and suddenly you'll be the reason Tessa and I break up next month."

Glancing around surreptitiously, Sasha pulled her hand back. "I think we're safe. So you guys are breaking up when you leave for Madison, then?"

"We haven't discussed that, either."

"Better get on it. The summer's half over."

"I know. I just have no idea what to say to her. I know what I want—"

"Which is?" Sasha prompted.

Eleanor released a breath. "A real relationship, as far-fetched as that might sound."

"It's not far-fetched at all. It has to mean something that you're the only woman she's ever been with openly. Or semi-openly."

"Maybe, but that doesn't mean she wants a future with me. She can be pretty hard to read."

"Duh, Elle, she's an actor. But what do you have to lose by telling her what you want? Better to lay your cards on the table now than, say, five years down the road after you've already wasted your best years on the cheating bastard. Oh, wait," she added, "sorry, that was me."

"You didn't waste your best years on Ben. Or not all of them. Kidding," she said, as Sasha glared at her. "Thanks for the advice, as usual, and for listening. Now, what's new with you? Any potentials out there on the horizon? It's been almost a year since you and Ben broke up. Don't you think it's time the mourning period ended?"

Sasha took a sip of the wine she'd ordered with lunch. "Actually," she said, "there's a new associate at the firm who might have potential."

"That's great," Eleanor exclaimed. "What's he like? Where's he from?"

"He's black, for once," Sasha said (she often blamed Smith's monochromatic student population for her post-graduate tendency to date white men), "and you're not going to believe this, but he's from Orange County. We think our parents might know each other."

"And you're okay with that?" Eleanor asked carefully. Her former roommate had long avoided romantic entanglements with anyone of whom her parents might possibly approve.

"I am," Sasha said, sounding surprised by this fact herself. "Told you, Elle. People do change."

"Apparently."

After lunch, Eleanor dropped Sasha back at work and checked her watch. She still had some time before she had to pick Laya up, so she headed down to Malibu and walked along the beach, dodging scantily clad teenagers and wondering where Tessa's old house was located. Sasha was right. At some point, she and Tessa were going to have to talk about September. But as she thought about declaring what she wanted—a future together, somehow—she also pictured Tessa rejecting the idea out of hand. What if they weren't on the same page? Then what?

She wasn't ready to lose Tessa and Laya, she thought as she walked along the ocean's edge, hands in the pockets of her capris. Not yet. She would have to be ready for that eventuality before she laid her cards on the table. That was the problem with gambling—you could never be sure what the other person was holding.

CHAPTER EIGHTEEN

Everything seemed to be going smoothly. Almost too smoothly, Tessa thought, which made her question when the other shoe would drop. Except she knew which shoe was readying to fall, and the exact date it would plummet out of her life.

The foundation kept Tessa too busy during the day to dwell on the steady approach of summer's end. The consultant she and the Byerlys had hired was helping tremendously. By mid-summer, they had written a mission statement, completed a business plan, and defined specific areas of funding interest. They'd also found an executive director, an experienced (female) professional from Seattle, and hired an attorney to incorporate the foundation and an accountant to oversee finances. In the next ten weeks, the plan was to identify candidates for the board of directors, choose a name, move into new offices downtown, hire staff, create a Web site and begin raising funds. The list sounded daunting to Tessa and the Byerly sisters, but the consultant assured them two and a half months was plenty of time to complete the tasks they'd set for themselves.

Tessa loved what she and the Byerlys were accomplishing, but she loved even more coming home each afternoon to Laya and Eleanor. The moment she walked in the door, Laya would drop whatever she was doing and fling herself into Tessa's arms, and she would kiss her daughter's hair and smile at Eleanor over Laya's head, seeing her own pleasure reflected in those open, blue-green eyes. Eleanor continued to captivate Tessa with her honesty and humor, her ardent responses, her generosity in lovemaking. Though as the summer wore on, they didn't necessarily have to devour one another's bodies as soon as Laya was asleep. While the sex had been remarkable right from the start, it wasn't the only thing between them. For Tessa, at least, it never had been, which was why she was trying so hard to forget about September.

In mid-July, she and Eleanor agreed it was probably time to branch out beyond their domestic bliss and finally have their friends over for dinner. Sasha and Will had been harassing them for weeks now, so they figured they might as well ante up and host a dinner party. For their first foray into public coupledom, the guest list would be small: Sasha and her date, Allen, and Will and his partner, Scott. Laya, meanwhile, would be spending the night at Rayann's house. Margot was out of town (otherwise she and her husband would have rounded out the list), but Olivia, Rayann's nanny, was a close friend of Ama's, and Tessa had no qualms about leaving Laya in her care. For her part, Laya was so excited about the exotic experience of sleeping over at Rayann's house that she quickly got over being left out of the dinner party.

The next to last Saturday of July, Tessa and Eleanor welcomed their guests into the inner lair, Eleanor's nickname for Tessa's house. Sasha and Allen, a fellow associate from her firm, arrived first, and Eleanor ushered them into the kitchen where Tessa had set up a small bar at the island.

"Sasha and Allen, meet Tessa," Eleanor said, smiling a little nervously. She was dressed in gray trousers and a silk shirt of Tessa's that brought out the blue in her eyes.

"Pleasure to finally meet you," Tessa said, setting down a wine rabbit to shake hands with the two attorneys. Allen seemed a bit shy, tugging on his tie as he squeezed her fingers, but Sasha's grip was firm, her eyes inquisitive.

"You too," she said. "Eleanor, of course, has spoken of you often."

Tessa knew the cliché she was expected to offer—*All good things, I hope?*—but she opted for the less schmaltzy, "I've heard a lot about you too."

"You have a beautiful home," Sasha went on.

"Thank you." Hoping she exuded calm, Tessa met the other woman's probing gaze. As Eleanor's closest friend, Sasha would probably be trying to gauge Tessa's worth as a mate, just as Will would be evaluating Eleanor. No pressure, Tessa thought, glad as she often was in social situations that she'd acted for so many years. Projecting fake serenity was a skill that came in mighty handy outside the film world.

As Eleanor opened the oven door to check on the salmon, her former roommate looked over her shoulder.

"What, no stir-fry?" Sasha asked.

Tessa watched in amusement as Eleanor turned and smacked her on the ass. Then the doorbell sounded again, and Tessa excused herself.

"Where's the hunky butler?" Will asked, leaning in to kiss her cheek as he entered the house.

Scott pecked her other cheek. "Don't mind him. He's just having a flashback to the last Chuck Platte party we went to."

Chuck Platte was a notorious flamer who hosted regular boy-only fêtes at his Beverly Hills mansion.

"Sorry to disappoint," Tessa said, accepting the bottle of wine they offered, "but you two are the only hunky homos here tonight."

"Somehow I think we'll make do," Scott said. "Now, where's this woman of yours? Will has been dying to meet the lesbian who could tame you."

"I haven't been tamed," Tessa insisted, but Will just looked at her.

In the kitchen, as Will tasted Eleanor's homemade salad dressing and Scott engaged her in a conversation about charter schools, Tessa felt herself begin to relax. They liked Eleanor, she thought, channeling Sally Field. They really liked her. While the two teachers talked shop, Tessa led Will out onto the patio where Eleanor had sent Sasha and Allen to watch the sunset.

"She's lovely," Will said, following her through the French doors. "So wholesome. So entirely un-L.A."

"My thoughts exactly," Tessa said, guiding him toward Eleanor's friends.

While the sky turned pink overhead, Tessa worked to draw out the lawyer and her date. She knew theirs was a brand-new affair, and that Eleanor wanted her friend to find someone more deserving this time around. As Allen chatted comfortably with flirty, flamboyant Will, Tessa mentally chalked a point in his column. Not all straight men were that secure.

Back inside, conversation seemed to flow easily about the dining room table. Tessa was seated at the end farthest from the kitchen with Allen and Will as her nearest neighbors. As the meal progressed, Tessa noted that not only was Allen more low-key than most of the attorneys she knew (in a good way), he also adored his many nieces and nephews, most of whom lived in Southern California. Eleanor would be happy about that. An only child, Sasha had apparently always wanted a big family. She was also hoping to have kids of her own, according to Eleanor, and soon. A boyfriend who liked kids seemed like a positive step.

At the other end of the table Eleanor was flanked by Sasha and Scott, who talked animatedly with little help from her. Every once in a while she jumped up to grab something from the kitchen, and Tessa would temporarily tune out to watch her puttering about. She was so cute, so concerned that the meal function just right. She needn't have worried. The food appeared to be a hit—the salmon tender and flaky, the apple pepper jelly she had glazed the fish with simultaneously sweet and tangy. Garlic mashed potatoes and a mixed green salad with homemade mustard dressing complemented the fish perfectly, everyone agreed, applauding the chef's culinary skills.

"Elle hasn't always had such refined taste," Sasha said toward the end of dinner, smirking at her former roommate. Eleanor gave her what Tessa clearly recognized as a warning look, but she continued blithely, "In fact, senior year she was known as the Ramen Queen of the on-campus apartment complex."

"Really?" Tessa asked. "What else has she been hiding?"

"Let's see," Sasha said, narrowing her eyes. Eleanor threw her napkin, but her friend just ducked. "Has she mentioned the Radical Debutante Ball junior year, when her girlfriend convinced her they should go dressed only in—"

"Ahem," Eleanor interrupted, standing up. "Would anyone like coffee or dessert? Or maybe you'd like to hear about Sasha's fondness for her favorite newspaper, the *Washington Post*?" she added significantly, staring down her roommate.

At this, Sasha pursed her lips. "Can I at least tell them what Rad Deb is?"

"Knock yourself out," Eleanor said, and started clearing plates.

Tessa rose to help, listening with one ear to Sasha's description of the semi-formal dance the Smith student Lesbian Bisexual Association used to hold downtown each spring at the Hotel Northampton. Rad Deb in the '90s, Sasha said, was an alcohol-infused soap opera that made the *L Word* seem tame. LBA dances in general usually had the best dance music outside of Black Student Alliance parties. Naturally.

Tessa surreptitiously checked Allen's face for any sign of discomfort. Whether he knew it or not, he was the only thoroughly straight person at the table—assuming he was straight. Eleanor had told Tessa about Sasha's college experimentation with one of their classmates, now a staff writer for the *Washington Post*, but Tessa wasn't sure Allen was aware of his date's past. Still, he appeared fine with the topic of Smith lesbians. That, or he was a good actor too.

"Maybe someone should write a script about Smith's Sapphic shenanigans," Will said, grinning wickedly.

Sasha snorted. "I can only imagine the uproar from the alumnae, the old straight white ladies in particular. They already bemoan the fact that lesbians and women of color are allowed to set foot on their sacred campus."

"Seriously?" Scott asked. "But Smith has such a liberal reputation."

"Looks can be deceiving," Eleanor said, carrying coffee and tea to the table. "When we were in school, there were rumors that one of the houses in the quad had it written into their constitution that only white students were allowed to live there."

"Unbelievable," Tessa said, shaking her head. One good thing about fame, she'd noticed, was that people rarely made the comments or asked the questions she'd encountered regularly growing up Asian American, even in a city as diverse as Chicago: "Your English is so good!" and "Where are you from? [Chicago.] No, where are you really from?"

Sasha smiled wryly at her. "Tell me about it."

"Can't we all just get along?" Allen quipped, eliciting groans from the group.

They lingered over coffee, herbal tea and raspberry cheesecake, discussing politics, education and the entertainment industry, which had employed most of the people at the table either directly or indirectly. Sasha, Allen, Will and Tessa knew many of the same people, and they gossiped for a bit about recent scandals around town. Fortunately Eleanor and Tessa's relationship was no longer considered news. Just as there was always a video, a new sex scandal was almost always brewing in Hollywood. Eleanor and Scott, meanwhile, seemed happy comparing notes on public and private school politics.

Only crumbs remained of the cheesecake by the time Sasha took advantage of a lull to announce that she and Allen should be going—they had to be at work early the next morning.

"On a Sunday?" Eleanor asked. "Both of you?"

"I know, God will be pissed," Sasha said, "but the courts wait for no one."

Scott and Will said they should be going too, not because of work but because they were an old married couple no longer accustomed to staying out past midnight. Protests of youth and goodnights were made all around, and Eleanor and Tessa walked the two couples out, waving from the front stoop as

Will's Jeep and Sasha's BMW started their descent down the long driveway.

"Well," Tessa said, turning to Eleanor as their friends' taillights faded into the night, "that was fun."

"Wasn't it?" She was bouncing in place, either from happiness or the two cups of coffee she'd imbibed after dinner, Tessa couldn't be sure.

"You are so cute," she said, smiling.

"I'm pretty sure America would say you're the cute one in this relationship," Eleanor said, then froze, staring at her.

"Is that what we're calling this?" Tessa asked, stepping forward to slide her arms around Eleanor's neck. "The R-word?"

"Well, yeah," Eleanor said, using the simultaneously tough-vulnerable voice that Tessa loved. She set her hands at Tessa's waist and looked down at her. "I think so. What about you?"

"I'm in," Tessa said, and kissed her, trying not to think about countdowns.

Lips tasting of wine and hazelnut, Eleanor backed Tessa inside the house and kicked the front door closed, never breaking the kiss. Then she maneuvered Tessa across the entryway and into the dining room.

As Tessa's legs bumped against the dining table, she broke away, laughing. "What are you up to?"

Eleanor gazed down at her, eyes already darkening. Tessa was still surprised sometimes by how quickly she could shift gears—from nanny to seductress, dinner party hostess to sexpot.

"We're completely alone, finally," she said softly, "and ever since I saw this table I've had this fantasy..."

"Ever since you saw it?" Tessa asked, nudging her thigh between Eleanor's legs. "Are you talking about the day I offered you the job?"

"Of course," Eleanor said, her hands steady at Tessa's waist. "You knew I wanted you the moment you walked into my classroom."

"I hoped," Tessa admitted. She could feel the warmth radiating outward from Eleanor, and a matching heat sparked inside of her, making her long for Eleanor to put her fantasy into action. "So what are you waiting for, then?"

Eleanor shoved the nearest dessert dishes out of the way and lifted Tessa onto the edge of the table, settling her hips between Tessa's legs. She slid both hands up the inside of Tessa's thighs, pushing the hem of her dress higher until she reached the silk of her underpants. Eyes intent on Tessa's, Eleanor cupped her hand over the thin material, then slid her fingers into the wetness beneath.

Tessa bit her lip, aware of the moan threatening to spill over. She'd fantasized about this too—maybe not about this table, exactly, but about the steamy look in Eleanor's eyes, the impatience in her movements as she pulled Tessa's panties down across her thighs, the eagerness in the hand she slid inside Tessa's dress to caress her nipples, the mouth that pressed against hers almost painfully. But Eleanor, Tessa knew, would never hurt her.

Knowing this allowed her to let go of the inhibitions she had always, until now, held carefully in place. Allowed her to spread her legs wider, to guide Eleanor's face first to her breasts, still covered by her dress, and then down further, until Eleanor knelt on the floor before her, still fully clothed, cupping Tessa's hips and pulling her toward her waiting mouth. In the empty house, Tessa gasped aloud, moaned, cried out as Eleanor's lips and tongue and fingers stroked her rhythmically, driving her rapidly to a climax that left her shaking and complete at the edge of the dining room table.

Still trembling, she pulled Eleanor back up. "I like your fantasies."

"So do I," Eleanor said, a self-satisfied smile on her face.

"My turn." And she reached for the buttons on Eleanor's shirt.

The dishes didn't get done that night, a fact that bothered neither of them in the least.

CHAPTER NINETEEN

This was it, Eleanor decided when she woke up in Tessa's bed the first Wednesday of August. July was over and she still hadn't found the courage to lay her cards on the table. She didn't have a place to live in Madison yet, either, and classes were due to start in just over a month. She and Tessa needed to talk, and not only because she had to tell Tessa about the flight to Chicago she'd booked for the coming weekend.

The itinerary had her leaving L.A. Friday afternoon and returning Sunday night, flying in and out of LAX, Tessa's least favorite airport in the city. She would be in Madison for two days, enough time to meet some of her future classmates and (she hoped) find an apartment for the fall semester. The ticket hadn't even put a dent in her checking account, overflowing from the most recent direct deposit from Tessa's business manager's account. Lately she'd had a hard time not thinking about the fact that she was in a relationship with the person whose signature was stamped on her paycheck. But whatever was happening between them, a job was a job.

As it turned out, though, Laya had her own agenda that morning. They were sitting at the kitchen island together as usual, Eleanor inhaling her coffee, Tessa reading the paper, and everything seemed normal. Laya was peppering them with questions about constellations and cancer. She and Eleanor had gone to a show at the Griffith Park Observatory the previous afternoon, where Eleanor had made the mistake of mentioning that her own mother had loved the Observatory, which had led to the mind-blowing discovery on Laya's part that Eleanor had once had a mother too, but that she'd died recently.

Eleanor had almost finished her first cup of coffee when Laya abruptly changed the subject. "I know you've been having sleepovers," she announced. "You don't have to pretend anymore." Then she shoved a large piece of toast in her mouth and began to chew, smiling encouragingly at them.

Tessa looked at Eleanor, who looked back at her, glad she wasn't the actual parent in this situation. She didn't have nearly enough caffeine in her system yet to defuse this particular conversational bomb.

Correctly interpreting the *This is so you* look Eleanor was sending her, Tessa folded the newspaper and leaned across the kitchen island. "What do you mean, sweetie?"

Laya kept exaggeratedly chewing the enormous bite of toast. Finally she swallowed and said, "I mean, I know Elle sleeps over. I was just wondering, could I sleep with you too?"

"No," her mother said quickly as Eleanor hid her smile behind her coffee cup. "You're right, Elle does sometimes stay in my room, but it's something that's just for adults."

Laya tilted her head sideways, kicking the top rung of her stool as she considered this. "Does that mean you're doing the sex?"

Tessa's jaw literally dropped, and Eleanor nearly spewed out her mouthful of coffee. Looked like that sex ed talk was going to be happening quite a bit earlier than either of them had anticipated.

"What?" Tessa shook her head. "Why would you even ask that?"

"Rayann said that Luke's brother told them that doing sex is how babies are made. I was just thinking maybe you and Eleanor might want to have a baby because I think I want to be a sister. But not if you're going to have a boy. I really don't want a brother."

If only they could have a baby together, Eleanor thought wistfully, not for the first time. She would love to combine her and Tessa's gene pool to produce a miniature version of Laya, despite the awkwardness of this parenting moment. Tessa was looking at her now wide-eyed, silently begging for help.

Eleanor relented. Calling up her teaching voice, she said, "No, we're not trying to make a baby. There are some things about making babies that it sounds like Luke and Rayann don't understand, and that's because you're still not old enough to learn about it yet. Remember how we talked about how some things are easier for grown-ups to understand because adults are bigger and so are their brains?"

Laya nodded.

"Well, how babies are made is one of those things. When you get a little bit bigger and your brain grows too, then it'll be the right time to think and talk about sex and baby-making. But for now, maybe you could just set those things aside for later and think about something else."

Laya nodded again. Apparently this made sense to her. Then she said, "If you're not baby-making, then what are you doing at night?"

Eleanor glanced at Tessa, who stepped in again. "Eleanor and I are very good friends, and we like to be close to each other. Sometimes we like to sleep in the same bed."

"But then why can't I sleep with you?" Laya asked.

"You just can't," Tessa said, not meeting Eleanor's eyes. "When you get bigger, like Eleanor said, I'll explain."

Not *we*, Eleanor noticed, but *I*. Did that mean Tessa thought she wouldn't be around when Laya was older? Did she not want Eleanor to be around? And did she really think of her as a "very good friend"? Laya already knew that some couples were made up of a man and a woman and others of two men or two women.

She lived in L.A., after all, and Tessa had purposely exposed her to a variety of different types of families. Why, then, didn't she want to tell Laya that they were a couple? Yet another reason why it was high time they had that talk.

But Tessa had a meeting downtown with a new member of the foundation's board, and Laya had a playdate with the infamous Luke and his brother. For now, clearly, any discussion would have to wait until after dinner.

Half an hour later, Eleanor buckled Laya into the backseat of the Escape and set her laptop carrier on the passenger seat. While Laya played and swam with her friends and perhaps learned additional fallacies about the human reproductive system, Eleanor intended to find a coffee shop with WiFi and browse Madison's Craigslist apartment listings. One of the current grad students in her program had e-mailed her a concise description of where to live and where not to. Armed with that information and her new iPhone (a necessity in this day and age, she'd convinced herself), she should be able to find her way around her future hometown this coming weekend.

Despite the turmoil that overtook her whenever she thought about leaving Tessa and Laya, she was starting to get excited about going back to school. Something she'd looked forward to for so long was now finally about to happen. She still wasn't sure she wanted to spend the next five years in plebian academic hell, but she owed it to herself to at least give the program a chance. After all, the University of Wisconsin only admitted a half dozen new students each year. Pretty cool they wanted her.

"You're coming in with me, aren't you?" Laya asked when Eleanor pulled up in front of the palatial Malibu house where Luke's father, a well-known director, lived.

Eleanor cut the engine and glanced back at her. "Not this time, kiddo. I have some errands to run."

"Oh. Well, I'll miss you." She leaned forward to peck Eleanor's cheek. "Bye!" And she exploded out of the car, slamming the door on her way to meet Luke on the front steps.

Eleanor waited until the housekeeper had ushered the kids inside before guiding the Escape down the long driveway to the gate. A motion-sensor caught her approach, and by the time she reached the end of the driveway, the gate was standing open, waiting for her to pass. *I'll miss you too*, she thought, watching the mansion disappear in her rearview mirror.

Eleanor was the first one to officially bring up the impending dissolution of their relationship. Not that she called it that, but that's what it sounded like to Tessa when Eleanor informed her that evening that she needed a few days off to fly to the Midwest to look for an apartment. A place, incidentally, she would be living while Tessa and Laya continued their existence in L.A. with the black hole she'd left to keep them company.

This was apparently the day for revelations, Tessa thought, given Laya's shocking pronouncement that morning. Tessa could only imagine the sorts of things Luke was reporting to his parents after spending the day with Laya. But tonight, instead of rehashing the bombshell Laya had dropped, Tessa had returned downstairs from putting her daughter to bed to find Eleanor pacing the family room, brow furrowed.

"We need to talk," Eleanor had announced abruptly, and things had—predictably—gone downhill from there.

"Why didn't you just ask me?" Tessa said now. She was curled up in the corner of the love seat, arms around her legs. "I would have given you the plane. You could have gone whenever you wanted instead of at the whim of the airlines."

Eleanor turned from the window to stare at her. "You're upset that I'm not taking your private jet? Seriously?"

When she put it that way... "No," Tessa said. "Or yes. I don't know. I have a meeting on Friday. What am I supposed to do with Laya?" Even as she said it, she knew she wasn't upset about the airplane ticket or Laya's babysitting schedule or even the thought of a weekend without Eleanor. This sudden jaunt to Madison to pick out an apartment was a reminder that soon Eleanor would be a permanent resident of the state of Wisconsin, while Tessa and Laya would still be here in this same house, chasing her ghost through the empty rooms.

"You'll muddle through somehow," Eleanor said, "like normal people do all the time."

And there it was. Took a few months, but finally it was out there between them: Eleanor didn't respect her. Tessa knew she'd grown overly accustomed to comfort. Giving away millions didn't change the fact that she spent millions on herself and her daughter. Many people believed money would make them happy, and Tessa had discovered that it did, in fact, make life much easier. It was as if she thought she was owed ease and comfort after a marked lack of such things early on. But that wasn't really the way things worked. She'd gotten lucky with acting, that was all. No more, no less.

"Damn it," Eleanor said, and knelt before her. "I didn't mean that."

"I know."

"No, I'm serious. I'm not angry with you. I'm just upset with the whole situation. I don't want to go to Madison, and yet at the same time, I really do. I'm just afraid of what it might cost me. What it might cost us."

Tessa looked into her eyes and saw the confusion there mirroring her own. She wanted to tell her not to go, to stay here with them instead, but she knew that wasn't the right thing to say or do, either. Eleanor had remained in Boston for a decade while her mother fought cancer, delaying the start of her career so that she could be close to her family, even as they pushed her away for having the courage to be who she was. That was one of the things Tessa loved most about her—her strength, her refusal to compromise who she was for anyone. Love, she repeated to herself. Crap.

"I'm not sure what to say," she heard herself venture.

Eleanor took her hands and held them between her own, eyes shadowed in the lamp-lit room. "Say you want this to work as much as I do. Say you want us to be together, to have a real relationship. Say you've never felt like this about anyone either."

Tessa stared at her. "But you're leaving."

"That doesn't mean we can't make this work. You own an airplane, remember?"

"I also have a daughter. I can't just take off whenever I want and leave her. Or drag her back and forth between L.A. and Wisconsin." Tessa had tried relationships with other actors a couple of times in her twenties, before Nadine, but they never lasted because one or the other of them was always heading out on location. In her experience, distance was rarely surmountable.

"I don't see what choice we have. I mean, either we do the long-distance thing or we break up," Eleanor said matter-of-factly.

Tessa closed her eyes and rubbed her forehead. She didn't want to lose Eleanor. Even if she hadn't admitted it aloud, she didn't think she ever had felt this way about anyone. But everyone thought that at the beginning, didn't they?

"There might be a third option," Eleanor said.

"What's that?"

"You and Laya wouldn't have to stay here, necessarily. You're always saying how you wish you could raise her outside the Hollywood fishbowl."

"Are you suggesting we move to Madison?" Tessa pictured Laya walking along safe, tree-lined streets with her friends to a school building not far from their comfortable but less than extravagant home. Then she stopped herself. It was a nice fantasy, but their lives could never be that simple. Anyway, she and Eleanor had only known each other a few months. Moving cross-country together would hardly be wise. Bad enough that they were basically living together now. Although really not bad at all. Quite nice in fact.

"Not necessarily Madison," Eleanor said, still kneeling before her. "But what about Chicago? It's only a couple of hours away and it has everything a city that size has to offer—museums, art, private schools, other famous people. Michael Jordan lives there, and so does Oprah."

"Chicago?" Tessa echoed. She stared at Eleanor disbelievingly for a moment, and then she snickered. She couldn't help it. Laughter just bubbled up inside of her and fell into the space Eleanor's suggestion had created between them. Immediately Eleanor started to pull away, eyes shuttered, but Tessa reached out and grabbed her hands. "Wait, I'm sorry. I didn't mean to laugh. It's just, well, there's something you don't know about me." She stopped. Should she tell her?

Eleanor wrenched her hands away and stood up, towering over her. "You think I don't know that? You know everything there is to know about me, but you, Tess, you're a fucking mystery. I don't even know your real name, do I?"

Tessa stared up at her, stunned by the vehemence in Eleanor's voice. She'd never seen her angry before. The hair rose at the back of her neck. After all these years, anger still possessed the power to scare the bejesus out of her. "No," she admitted.

"Great. Just great. I don't need this," Eleanor said, turning away. "I didn't ask for any of this. I was doing fine before you." And she stormed out through the patio doors, headed for the carriage house.

"It's O'Neil," Tessa said. But by then, Eleanor was halfway across the patio.

Shit. She slouched down on the couch and covered her eyes. That had gone incredibly badly. She should have been overjoyed that Eleanor wanted to try to make things work even after the summer ended, but instead, all she could do was laugh at the idea of returning to Chicago. How had she managed to fall in love with a woman whose destiny led to the part of the world she had worked so hard to escape? For all she knew, if she returned to Chicago, she could very well run into ghosts from her past. Ghosts, unfortunately, who were all too real.

Eleanor was right about one thing. She did fantasize about leaving L.A. In an ideal world, she would raise Laya someplace where surface appearances weren't a central concern, where who you were mattered as much as, if not more than, what you looked like.

She was tired of people, tired of crowded streets and the constant white noise of urban life. There was a reason 9/11 had happened in New York, a reason L.A. was considered a likely West Coast site for terrorist activity. Few paparazzi lived in the Midwest because stars rarely lived in the fly-over states. But she wasn't a star anymore. And despite her fears, part of her longed to go home, to revisit where she had come from. Possibly, even, who.

Instead of acknowledging all of those difficult things, she'd rejected Eleanor, laughed in her face seemingly at the idea of continuing their relationship beyond the boundaries of the summer. Instead of meeting her halfway and saying yes, she wanted this to work too, yes, she loved her too, she'd turned away, stonewalled her, even appeared to deride Eleanor's bravery in taking the first step. All because she was afraid that if Eleanor knew who and what she came from, she might not love her after all.

"Coward," she muttered to herself as she walked through the house checking doors and windows, a nightly ritual she'd let slide since the Hawaii trip. At the patio doors, she hesitated, then turned the bolt. She could see lights on in the carriage house. She pictured Eleanor settling alone into Ama and Dani's old bed, and then imagined herself crawling in beside her, begging her not to leave. But she couldn't do that. Couldn't ask Eleanor to give up her dream; didn't, if she thought about it, even want to. Which left the three options Eleanor had outlined: a clean break now, a long-distance relationship, or a move back to the Midwest. But Tessa couldn't go back to Chicago, either. She wouldn't.

She rubbed her bare arms, suddenly chilled despite the August heat. The house was cooler than usual because Eleanor, pale-skinned Vermonter that she was, liked it cold at night. This would be their first night apart since they'd returned from Kauai. She would miss Eleanor's warmth.

Might as well get used to the feeling, she thought, and turned away from the carriage house lights. Soon enough Eleanor's absence, and her own regret for what might have been, would be permanent.

CHAPTER TWENTY

Thursday morning, Tessa left for work early, which suited Eleanor fine. After what had happened between them the night before, she didn't have anything to say to Tessa. She took Laya hiking near Santa Barbara for most of the day, careful to hide her anger and disappointment. After all, Laya wasn't responsible for her mother's behavior. Back at the house that evening, Tessa tried to catch her eye as they made dinner and chatted about their days, but Eleanor pretended not to notice. She couldn't wait to get out of L.A. A few days in Madison was just what she needed.

As soon as Tessa took Laya up to bed, Eleanor slipped out the patio doors and returned to the lonely carriage house, where she failed to sleep well for a second night in a row. The next morning, she ate breakfast alone, then said a hurried goodbye to Tessa and Laya. Tessa's hug was short, impersonal, mostly for Laya's benefit, Eleanor suspected. After all, they were supposed to be "very good friends."

Good friends, however, didn't ridicule each other, she reflected on the way to LAX. She still couldn't believe she'd laid her cards on the table only to be so heartlessly rebuffed. Tessa had actually laughed at the idea of continuing their relationship past the summer—the reaction Eleanor had feared most. No wonder Tessa had never wanted Laya to know about their relationship. When it came down to it, Eleanor was apparently nothing more than a convenient, temporary diversion. Before the other night, she would have sworn that the real Tessa Flanagan was warm and funny and loved faded jeans and hanging out at home. And, possibly, her. Clearly she'd been wrong. Come fall, Tessa would be able to pick from a whole fleet of lipstick lesbians who were more like her, women who shopped on Rodeo Drive and wouldn't be caught dead flying coach.

Fortunately, Madison was nothing like L.A. Wisconsin would be the perfect place to get over Tessa, she decided glumly that weekend as she explored her future home. The small city was hot and humid in mid-August, but lush and green too, with miles of lakeshore paths and a vibrant downtown built on a narrow isthmus between a pair of tree-lined lakes. A college town best known for frat parties and social activism, Madison offered a picturesque central square crowned by the state capitol building, an impressive farmers' market with locally grown organic produce, and laidback, friendly people who, luckily, seemed ignorant of her relationship with Tessa.

On Saturday morning, she met up with a couple of students from her program, Josh and Bryn, who gave her a tour of the university and assorted neighborhoods nearby. Then, iPhone in hand, she went apartment hunting. It was grueling, but by the end of the day, she had signed a six-month lease on an upstairs unit in an old Victorian house on a residential street not far from campus. To celebrate, Josh and Bryn took her out on the town that night. As she drank beer and sampled cheese curds at a hipster restaurant with her soon-to-be fellow students, both of whom were several years her junior, Eleanor decided she could picture herself with these people in this place for the next few years. It could work—which was good, seeing as she'd just dropped fifteen hundred bucks on first and last month's rent.

But even as she imagined herself assuming the life she'd planned for so long, she couldn't stop thinking about the one she'd put on hold back in L.A. While she sat in an honest-to-God Western-style saloon after dinner with Josh, Bryn and some of their friends listening to a local band jam onstage, she could picture Tessa and Laya cooking dinner without her, washing up afterward and reading a few stories until Laya finally drifted off midsentence in her tree house bed. She could imagine them at breakfast the next morning, Tessa with her obligatory newspaper, Laya cutting animal shapes out of her pancakes and providing detailed descriptions of each creature's life cycle. As Eleanor sipped her beer and smiled at the students she was bound to get to know possibly too well in coming years, she understood that this was how Madison would be at first—her mind only half present, the other half somewhere she wasn't even wanted.

On Sunday morning, she met Bryn and a handful of her friends for brunch at a downtown restaurant that served food primarily sourced from local farms. As she waited for her eggs and hash browns to arrive, Eleanor listened to the conversation flow around her and checked out the women Bryn had invited along. Most looked the same—smart young white women who cared more about what they read than where they bought their shoes. But Reed, a music student sitting beside her at the very end of the table, set her gaydar pinging—androgynous name and figure, short dyed blond hair molded into a faux hawk, baggy shorts and a multitude of tattoos visible beneath her tank top.

"So, Reed, what instrument do you play?" Eleanor asked after the server had poured their coffee.

"Piano and harpsichord," the younger woman said. "What about you? Any music lessons in your past?"

"Violin," Eleanor admitted, "but I haven't played in a while. I've always wanted to learn guitar, though. Me and every other lesbian, I guess."

Reed's eyebrows rose for a second, then evened out. "Totally," she said. “Half the women I know already play the guitar, and the others all want to.”

Bingo. “What’s the women’s community like in Madison?”

“It’s actually great,” Reed said, and launched into a description of the bookstores and student groups and clubs available to women of their persuasion. But after a minute, she stopped midsentence and stared at Eleanor. “Wait, did Bryn say your name was Eleanor?”

“Yeah, why?” A thought occurred to her, but she pushed it away. She was not about to be recognized by a virtual stranger.

“And you’re here from L.A.?”

Then again… Eleanor nodded slowly.

Reed snapped her fingers. “I thought you looked familiar. You’re the woman who outed Tessa Flanagan, aren’t you?”

This was definitely a first. All at once, Eleanor felt a flash of empathy for Tessa, who rarely went anywhere without being recognized. “I’m not sure *outed* is the right word, exactly.”

“No way! I can’t believe I’m having brunch with Tessa Flanagan’s girlfriend!” She glanced around the table, trying to catch the eye of one of the other women.

Girlfriend wasn’t the best word choice, either. Eleanor touched Reed’s arm. “Wait,” she said, her voice low. “Please don’t say anything right now. I’d really like to get through the weekend with everyone thinking of me as just another new student, not Tessa Flanagan’s girlfriend. Or whatever,” she added, stumbling over the blatant untruth.

After a moment, Reed nodded. “I can understand that,” she said. “I just moved out here from New York last summer. It’s hard to start over, especially if people already have a certain view of you. Those articles probably didn’t get much right, did they?”

“Almost nothing,” Eleanor agreed, relieved that Reed was willing to keep her identity under wraps for now.

“Can I just say, you rock. I’m serious. Bringing a woman like her over to our side has got to be the coup of the decade.”

Eleanor sipped her coffee. “I can’t take any credit.”

“You mean she was already…?”

“Practically a gold-star lesbian.”

"I heard those rumors but I never believed them. I mean, what are the odds someone like her would dig chicks?"

"Someone like who would dig chicks?" Bryn put in, and conversation around the table paused as all eyes swiveled to Reed.

"Portia de Rossi," she said, exchanging a significant look with Eleanor. The conversation settled briefly on Ellen DeGeneres and her gorgeous, funny girlfriend before skipping on to more pressing concerns, such as the professor in the English department who was currently cheating on his wife with a grad student. A male grad student.

As Eleanor worked on her hash browns, she reflected that Reed was going to be disappointed when she found out they weren't a couple, after all. At least her relationship with Tessa had made her a sort-of star by association in the lesbian community. She probably wouldn't have any problem finding women in Madison who wanted to be friends with the woman who had outed Tessa Flanagan, as Reed had put it. That had to be something, didn't it?

On the flight back to L.A. that evening, as the airplane chased the sun westward, Eleanor counted the days until she was due to return to Madison. Twenty, she realized, that was all. Then she would pack up her car and drive through the states the jet was currently flying over. Sasha had offered to take time off and accompany her—reluctantly, because she was not a fan of Mormons (Utah) or cowboys (Colorado), and Eleanor shouldn't even get her started on redneck states like Nebraska and Iowa. But for her best friend, she was willing to risk life and limb traversing the middle west of their great nation.

Watching the clouds darken beyond her narrow window, Eleanor wondered how she was going to get through the next few weeks. She still loved Tessa just as much as she had before Wednesday's harsh reality check. How was she going to manage around Tessa at meals, in the evenings, between now and the end of the month? Maybe she wouldn't. Maybe she should tell her that their current arrangement no longer worked. She could move back in with Sasha and only come up to the house during the day while Tessa was down in the city, like they'd talked about before.

That would probably work, she thought, closing her eyes. Why, then, did she wish she hadn't thought of it?

On Sunday evening, Tessa dropped Laya off at Margot's house for an impromptu sleepover. Eleanor was due home in a few hours, and Tessa didn't want her daughter distracting her from what she knew she had to do.

"You're in rough shape," Margot said as soon as Laya and Rayann ran off to the downstairs playroom of the Trivers' mansion.

"What gave it away?" Tessa asked, knowing that her hair under the makeshift bandana was disheveled, her mascara-free eyes looked like someone had punched her, and her threadbare UCLA T-shirt had seen better days. Meanwhile Margot, closer to fifty these days than forty, looked well put together as usual in a stylish dress shirt and tailored pants, her makeup flawless and hair carefully coiffed.

"You know I don't usually tell you what to do," Margot said as they stood in the entryway to her Malibu home, the Pacific sparkling in the near distance, "but I don't think you should let this one go. She's different, Tess. You're different with her, in a good way. Though I don't suppose I have to tell you that."

The older woman was everything Tessa liked about Hollywood—ethical, brilliant and hard-working. When Tessa told Margot she was retiring from acting, she'd expected the producer to react like everyone else. Instead, Margot had considered Tessa with her piercing hazel eyes and nodded once. "Good for you," she'd said, cementing Tessa's eternal admiration.

"I don't want to let her go," she told Margot now. "I'm just not sure how to keep her. Or if I'm even the one to do the keeping."

For four days Tessa had sleepwalked through work, time with Laya, nights alone, wondering all the while what Eleanor was doing, thinking, feeling. For four lousy nights she'd slept by herself in a bed that suddenly felt too big. Or not slept, as the marks beneath her eyes clearly attested. Mostly she had lain in the dark missing Eleanor and trying to decide what to do. No one had ever gotten this close before. Certainly not Nadine, and not even Tory, who she had loved blindly with the ease of youth. But she and Eleanor weren't kids. Hadn't been for a while.

Back at home, she took a long hot shower and tracked Eleanor's flight on her BlackBerry. When it was safely on the ground, she poured a glass of wine and headed out to the patio to watch the sky darken as the solar lights automatically lit up. She was sitting by the pool when Eleanor slipped in through the garden gate, avoiding the main house as Tessa had known she would.

She rose in the near-dark. "Elle."

"Jesus!" Eleanor stopped suddenly, her wheeled carry-on running up the back of her leg. "Ouch! Damn it."

Not the beginning Tessa had hoped for. "I'm sorry, I didn't mean to scare you."

"What are you doing out here? Is Laya okay?"

"She's with the Trivers for the night," she said, and folded her arms across her chest. In the patio lighting, she could just make out Eleanor's features. She didn't look happy. "Can we talk?" She waited a long, agonizing moment as Eleanor looked out over the pool.

"Okay," she said finally, glancing back at Tessa. "But I need to get out of these clothes first. I'll come over in a little while, all right?"

"Of course," Tessa said, inclining her head. "Take your time."

Eleanor apparently took her at face value. Tessa paced the family room for twenty minutes, swallowing more wine than she'd intended as she waited for Eleanor to appear. All weekend she had pictured Eleanor falling in love with Madison, the University of Wisconsin, her new Flanagan-less existence. Maybe she hadn't even wanted to come back to L.A. tonight. Maybe she was only back to pack up her things and leave again as soon as she possibly could.

The French doors opened and Eleanor was suddenly there, damp hair curling about her shoulders, eyes wary. She didn't quite look at Tessa as she stood just inside the doors, hands in the front pocket of her Smith hoodie.

"Sorry," she said. "I really needed a shower."

"Of course." Tessa set her empty wineglass on the coffee table and approached Eleanor, who shifted away slightly. Tessa ignored this and launched into the prepared speech that she'd memorized as if it were a script. "But I'm the one who should apologize. I know it seems like I laughed at you the other night, but it didn't have anything to do with you or what you said. You couldn't know this but I actually grew up in Chicago. I was born and raised there." It was easier to say than she had imagined. Nothing changed outwardly, but inside, she felt lighter. Finally, after all these years, she wanted someone else to know her story.

Eleanor was watching her more closely now, mouth still unsmiling but eyes no longer quite as flat. "I thought you were from New York?"

"No, and my parents weren't killed in a car accident, either. My mother's gone, but my father is very much alive and still in Illinois, last I heard."

"I don't understand," Eleanor said. "What do you mean, last you heard?"

She didn't have to tell her. She could still back out. But as she saw Eleanor frowning, shoulders hunched forward in her faded sweatshirt, Tessa realized she wanted Eleanor to know all of her, not just the film star with the house in the Hills and more money than she knew what to do with. She wanted Eleanor to know the scared kid who had possibly never fully recovered from the moment that had changed her life into a before and an after.

"We're not in touch anymore because my father is in prison," she said. "When I was nine, he killed my mother during an argument. I ended up in foster care and went through half a dozen placements. I left Chicago as soon as I turned eighteen. I've never gone back. I don't even like to fly through O'Hare." All these years later, saying what her father had done felt impersonal, as if she were relating something that had happened to another person. Which, in a way, it had.

"My God," Eleanor said, her face pale. "I had no idea." She pulled Tessa into her arms, into a warm, solid embrace. "I'm so sorry, Tess."

Tessa hid her face in Eleanor's neck. Thank God, she didn't hate her or, apparently, feel repulsed by her family history. Tessa's throat tightened, and she breathed in deeply. Eleanor smelled familiar—of soap and minty shampoo and a scent that was all hers. And now she was kissing Tessa's hair, her cheek, her lips. Tessa was drowning, dizzy from red wine, exhaustion, relief.

"I missed you so much," she murmured.

Eleanor leaned her forehead against Tessa's. "Tell me about it."

"How was Madison?"

"Good, but lonely. How's Laya?"

"Mad at me for not letting her be here when you got home. She missed you too." Tessa tightened her grip on Eleanor's waist. "You're not still angry with me?"

"Does it look like I'm angry?"

"No. But can you understand why I reacted like that when you brought up Chicago?"

Eleanor hesitated. "I think so. Going back might feel like returning to who you were then."

"That's exactly it. I wasn't laughing at you. I just couldn't believe you were suggesting I go to the one place I promised myself never to set foot in again. I'm so sorry. I should have told you I wanted to be with you because I do. So much, Elle. I don't want to lose you."

"That's all I wanted to hear," Eleanor said, pulling her close again.

Later, upstairs in Tessa's bedroom, they lay together in the dark under the sheets, holding onto each other as Eleanor asked questions that Tessa, for once, answered candidly: what her foster families were like, how she survived, where she went to junior high and high school. Tessa asked questions too: what was Madison like, did she find an apartment, what did she think of the people she'd met? When Eleanor told her about Reed's comments at brunch, Tessa felt herself bristle.

"Coup of the decade, my ass. I hope you corrected her."

"Maybe," Eleanor responded, a teasing glint in her eyes.

"You better have," Tessa said, but a massive yawn ruined the tough tone she was aiming for.

She was almost asleep when she heard Eleanor ask, "How did your mother die?"

Tessa had been at school when it happened, but she knew the basics, and that was what she shared with Eleanor now: Her mother was angry with her father because two of her friends had called to say they'd seen him out with a woman from the neighborhood. She waited up all night at the kitchen table, smoking cigarettes (which she usually didn't do inside the apartment) and drinking Tessa's father's favorite bottle of whiskey, reserved for special occasions. He still hadn't come home the next morning, so Tessa got herself ready and off to school. The last time she saw her mother alive, she held a cigarette in one hand, a half-full glass of whiskey in the other. She looked like a stranger. Tessa wasn't sure her mother even saw her leave.

In his deposition, her father claimed he acted in self-defense. As soon as he entered the apartment that morning, she'd flown at him, he said, shrieking and striking him about the head and chest. When he pushed her away, she fell and her head slammed into the hall table. He'd called 911 and waited for the ambulance with her, but she never regained consciousness. She was pronounced dead at the hospital. An immigrant with no family support and little financial resources, he couldn't afford a lawyer. The public defender assigned to his case convinced him to accept a murder plea, and the judge sentenced him to thirty years in prison. Tessa, already in foster care, officially became a ward of the state.

"Pretty incredible you've kept a secret like that all these years," Eleanor said. She was lying on her back now, one arm under Tessa's neck, stroking her hair gently, rhythmically.

"It is," Tessa agreed. "I always thought someday I would get a call from Melody, that a reporter would be asking for a comment on a story they were writing about my real name, my real family. Apparently there were a couple of close calls, I don't know, maybe more. Michael and Melody have done an impressive job keeping everything under wraps."

"I'd say so." Eleanor's hand stilled. "What I don't understand, I guess, is why you decided to keep everything hidden. What would be so terrible about people knowing the truth?"

Tessa propped herself up one elbow. She'd almost been

expecting the question. Eleanor had never had to hide anything about herself. Not a surprise, then, that she wouldn't understand why someone else might. "I'd rather not be the star of my own made-for-TV movie, thanks very much."

"It wouldn't have to be like that. Think of all the kids going through the same kinds of things you went through, the foster kids feeling alone and scared and totally hopeless. You could go on TV and share your story, and think of what it would mean to those kids to know it's possible to start over again."

But was it possible? Tessa wasn't so sure. Despite her success, despite her career and the money and the years of therapy, she'd never quite been able to outrun the pain of losing both of her parents in a single moment of violence.

"That's a sweet idea, Elle, and if I thought that was what my coming out, so to speak, would accomplish, I'd do it." Would she really? She ignored the flicker of self-doubt. "But it wouldn't be like that. And anyway, talk about false hopes—the odds of any of those kids coming to L.A. and making it big are pretty slim. Plenty of well-adjusted people never achieve their dreams here, let alone the ones hauling around overwhelming emotional baggage."

"The point isn't that they'll think they can make it in Hollywood," Eleanor insisted, "although I did hear a story on NPR recently about how the American Dream has shifted from owning a house and raising a family to becoming rich and famous. But the point is that you could give throwaway kids the hope that someday their lives will change. I mean, look how much yours has."

She had a valid point, but Tessa didn't want to hear it. As an A-list star, she hadn't enjoyed privacy in more than a decade. One of the things about being famous was that you didn't get to control the conclusions people drew about you. Each bit of information that leaked out was used by a hundred different people in a hundred different ways, but all for the same motives: profit and publicity, which, when you came down to it, were basically the same thing. If she revealed her family history publicly, she would then have to watch as the media dug deeper and probed painful memories and twisted things to make a better, more dramatic story. Because drama sold, whether it was true or not.

"I'm not going to tell the world about poor little Mary Therese and her dead mother and abusive father," Tessa said. "It's my family, not some script that can be tied up neatly and packaged to the masses. You have no idea what it's like. It's my decision, and I would hope you would respect that." She rolled away from Eleanor and hugged a pillow to her body, closing her eyes against the tears threatening. She was so tired. It had taken so much energy to tell Eleanor the truth, and now all she wanted was sleep.

Behind her, she felt Eleanor shift until they were spooning. "I'm sorry," Eleanor whispered, her arms tight around Tessa. "Of course it's your decision. And you're right, I can't possibly know what it's like. I can just tell you that I love you and I want to be with you. I'll keep your secret, Tess. You don't have to worry."

Tessa opened her eyes to the dark room, aware of Eleanor's body pressed against hers from behind, Eleanor's breath stirring her hair. "Did you just say you love me?"

"Among other things."

She turned over to face her again. "Even though you don't know my real name?"

"Even so."

"It's O'Neil," Tessa said for the second time that week. "And I love you too."

They fell asleep in each other's arms a little while later, the house shifting quietly around them.

CHAPTER TWENTY-ONE

Over the days that followed, Eleanor vacillated between joy—*she loves me!*—and unease. What did it mean that Tessa had kept hidden such a big part of her life? Was it only habit, or did she really not trust Eleanor? Faced with losing her, Tessa had, in fact, trusted her enough to reveal the details of her nightmarish childhood, and Eleanor now felt the pieces of the Tessa puzzle falling into place. No wonder she was so careful all the time. It wasn't just that the press and her fans had followed her every move since she'd become famous. She'd lived for years with the fear of being found out, and not just as a lesbian.

Whenever Eleanor remembered her own exhortations for Tessa to bare all on behalf of foster children everywhere, she had to acknowledge that her timing could have been better. She still believed Tessa should open up and share her story. In a psych class at Smith she'd learned that people who carried secrets for long periods of time suffered ill health effects, both physically and psychologically. Her professor had noted that the state motto of nearby New Hampshire, "Live Free or Die," was surprisingly accurate when applied to the human psyche. Still, she probably wasn't going to convince Tessa overnight that it was in her own best interests to reveal to the world that her father had murdered her mother, and that she herself had endured almost a decade in Chicago's foster system.

September wasn't far off now, and Eleanor had other things to worry about as the days followed one after another. The middle of her last month in California passed in a blur of day trips with Laya and, increasingly, Tessa; poignant moments in the darkness of Tessa's bedroom; the inevitable arrangements that preceded Eleanor's move to Madison. She found herself spending hours on the phone and online, when she would rather have been with Tessa and Laya—classes had to be registered for, tuition paid, a portable steel storage container with all of her possessions shipped from Boston to Madison. In her new apartment, she would once again have her insanely cushy couch from (of all places) Sears, her many books, her favorite art prints picked up for cheap at assorted Boston street fairs, her framed family photos. She had plenty of digitized reminders on her laptop, but it would be different to be in a home of her own again and see images of her parents and Julia arrayed about her, silent witnesses to her everyday life.

She'd missed that sensation these last months, just as she would miss others in the months to come. She and Tessa had decided almost by default to do the long-distance thing, but Eleanor still wasn't certain how often they would see each other. Thanksgiving and Christmas for sure, they'd agreed. But other than the holidays, visits were still TBD. And what about Laya? Eleanor knew how much a six-year-old could change in the space of a month, let alone a semester. In grad school half a continent away, she would miss so much of Laya's life, with no resolution in sight.

For her part, Laya was considerably more stoic than the adults in her life. They'd known all along that Eleanor was leaving, she pointed out whenever they broached the topic, and it wouldn't be forever. They could talk on the phone and e-mail and even Skype on the new webcam-equipped laptop Eleanor had purchased for just that purpose. Besides, taking chances was a good thing, Laya reminded them—like in one of her favorite books from Eleanor's class, *Chipo's Gift*, in which Chipo the mopane worm from South Africa learns that new places help you grow. Eleanor just shook her head, impressed as ever by Laya's ability to remember uncommon worm species and where they hailed from.

As the days and nights dwindled away, Tessa took a break from work on the foundation to spend time with her "two favorite females," as she now referred to Eleanor and Laya. They swam in the pool and hung out with Sasha and Allen, Will and Scott, Margot and Rayann. They went school shopping in town and screened new movies in the den and read aloud from Harry Potter on the patio, and it was just like the first days after they returned from Kauai only with the specter of fall hanging over them all. Eleanor fell asleep each night next to Tessa wishing summer could last a few more weeks, another month. But each morning she awakened knowing she had one fewer day in California.

And then, as it was always going to do, the countdown dropped below a week.

The last Friday of August, they were sitting on the patio playing a seemingly never-ending round of Uno when Tessa announced, "Laya, I was thinking of borrowing Eleanor tonight. Is that okay with you?"

"Maybe," Laya said. "What for?"

"I thought I would take her out to dinner at a nice restaurant. You know, as a thank you for everything she's done for us this summer." She smiled at Eleanor, her eyes glowing with the bittersweet look Eleanor had grown accustomed to in recent days.

"Can I come?" Laya asked.

"Sorry, sweetie, but this restaurant is for grown-ups. You wouldn't have any fun. Besides, they don't have french fries."

Laya frowned. "Which restaurant?"

"It's a surprise," Tessa said. "Can you keep a secret?"

"Duh, Mom."

Tessa leaned over and whispered in her ear, and Eleanor hummed softly to herself so she wouldn't accidentally overhear. She liked surprises. At least, the L.A. her liked surprises. The Boston Eleanor not so much.

Apparently the restaurant passed muster. Laya nodded and said, "Okay. But I get to help pick out your clothes, right?"

"Of course," Eleanor put in, and held up her hand for a high five. As Laya slapped her palm, she wondered where Tessa was taking her. They had spent so much time avoiding camera phones, gossip bloggers and paparazzi that they'd never been on an actual, real-world date.

Upstairs, they opened the side of the walk-in closet that contained Tessa's movie premiere and award show outfits. For Eleanor, Laya selected a V-neck silk dress that brought out the green in her eyes, while for Tessa she suggested a deep red backless dress. In addition to flora and fauna, the kid knew fashion, Eleanor thought. But then she was the daughter of a movie star. She'd been weaned on Dolce and Gabbana.

Before they left the house, Tessa helped Eleanor with her hair and makeup, managing to hide her freckles without the appearance of anything but the barest of foundations. Eleanor surveyed her up-swept hairdo and flawless skin in the mirror, slightly shocked to realize that she was, in fact, the seemingly sophisticated woman staring out of the glass.

"You learn things when you spend half your life on a movie set," Tessa said, pursing her lips as she applied a shade of lipstick that matched her dress perfectly.

"You look fabulous," Laya said, winking at them in the mirror. Only she couldn't quite get the hang of the single eyelash dip and ended up blinking owlishly instead. Eleanor was careful not to laugh, and not only because she was afraid it might ruin her makeup.

Nancy, Ama and Dani's oldest daughter, showed up at five thirty to babysit. She whistled appreciatively when she saw them and took a picture on her camera phone to send to her parents. Laya had her snap a few shots on the family digital camera too.

Then the limo arrived and Eleanor and Tessa climbed into the backseat, waving at Laya and Nancy as the driver closed the door behind them.

"I've owed you a real date for a while now," Tessa said as the limo glided down the canyon toward Beverly Hills. "We've spent so much time hiding out at home that I haven't even wooed you properly."

"I'm not really the wooing type," Eleanor said, clasping Tessa's hand in hers. They were seated at the back of the long car, both dressed like movie stars (which, of course, Tessa was), privacy shield in place. While they could see out the tinted windows, no one could see in, not even the driver, and she liked the sense of opulent anonymity the limo afforded.

"Neither am I," Tessa admitted. "But we have to show the world we're a happy couple. As soon as you leave, the headlines will announce the tormented end to our relationship. No matter who Perez Hilton claims I'm rebounding with, just remember it's all lies."

"I wouldn't buy it anyway. I've seen how slow you are on the uptake."

"Hey, now," Tessa said, laughing. Then her smile dimmed. "I was slow, wasn't I? I can't believe how much time we wasted."

"I wouldn't say *wasted*, necessarily," Eleanor said, though similar thoughts had occurred to her.

They looked out the window at the shiny storefronts rolling past, at the tourists and locals alike out on the streets enjoying a warm Friday night in late summer.

"We're almost there," Tessa said, squeezing her hand.

When the limo stopped on the narrow street behind Spago, Eleanor almost clapped her hands. She had hoped the swanky restaurant might be Tessa's intended destination. They entered through the back door to avoid oglers—their table was reserved under her agent's name, Tessa said, but you never knew who might be out front hoping for a lucky sighting—and were escorted immediately to a well-placed table in the restaurant's interior far from the front windows. As they wound through the seating area, Tessa nodded and said hello to various patrons, and even stopped once to introduce Eleanor to a sharp-faced woman and her husband, both higher-ups at some studio or another. Eleanor was having a hard time focusing due to the tenor of her thoughts—*I'm at SPAGO! With TESSA FLANAGAN!* She wished her mother were still alive. Sarah Chapin would have been impressed by this date. But if her mother had been alive, Eleanor probably wouldn't have come to L.A., which meant she would never have met Tessa. Not a syllogism she wanted to spend much time analyzing.

Dinner was wonderful—the food was strikingly named and presented, and Eleanor happily devoured the delicious seafood and vegetarian concoctions placed before her. Soon she would be subsisting on bagels and soup, though not ramen, trusty student fare that it was. She had sworn after Smith never to touch the stuff again. Spago's chef had likely never sampled ramen noodles, judging from the rich inventions the waiter kept bringing.

After an initial hesitation, Eleanor drank deeply of the four hundred dollar bottle of wine Tessa ordered, telling herself that it was okay to dine like this once in her life. Besides being unimaginably flavorful, the wine was quite effective at dulling the guilt eating away at her. New Englanders were typically spendthrifts. Blowing cash on such transitory items as food and alcohol was not a family value where she came from. But she had to admit, the food and the wine and the ambience easily surpassed any and all of her previous (and likely future) dining experiences.

As did the company—for once in public, Tessa wasn't hiding behind an impersonal mask. They were barely seated when she reached across the table and took Eleanor's hand, holding it lightly in her own, thumb rubbing her wrist gently. Throughout the meal, she gazed deeply into Eleanor's eyes, laughed unrestrainedly at her jokes, fed her bites of salad and halibut and crab cakes, appearing to ignore the surreptitious looks Eleanor caught nearby diners casting their way. This was how their life together could be, she seemed to be saying—open, honest, affectionate. At least, here at Spago where the clientele was of a certain class and the paparazzi couldn't reach.

Distracted by this uncustomary attention, Eleanor drank too much, and when they exited through the rear of the restaurant a full two hours after they'd arrived, she nearly stumbled as flashbulbs exploded in her face. Tessa gripped her arm tightly and gave the gathered photographers a tight-lipped smile as she hustled Eleanor to the limo.

"Give us a kiss!" someone shouted.

"Come on, show us your teeth!" another called.

Eleanor thought this last comment was particularly strange, as the one making it was the piranha, after all. Giggling at the thought, she waved over Tessa's shoulder as the limo door closed on the amassed photographers.

"Did you just wave at them?" Tessa asked as the car pulled out onto the quiet Beverly Hills street.

"Maybe," Eleanor said, and hiccupped.

"You're a lightweight, Miss Chapin, you know that?"

"You can call me Eleanor."

"Thanks." Tessa smiled indulgently. "So what did you think of Spago? Or do I even need to ask?"

"Scrumptious and delectable and lip-smacking." Her tongue felt heavy, due no doubt to the half bottle of wine she'd consumed.

"Really. Is that your official review?"

"No, it's your Facebook status," Eleanor said, giggling some more. That reminded her—should she change her relationship details on Facebook? Was she officially no longer single? "Hey, what am I supposed to call you when people ask me about you?"

"Tessa. No one's called me Mary Therese in decades."

"No, I mean, are you like my girlfriend, or what? Because I really don't like the word lover. Did you ever see that skit they used to do on *Saturday Night Live*? Oh my God, it was so painful."

"I remember," Tessa said. "Why? Do you want to be my girlfriend?"

"Dude, heck yeah," Eleanor said, craning her neck to look at her. "I love you, babe."

"All right, then, we're officially girlfriends."

"Score," Eleanor said, and kissed her. Tessa's tongue flicked lazily against hers, and Eleanor felt her body begin to hum expectantly. She didn't think she'd ever get tired of making out with Tessa.

The delicious wine haze presented a problem when they got

home. They'd said goodnight to Nancy and turned on the alarm and checked on the sleeping Laya, and were headed down the hall to the master suite when Tessa's BlackBerry pinged. She quickly set it to mute, then frowned as she held up the glowing screen in the dimly lit hallway.

"Don't answer," Eleanor said, hands on Tessa's hips ushering her forward. She'd passed the ride home picturing everything she would do to Tessa in the confines of their bedroom.

"I won't," Tessa said, turning to her. Phone still in hand, she pushed Eleanor back against the wall and kissed her deeply, her tongue sliding into her mouth as the sleek material of their dresses rubbed together. God, Eleanor thought dimly, she was going to miss this.

Before things could get out of control, they took the last few steps to the bedroom and closed the door behind them. But just as Eleanor was pushing Tessa toward the bed, the BlackBerry vibrated. And then the land line on the bedside table rang, soft but insistent.

"You should probably answer," Eleanor said reluctantly. No one would call Tessa this late without good reason.

"Yeah, okay," Tessa said absently, reaching for the cordless phone.

Eleanor stripped out of the dress Laya had picked for her and hung it back in the closet, only half-listening to her girlfriend's—ha!—end of the conversation. It was Melody, her publicist, and from the sound of Tessa's voice, the news was not good. As Eleanor returned to the bedroom in only a lacy bra and a thong Tessa had ordered for her (surprisingly comfortable, she'd discovered, and good for outfits where a panty line was undesirable), she thought about sneaking up on Tessa and planting a kiss on her free ear. But at that moment, Tessa turned away from the curtained window and looked at her so bleakly that Eleanor froze.

What had happened? Ama and Dani, she thought immediately, but that didn't make any sense. Nancy would have said something, and besides, Melody wouldn't know anything about them. Which left a PR calamity of some kind. Everyone already knew they were together. What else was there?

"Did they say where the story came from?" Tessa asked, her eyes on Eleanor. "No? Well, try to find out." She turned away, pacing toward the window again.

Goose bumps rose on Eleanor's skin. It couldn't be, could it? She racked her mind. Had she told anyone about Tessa's past? Somehow let even part of the story slip in front of someone she shouldn't have? But there was no one. She hadn't told or e-mailed or texted a soul, not even Sasha.

"I can't," Tessa said after a minute, her back to Eleanor. "There is no plausible deniability here, Mel. If they've got my birth certificate and school photos, they have everything." She listened, then made a fist with her free hand. "No! Absolutely not! I am not going on the record with this. Tell them no comment... I don't care. Just do it." And she hit the off button on the phone.

For a moment, neither of them moved. Then Eleanor swallowed past the knot in her throat and asked, "Are you okay?"

"No," Tessa said. "I'm not okay."

Suddenly sober, Eleanor folded her arms across her chest. She was starting to shiver. But maybe she was wrong. Please God, let her be wrong. "What happened?"

"What happened?" Tessa spun around to face her. "What happened is that Katie Evans from *Entertainment Tonight* called Melody for a comment on the story they're about to run. Seems someone found my birth certificate in Chicago."

Eleanor was trembling now, hands rubbing her upper arms. "But how?"

"I don't know, Elle. Why don't you tell me?"

She stared at Tessa. "You don't think I have anything to do with this, do you?" But even as she delivered the line, she knew it was unnecessary. Of course Tessa thought she was at the root of the leak. For nearly two decades she'd kept her past secret, and then suddenly it came out only a matter of weeks after she told someone for the first time? She'd be crazy not to wonder.

Tessa's eyes were glowing in the lamplight, and it took Eleanor a second to realize she was crying. "I don't know what to think," she said, and sat down on the bed, head in her hands.

Eleanor wanted to go to her but couldn't stand her own

nakedness another second. She went into the closet where she'd left her clothes what felt like ages before, dressed silently, and returned to the bedroom, trying to figure out how she might bridge the impossibly wide gulf that had somehow opened between them.

Tessa was lying on her side of the bed in her red dress, face buried in a pillow. Eleanor hesitated, then went to sit beside her. "I'm so sorry," she said, touching Tessa's hair. She had never seen her cry before.

Quickly Tessa looked up, mascara running everywhere, and Eleanor added, "Not because—I don't have anything to be sorry for. But I know how it looks and I know how devastated you must be. I can only tell you that I would never, ever, do anything like this. You have to know that. I love you."

"I know you do," Tessa said. Then she closed her eyes and turned her face toward the pillow again. "I just don't know what to think."

Think the best of me, she wanted to say. *Believe me. Love me.* But in the brief moment Tessa had looked back at her, Eleanor had read the doubt in her eyes, shuttered in a way that reminded Eleanor of her mother. It was obvious—Tessa didn't trust her. Probably, she didn't trust anyone. But the distinction didn't make the reality any easier to accept. The way they felt about each other didn't matter, not if Tessa believed she was capable of something like this. And all at once the loss was too much—her mother, Tessa, Laya too, sleeping soundly just down the hall unaware of what was happening.

"I'm sorry," Eleanor said again as her own tears spilled over. Then she stood and headed for the hallway.

She moved slowly down the stairs and through the house, waiting for Tessa's tread behind her. She would come after her, wouldn't she? Tell her she knew it couldn't possibly have been her? But Eleanor made it out of the house and across the patio alone, and then she was in the carriage house, still keeping an ear out as she undressed, brushed her teeth, washed off the makeup Tessa had so carefully applied only hours before.

Spago seemed like a dream now, an impossible fantasy as Eleanor lay in bed, waiting for a sound that didn't come.

CHAPTER TWENTY-TWO

Tessa was only partially awake when she detected the sound of tires crunching across the driveway. She lay against her pillow, blinking at the dim light leaking in around the edges of the curtains. It wasn't even six yet. Who was in the driveway this early?

Laya traipsed into her bedroom just then, dragging both Moo and Gerri in her wake. "Eleanor's gone," she announced. "She came in to say goodbye. Did you see her too?"

Tessa sat up in bed. "Uh-huh," she murmured, hoping the vague sound would satisfy her daughter. Eleanor must have turned off the baby monitor in Laya's room. Where was she off to at this time of day? Tessa was a little miffed that Eleanor had taken off without a word to her on today of all days, but she couldn't blame her for needing space, not when she'd all but accused her of betrayal the night before. Soon the source of the leak would be revealed, if it hadn't been already, and then they could put this whole episode behind them. Just in time for Eleanor to leave for grad school on Monday.

"Are you sad Elle has to go, too?" Laya asked.

"I am," Tessa answered.

"Poor Mama," her daughter said, and climbed up next to her on the bed. "It's okay. She'll be back. But for now, maybe you should take Moo."

"Thanks, sweetie." She embraced the large stuffed animal. Moo's brown eyes gazed up at her steadily, comfortingly.

"Do you want me to bring you breakfast in bed?" Laya asked.

They'd brought Eleanor breakfast in bed the morning of her thirty-fourth birthday the previous month, at Laya's insistence. The logistics had presented some difficulty, since Eleanor's birthday had come several weeks before Laya had announced she knew about their sleepovers. But given a heads-up the night before, Eleanor had sneaked out the morning of her birthday and arranged herself in bed in the carriage house, acting suitably surprised when Tessa and Laya showed up with a tray of waffles garnished with flowers Laya had picked from the garden.

"That's okay," Tessa said now, and forced herself to push back the covers. "I'll make breakfast. I was just about to get up anyway." Staying in bed would only make matters worse. She might as well face what the day had to offer. Reaching for her BlackBerry, she quickly scrolled through her text messages. Nothing from Eleanor, and only one from Melody that read, "Still asking around."

Downstairs, she went outside to pick up the paper at the foot of the driveway, heartened to see that no photographers were loitering about her gate. Back inside she leafed through it quickly, but there was nothing—apparently *ET* was sitting on the story for now. Why? It wasn't like they needed to worry about future slights. She was hardly a hot commodity on the red carpet interview circuit these days.

Over a breakfast of cereal and toast, Laya asked if they could go for a walk on the beach. Eleanor sometimes took her to the ocean, and she thought maybe she'd like to see some seagulls today.

Tessa paused. Soon enough the story would break, and then it would be difficult coming and going again. She was going to have to warn Laya, she realized, and not just about the press. Laya was due to start school this week and would have to be prepared for the things the other kids might say. Tessa knew she should probably wait for Eleanor to get back—she always knew what to say. But she decided to forge ahead on her own. Soon she'd be handling everything related to Laya by herself. Might as well start now.

She led with, "Do you remember how we needed to stay home for a little while after Hawaii because the people with cameras wanted to follow us around?"

"Those cockroaches," Laya said, slurping milk from her spoon.

It felt like too much work to chastise her on either account. "Well, the photographers are back. Or they will be soon."

Her daughter frowned. "Is that why Eleanor left? To avoid them?"

"No, it's not. It doesn't have anything to do with why she left." Which wasn't entirely true, but there was only so much you could tell a six-year-old.

"Don't you think it's a coindi-coinki—"

"Coincidence," Tessa supplied.

"Exactly!"

Eleanor liked the word *exactly*. She was the one who had taught Laya to call the paparazzi cockroaches, too. Tessa pictured the two of them giggling over their nickname for the photographers, and almost wished that Eleanor were there now. But at the same time, she wouldn't have known what to say to her this morning, not yet. While she didn't want to believe Eleanor was capable of something like this, the timing was too suspect.

"Sometimes there are just coincidences," she told her daughter, resolutely ignoring the irony of the sentence crossing her lips. "This is one of those times."

Laya seemed to accept this pronouncement. "Then why are the camera people back?"

"Because they found out some information about my mom and dad and now they want to know more. Remember how I told you my mother died and I don't really know my father, sort of like how you don't know yours?"

Laya nodded, cereal momentarily forgotten.

"Well, there's a reason I don't know him. He made a mistake once a long time ago." She took a deep breath, steeled herself, and told Laya the barest of details about Chicago, careful to make her mother's death sound like more of an accident than the judge who sentenced her father had apparently believed.

"But if it was an accident, why don't you talk to him?" Laya asked, frowning. "Elle says we should forgive people when they make mistakes."

Another question she didn't know how to answer. "It's complicated," she said. "You know how Eleanor says some things are easier for adults to understand? This is one of those things. When you're bigger, you and I can talk about my father and why I decided not to be in touch with him."

Laya sighed dramatically. "I'm sick of being little."

"Oh, yeah? Well I, for one, think you're the perfect size." And she slid off her kitchen stool and hauled her daughter into her arms, inhaling her familiar scent. "I love you, Mahal."

"I love you too," Laya said, her voice subdued.

Tessa planted a wet, noisy kiss on her neck, the kind her own mother used to give her before bed each night. Squealing, Laya squirmed away from her and went running from the room.

Well, at least that part was over, Tessa thought as she leaned against her stool. No doubt Laya would be full of questions in the coming days, especially when school started and ill-informed first graders or other, older children at the Barclay School talked about what they thought they knew but didn't remotely understand. Still, she wouldn't be blindsided when the first kid walked up to her on the playground and announced that her grandfather had killed her grandmother. That had to be a good thing.

As Laya ran back down the hall, Tessa glanced out across the patio. Where was Eleanor now? At Sasha's apartment on Beechwood, only a few miles away? This wasn't supposed to happen. They were supposed to spend their last few days together in mournful bliss, not apart. Maybe she should call her, she thought as Laya burst back into the room and collapsed on the love seat. They had to figure out a way to get beyond what had happened the night before. Time was nearly up.

But Tessa didn't call her, and Eleanor didn't call, either. She stayed away from the house and Tessa let her, waiting impatiently for news from Melody. The publicist called twice that morning, both times to tell her that she was still working on tracking down the source. Work harder, Tessa thought, but it wasn't Melody's fault that her past had refused to stay hidden. The problem was they didn't know whose fault it was.

Tessa didn't notice the envelope on her bedside table until after lunch, when Laya went down for her nap. In her own bedroom, she was just starting to strip the sheets from her bed (cleaning was an excellent distraction, she found) when she glimpsed the white envelope leaning against the lamp, her name printed on it in Eleanor's neat script. For a moment she paused in the act of tossing the comforter to the floor. Then the fabric slipped from her hands.

She sat down at the edge of the bed and pulled a folded sheet of notebook paper from the envelope.

Tessa,

It's five a.m. and I can't sleep. I keep seeing your face last night when you told me you didn't know what to think. Lying here in Ama and Dani's room, I haven't been able to picture anything else. I understand, I really do. I know I've said that before, and you've said I couldn't possibly, but I get why it's so hard for you to trust anyone. It's just, I'm not anyone, and you should know that—after all, what do I have to gain from telling anyone about your past and what do I have to lose?

But you don't know, so now I'm left remembering the options we discussed—a clean break, a long-distance relationship, or my original, lousy idea for you and Laya to move to the Midwest. I know we decided on option B, but right now, I don't have any idea what that would look like. Too much has happened. And option C was never a real possibility.

What I would like is to forget the way you looked at me last night, to stop time at the moment you picked up the phone. I'd like to pretend that we had one amazing summer together (we did—at least, I thought so) and that we parted on good terms, cleanly, without any drama. I'd like to say that we were good to and for each other for the short amount of time we had together, and that we're moving on now but we'll both treasure the time we shared. Because as incredible a dream as it was to be with you, to love you and Laya, you were right in June when you warned me what it could be like. Until last night, the only part I didn't understand was how what other people think and say could drive us apart.

I'm sorry that you're hurting right now. I wish I could change that. But I can't, and I also can't be part of your life if you don't trust me. I think you know that. I'm also sorry that we won't get to spend my last few days in L.A. together. I'll be thinking about you. I think you know that, too.

But for now, please don't contact me. I don't know how to do this except as option A—a clean break. I hope you'll respect my wishes on this. And make sure Laya knows I didn't leave because of anything she did or didn't do. I love her with all of my heart, the same way I loved you.

Eleanor

Tessa's tears started when she was only halfway through the letter. Eleanor leaving this morning wasn't just her taking some time away until the situation was resolved. It was permanent. Comprehension swept through Tessa and she lay back on the bed, curling into a ball as sobs wrenched her. Eleanor was gone. She had left early, and Laya was wrong. She wouldn't be back.

Hands clenched into fists, Tessa wondered what was wrong with her that no one she loved stuck around. At least she still had Laya. As long as they had each other, they would always be okay, she reminded herself. But somehow the old mantra didn't feel like enough anymore.

She was still crying softly when her BlackBerry, wedged into the back pocket of her yoga pants, vibrated. An irrational hope welled up in her as she checked caller ID, but it was only Melody. Swallowing, Tessa rubbed her eyes and tried to control her breathing. Just before the call went to voice mail, she answered.

"I've got some news," her publicist said, voice uncharacteristically reserved, "but I was hoping I could come by to share it with you in person."

Eleanor, Tessa thought, disbelieving. But it couldn't be. Eleanor wasn't responsible for this debacle. If Tessa'd had any doubts (and she had), the letter had erased them. "What did you find out?"

"It's not something we should discuss over the phone, Tess. I can be there in thirty minutes."

"Fine," Tessa said. Laya should be asleep for a while yet, and a half hour would give her time to shower and repair her face. Melody had seen her at her best and worst over the many years of their professional relationship, but Tessa didn't want anyone to see her like this.

She set the phone down and picked up the letter again, skimming its contents once more. She should have trusted Eleanor, that much was clear. But working in the film industry, where deceit and betrayal weren't uncommon, had warped her view of what other people were capable of. She was tempted to throw Laya in the car and drive down to Beechwood and camp out at Sasha's apartment until Eleanor agreed to see her. But the letter was clear—Eleanor didn't want to see her. And anyway, Melody was on her way over. She would have to figure out what to do about Eleanor later.

Tessa managed to clean herself up before Melody drove her Mercedes up the long driveway. After exchanging the barest of greetings, they went straight to the patio where Tessa had placed a pitcher of iced tea, Melody's favorite beverage, and two glasses.

"You make a mean iced tea," Melody commented after her first sip. Even on a Sunday she was dressed in a sleek Armani suit, her makeup fresh.

"Or Trader Joe's does, anyway." Tessa held her own glass tightly, the ice cooling her skin. "What's going on, Mel? Why the kid gloves?"

Melody, a former Manhattanite a decade her senior, bit her lip and looked down. Long a PR maven to Hollywood's A-list, she was rarely anything other than confident to the point of brashness, in Tessa's experience.

"I have some bad news," she said. "Something of an extremely personal nature."

"What is it?" Tessa asked again, trying to control her impatience. "Did you find the source?"

"I did. I basically arm wrestled Katie Evans into revealing the story along with her source, but it's not anything you're going to want to hear."

"Just tell me."

"I'm not sure it should come from me," she said, then added quickly as Tessa glared at her, "but it looks like we don't have a choice. I'm sorry to be the one to tell you, Tess, but your father died last week."

Tessa leaned back in her chair. This was not at all what she had expected. "What are you talking about?"

"He had a heart attack at the correctional center in Joliet," Melody explained, tapping her foot against the wicker table, "and died in his sleep. His death is at the root of the story. It seems the prison officials found some indication in his personal effects that you were his daughter."

She hadn't even known he knew. She'd decided when she left Chicago that her old life was over, including any contact with her father. It wasn't like they'd been close. Tessa's social worker had sent him her school pictures each year, and she'd dutifully written letters and visited him every few months. But the last time she visited him in prison, right before she left for California, she informed him that she was an adult now and had decided she didn't want a relationship with him anymore. He'd looked at her for a long moment, and then he nodded. He told her that he understood and wouldn't try to contact her. If she changed her mind, though, he would be there for her. He would always be sorry for what he had done. He would always love her, and her mother too.

Tears pricked Tessa's eyes (Christ, again?) as she remembered the way he had looked at her in the gray-walled visitor's room at Stateville, slope-shouldered and defeated, so different from the young man who had pushed her on the swings and argued passionately with her mother and danced with both of them around the shabby living room of their apartment while the El roared past, the walls of their brick house shuddering. That day, only a few years older than Tessa was now, he'd seemed ancient and not a bit surprised by her decision. Judging from the well-rehearsed quality of his speech, he'd been expecting it.

That was the last time she would ever see him, she realized. She couldn't make contact when he got out of prison, a possibility that had always lurked somewhere at the back of her mind. He was gone, just like her mother. The last thing he'd said to her was that he loved her, but she wasn't sure now if she'd even told him goodbye.

"I'm sorry," Melody said again, leaning across the wicker patio table to touch her leg. "Particularly because the leak seems to have come from my office. One of my junior associates fielded the call from the prison and, well, you know how this town works. I've fired her, so you won't have any additional problems on that account. I'm just sorry someone from my staff has caused you grief."

"It's not your fault," Tessa said, wiping her eyes again. "But thank you for telling me, Mel. It couldn't have been easy."

Melody waved Tessa's thanks aside. "Is there anything I can do for you?"

"No, thanks." She stood up. "I think I'd like to be alone with Laya." And Eleanor, she thought, but that wasn't an option, and she had only herself to blame.

"Of course," Melody said, rising too. "But I do think we should talk about how to handle things. I practically bludgeoned Katie into delaying the story, and I have some ideas I'd like you to consider."

"Let's talk later, okay?" Tessa said as she walked the publicist out. "I need some time to let it sink in."

"All right," Melody said reluctantly. "But Katie's going public in the next twenty-four hours, so if you want to get a head start on this, you'll call me sooner rather than later."

"I will," Tessa promised, and they air-kissed, Melody's hand on her shoulder comforting.

The Mercedes had just pulled away when Laya came stumbling down the stairs, blinking. "Who was that? It wasn't Eleanor, was it?"

"No, baby." If only Eleanor would change her mind and come back, Tessa thought wistfully. She looked down into her daughter's wide, trusting eyes. With the story of her father's death about to break, she would have to tell Laya. But not yet. Right now she needed to curl up with her daughter in a dark room and escape into someone else's version of happiness. Right now, she needed a movie break.

"What do you think, kiddo—feel like a movie?"

"Okay," Laya agreed readily. "Can we watch *Nemo*?"

Tessa paused, remembering the last time they'd watched *Finding Nemo* in Kauai with Eleanor as rain poured down beyond the windows of the darkened studio. "Actually, I was thinking of *Dr. Doolittle*," she said. The 1960s version, starring Rex Harrison and shot partially on location in the Caribbean, had been one of her mother's favorites.

"Oh, yeah," Laya said. It was one of her favorites too. When she grew up, she often said, she wanted to be Dr. Doolittle.

By escaping into movieland, Tessa hoped to give her mind (and her emotions) a well-needed rest. If she could project herself out of her own consciousness for just a little while, she might be able to return with a better idea of what to do next. That was what she loved about movies, and books, too—the best ones allowed you to become someone else and then brought you back afterward refreshed, ready to deal with whatever lay in your path.

They stopped in the kitchen to microwave a packet of buttery popcorn, their usual screening fare, then headed toward the downstairs den where Tessa had had surround sound and a retractable screen installed shortly after she moved in.

"Race you," Laya called, sprinting across the hardwood floor in her stocking feet.

Careful, Tessa thought. But she said only, "You're too fast for me," as she carried the steaming bowl of popcorn down the hall after her daughter.

CHAPTER TWENTY-THREE

Eleanor hadn't managed to finish all six of Jane Austen's novels over the summer as intended. Somewhere along the way the plan had lost impetus, and now as she settled into life in Madison without Tessa and Laya, she was glad she'd left *Northanger Abbey* for last. Its purposeful melodrama and tongue-in-cheek discussion of what made a suitable heroine perfectly suited the way she felt as, each night after she'd made a dent in her abundant homework, she opened Austen's earliest novel and read until her eyes drooped and she could no longer hold up the book. Often during those first weeks in Wisconsin she awoke to her alarm only to find the novel resting on her chest, bedside lamp still shining. Each time this happened, she remembered the light in Tessa's bedroom ingeniously hooked up to The Clapper.

Despite the fact that she was in an entirely new location,

somehow nearly everything still managed to remind her of L.A., a situation not helped in the least by the prevalence of Tessa's face and story in the news. Eleanor had learned of Tessa's father's death while driving along the 15 near Rancho Cucamonga on the Sunday morning she and Sasha left L.A. (a day earlier than planned) when Allen called to see if they'd heard. She'd actually considered turning the car around and going back to L.A. to comfort Tessa, but Sasha had squeezed her hand and cast her a look that reminded her of her mantra: "Clean break, clean break, clean break." As if there could be a word more appropriate than "excruciating" or "agonizing" to modify "break."

The drive across the western half of the country had seemed to take forever, but now that it was over, she didn't remember most of it. She and Sasha had taken turns at the wheel, and Sasha had done a tremendous job at keeping her mind off what she was leaving behind, partially by gamely staying awake most of the hours she wasn't driving and partially by bringing along a variety of entertainment options. There were plentiful books on tape (many pinched from the holdings at her firm, which provided audio books as a service to its employees to help prevent road rage), several boxes of Trivial Pursuit cards, and assorted road trip games they vaguely remembered from childhood and modified now as they saw fit.

But Sasha couldn't be expected to stay awake the entire time, especially not crossing the monotonous western plains where an occasional abandoned farmhouse was often the only object to break the otherwise flat landscape. The day they crossed Nebraska, Eleanor was alone for hours at a time with only her thoughts and whatever iPod playlist Sasha had selected before dozing off. She watched the miles roll past and thought about Tessa and Laya and wondered if a clean break was really what she wanted, after all. Wasn't she being a coward by turning tail and running? Shouldn't she have given Tessa another chance, or at least said goodbye in person?

The night after she left Tessa's, Eleanor had gone out for sushi with Sasha, Allen and Luis, all of whom had assured her that she was right to walk away. In fact, they agreed, it was really her only choice. While trust might be a hard commodity to come by in cynical Hollywood, it was nevertheless a basic requirement for any serious relationship. Eleanor and Tessa had had a good time, and they'd even fallen in love, Sasha had pointed out, Luis and Allen nodding in agreement, but Tessa evidently wasn't ready or able to commit to the next level. Eleanor couldn't do all the committing. Better to learn now than later.

Intellectually, Eleanor suspected that she had made the right decision. As soon as Tessa had admitted she wasn't sure what to think, their relationship was basically over. Eleanor just didn't feel like it was over. What was more, she didn't want it to be. She still wanted to fall asleep next to Tessa every night and wake up to the sound of Laya's footsteps in the hall. She missed them both so much, more than she missed her mother, more than she'd ever missed anyone. She had fallen in love with them both, and now a life without the Flanagans seemed dismal, colorless.

At least she still heard from Laya regularly. Tessa's daughter called her every few days and Skyped her at least once a week. The first time she'd heard the "Life in the Fast Lane" ring tone, she and Sasha had been crossing Utah. Eleanor had literally gasped (a reaction Sasha had kindly ignored) and let the call go to voice mail, simultaneously relieved and disappointed a few minutes later when she heard Laya's childish tones through her Bluetooth headset. Laya sometimes e-mailed too, her typing skills as freakishly advanced as other kids of her socio-economic status but her spelling and vocabulary skills clearly signaling her age. The day she arrived in Madison, Eleanor received an e-mail to which Laya had attached one of the pre-Spago photos of Eleanor and Tessa in their Oscar finery, Laya between them, all three looking so happy as they posed together that Eleanor promptly burst into tears.

Fortunately, she managed to hold it together during her regular chats, video and otherwise, with Laya. She knew that Tessa had to be involved in these contacts, monitoring her daughter's technology usage, but Tessa stayed in the background, apparently respecting the instructions in the Dear John letter Eleanor increasingly regretted leaving on the bedside table that last morning.

Grad school, once it started, took up significant space,

ably distracting her from her broken heart for whole hours at a time. There were meetings and classes to attend, names to learn, endless studying. She was only taking two classes this first semester, but they were doozies: "Advanced Psychological Statistics" and "Applied Behavior Analysis." The older grad students assured the handful of newbies that the first semester was the hardest, both in terms of work levels and expectations. The professors wanted to weed out anyone who wasn't entirely committed. As long as the new cohort of students attended every class, did their reading and turned in the requisite work on time, the older students told them, they would be fine. So Eleanor willingly plunged into the work and used *Northanger Abbey* to fill in the odd moment when she wasn't reading or thinking about high-level statistics or experimentally derived principles of behavior.

Her fellow classmates were all younger, as anticipated, and prone to complaint, she'd discovered when she attended a group study session in the library the first week of classes. Three others were women and two were men, and they all seemed more interested in gossiping about their professors and the older students and complaining about the massive workload than actually tackling the statistics project they were supposed to complete by the following class meeting. After inventing a headache, Eleanor went home to her mostly unpacked apartment and decided that studying was probably going to be more of a lone-wolf endeavor. Good thing she loved her apartment—its high ceilings made the space seem bigger than it actually was, and the kitchen and bathroom had both been recently remodeled. As she'd predicted, it was nice to be surrounded by her own furniture and family photos again, even if she wasn't surrounded by the people she'd come to think of as family.

While her classmates seemed uniformly uninteresting, Reed, the music student she'd met in August, had invited her to brunch with a handful of local lesbians her first weekend in town. Some were grad students at the university, others professionals of varying ilk who had moved to Madison to enjoy the college town's reputation as a lesbian-friendly community, an apparently rare commodity outside of the region's big cities. She was just getting to know these women, but already Eleanor sensed the possibility of a social network similar to the one she'd enjoyed in Boston, where Smith and Mt. Holyoke and even Wellesley alums had congregated in great numbers, their petty Seven Sisters rivalries forgotten in the face of a world that didn't particularly prize recent women's college graduates.

At the end of brunch, Reed had asked her about Tessa, and Eleanor had smiled tightly. "Neither of us is the long-distance type," she'd said, and Reed let the subject drop, for which Eleanor was grateful. The news about Tessa had focused on her father's imprisonment and death. Seemed the press hadn't yet discovered that Eleanor was no longer living with the Flanagans.

By the time the third Friday in September rolled around, she still wasn't any closer to getting over Tessa, but she was becoming more settled in her new life. Neither of her classes met on Fridays, so she slept in that morning, got up late, and went for a run along the shores of Lake Mendota, loping along the imaginatively named University Bay Marsh and out along the heavily forested Picnic Point. With its downtown built along the lakefront, Madison reminded her of a larger, more cosmopolitan version of her hometown, Newport, minus the green mountains hulking in the distance. But the air along the lakeshore smelled the same, and it was just as cool on a late September morning in Wisconsin as it would have been in Vermont. Meanwhile, L.A. was probably still stifling. She pictured herself jogging up Runyon Canyon slowly in the sweltering desert heat, weighed down by a half gallon or more of water. She much preferred this type of run. Of course, L.A. offered something Madison couldn't.

Eleanor allowed herself to imagine what the Flanagans would be doing on a Friday morning. Laya would be in class at Barclay, probably reading or practicing numbers or drawing. She'd been assigned to Mrs. Blakely, an older English woman who had been exceedingly kind to Eleanor during her short tenure at the school. Tessa, meanwhile, would probably be downtown in the high-rise she'd pointed out to Eleanor as future home of the as-yet unnamed foundation. Or maybe they'd named it by now. Eleanor was still trying to steer clear of media coverage of her now ex-girlfriend. Given the usual span of the celebrity news cycle, the story of Tessa's family history had blown over by now. Which was good and bad, Eleanor thought—good because she didn't have to accidentally encounter repeated images of Tessa everywhere she turned, bad for the same exact reason.

The previous weekend, she'd fallen off the wagon and spent Sunday afternoon watching the comic book trilogy Tessa had starred in, back-to-back on DVD. How was she supposed to forget about Tessa when all she had to do was load a disc in the DVD player and suddenly there she was, dashing across the screen looking gorgeous and a tad butch in close-fitting cargo pants and a safari shirt unbuttoned lower than it really needed to be. Midway through the film fest, Sasha had called to see what she was up to, and Eleanor had muted the television and said, "Homework." Sighing audibly, Sasha had ordered her to turn off the TV that instant and go for a walk. Obediently, Eleanor had done so. But she'd returned to watch the third movie before falling asleep that night and dreaming of Mele Honu'ala. What she wouldn't have given for a glimpse of the lagoon from the soothing waters of the hot tub there, the feel of Tessa's skin slick against hers, the scent of chlorine and jasmine rising about them…

Pushing thoughts of Hawaii from her head, Eleanor tried to focus on her breathing and the dappling of sunlight through the oak and elm trees and off the lake as she ran. She was happy, she told herself. Or if not now, she would someday be happy here in her new home.

Back at the apartment, she showered and fixed herself a veggie omelet with the last few slices of smoked gouda. Sasha had taken her shopping before she flew back to L.A., splurging on all of Eleanor's favorite foods as a housewarming gift. When mending a broken heart, Sasha had reminded her, it was important not to skimp on the little things that made you happy.

As she dug into the omelet at her kitchen table, an IKEA purchase now seeing her through a third breakup, Eleanor cracked open her Applied Behavior textbook and picked up reading where she'd left off. The weekend stretched dauntingly before her. Except for drinks with Reed and her girlfriend tomorrow night, she didn't have any plans for the other sixty-odd hours facing her between now and Monday. Probably she should call someone in her class. One of the women, Rachel, a twenty-five-year old from Chattanooga, seemed okay one-on-one, away from the group. Maybe she would want to check out the local indie movie theater. Assuming she didn't worry Eleanor was hitting on her.

In the first week of classes, she'd discovered that out of the thirty or so students in her program, she was the only lesbian, a fact that neither surprised nor thrilled her. Her graduate experience in Wisconsin was going to be very different from her undergrad experience, she'd already deduced, for a variety of factors—most notably the size of the student body (40,000 at U-W versus 2,800 at Smith), gender makeup and sexuality, in that order. There was an active GLBT group on campus, she'd learned, but she didn't walk around campus with her gaydar going off constantly like she had at Smith. Definitely different.

She spent the next few hours on her Applied Behavior reading, only stopping for food and beverage breaks, and was finally feeling reasonably caught up to the rest of the class, all of whom were much closer to their undergraduate studies and none of whom appeared to be suffering from a broken heart, when her cell phone rang. Sasha.

"Yo, sistah," Eleanor said, just to mess with her.

But Sasha only said, "Did you ever hook up your cable?"

"Right after you left. Why?"

"Do me a favor and pull up the onscreen guide."

"Yes, ma'am," she said, but Sasha didn't respond to this comment either. Something was clearly up.

Eleanor moved the five paces from her kitchen table to her coffee table (the kitchen and living area were opposite ends of a single extended room) and picked up the universal remote. "What am I looking for?" she asked as she pulled up the guide. Cable came with the apartment—Jonah, the young econ professor who owned the house and lived on the first floor, let the upstairs tenant piggyback off his cable for free. A techie, he had outfitted the house with broadband wireless Internet access, also free. This was one of the reasons Eleanor felt okay paying a slightly higher monthly rent.

"I want to confirm when *Noelle* airs in your little Podunk town," Sasha said.

Noelle Robinson was a former model turned talk show host trying her best to rival Oprah and Ellen for daytime supremacy. An out lesbian and lifelong Chicago resident, she had dated Tempest Maxwell, one of the leading point guards in the WNBA, throughout the late 1990s and well into the 2000s. Until they split up, she and Tempest had been one of the best-known African American lesbian power couples.

Eleanor scrolled through the guide. "She's on in fifteen minutes. Since when are you interested in *Noelle*?"

"It's for you, not me," Sasha said. "Check the info on the show and make sure it's not a repeat."

Eleanor read the description of the episode aloud: "All new. Stars of Reality TV, plus the best omelet ever—a little late for that—and how to find a bathing suit that fits. Okay, Sash, what gives? You know I don't watch reality TV, so that can't possibly be the draw."

"You're going to want to watch this one, Elle," Sasha said. "Or so my sources tell me."

Her sources? She didn't mean… Eleanor stopped the thought before it could leech into her consciousness. "I can't. I have a ton of reading."

"And zero social plans for the weekend, I'm guessing."

"Wrong. I'm going out for drinks with Reed and her girlfriend tomorrow night."

"Ooh, look out Madison."

"I'm hanging up now."

"Wait," Sasha said quickly. "Just promise me you'll give the show a chance. Please? I gave someone my word, and I don't like to lie."

"You're an attorney. You live to lie."

"At work, yes. But this is personal."

Eleanor allowed her earlier suspicion its full form. "Does this have something to do with Tessa?"

"I'm not at liberty to say," Sasha obfuscated, "but it would behoove you to find out. Gotta run. Call me later." And the line clicked.

Eleanor turned off the TV and went back to her textbook. She wasn't about to watch daytime television. She had better things to do with her day. Things that apparently didn't include studying, she realized as she read for the third time a paragraph about specifying criteria for evaluating the significance of behavior change, the words trying valiantly but failing utterly to penetrate the brain fog Sasha's call had induced. Eleanor stared at the blank TV screen, still glowing slightly, and hit the power button on the remote. Wasn't like she had to watch the whole episode.

And yet, that's exactly what she did. Because as the credits rolled across the screen, the camera panned back and showed the stage with its postcard image of the Chicago skyline, Noelle in her customary armchair chatting with a guest who was most certainly not a Reality TV star. Tessa sat in a matching chair beside her, dressed in a collared shirt and familiar gray trousers, looking wonderful and significantly calmer than Eleanor felt.

"What are you doing?" she demanded of the TV Tessa, and then sat back against her comfy couch to watch as Noelle proceeded to interview her ex-girlfriend about her childhood in Chicago.

Photos accompanied the interview, youthful pictures of Tessa that Eleanor had never seen before, shots in which she looked shell-shocked and sick, pale and overweight, nothing like the healthy, well-adjusted adult Eleanor had come to know. Noelle asked her about the years before she lost her parents, her experiences in the foster system, what it was like growing up knowing that her father had caused her mother's death.

"Difficult, of course," Tessa said, her knuckles white on the chair arms. *Relax*, Eleanor thought, and as if on cue, Tessa took a breath and loosened her grip. "I loved both of my parents and I know they loved each other. I genuinely believe my mother's death was an accident."

"And your father?" Noelle prodded. "He died of a heart attack, is that right?"

"Technically. It may sound strange, but I think he really died of a broken heart. His life had become unrecognizable. I think he became unrecognizable to himself." She looked down, and

Noelle nodded sympathetically before asking the next tough question.

She made it a statement: "But you chose not to see him again once you finished high school."

Tessa lifted her chin bravely. "I decided when I left Chicago fifteen years ago that I wanted nothing more to do with that part of my life. That included my father. I didn't write to him or see him or speak to him again, not even once. In hindsight, it's a decision I regret. My refusal to forgive him meant he died completely alone. He was only fifty-eight. I think I thought there'd be more time."

Noelle nodded understandingly and the audience made sympathetic noises. Then Noelle said they needed to take a break, but to stay tuned for more from Tessa Flanagan after these messages.

Alone in her apartment, Eleanor sat on her couch, stocking feet curled under her, stunned. "You could go on TV and share your story," she vividly recalled saying the night Tessa told her about her parents. And now here Tessa was, reaching out to the throwaway kids in America. Did that mean she was on-set in Chicago right now? Or had she taped the show another time? Eleanor suddenly wished she'd learned more about the television industry during her sojourn in L.A. Maybe then she'd know the odds of Tessa currently being within driving distance.

There was one way to find out, of course. She glanced at her iPhone resting innocently on the kitchen table a few paces away. She hadn't deleted Tessa's cell phone number yet, even though Laya only ever called from the land line. Now she wished she had. The temptation to call was nearly overpowering, just as it had been the day she'd watched six hours of action adventure starring the woman she still wasn't even close to getting over.

When the show resumed, Noelle inclined her head toward Tessa and said, "I'm sure our audience is asking the same question I asked you during the break. Why now? Why give this interview on national television when you've always been so private before?"

"For one thing," Tessa said, "it's a little late for privacy. The entertainment press has already 'pursued the story to its natural conclusion,' as they like to say. But for another, someone very special to me—"

Eleanor couldn't help noticing that Tessa's phrasing made it sound as if this special someone was still in her life.

"—suggested that I might be able to offer hope to kids in similar situations, kids living in foster care without families of their own, who aren't sure where the next blow will come from. Because I was like that. I didn't have hope myself."

"Then what got you to where you are today, if not hope?"

"Stubbornness."

The audience laughed.

"I'm sayin'." Eleanor jabbed a finger at the television.

"That's the Irish in me," Tessa continued. "And assimilation—that's my Filipino blood. I kept telling myself that if I could just make it out of high school, get away from Chicago, then everything would be okay. And as it turns out, I was right. I've been lucky enough to have a career I loved, I have a beautiful daughter I love even more, and I recently partnered with two terrific women in L.A., Jane and Elizabeth Byerly, to start a charitable foundation that will provide financial assistance to the causes closest to our hearts: HIV/AIDS education and prevention, poverty assistance, domestic violence prevention and aid, anti-bullying programs and other children's issues."

"Does this organization have a name?" Noelle asked.

"It does. We've decided to call ourselves The Mercy Foundation, for my mother, Benita Reyes. Her middle name was Mercidita."

"The Mercy Foundation," Noelle said, nodding at the audience. "I like that."

They talked about the foundation for a few minutes, then took another break, during which Eleanor called Sasha. She reached voice mail and left a lengthy, slightly rambling message about how this wasn't helping the clean break and remember, Sasha was the one who had convinced her to remain incommunicado with Tessa. Damn it.

When the show came back again, she dropped back down on the couch and listened attentively as Noelle said, "Now, you told me during the break that this is your first time back in Chicago in more than fifteen years. Is that right?"

"Yes," Tessa said. "I had the opportunity to do some film work here, but my agent knew I wouldn't accept a job if it required me to be on location in the city."

"Wow. You weren't fooling around," Noelle said, glancing at her audience who provided the requisite laughter. "What changed your mind? Let me guess—was it that same special someone?"

Tessa nodded, glancing at the audience.

"And is that someone very special still in your life today?"

Tessa paused, and Eleanor held her breath. "No, she isn't. Not currently."

Not currently. What did that mean?

But Noelle was interested in a different angle on what Tessa had just said. "*She*," she repeated. "Does this mean the tabloid rumors about your sexuality are true? You haven't commented one way or another."

"Yes," Tessa said, and looked into the camera. "I'm a lesbian. I always have been." And she shrugged nonchalantly, offering one of her trademark raised eyebrow smiles.

"Dang, girl," Noelle said, fanning herself with her note cards. She exchanged another look with her audience, who tittered nervously. "When you decide to give an interview, you don't kid around, do you?"

In her apartment, Eleanor wished she had someone to exchange a high five with. Tessa had just come out publicly on national television—the first American A-list movie star ever to do so. People would be talking about this moment for years. It was almost too much to fathom.

Onscreen, Noelle was asking Tessa why coming to terms with her sexuality had taken so long, and Eleanor winced. She knew that this often incorrect assumption was a sore point for gay and lesbian actors, the same way GLBT teachers fumed over accusations of pedophilia.

"In fact," Tessa said, her smile nowhere to be seen, "it was never much of an issue from my point of view. It was probably easier for me than for other people, to be honest."

Noelle gave one of her trademark *What you talkin' about, Willis?* looks, and Tessa continued.

"What I mean is, I didn't have parents to disappoint, or

anyone else to disapprove of me. The first time I fell in love, shortly after I moved to L.A., it was wonderful. I finally felt like I knew who I was."

"If you knew who you were all those years ago, then why are you just now sharing the news with the rest of the world?"

"What kept me from being open was the same thing that keeps other gays and lesbians firmly in the closet—the fear of losing my job. In Hollywood there's this belief that coming out ruins careers. Studio executives are convinced that the public won't buy a gay actor in a straight role. The thing is, American audiences certainly accept straight actors who play gay for pay. Why not the reverse?"

"Gay for pay," Noelle echoed. "Admit it, you stole that line from the *L Word*."

Tessa's eyebrow quirked. "You got me." Then she turned serious again. "But just look at *Brokeback Mountain* and *Milk*, both of which won multiple Oscars. Or Felicity Huffman's brilliant performance in *Transamerica*. Why is it that sexuality doesn't matter when a straight actor plays a gay character, but it does when a gay actor plays straight? Success in Hollywood is supposed to be based on the performer's ability to play a convincing game of pretend. Shouldn't I be proof enough that gays and lesbians can successfully play it straight on the big screen, just as Heath and Sean and Felicity showed the opposite?"

"You're preaching to the choir here, my friend," Noelle said, nodding. "But I guess we'll have to let American audiences decide the answer to that one."

The show wound down then. As the end credits rolled and the camera panned out from the stage, Eleanor leaned back against her couch and released a pent-up breath. Could people really change, she thought, remembering Sasha's claim. Tessa had seemed warm and open on Noelle's show, as if she truly had nothing more to hide nor any desire to do so. What did it mean? Other than she had retired from acting too soon.

She knew Tessa had learned early on that she'd had nothing to do with the leak. Luis had called while they were still in Utah to tell them that prison officials had found certain documents in Tessa's father's personal effects indicating that she was his daughter, Mary Therese O'Neil. The information had found its way to the press from an enterprising member of Tessa's own publicist's staff, who had promptly been fired and even more quickly snapped up by a rival agency and given the promotion such a stunt usually earned in Hollywood. Typical, Sasha and Luis had agreed.

Eleanor had wondered if she would hear from Tessa when the source of the leak had been publicly identified, but no dice. Tessa was thoroughly respecting the wishes outlined in a letter Eleanor had written at five in the morning on an hour's sleep, tops, with a hangover impairing any and all judgment. When the sun had come up later that morning, she'd already been at Sasha's. As the day arrived and things didn't seem quite as desperate as they had in the middle of the night, she'd wished she'd observed the same rule she used with e-mail—she never allowed herself to send a potentially contentious or emotional e-mail until a twenty-four hour cooling period had passed and she'd reread her missive from a more rational space. But Sasha and Allen and Luis had assured her she'd done the right thing, and Tessa had maintained complete silence even as the story of her hidden history boiled over and then abated.

Curling onto her side, Eleanor closed her eyes. She was happy for Tessa that she had finally freed herself from the burden of her secrets, proud of her for using her experiences to try to help those who were considerably less fortunate in circumstance. But the "currently" Tessa had invoked during the interview kept coming back to Eleanor. Did Tessa think she would be back in her life at some point?

Her phone beeped, alerting her to a new text message. Sasha—the little shit hadn't even had the nerve to call back. She grabbed her phone from the coffee table, then almost dropped it as she read the sender's name: Tessa. Eleanor licked suddenly dry lips, opened the message and read, "Just wondering if you wanted to talk about the show? I have it on good authority that you got a chance to see it this afternoon."

Eleanor knew exactly who the authority was. What she didn't know was why Sasha had all of a sudden changed teams. She stared at the words inscribed on the iPhone screen. She didn't have to answer. There was nothing to prevent her from deleting the message and pretending she'd never read it. But New Englanders weren't very good at playing pretend. Not even the ones who made a career out of teaching kindergarten.

"I wouldn't call her good," she typed in reply. "But congratulations on the show. You did beautifully." She hesitated, then hit send.

"You didn't answer my question," the reply came back almost immediately. "Do you want to talk? Please. I'm sorry about L.A. I've missed you. Terribly."

The neat words flashing on her iPhone screen melted Eleanor's resolve, but she shored it up again. Tessa had all but accused her of betrayal. Although now, in hindsight, it was possible she'd overreacted. Just possible that she'd been so worried and upset about leaving L.A. that she'd subconsciously used their disagreement as a means of lessening her guilt at leaving Tessa, who had been abandoned by everyone who had ever loved her. Possible, though not likely.

"Maybe," she typed. She hesitated again. "Are you in Chicago?"

"Not anymore." The answer came back immediately, and Eleanor tried not to notice that Tessa had come within a hundred and fifty miles of Madison without even trying to get in touch with her.

Then the phone beeped again, and she read, "Come outside."

It only took her a second to realize what the message meant. She leapt off the couch, then looked down at her pajama pants and ratty Smith T-shirt with holes in both armpits. This would never do.

"Just a sec," she texted back, and raced into her bedroom. Good thing she'd taken a shower after her run. Two minutes, a pair of jeans and clean shirt, and a quick brushing of teeth and hair later, she was opening the hall door and jogging down the steps to the main hallway she shared with her landlord. Taking a deep breath, she turned the doorknob and stepped outside. Parked at the end of the stone walkway beneath the elm trees that shaded the front yard was a limo with tinted windows. As Eleanor watched, Tessa emerged from the car clad in the same outfit she'd worn on *Noelle*, and gazed up at her with eyes that Eleanor could tell even from here held nothing but hope.

She stood motionless on the porch, trying to fix the image in her mind. She wasn't sure what would happen next, couldn't have said for certain what she wanted. But that wasn't entirely true. She just didn't know what Tessa wanted, or if their individual desires would fit together again the way they had before she'd left L.A.

One way to find out. She started down the steps.

What do you do when your worst fears are realized? Sometimes you figure out that what you dreaded all those years isn't nearly as powerful as your fear itself.

Over the past few weeks, Tessa had buried her estranged father, withstood yet another press onslaught into her personal life, and gradually come to realize that the revelation of her family's history had not led to any particular earth-shattering change other than Eleanor's disappearance.

Only she wasn't ready to let go of this sweet, intractable woman she'd come to love and rely on. So, with Melody's assistance, she'd devised a strategy that would allow her to reach out in the exact way Eleanor had suggested. The foundation was designed to help people in need, but it offered a form of assistance that would allow her to maintain a careful distance from the people it served. The route Eleanor had advocated was necessarily messier and meant revealing more of herself than she really wanted to. But perhaps by embracing the disparate halves of her life and holding them out for the world to see, she would be able to meld the distinct before and after chunks into a single, seamless entity.

And if she didn't manage such a transformation, at least this way she might be able to help someone other than herself even as she attempted to convince Eleanor she was worthy of a second chance. She wasn't sure that baring all would be interpreted as anything other than an exercise in typical Hollywood narcissism, but Eleanor seemed to think she had something to offer. That was enough for Tessa.

Now Eleanor was walking toward her down the walkway Tessa recognized from the Google street view images she'd pored over these last weeks, imagining Elle going about her new life in the green, lake-strewn Midwestern city. As she drew closer, Tessa stared at her, drinking in the way she walked quickly but not too fast, the look on her face simultaneously tough and vulnerable. She looked different in warm-weather clothes—jeans and a long-sleeved shirt—instead of the summer gear Tessa was used to, her hair fastened back from her face in a single barrette. She looked wonderful. She looked like herself.

They met at the gate, and Tessa smiled hesitantly. "Hi," she said, the apology she'd planned slipping away as her gaze found Eleanor's. She'd forgotten what a look from those clear, open eyes could do to her.

"Hi," Eleanor said.

Then, before Tessa had a chance to work her way into her prepared apology, Eleanor was throwing her arms around Tessa and covering her lips in a fervent kiss. She tasted like toothpaste. Tessa wrapped her arms around Eleanor's neck and kissed her back, moaning a little as their tongues met. God, even better than she'd remembered.

Eventually it occurred to her that they were making out in broad daylight on a Wisconsin city street in broad view of anyone who happened by. She pulled back, keeping her hands locked behind Eleanor's neck. "I missed you so much."

"I missed you too, you shit."

"I was a shit, wasn't I? Can you forgive me? Again?"

"Of course," Eleanor said. "It's one of the first lessons I teach my kids—everyone makes mistakes. But is this what you meant when you told Noelle I wasn't 'currently' in your life? Were you planning all along to show up here and sweep me off my feet?"

"Planning's a bit strong, but I was hoping. I thought I better not give you a heads-up, though. I wasn't sure how you'd feel about seeing me."

"I'm thrilled to see you," Eleanor said.

"Ditto, pal," she said, smirking, then laughed as Eleanor pushed her away.

A few minutes later they were upstairs sitting cross-legged

on the couch facing each other and trying to get caught up on everything that had happened during their few weeks apart. Tessa informed Eleanor that Laya was adjusting to first grade and liking her role as a bigger girl and presently enjoying a few days at Rayann's house. The foundation was open for business, she added, and Eleanor congratulated her on the milestone and complimented her on the name choice. Tessa asked her how school was going and listened as Eleanor explained that even though classes were only a couple of weeks in, they were already harder than she'd expected. But Reed, the lesbian she'd met back in August, and her girlfriend were nice and had introduced her to some other cool women. So far, she said, Madison was living up to her expectations in a mostly good way.

"I'm glad to hear that," Tessa said, tracing the back of Eleanor's hand with a finger. "I've been trying to get information out of Laya after every call. I was hoping what happened between us wouldn't muck up things for you here."

Eleanor turned her hand over, intertwining their fingers. "I'm sorry I left like I did. I could have at least said goodbye instead of leaving you that awful note."

"You don't have to apologize. You were right to leave, Elle. I didn't deserve you." Tessa leaned in to kiss her again, slowly, lingeringly. She wanted to deserve her now. She needed to deserve her. Life made more sense when Eleanor was in it.

They made out for long minutes, tongues dipping into each other's mouths languidly before retreating, lips touching lightly then more firmly as the kiss deepened. Tessa lifted her hands to Eleanor's collarbone, then trailed her fingers downward, feeling Eleanor's nipples tauten and strain beneath her touch. As Eleanor caressed her breasts in return, Tessa moved one hand between Eleanor's legs, feeling the damp heat through her jeans. She stifled a groan against Eleanor's mouth. It had been way too long. She didn't think she could wait any longer.

"I need to taste you," she murmured against Eleanor's mouth.

"God, yes," Eleanor returned, her breath coming quicker.

Tessa slipped to the floor and knelt before her, helping as Eleanor quickly pushed her jeans and panties down. Then she slid her hands beneath Eleanor and pulled her forward to the edge of the couch. A familiar scent reached her, and she breathed in deeply as she pressed Eleanor's legs apart. She lowered her face to Eleanor's wet center, parting the folds and stroking her with her tongue first lightly, then more firmly, sliding from the tip of her clit to the slick opening below and back again. She'd barely even started when suddenly, Eleanor's hips rose up off the couch and she cried out, sounding nearly as surprised as Tessa felt. Whoah. That was not part of the plan.

Above her, Eleanor was laughing sheepishly. "Well, shit," she said. "Is this what guys feel like when they ejaculate too soon?"

"Ew," Tessa said as she resettled on the couch beside her. "Thanks for that mental image."

"You should be flattered," Eleanor said, leaning her forehead against Tessa's. "Shows how much I missed you."

"Or what a hussy you are."

"Hey, now." Eleanor smacked the side of her hip lightly.

"You can do better than that," Tessa said teasingly.

The next thing she knew, Eleanor had flipped her over onto her stomach and was tugging her trousers and undies down over the back of her legs. Tessa lifted her hips helpfully, burrowing further into the obscenely comfortable couch. This was the infamous Sears find? And then she forgot about the couch as Eleanor lay back down and slipped one hand between her legs. Tessa closed her eyes, the ache inside growing as Eleanor's fingers explored her, brushing here, rubbing lightly there. Then she felt the tip of Eleanor's thumb circling her opening, sliding in a little, then retreating, entering again a tiny bit, pulling out once more. Tessa bore this teasing for as long as she could, and then all at once she pushed back against Eleanor's hand, taking her thumb as deeply as possible and rubbing her clit against Eleanor's fingers. Almost immediately Eleanor withdrew, tormenting Tessa again with feather-light touches. Finally she moaned in frustration.

"What was that?" Eleanor breathed against her neck.

"Please," Tessa whispered. "Please, Eleanor."

She felt Eleanor shift, and there was her thumb again, her beautiful, talented thumb filling Tessa, withdrawing, surging into her again as her long fingers caressed her clit. There was nothing teasing about her touch now, only purpose, and Tessa surged back against her on the couch, then forward, then back again in a rhythm they set together, waves of feeling mounting inside her until the pulsing built to a climax and she thrust herself back on Eleanor's thumb one last time, her muscles tensing and releasing as colors broke against her eyelids and she heard her own voice, as if from a distance, raised in wordless exclamation.

"Sweet Jesus," she murmured as her heartbeat slowed and Eleanor kissed her shoulder.

Beside her, Eleanor slipped an arm around her waist and said, her voice low, "I love you, you know."

"I love you too," Tessa said, her breath evening out. She smiled, eyes still closed. "Even if your parents gave you a lame middle name."

"Watch it," Eleanor said, and pinched her ass lightly. "I do have one question, though."

"What's that?"

"How did you get Sasha to come over to the dark side? She was pretty set against you, especially after the road trip out here."

"She was a tough sell," Tessa admitted. "But in the end she saw the light. She wants you to be happy and so do I."

A little while later they moved into Eleanor's tiny, high-ceilinged bedroom, where they shed the remainder of their clothing and made love again, Indigo Girls playing in the background. The first time, they'd been unable to get close enough as fast as they both needed, but now they moved together more slowly, taking their time as they relearned curves and slopes and sensitive spots. Afterward they lay on their backs talking in low voices, touching each other as if they couldn't bear the thought of separating.

"Did you know," Tessa said, her head on Eleanor's shoulder, "that your school here has the first-ever program for the study of wildlife management?"

"Laya told you that, didn't she."

"She did. Looks like Smith might have some competition for her future allegiance."

"Oh, we'll see about that."

They were a *we* again, Tessa thought, breathing in the familiar scent of Eleanor's skin. She had missed her so much, and she would miss her again when it came time to fly back to L.A., to Laya and their life in California. For now, distance and loneliness would remain a necessary part of her relationship with Eleanor. But not the way it had been the last few weeks. Now when she went to bed alone in her house thousands of miles away, she would know that Eleanor was here in Madison thinking about her, missing her, loving her.

The distance wouldn't last forever. There were holidays and summer breaks and maybe even, somewhere down the road, a move for Tessa and her daughter to someplace that would feel more like home. The foundation would practically run itself soon, and she could do fundraising work from anywhere. Noelle had hinted just that morning that with Tessa now embracing her Chicago roots, the Windy City might present "a unique opportunity" for the Mercy Foundation. She and Laya and Eleanor would be a family again at some point, and maybe eventually they'd even add a fourth. After all, Eleanor had mentioned she might like a child of her own, and Tessa had all that sperm banked in Switzerland…

But she was getting ahead of herself, ahead of the two of them. She didn't want to think about the future. For now she wanted to enjoy the sensation of lying naked and entwined with her girlfriend in her upstairs apartment, surrounded by Eleanor's books and clothes and belongings. For so long their relationship had taken place in L.A., where Tessa's history and the expectations of her former profession had formed a dual albatross about their necks. It was a relief to be someplace new with Eleanor, a place where they could be new together.

"How does it feel to be out in every meaning of the word?" Eleanor asked.

"Awesome," Tessa said, and smiled at her in the autumnal light that slanted through the window above the bed. "How does it feel to you?"

"Not bad." Eleanor stretched. "I just wish my mom could have met you."

"I know what you mean."

They lay quietly together for a little while longer until almost in unison their stomachs began to growl. Then they pulled on clothes and padded out to the kitchen to scrounge up dinner.

As they leaned together looking into the open refrigerator, Eleanor asked, "Can we call Laya?"

"Of course. She would love it."

"Was she upset after I left? I couldn't really tell on the phone."

"Nah, she kept saying that everything would work out and we would see you again soon."

"Smart kid," Eleanor said. She focused on the refrigerator again and pursed her lips. "How about—"

"Tofu stir-fry?"

"I was going to say shrimp stir-fry."

"Even better."

They set about making dinner in the warm kitchen at the back of the old house, while outside the sun set and the air cooled and the leaves on the trees rustled in the breeze. And it was just like the summer they'd spent together, only better, Tessa thought, pausing to kiss the back of Eleanor's neck as she drifted past in the open kitchen. The only thing missing was Laya, and soon enough they'd all be together again.

"I love you," Eleanor said, smiling over her shoulder.

"Good thing," Tessa said, and kissed her again.

Publications from
Bella Books, Inc.
Women. Books. Even Better Together.
P.O. Box 10543
Tallahassee, FL 32302
Phone: 800-729-4992
www.bellabooks.com

THE GRASS WIDOW by Nanci Little. Aidan Blackstone is nineteen, unmarried and pregnant, and has no reason to think that the year 1876 won't be her last. Joss Bodett has lost her family but desperately clings to their land. A richly told story of frontier survival that picks up with the generation of women where Patience and Sarah left off.
978-1-59493-189-5 $12.95

SMOKEY O by Celia Cohen. Insult "Mac" MacDonnell and insult the entire Delaware Blue Diamond team. Smokey O'Neill has just insulted Mac, and then finds she's been traded to Delaware. The games are not limited to the baseball field!
978-1-59493-198-7 $12.95

WICKED GAMES by Ellen Hart. Never have mysteries and secrets been closer to home in this eighth installment of this award-winning lesbian cozy mystery series. Jane Lawless's neighbors bring puzzles and peril--and that's just the beginning.
978-1-59493-185-7 $14.95

NOT EVERY RIVER by Robbi McCoy. It's the hottest city in the U.S., and it's not just the weather that's heating up. For Kim and Randi are forced to question everything they thought they knew about themselves before they can risk their fiery hearts on the biggest gamble of all.
978-1-59493-182-6 $14.95

HOUSE OF CARDS by Nat Burns. Cards are played, but the game is gossip. Kaylen Strauder has never wanted it to be about her. But the time is fast-approaching when she must decide which she needs more: her community of Eda Byrne.
978-1-59493-203-8 $14.95

RETURN TO ISIS by Jean Stewart. The award-winning Isis sci-fi series features Jean Stewart's vision of a committed colony of women dedicated to preserving their way of life, even after the apocalypse. Mysteries have been forgotten, but survival depends on remembering. Book one in series.
978-1-59493-193-2 $12.95

1ST IMPRESSIONS by Kate Calloway. Rookie PI Cassidy James has her first case. Her investigation into the murder of Erica Trinidad's uncle isn't welcomed by the local sheriff, especially since the delicious, seductive Erica is their prime suspect. 1st in series. Author's augmented and expanded edition.
978-1-59493-192-5 $12.95

BEACON OF LOVE by Ann Roberts. Twenty-five years after their families put an end to a relationship that hadn't even begun, Stephanie returns to Oregon to find many things have changed... except her feelings for Paula.
978-1-59493-180-2 $14.95

ABOVE TEMPTATION by Karin Kallmaker. It's supposed to be like any other case, except this time they're chasing one of their own. As fraud investigators Tamara Sterling and Kip Barrett try to catch a thief, they realize they can have anything they want--except each other.
978-1-59493-179-6 $14.95

AN EMERGENCE OF GREEN by Katherine V. Forrest. Carolyn had no idea her new neighbor jumped the fence to enjoy her swimming pool. The discovery leads to choices she never anticipated in an intense, sensual story of discovery and risk, consequences and triumph. Originally released in 1986.
978-1-59493-217-5 $14.95

CRAZY FOR LOVING by Jaye Maiman. Officially hanging out her shingle as a private investigator, Robin Miller is getting her life on track. Just as Robin discovers it's hard to follow a dead man, She walks in. KT Bellflower, sultry and devastating... Lammy winner and second in series.
978-1-59493-195-6 $14.95

LOVE WAITS by Gerri Hill. The All-American girl and the love she left behind--it's been twenty years since Ashleigh and Gina parted, and now they're back to the place where nothing was simple and love didn't wait.
978-1-59493-186-4 $14.95

HANNAH FREE: THE BOOK by Claudia Allen. Based on the film festival hit movie starring Sharon Gless. Hannah's story is funny, scathing and witty as she navigates life with aplomb -- but always comes home to Rachel. 32 pages of color photographs plus bonus behind-the-scenes movie information.
978-1-59493-172-7 $19.95

END OF THE ROPE by Jackie Calhoun. Meg Klein has two enduring loves—horses and Nicky Hennessey. Nicky is there for her when she most needs help, but then an attractive vet throws Meg's carefully balanced world out of kilter.
978-1-59493-176-5 $14.95

THE LONG TRAIL by Penny Hayes. When schoolteacher Blanche Bartholomew and dance hall girl Teresa Stark meet their feelings are powerful--and completely forbidden--in Starcross Texas. In search of a safe future, they flee, daring to take a covered wagon across the forbidding prairie.
978-1-59493-196-3 $12.95

UP UP AND AWAY by Catherine Ennis. Sarah and Margaret have a video. The mob wants it. Flying for their lives, two women discover more than secrets.
978-1-59493-215-1 $12.95

CITY OF STRANGERS by Diana Rivers. A captive in a gilded cage, young Solene plots her escape, but the rulers of Hernorium have other plans for Solene--and her people. Breathless lesbian fantasy story also perfect for teen readers.
978-1-59493-183-3 $14.95

ROBBER'S WINE by Ellen Hart. Belle Dumont is the first dead of summer. Jane Lawless, Belle's old friend, suspects coldhearted murder. Lammy-winning seventh novel in critically acclaimed cozy mystery series.
978-1-59493-184-0 $14.95

APPARITION ALLEY by Katherine V. Forrest. Kate Delafield has solved hundreds of cases, but the one that baffles her most is her own shooting. Book six in series.
978-1-883523-65-7 $14.95

STERLING ROAD BLUES by Ruth Perkinson. It was a simple declaration of love. But the entire state of Virginia wants to weigh in, leaving teachers Carrie Tomlinson and Audra Malone caught in the crossfire--and with love troubles of their own.
978-1-59493-187-1 $14.95

LILY OF THE TOWER by Elizabeth Hart. Agnes Headey, taking refuge from a storm at the Netherfield estate, stumbles into dark family secrets and something more... Meticulously researched historical romance.
978-1-59493-177-2 $14.95

LETTING GO by Ann O'Leary. Kelly has decided that luscious, successful Laura should be hers. For now. Laura might even be agreeable. But where does that leave Kate?
978-1-59493-194-9 $12.95

MURDER TAKES TO THE HILLS by Jessica Thomas. Renovations, shady business deals, a stalker--and it's not even tourist season yet for PI Alex Peres and her best four-legged pal Fargo. Sixth in this cozy Provincetown-based series.
978-1-59493-178-9 $14.95

SOLSTICE by Kate Christie. It's Emily Mackenzie's last college summer and meeting her soccer idol Sam Delaney seems like a dream come true. But Sam's passion seems reserved for the field of play...
978-1-59493-175-8 $14.95

FORTY LOVE by Diana Simmonds. Lush, romantic story of love and tennis with two women playing to win the ultimate prize. Revised and updated author's edition.
978-1-59493-190-1 $14.95

I LEFT MY HEART by Jaye Maiman. The only women she ever loved is dead, and sleuth Robin Miller goes looking for answers. First book in Lammy-winning series.
978-1-59493-188-8 $14.95

TWO WEEKS IN AUGUST by Nat Burns. Her return to Chincoteague Island is a delight to Nina Christie until she gets her dose of Hazy Duncan's renown ill-humor. She's not going to let it bother her, though...
978-1-59493-173-4 $14.95